BRIAN FLYNN

MEN FOR PIECES

Brian Flynn was born in 1885 in Leyton, Essex. He won a scholarship to the City Of London School, and from there went into the civil service. In World War I he served as Special Constable on the Home Front, also teaching "Accountancy, Languages, Maths and Elocution to men, women, boys and girls" in the evenings, and acting in his spare time.

It was a seaside family holiday that inspired Brian Flynn to turn his hand to writing in the mid-twenties. Finding most mystery novels of the time "mediocre in the extreme", he decided to compose his own. Edith, the author's wife, encouraged its completion, and after a protracted period finding a publisher, it was eventually released in 1927 by John Hamilton in the UK and Macrae Smith in the U.S. as *The Billiard-Room Mystery*.

The author died in 1958. In all, he wrote and published 57 mysteries, the vast majority featuring the super-sleuth Antony Bathurst.

BRIAN FLYNN

MEN FOR PIECES

With an introduction
By Steve Barge

DEAN STREET PRESS

Any work of fiction whose language is entirely cleansed of the idioms and expressions of its time would rightly be condemned—by that fact if by no other—as being an unfaithful witness to the world it seeks to portray. Therefore, no apology can be considered necessary for the occasional term or phrase that reflects the era of this book's original publication, even if some may now view such words with unease.

It is hoped that modern readers will approach these passages with an understanding of the historical context, and with the assurance that no malice was intended then, nor is any endorsed now.

INTRODUCTION

"Having once constructed my main plot, I sit down to write and permit the puppets to do their own dancing."

Thus wrote Brian Flynn in an article for Crime Book Magazine. They had awarded Black Agent (1949) the Society's Selection for that issue and asked Brian to introduce himself. While Brian had, until recently, been long forgotten as a crime writer, it is unclear how unknown he was when he was writing his fifty-seven mystery novels. From the tone of the article, it would seem that he viewed himself as something of a lesser author—when mentioning *"the distinguished authors who now write detective stories"* and *"the brilliant examples they constantly offer"* he refers to his own *"comparative unworthiness for the fire and burden of the competition."* However, he ends that section on a positive note:

"The stars have always been the most desired of all goals, so I allow exultation and determination to take the place of that but temporary dismay".

At this stage of his writing career, Brian was writing exclusively for John Long, a publisher that focussed primarily on the library market. His first book, *The Billiard Room Mystery* (1927), was published by John Hamilton, as were the next four, and then he moved to John Long for the rest of his career. (For the sake of accuracy, I feel that I should note that the first John Long book, *The Five Red Fingers* (1929), was actually published before the last Hamilton book, *Invisible Death* (1929).)

A selection of books was published in the US as well, the last of these being *The Case Of The Purple Calf* as *The Ladder Of Death* in 1935. A few other titles were translated into French (*The Case Of Elymas The Sorcerer* (1945) as Bryan Flynn), German (*The Mystery Of The Peacock's Eye* (1928), *The Horn* (1934) and Swedish (*The Case Of The Black Twenty-Two* (1928)). There is, according to a comment by Brian in an article, also a Danish translation, but I am yet to discover any evidence of this.

In the UK, there were some paperback reprints, all by John Long. A few appeared in their Four-Star Thrillers series, and some later titles such as *Such Bright Disguises* (1941), *Reverse the Charges* (1943) and *The Swinging Death* (1949) in the company's Pocket Editions, alongside such authors as Edgar Wallace, John Creasey and Frances Durbridge. By the time of *Men for Pieces* (1949), Brian's books were solely being printed in hardback, destined primarily for library shelves. Of course, this is one reason why copies of his books are particularly hard to find . . .

For those of you who are new to Brian's work, the majority of his output, fifty-three of his books, featuring the gentleman-detective Anthony Bathurst. One other is a children's book, *Tragedy at Trinket*, which can be recommended if you think most schoolboy murder mysteries don't have enough schoolboy cricket in them or vice versa (and features Bathurst's nephew, despite being published by a different company, Nelson). The final three are the Sebastian Stole mysteries, written under the pseudonym Charles Wogan. Stole is the exiled Crown Prince of Calorania, but his exploits only last three books. While the first book is quite distinctive from the Bathurst mysteries, the third one, *Cyanide For A Chorister* (1950), could have easily been one of Anthony's adventures with only minor alterations, and perhaps that is why this one, published between *Men For Pieces* (1950) and *Black Agent* (1951) was the final case for Stole and thereafter Brian focussed exclusively on Bathurst.

Writing exclusively for one sleuth might be seen as problematic, but it is notable how the style of the books varies as the series goes on, which may well be a reflection of the times as well. The country house settings of some of the early titles has long since gone by the time *Men For Pieces* (1949) is published, and there have been some changes to Brian's writing style. While Bathurst's character remains constant, there are far fewer books that are narrated by a third party—all of the five books from *Men For Pieces* (1949) to *The Ring Of Innocent* (1952) are written in the third person. As the series progresses, there are some books that veer away from the whodunit element as well.

A case could be made for the first such deviation from the norm being the inverted mystery *Such Bright Disguises* (1941), but there is still a whodunnit element at the end of the tale. The first of the out-and-out thrillers, however, was *The Grim Maiden* (1944), swiftly followed by *Conspiracy At Angel* (1947) and *Where There Was Smoke* (1951), all of which being tales of a criminal conspiracy where the story is more about the puzzle of what exactly is going on, rather than the identity of the villain of the piece. There are earlier examples of these conspiracy stories—*The Case Of The Purple Calf* (1934) and *They Never Came Back* (1940) for example, but these also have an unmasking at the end of the tale.

This is a reflection, though, of Brian's overall style at this point. The third person focus on primarily Bathurst and occasionally his co-investigators means that the focus of the book is on the investigation. Once Bathurst arrives on the scene, there are few scenes depicting suspects discussing things—we are exclusively seeing what Bathurst sees. One local newspaper review made comparisons to Freeman Wills Crofts, the creator of Inspector French, and this comparison is a reasonable one. Of course, that may not inspire some readers, as Crofts is one of the authors who has been in the past dismissed as "humdrum", thanks in part to Julian Symons' critique, but the Inspector French books are another until-recently-lost highlights of the Golden Age and I do recommend that readers who have dismissed him give him another go. Once you've read all the available Brian Flynn books, of course. After all, an entire narrative spent in Anthony Bathurst's company is no bad thing.

As there were no reprints of the titles from *Men For Pieces* (1949) onwards, we are lucky to be able to bring these five books to you. We have to thank Brian's estate for *Men For Pieces* as in my eight years collecting his work, I have never seen a copy for sale on the second-hand market. I can see why, as it's a really fun mystery, with Bathurst himself all but dismissing a dead body as suicide (he clearly doesn't realise that he's in a detective novel) until the victim's sister spots that the plug from the bath is in the wrong place! That's enough for our hero to dive into a mystery involving stolen and returned money, a plethora of suspects and a genuine surprise at the end. The original cover billed it as "Tense and Exciting" and they are not far from being wrong.

Black Agent (1950)—at this point Brian was clearly using his Big Book Of Quotations to find his titles—has a typically odd set-up for a Bathurst mystery. Barbara Marsden disappeared without trace from a New Year's party in her village. The only trace is spotted a month later when the distinctive yellow dress she was wearing is spotted being used as a costume in a play, only for the woman wearing it to also disappear . . . It's an original (if odd) concept and once the inevitable bodies appear, Brian does a great job of ratchetting up the tension. We also get another appearance of Bathurst's sort-of love interest and one of the earliest examples of a female Scotland Yard officer, Helen Repton.

The aforementioned *Where There Was Smoke* (1951) goes even further with the odd set-up. Donald Finney, a chemist, is offered work by the mysterious Mr Rehoboam, only for Donald's body to be discovered with no obvious cause of death. Questions abound however. Why was his skin discoloured? How did he have a printed note with the local Inspector Stire's name on it? And why was a piece of cooked bacon rind hidden in his belly button? A thriller following Bathurst's investigations—and there are some impressive Sherlockian deductions that Bathurst makes just from the crime scene—and a really fun adventure. Oh, and there's the only creative use of Alphabetti Spaghetti that I've aware of in a mystery novel . . .

Another Macbeth quote provides the title for *And Cauldron Bubble* (1951) although a reader hoping for a witch related mystery may be disappointed. Back to the whodunnits, and this time Bathurst is investigating a disappearance and a murder. Lady Blanchflower and her companion Mrs Whitburn left *The Red Deer* together after dinner, only for Lady Blanchflower to be found strangled and of Mrs Whitburn, there is no trace. And under Lady Blanchflower's body is, for some reason, a man's wig. This is one of the books where we see Bathurst being more fallible. With mostly just his intuition to go on, he follows several dead ends until the truth is revealed. This is similar to the later serial-killer title, *The Seventh Sign*, although we don't see Bathurst sinking to the same levels of frustration and despair here.

The final book in this set of re-releases is *The Ring Of Innocent* (1952) and we kick off with that old chestnut, the overheard conversation. Martin Scudamore overhears a mention of four rings and that if a certain Mr Lovelace interferes, "I'll slit his throat—without the slightest compunction or hesitation". Scudamore mentions it to Helen Repton, who promptly tells Bathurst, they arrive in time to hear Lovelace's dying message—the two words "*innocent*" and "*teaspoon*". It's a good mystery and moves along at a rapid pace, and, most importantly, is probably the title where we get the most insight into the Bathurst-Repton "relationship".

It brings me great delight that we are able to continue to bring the adventures of Brian Flynn back to the masses. I need to thank the many people who have helped along the way to revive Anthony Bathurst, but most importantly the late Rupert Heath, without whom Brian Flynn—and many other authors—would still be naught but a memory.

Steve Barge

CHAPTER 1

1

It was Easter Tuesday—one of the most beautiful April mornings that could possibly be imagined—and the members of the staff of the Lombard Street branch of Delaney's bank seemed more than ordinarily conscious of the fact. The Easter break was over, worse luck, and Whitsun seemed a hell of a way ahead. Some yawned as they pored over ledgers, one or two shivered at certain persistent thoughts which refused to be allayed, others appeared to be contented to be sullenly discontented.

Even Andrew Murray, the imperturbable and habitually good-tempered manager, had frowned heavily at the various papers in possession of his table when he had seated himself in his customary chair upon his arrival.

Murray was tall, broad-shouldered, and good-looking for a man in the early fifties—happily married and eminently capable on his job. His son was out in Kenya supervising an intensely efficient and extremely modern engineering scheme, and his daughter had very recently been appointed as Languages Mistress at the Girls' Grammar School at Horton Hatch, that charming suburb of Wimblefield where he had lived for the past thirteen years.

We will contemplate Andrew Murray again as he sits in his private room and we notice immediately that a second frown has quickly followed the first. The object to occasion the later frown was Murray's large desk diary which seemingly had just caught his eye. Or, more particularly, an entry upon it rather than the diary itself. An entry under date, Easter Tuesday, April 19. The entry read, "Oliver—re F.S." Murray pushed back his chair a little, frowned again heavily and picked up the internal telephone. His brows contracted as he spoke.

"Send Oliver in to me, will you? And remind him to bring in the foreign securities register. The fact that I instructed him on Saturday to see me at 9.30 sharp this morning seems to have escaped his attention."

There was a grimmish smile on Andrew Murray's lips and an acid tone in his voice as he replaced the receiver. The smile was that of the efficient chief about to interview an erring subordinate and to tear him off a strip.

2

Murray drummed with his fingers on the surface of the table as he awaited Oliver's entrance. As the period of the waiting lengthened, the drumming increased in impatience.

"I really don't know," said the manager aloud, "what we're damned well coming to. Very different when I was a junior. If I'd kept my old man waiting like this—when I'd been specially sent for—he'd have chewed my b—"

The door of the manager's room opened to check the reminiscent soliloquy and to admit a member of the staff. Murray saw with some annoyance that the man who had entered was not the officer whose presence he had just requested.

"Good morning, sir."

The tone of voice was cheerful and buoyant. "Good morning, Lester. I didn't send for you. Where the hell's Oliver?"

"I'm sorry, sir, but Mr. Oliver's not here this morning."

"What do you mean—not here?"

"He's not turned up, sir. He's . . . absent. Nobody's seen him and I've checked up on the time-book. He's not signed on, sir . . . "

The manager caressed his chin. Lester felt that he had been cheated of his prey.

"I see. Must be sick, I suppose. That puts a somewhat different complexion on the matter. All the same, either Oliver or his people should have 'phoned through to the bank and given the reason for his absence. Courtesy costs nothing— that's why you never get it these days, I suppose."

Murray looked up at his junior as though expecting confirmation of his remark.

"Yes, sir," replied Lester, dutifully. He turned as though about to go, but a word from his chief halted him.

"If any message come from Oliver, or about Oliver, let me know at once. His absence to-day's decidedly awkward. There was a special matter I wanted to see him about—in relation to the foreign securities register. He seems to have been keeping the book for some months now."

"Yes, sir. He has. Since you took him off the counter, sir."

Murray nodded. "Yes. I remember. How long ago is it that I made that change, Lester?"

Lester thought over the question. "Last October, sir. Just after you returned from your holiday."

Murray was groping for an elusive memory. "That's right. Now let me see, why did I do it? I had a reason at the time. Why did Oliver come off the counter? He was third till then, if I remember correctly?"

"That's so, sir. The change was made, in all probability I should think, sir, because of Mr. Lovell's promotion to the Putney branch. You had to have a sort of general shake-up, sir. Don't you remember?"

Murray rose from his seat and smiled. "Quite right, Lester. That was the reason. Lovell going to Putney. It's all come back to me. But Oliver choosing this morning to be away sick is a damned nuisance. It's upset all my arrangements. And that's putting it mildly." Murray looked at his wrist-watch. "O.K., Lester. That's all right. Get back to your job."

"Very good, sir. There is one thing, sir, before I go—shall I bring you the 'F.S.' register? Or would you rather—"

Murray stood for a moment or so and then shook his head. "No I don't think so, Lester. Don't bother. I'll wait until Oliver turns up. The one, you see, isn't much value without the other. I wanted to go through it with him. But you can tell Mr. Fitzgerald I'd like a word with him."

"I understand, sir." Lester walked to the door of the manager's room and closed it quickly behind him.

3

The day wore itself out—both in the Lombard Street branch of Delaney's bank and everywhere else. The pale-gold sunshine of April had warmed the hearts of London's millions. Almost all of them, influenced by April's meretricious promise, looked forward eagerly to the even greater climatic delights that were to come. May . . . June . . . July . . . August and their attractive concomitants . . . cricket . . . the Derby . . . Ascot . . . Henley . . . Wimbledon . . . Goodwood . . . holidays in the green country and by the sea.

Andrew Murray, with the clock in his room pointing to half past four, closed a drawer of his desk-table and simultaneously thought once again of Oliver, the man on his staff who was absent, and of whom he had heard nothing. He spoke on the telephone to Lester.

"Any news from Mr. Oliver, Lester?"

"No, sir. Nothing at all, sir."

For some reason, Murray became unusually angry.

"Well, it's a piece of damned cheek—a man away from duty for a whole day and not a blind word—Murray pulled himself up abruptly. He appeared to remember to whom he was speaking. After all, Lester was Oliver's junior. What he was saying was, from that particular angle, unseemly. "O.K., Lester," he concluded, "we shall probably know all about it by tomorrow morning. Either Oliver will turn up smiling somewhere round nine o'clock, or there'll be a letter in the post explaining everything."

The manager hung up. "There's too much taken for granted in this ruddy bank," he growled.

4

Stella Forrest, the cashier in Lambert's restaurant, situated something less than half a mile's distance from the Lombard Street branch of Delaney's bank, had, during that same Easter Tuesday, shared Andrew Murray's anxiety with regard to the absence of Peter Oliver.

The anxiety, however, in her case, was foundationed upon, and occasioned by, an entirely different cause. For whereas the misgivings of Andrew Murray originated from Oliver's absence from Delaney's bank, Stella's worry and forebodings had their origin in the beating of her heart.

For Stella Forrest was hopelessly head over heels in love with Peter Oliver, and for over a month now she had known that her passion was reciprocated, everything in the mutual garden was absolutely lovely and all set in due and inevitable course for the world of melody of merry wedding bells.

On this Tuesday in Easter week, however, by date April 19th, Stella had been, since approximately 2 p.m., in an agony of acute distress and suspense. For Peter had failed to put in his customary appearance for lunch. Such a thing had not happened for months. Certainly not since she and Peter had first fluttered love at each other over the cashier's desk at Lambert's restaurant.

Stella Forrest, at the age of 22, was an authentic "lovely". She was an ash-blonde, with dark violet-blue eyes, and whether you looked at her for the first time, full face or in profile, you caught your breath, went down three times and as often as not left your change on the ledge in front of her.

With Stella in the cash-desk, old man Lambert could traffic in equine steaks, wallow in whalemeat delicacies, serve megrims as Dover soles and not a customer complained or even murmured. They all came back for more, but the more was an eyeful of Stella Forrest and not, as old man Lambert kidded himself, the pleasure of the piled plate.

As Stella watched the people make their way in and out of the restaurant, hour after hour on this Easter Tuesday, with still no sign of Peter Oliver, she became more and more certain that all could not be well with him. She had valid reasons for this feeling of certainty. The chief of these was that when she had kissed Peter good night on the previous evening he had said to her (as he invariably said to her after their last kiss), "see you at lunch-time tomorrow, darling."

Inasmuch as he had said that to her on the Bank holiday evening, she argued to herself, as she went on mechanically accepting money and equally automatically giving change, he must have *intended* to come to the restaurant for lunch. Otherwise there had been no need for him to say it.

Therefore, as he *hadn't* come in for lunch, one of three dreadful things must have happened. One—the epitome of all suffering as far as she was concerned—Peter had ceased to love her and by this time was already loving another. Two—almost as awful for her—Peter was dead. Three—not so bad, but certainly agony enough—Peter was ill. On the whole, she considered the third possibility as perhaps the most likely.

As soon as she could get the chance, she would ring his house from the 'phone at the back of the restaurant. If only she could hear his voice even, it would reassure her. Then a wave of doubts assailed her again. *Was* he at the bank in Lombard Street after all? Keeping away from her because he had no wish to see her any more? Should she telephone to the bank, and not to the house? Would that be better? Would they know what she wanted to know?

She tossed and turned the questions in her mind. If only this eternal procession of customers would stop for a few minutes! The fed and the to-be-fed. And all looking equally fed-up.

Stella kept glancing anxiously at her watch. There should be a lull in the restaurant in the region of three o'clock. There almost invariably was.

Directly it came and the chance presented itself, she'd dash to the telephone and try to get through to Peter's house. At 3.10 precisely, Stella got the chance for which she had been waiting so anxiously and literally flew to old man Lambert's telephone in the far corner of the back of the restaurant.

Hastily—almost feverishly—she dropped in the coins, dialled MID 5557 and waited in an agony of impatience. The ringing tone reached her ears—not long now, she comforted herself, before I find out *something*. And then she chilled. Suddenly her optimism vanished. For no answering voice came to take the place of the ringing tone.

Stella pressed the receiver to her ear, hoping against hope that the voice she yearned to hear would come suddenly and briskly like the draught of fresh water which slakes the thirst and cools the fevered mouth. She clung to the receiver almost desperately.

But no voice came, only the ringing tone continued—relentlessly, impersonally, horribly! Stella, acting mechanically again now, pressed button B and collected the coppers she had inserted. *There was no reply*. Stella almost recited the words aloud. No reply from 8 Mayblossom Avenue, Puck Willow. The house of the Olivers. Where Peter and his family lived. Where Peter would be if he were away from the bank by reason of illness. No reply from *anybody*! Stella stumbled back to her chair at the cash-desk. She saw with a numbed relief that nobody was waiting for her with frowning impatience.

As she took her seat again at the receipt of custom, she began to sort things out. To *try* to sort them out!

CHAPTER 2

1

There was only an occasional customer now for Stella's attention, because the midday rush was over and the resultant breathing-space gave her the opportunity to do the "sorting-out", as she had mentally described it. To her knowledge there were five in the Oliver family. At least that was her understanding of what Peter Oliver had told her from time to time.

She herself had not yet visited the Oliver house. There were reasons for this. To tell the truth, no invitation from Peter's mother had so far been forthcoming. Peter's original excuse had been that he wasn't keen on breaking the news of his engagement to Stella to his parents for a month or so, and all through the stages of their love-affair they had done their best to keep it as secret as possible. Although a few weeks before Easter Peter had whispered something to his mother.

So Stella was forced to rely on what Peter had told her for details of his family. Stella was going to try to account for them now, one by one. Because she was remembering one thing all the time. *There had been no reply from the house* when she had telephoned.

First of all there was Peter's father. His name was Richard. Richard and something else. Stella could remember that. Yes, he was in Scotland for Easter week—Stella recalled that fact—it was something to do with the recent death of his sister. Business he had to transact with the solicitors concerning the estate. Peter had told her how his father had decided to use Easter week for the particular purpose.

So *he* wouldn't be at home. Then there were Peter's mother and sister. Margaret was his sister's name, but Stella wasn't too certain of Peter's mother's name. She thought it was either Edith or Evelyn—still, it didn't really matter. And, of course, Mrs. Oliver and Margaret were away on holiday together. For the whole week. They were staying at Bournemouth. At the "Suffolk Hôtel". They wouldn't be back until next Saturday afternoon or evening. Peter had told her that once or twice over the recent holiday. So that *they* wouldn't be at home. Well, that only left David, Peter's brother. Now where was he?

Stella puckered her brows in an attempt to remember. Peter had definitely told her something about him—with regard to the Easter holidays. Now what was it? Stella cudgelled her brains. David was away! David was away somewhere, she felt positive of that. But where was it—and for how long? After some moments' intensive thought, which got her nowhere, Stella gave up the problem. Anyhow, he wasn't at the house at Puck Willow, which meant in effect that *nobody* was there. Nobody who could answer the ringing of the telephone if Peter were in the house somewhere, lying ill, unconscious perhaps, from an accident. Lying there, bleeding to death! Nobody there to look after him or help him in any way! This last thought brought Stella Forrest to a sudden decision. Something must be done about it! *She*—Stella Forrest—must do something about it. And as quickly as possible!

But what, and how? She was on duty in the restaurant till seven o'clock on this particular Tuesday, but with a three-quarters of an hour's break at half past three. That is to say, within a few minutes' time. During the period of that break she'd telephone and contact—and then, abruptly, suddenly and almost shatteringly, a wave of optimism came flooding over her, and completely engulfed the pessimism and despondency which had so recently possessed her. Peter was all right. Of course he was! He must be! And there was a perfectly simple explanation of his absence. He must have been sent somewhere on official business by the bank at which he worked. Which had caused him to alter or forgo his normal lunch-time break. Of course that was it! Why hadn't she realized it before instead of worrying her guts out as she'd been doing?

And then the complete *volte-face* occurred and Stella began to chide and to castigate herself for her previous foolish forebodings and silly misgivings.

Her optimism ran high and rioted. Her doubting mind clarified. She saw without any obscurity or hesitation the course of action she would take. Why she hadn't thought of it before she didn't know. When she had finished her day's work, at seven o'clock that evening, she would go straight to Peter's house at Puck Willow. His parents would not be there to bite her head off. Neither of them would have yet returned home. She was certain of that. In all probability Peter would be there alone, overjoyed to see her in advance of the evening-time when they had arranged to meet.

He'd explain to her the reasons that had prevented him turning up for lunch . . . such ordinary commonplace reasons and then Stella would tell him of the suspense and distress which she had suffered by his absence . . . and they'd have a jolly good laugh over it . . . and Peter would take her in his arms and kiss her!

2

Stella flew out of the restaurant and caught a train from Cannon Street a few minutes after seven o'clock. The journey took nearly three-quarters of an hour. Puck Willow was two stations beyond Wimblefield.

When she left the station at Puck Willow, she knew the direction to take for Mayblossom Avenue because Peter had often described to her his morning walk to the station and the local landmarks he passed on the journey. According to him, the house was about eight minutes' walk from Puck Willow station. You could do it on your head in eight minutes—that was his way of putting it.

It was a beautiful Spring evening, equally lovely with the day that had preceded it.

Stella walked on, past the old-fashioned public-house on the corner, "The Viper", until she came to the big chestnut tree in the middle of the road.

She had heard about this tree from Peter many times, so that directly she saw it she knew she was on the right road. Soon she saw the turning for which her eyes had been searching—Mayblossom Avenue.

Stella swung round it. It was a short road. Of large, modern, semi-detached, suntrap-fronted villas. There were about a dozen of them on each side of the road.

Stella moved quickly up the crazy-pavement path that led to the front door of the house she wanted and lifted the lion's-head knocker. She knocked three times, fairly lightly, and noticed as she knocked that there was a bottle of milk standing in a corner by the door.

She heard the knocking resound through the house. She listened for Peter's quick, alert, eager step up the hall to open the door. But she listened in vain. For not a sound came from this house of the Olivers. She had evidently not knocked loudly enough. Perhaps Peter was in the garden.

Stella knocked again—loudly and more insistently this time. Still no response came to her. Only the echoes of her own knocking. Stella tried to peer through the leaded-glass panel set in the side of the front door. All she could see, vaguely, were two closed doors.

It was then that Stella Forrest began to tremble a little—but she raised the knocker again and knocked for the third time. On this occasion she knocked sharply, almost imperiously but again to no avail. The house of the Olivers remained deaf . . . stoically impervious . . . to all her entreaties.

It was at this precise moment that all Stella's doubts receded. That is to say they no longer remained *doubts*—they vanished completely for something worse to take their place. The silence of the house and the bottle of milk were the last straws as far as she was concerned. They left no doubt in her mind! She was absolutely *certain* now that something was wrong. The doubts were swamped by this certainty. And she felt that whatever it was, that *was* wrong, had to do with Peter Oliver. Her Peter.

But what could she do about it and how could she do it? They were the questions which gnawed at her as she stood there that evening outside the front door of No. 8 Mayblossom Avenue, weighing all sorts of possibilities.

And then something happened. Something which she hadn't been expecting. The front door of the house adjoining opened and an elderly lady came out into the porch. She began to speak to Stella, before Stella quite realized the fact.

3

"Good evening. Were you wanting Mrs. Oliver?" asked the elderly lady.

"Er . . . no . . . not exactly," said Stella.

"Because if you were—she's away. She's at the seaside for the week. With Miss Oliver. They won't be back till Saturday." Stella plucked up courage. "Yes. I know that. They're at Bournemouth. I really wanted young Mr. Oliver. Mr. Peter Oliver."

The elderly lady shook her head. "I don't *think* he's home from business yet. I haven't heard him." Her features brightened considerably as she appeared to think of something additional. "As a matter of fact, I don't *think* he's been back since he went out last night."

Her words made a great impression on Stella. So much so that she determined to take part of a plunge, at least.

"I'm rather a special friend of Peter's—in fact I was with him yesterday evening until about nine o'clock and have an appointment with him later on this evening. But something's happened to-day that has . . . sort of worried me. He should have met me at lunch-time, but he didn't. Would you mind telling me the time you heard him go out?"

The elderly lady smiled. "I don't mind, my dear. If it will help you at all and, perhaps, ease your mind. He went out, I should say, just after eleven o'clock last night. My husband and I heard the door slam. That's how I know. It must have been Peter, because all the rest of the family are away. He's the only one there. Until the end of the week."

Stella wrinkled her brows at the information. There was something here that she couldn't understand.

"Just after eleven o'clock last night? Couldn't that have been Peter *coming in*—not going out? Because he had said good night to me . . ."

The elderly lady promptly disposed of Stella's suggestion. "Oh, no. It couldn't have been him coming in. Because we'd heard him in the house for some time before that."

Stella glanced at the two houses and her eyes were the obvious clue to what she was thinking.

The elderly lady picked up the clue. "Perhaps I should explain to you, my dear. I expect you're wondering what I mean. Peter had a bath before he went out. We heard the bath-water running away. Down the waste-pipe. You can, you know."

Before Stella could find words to reply, the elderly lady had gone on talking.

"And I'm almost certain that Peter *didn't* come back here last night. I mean I think that he must have slept somewhere else. For these reasons. Neither my husband nor I heard him again. The milk-bottle, you can see for yourself, hasn't been taken in, and this morning's newspapers were showing in the letter-box when my husband went out soon after eight o'clock this morning. Actually, he pushed them through the letter-box- it's just as well to do that, you know, these days, there seem to be so many burglaries taking place when houses are obviously left unoccupied."

Stella had no words now. They had all left her. Her thoughts were rioting and her mind was in a whirl. It was impossible for her to think clearly. This was even worse than she had anticipated.

The elderly lady, however, continued to smile. The smile was intended to be one of reassurance.

"I expect he'll be back this evening sometime. You know what young men are nowadays. Probably went to a friend's house for the night and then went straight on from there to business this morning. You'll find there's no cause to worry, my dear."

There were signs here of the termination of the interview. Unmistakable signs. Stella Forrest nodded mechanically. If all these things that she was hearing were true, why hadn't Peter told *her* something of them? Given *her* some indication? Had he gone back to that other girl—the girl he had known before he had met her? Taken advantage of the fact that his parents were away from home? But even allowing for that deceit, he could still have come to the restaurant for lunch at midday. Unless of course he had finished with her for good . . . called it a day.

Stella thanked the good-natured neighbour for her consideration and information and turned slowly away. She would go back. Back to Puck Willow station and her own room in Hammersmith. Peter was supposed to meet her at their usual place at nine o'clock. But she knew that he wouldn't. There would be no Peter for her that night. To-morrow would come . . . eventually . . . and all that she could do, it seemed, was to wait for it. She would get no sleep, of course awake. And fret . . . and worry . . . and toss and turn.

4

Just as she opened the door of her sitting-room that evening, Stella remembered something. Something which flashed out of the dark, as it were, and terrified her. It terrified her so much that directly she thought of it she began to tremble violently. Supposing she and Peter *had* been seen after all . . . despite all the precautions they had taken to keep their love-affair just a secret between their two selves? Supposing . . . Stella began to work things out quickly . . . hundreds of memories rushed helter-skelter into her mind . . . Peter *had* made a mistake that evening he had taken her to that South American gentleman's—Stella couldn't think of the man's name . . . Peter had left the bank that evening and picked her up on the way . . . that was the only occasion he had ever done that . . . told her there was nothing whatever to worry about . . . that the man was as safe as houses and wouldn't give them away. To anybody.

She herself had by no means shared Peter's confidence. You could never tell with foreigners. There was something "different" about them. Different from English people. They had different standards. They "talked" a great deal more. Supposing—

Stella found for herself, in those few moments of reflection and remembrance, torment after torment. From nowhere came comfort or solace.

When she eventually went to bed, matters remained just the same. No respite of sweet sleep came to her tortured mind. Until the early hours of the morning, when she suddenly slid into a species of semi-feverish doze.

CHAPTER 3

1

The Wednesday of this Easter week, as far as the disappearance of Peter Oliver was concerned, ran on almost similar lines to the Tuesday which had immediately preceded it.

Andrew Murray, the genial and efficient manager of the Lombard Street branch of Delaney's bank, repeated his activity of the day before and made an almost immediate request for the attendance of Peter Oliver in his room, upon his arrival at the offices of the bank in question. The request, as on the Tuesday, was elaborated with an expressed desire to inspect at the same time the foreign securities register.

Lester, the junior, answered his chief's inquiries exactly as he had answered them twenty-four hours previously. Oliver had again not reported for duty, he told his chief, and Lester didn't think there was any news of him. No telephone message had been received as far as he knew and Lester didn't think there was any communication from Mr. Oliver in the morning post.

By this time, Murray's frown had assumed prodigious proportions, and language unbefitting the highest standard of bank managership was allowed to escape from his lips.

In fact Lester felt that the terms of his chief's verbal censure were distinctly unfair to Oliver's parents. After all, if Oliver were seriously ill "the old man" shouldn't say things like that. And, say what you like, there were such things as marriage certificates. Besides.

"Very well," concluded Murray, "don't stand gaping there, looking more daft than you actually are. If Oliver's not here he's not here. Go and get on with your work. And tell Mr. Fitzgerald I want him. That is to say if *he's* condescended to turn up."

"Very good, sir," replied Lester, "and will you still be wanting the F.S. register?"

"No, I won't," thundered the manager, "and it's a pity: some of you can't remember what you're told! Fact is you're spoon-fed, that's the ruddy trouble, coddled and cosseted from the cradle to the grave. When I was a junior—

"Yes, sir," said Lester, who put into process an exercise of immediate self-effacement. When he resumed his seat at his desk in the outer office he took a handkerchief from his sleeve and wiped his forehead. "For cryin' out loud," he muttered.

2

As it had been with Murray, Lester, and other members of the staff of Delaney's bank, so it was with Stella Forrest, at the cash-desk in old man Lambert's restaurant not so very far away. She had hoped against hope that this Wednesday luncheon-hour would bring Peter in for his customary meal, but, as deep down in her heart she knew it would be, the joy was denied to her.

The hands of the clock dragged on until twenty minutes past two. Stella had just rectified a bad mistake she had been about to make in respect of giving change, when she saw two men enter the restaurant. And one of the two men immediately arrested her attention because she *recognized* him. His name was Bathurst—Anthony Bathurst. She remembered it at once. On one occasion about a year ago she had gone to the Court of Criminal Appeal with a friend and this friend had pointed Anthony Bathurst out to her. And Stella remembered something else.

"If ever I were in a jam," Stella's friend had said, "that's the man I'd choose to scoop me out of it. And I'm not talkin' out of the back of my neck, either."

Stella's eyes now followed the tall form as it made its way down Lambert's restaurant in the company of a much shorter figure. And at that moment an idea was born within her. It was a perfectly wizard idea. She would enlist Anthony Bathurst's help in this matter of the missing Peter Oliver.

For one thing, Stella liked Anthony's face. It was clever and intelligent and had all those qualities which Stella knew a man's face should have—and, moreover, it had kindness in it, too. Every clever man didn't have that. But how could she best put her plan into effect?

A moment's thinking and Stella thought that she saw her way. She scribbled a note on a sheet of paper and signalled to one of the waitresses hovering near the cash-desk. The waitress saw the sign and edged up to Stella.

"Rose," whispered Stella, "you see that table over on the left there? The fourth row from the back and the third table from the wall? Two gentlemen. Do you see where I mean? They've only just come in. Be an angel and give this note to the tall one? The one with the grey eyes?"

Rose grinned as she took the slip of paper. "More of your 'come hither'—some of you kids are never satisfied, upon my word."

Stella shook her head faintly. "No, it's not what you think, Rose. Please give it to him for me."

"O.K., beautiful. I'll see that he gets it."

"Thank you, Rose."

The waitress slipped off in the approved direction and Stella watched with anxiety the voyage of her white-aproned argosy down the restaurant.

But a line of diners passing out momentarily obscured her vision and Rose was lost sight of. Within a few minutes, however, Rose was back at the cash-desk.

" 'Salright," she breathed to the cash-desk as she flitted by, "I gave it to him. And I must say, kid, I admire your taste. Very 'andsome indeed. Just my cuppa. And I was always reckoned a good picker, myself."

Stella breathed a sigh of relief at Rose's remark and settled herself to wait.

But she felt positive that this man to whom she had appealed would not let her down.

3

Anthony Lotherington Bathurst, not too fit after a most prolonged and persistent attack of urticaria, read the note which the rosy-cheeked waitress had placed in his hand and then flicked it gently across the table to his companion.

"Read that, Andrew," he said. "There's no doubt that I must be the stormy petrel of crime. It's becoming increasingly obvious. Some are born to it, others achieve it—I appear to have it thrust upon me."

Chief Detective-Inspector Andrew MacMorran, of the "Yard", grinned at Anthony, picked up the note and read it. It ran as follows:

Dear Mr. Bathurst,

Please forgive me taking this great liberty. You don't know me but I do know you by sight. I am the girl in the cash-desk. I am also in great trouble. I implore you to help me. I feel certain that somebody I love is in great danger. It may even be that he's already been murdered. I am not just a silly girl and I feel sure that I am not just imagining things. Will you please let me talk to you for just a few moments when you have finished your lunch? Please do this for me. I feel certain that I shall be able to convince you—I assure you will never regret it.

Yours imploringly,

Stella Forrest.

Andrew MacMorran grunted and handed back the note. "I've seen this sort of thing before, I'm afraid. Usually, there's nothing in it. Hysteria takes all sorts of forms, you know. And with these girls of a certain age . . ."

Anthony made no reply. As the waitress brought the soup to the table, he picked up the note again and re-read it.

"I don't know that I entirely agree with you, Andrew. In this particular instance. It's difficult to tell, of course. From a mere first impression. Have you seen the girl? Been here before? You know that I haven't—because I told you so when we came in."

"Been here two or three times. Not many. Less than half a dozen times all told, I should say. I rather fancy, from memory, though, that she's extremely easy on the eye. If that's any incentive to you. Not being a ladies' man myself—"

Anthony grinned. "I regard the condition you ascribe to her as usually preferable to the reputed but often extremely problematical heart of gold. *Pour passer le temps*, of course. No more than that."

Anthony finished his soup. "All the same, Andrew," he continued, "I shouldn't like it said of me, when I am but an echo or a shade, that I ever refused to help anybody in trouble. Especially on a day like to-day when you're with me. Nothing, from the little lady's point of view, could be more propitious. And if somebody *has* murdered her—"

MacMorran grunted non-committally as he interrupted. "Don't drag me into it. Leave me out. The note was addressed to you, not to me."

"Only because she knew my face, and, being a virtuous girl, had never made *your* acquaintance. Had the latter contingency ever taken place, I haven't the slightest doubt that the appeal would have been addressed to you and not to me.'

"Skip it," said the Inspector, "and get on with your lunch."

Anthony smiled and began to unscrew the top of his fountain-pen. He found a sheet of note-paper in his wallet.

"Chance it, Andrew, I'm going to cross the Rubicon. For better or worse and all the rest of it. You heard what I said to you just now. I shall pass through this world but once—I'll tell you the rest of that on a later occasion." Anthony scribbled a short note. When the waitress came to the table again, he handed it to her.

"As a great favour to me, Phyllis, will you please give that to the lady in your cash-desk?"

The girl smirked. "Cupid's little messenger—eh? Don't know what my union'll say about it, I'm sure! Suppose 'Erbert Morrison gets to 'ear what I've done? Also, for your information, I don't happen to be Phyllis. She took the wrong turning and left last December."

Anthony grinned back. "See my finger wet—see my finger dry—I promise you faithfully you shall dance at the wedding. But I don't necessarily say whose."

MacMorran attacked his roast lamb with gusto and alacrity. "What did you say? In the note, I mean?"

"To the beckoning siren? That I'd listen to her story when we'd finished our lunch. I didn't tell her who you were."

"Why not?"

"I thought she'd better get used to you—gradually. You know the idea. Like the little girl who first saw the giraffe."

MacMorran grinned as he peppered his potatoes. "And where do you propose to listen to the tale of woe? Have you considered that point?"

"My dear Andrew, *l'homme propose—mais Dieu dispose.* In this case-*la femme.*"

"I know all about that—but you can't very well have a sobbing lovely on your shoulder chattering crime and mumbling murder in a crowded city restaurant at peak-load hour. Even you won't care for that. It'll all get mixed up with the roast beef and two veg."

Anthony's imp of mischief still played his cards. "Why not? People would almost certainly think it was a new film being shot. They'd take you to be Boris Karloff, the girl, Hedy Lamarr—"

"You've slipped up. She's a blonde. The girl in the desk, I mean."

"What does that matter? Andrew, I'm surprised at your simplicity. The blonde of this morning is the brunette of this afternoon and the—"

The waitress spoke into Anthony's sentence. "The girl friend said 'Thank you very much'. I told her about the dancing engagement but it didn't seem to sink in."

"No it probably wouldn't. But you leave it all to me, Mustardseed. A promise is a promise and my word is my bond."

"O.K., Salt-cellar. I'll make a note in my engagement-diary. What sweets does your Royal Highness require?"

"Boiled jam roll-twice," replied Anthony; "*facilis descensus Averno.*"

The waitress threw back her head and regarded him critically. Gertcher," she said, as she departed.

"I entirely agree with you," said Anthony.

4

Stella Forrest closed the door of one of the upstair rooms. Old man Lambert sometimes let it for the evening. For one thing it had a piano and for another there was plenty of space in it. On this particular Wednesday afternoon she had prevailed on her employer to allow her to use it for half an hour.

Old man Lambert was a bit bewildered when she had gone to him upon receipt of Anthony's reply, but he had a softish corner in his heart for his pretty blue-eyed cashier.

So he acceded to her request—she told him with an excess of emphasis and entreaty that it was vitally important for her—and then instructed one of the waitresses to take Stella's place in the cash-desk until Stella herself came back.

When Stella Forrest closed the door she came forward to Anthony and MacMorran, who were already seated in the chairs that she had found for them. By this time, Anthony had noted that MacMorran's description of Stella Forrest did her less than justice.

"Lovely eyes," he commented to himself, "attractive profile and, from the looks point of view alone, a girl in a thousand. I'm surprised she hasn't had a wedding-ring put on the appropriate finger before this. Maybe she's 'choosy'. Well, she's every right and reason to be. With beauty like that, there's no knowing where she might climb eventually."

He spoke to her as she closed the door and came forward. "Sit here on this chair, will you, Miss Forrest? I understand from your little note that you already know me. I don't think, though, that you know this gentleman who's here with me. So I'd better introduce you as a start-off. Chief Detective-Inspector MacMorran of New Scotland Yard."

Andrew MacMorran half rose and gave the girl a clumsy sort of bow. But the effect on Stella Forrest was almost electrical. Her eyes opened wide and the tears came into them. "I'm pleased to meet you . . . and thank you . . . thank you," she said conventionally, "but I wish . . . I wish—"

The words she sought for refused to come. Anthony saw her distress and helped her out.

"Now you sit down here, Miss Forrest and tell us all your troubles. Then perhaps you'll feel better." Stella heard him, drew a deep breath and jerked herself back to recovery.

"First of all—please let me thank you for your—"

"Forget it," said Anthony laconically, "only too delighted to help. And that goes both for me *and* for the Inspector. You just sit there and tell us what it's all about."

CHAPTER 4

1

Stella Forrest looked at Anthony gratefully. "That's what I'd like to do. It's what I want to do. But it's all so puzzling and perplexing. And I must be so careful. To tell you everything properly, I mean. I know I mustn't confuse you. Oh, dear—I don't know the best way to start."

"Tell your story in your own way, Miss Forrest. Don't worry. And if it will help you, Inspector MacMorran and I will promise not to interrupt you. We'll reserve all our questions until you've finished."

Stella sat there, tight-lipped and unsmiling. Then a quick glance she gave at the clock seemed to frighten her. She drew another deep breath and started to talk.

"I'm the cashier downstairs, as you know. And I've recently become engaged to a boy named Peter Oliver. His full name is Peter Wilton Oliver. He works at Delaney's bank in Lombard Street. He used to be on the counter, as they say—a cashier—but for some months now he's had other work. They had a sort of change round in the Autumn because one of the staff had a promotion and Peter was shifted. In the same bank, I mean, of course."

Anthony nodded encouragingly. Stella went on.

"Peter lives with his father and mother, a sister and another brother at Puck Willow. His father's a book-keeper under the Wimblefield Corporation. I think he's in the Borough Treasurer's department. This Easter, the Oliver household has been unusually—how shall I put it—'split up'." Stella saw MacMorran's eyebrows lift. "No, I don't mean anything in the nature of quarrels, don't think that, but just their various ways of spending the Easter holiday."

"I get you," said the Inspector. "Sorry."

Stella continued. "I'd better explain what actually took place. Mr. Oliver, senior—that's Peter's father, of course—is at the present moment in Scotland. He travelled north the evening before Good Friday. Some little time ago, his sister died. In Aberdeen. Mr. Oliver is her executor and had to go there over some legal business to do with her estate. That's what Peter told me. I know there are some houses that are being sold which used to belong to the lady that's dead. Mr. Oliver isn't expected to return from Aberdeen until the end of the week. So you see *he* isn't at the house at Puck Willow. I want you to remember that, because it's important." Stella paused, took another of her deep breaths, and started off again.

"That's one. Now, besides that, Mrs. Oliver, Peter's mother, and Margaret, his sister, have gone to Bournemouth for Easter week. It was convenient, you see, with Mr. Oliver away up in Scotland. They won't be back until next Saturday evening. So you see, *they* aren't at Puck Willow either. That brings me to David, Peter's brother. He's away somewhere for Easter, but I can't remember where it is. Peter did tell me, but it's faded away. Anyhow, you can see that David isn't at his father's house, either. Which is the main point I want to make to you. In other words, Peter has been left on his own. He said he didn't mind, it was only for a week, and that he could manage on his head. Have I made it all clear, so far?" Stella's tone was anxious.

"You're doin' fine, Miss Forrest," said Andrew Mac- Morran, "now keep it up."

The blue eyes thanked him and Stella Forrest was in her stride again.

"Well I was off duty from here on Good Friday, Easter Sunday and on the Bank Holiday Monday. Peter's leave from the bank coincided exactly with mine. On the Saturday we were open and I came in. So was the bank, and he went in. On Good Friday Peter and I went to Hampton Court, Saturday evening we did a 'flick' at one of those cinemas in the Haymarket, Easter Sunday Peter took me to Southend by motor-coach for the day, and on the Bank holiday we went to Kew Gardens. Now please listen carefully—because I'm coming to the dreadful part."

Anthony glanced at her sharply. This girl seemed pretty sure of herself and he had heard and noted specially the adjective she used.

But Stella was in the saddle again and the pace was accelerating.

"We came back from Kew late on Easter Monday afternoon, had a little dinner at a restaurant in Hammersmith, and Peter said 'good night' to me just about nine o'clock. At Hammersmith station. As he left me he said 'Usual time tomorrow.' They were the last words he spoke to me.

That meant he would be in here, in this restaurant, to lunch, from the bank on the following day at some time between half past twelve and two o'clock. 'Usual time tomorrow' *always* meant that to us. It referred to our first meeting at lunch-time on the next day. Well, he didn't come yesterday, he hasn't been to-day, and I haven't set eyes on him or heard a whisper from him since we said 'good night' on Monday."

MacMorran was about to speak, but Stella recognized the indication and checked him.

"Please wait, there's more to come—and it's the awful part. And please go on listening as carefully as you can. I feel that so much depends on it. On Tuesday evening, I was so desperately worried at Peter's absence (I don't mind telling you that I nearly worried myself sick) that when I finished here at seven o'clock I went straight along and took the train from Cannon Street to Puck Willow. I went to Peter's house. I felt that I simply *must* get news of him somehow. That *anything* was better than the gnawing suspense. There was nobody there. Not a soul. I knocked and knocked and knocked—nothing doing. Then an old lady came out from next door. She was a decent old soul and besides being a bit 'nosy', I really think she wanted to help me. Please . . . please . . . listen to what she said. Because I feel it's frightfully important."

Stella's hands were trembling now and her fingers moving nervously. "According to her, Peter had gone home after he had left me. Just as I understood he intended to. That was all right. The old lady then said that she and her husband had heard him in the house. I found out later from her that what she really meant was that they had heard the bath-water running away—that Peter had had a bath. Then she said that he had gone out again just after eleven o'clock—they had heard him slam the front door—that he didn't come back to the house that night, and that he must have slept somewhere else. I'll tell you why she said the last thing. The milk-bottle was still on the step and her husband, when he went out that morning, had pushed the newspapers through the letter-box. Apparently they were showing where the boy had delivered them. Now, to finish up on all that, please remember one fact of the utmost importance."

Anthony came in quickly. "Which one's that, Miss Forrest?"

"That I haven't seen Peter Oliver since nine o'clock on Monday evening."

Anthony looked at her appraisingly. Stella's mood faltered. and her voice changed. "Oh, Mr. Bathurst, Inspector—Peter's either dead or in great danger. I know it. I am certain of it. Please believe me."

Anthony looked across at MacMorran and MacMorran's glance met his. Anthony nodded just perceptibly. MacMorran knew what the glance and the nod meant.

"Just a question or two, Miss Forrest, if you don't mind. Don't worry about your employer and the time—it hasn't all gone yet. And my questions won't take very long. Just a minute or so that's all. First of all—how old's this Mr. Peter Oliver?"

"Twenty-five, sir. Nearly twenty-six. He was twenty-five on the 22nd of July."

"Thank you. Now give us a rough description of him. Nothing elaborate. Just the main points."

"He's dark. Dark hair, dark eyes. Not so very tall. Just above what you'd call middle height. Not so very robust, either. Slim, not heavy in build. Clean-shaven. Left-handed. I don't think there's much else—"

"That's all right, don't worry, that'll do very nicely, just to be going on with. Now a slightly more unpleasant question. Was this gentleman, Mr. Peter Oliver, in any trouble? That you know of? In *any* sort of jam that he may have mentioned to you? Anything, mind—no matter how trivial it may appear to be? And don't be frightened to tell the truth."

"Nothing," answered Stella firmly, "that he has ever told me about. And judging from his high spirits when we said 'good night' on Monday evening, I should say that nothing could be more unlikely. He didn't seem to have a care in the world."

MacMorran nodded. "Thank you, Miss Forrest. Now the business angle, Delaney's bank. The place where your young gentleman works. The Lombard Street branch, I think you said. What do *they* say about it all?"

Stella looked dismayed at what, after all, was a perfectly natural question. She shook her head rather shamefacedly, Anthony thought.

"But I haven't inquired there, sir."

"Why not? Surely the bank's the place to inquire and the people there can—"

"But don't you see, Peter's not there! He can't be there! He hasn't been there for two days.".

"How do you know he's not there, young lady, if you haven't inquired? Can you be *so* certain?"

"But don't you see"—Stella began to twist her fingers almost desperately—"if he'd been there, he'd have come in here for lunch? To see me. That's just my point." The "Yard" Inspector was just about to continue the discussion when Anthony Bathurst intervened.

"Miss Forrest's point is an excellent one, Andrew. From her own particular angle. She's fortified by two conditions, don't forget that. Which at once give her two advantages over you and me. Firstly, she knows this Mr. Peter Oliver—and he is a stranger to us. Secondly, she has the intuition that is always linked inseparably with her sex. And, personally I'm distinctly impressed with what she has told us. All of it. Anyhow, it will be a simple matter for us to do now, Andrew, the very thing which you suggest Miss Forrest might have done before us. Ring the Lombard Street branch of Delaney's bank. And inquire if Peter Oliver is on duty. You do it, Andrew. From here. Do you happen to know the name of the manager, Miss Forrest?"

Stella thought it over. She answered rather slowly. "No, I don't think I do. Peter may have mentioned it to me at some time or the other but—"

MacMorran got up from his chair. "That's all right—the 'phone's downstairs, isn't it? I'll go and have a 'bash' at Delaney's bank."

Stella and Anthony heard the sound of MacMorran's footsteps as he made his way downstairs. The girl turned to Anthony plaintively.

"Mr. Bathurst, to ring up the bank is just waste of time," she said tremulously; "*of course* Peter can't be there."

"My dear young lady," replied Anthony, "in that case, it will, to a certain extent, confirm your story. Nothing will be lost as a result of our telephoning. And by that time Inspector MacMorran may be as impressed by your story as I am."

Stella made an impatient movement with her hands. Anthony smiled. "Ah-but don't forget he's a much bigger noise than I am. Besides being a credit to Scotland Yard. And the 'Yard's' an amazingly efficient institution, believe me."

There was a silence. Stella was quiet and Anthony was content to respect her quietude. Eventually, they heard MacMorran ascending the stairs. The door opened and he came in. Anthony saw at once that his face was grave and troubled. MacMorran sat down in the chair he had recently left.

"Peter Oliver," he announced, "has not reported for duty at Delaney's bank since last Saturday. I had a chat with the manager. He's wondering if the man's ill. But he can't understand his silence. He's actually sending a letter to him this afternoon asking him for an explanation. He told me that he'd already dictated it. He's inclined, very naturally of course, to go off the deep end. Calls Oliver's conduct the height of discourtesy. For one thing, he's broken the bank regulations re notifying absence."

Stella looked indignant but terribly white. Anthony rubbed the ridge of his jaw.

"Well, Andrew, that's that. But quite frankly, where are we now?"

"What do you mean—where are we?"

"Well, what's the next step? Where do we go to from here? If we're going to help Miss Forrest?"

"Well, it seems to me that we must wait for—"

Anthony quickly cut him. "I'm sorry, Andrew, the last thing I want to do is rush in, but I think that anything like waiting's the very last thing we should do." His voice changed as he continued, "I feel that I should tell you at once that I entirely share Miss Forrest's fears concerning the well-being of Peter Oliver."

A low cry broke from Stella Forrest. MacMorran rose, grim-lipped. "Perhaps you're right. Have you anything in mind?"

"Yes. I think the first thing we should do is to search the premises at the Olivers' house at Puck Willow. Looking back on what Miss Forrest has told us I don't know that I feel altogether satisfied over one or two points in connexion therewith. Miss Forrest here can give us the address."

MacMorran turned to Stella. "No. 8 Mayblossom Avenue," answered Stella mechanically.

"No. 8 Mayblossom Avenue," repeated MacMorran equally impersonally. He glanced down at the seated Stella. "Now you be a good girl," he said avuncularly, "and go and collect some more money at your cash-desk. It'll take your mind off things a bit. No doubt old Lambert can do with it—all these favourites going down lately. And if there's any good news, I'll see that you don't have to wait for it."

Stella stood up. "Thank you," she said, "thank you—for everything."

But Anthony saw her eyes fill with tears as she turned away from them.

2

"I don't think," said Inspector MacMorran, as he and Anthony left Lambert's restaurant, "that I shall trouble to communicate yet awhile with either of this man Oliver's parents."

Anthony made no reply. MacMorran went on to amplify his statement. "I had another word with the little lady before we came away. With regard to the *actual whereabouts* of these various people. In the family. The mother and sister are at Bournemouth. 'Suffolk Hôtel.' But she's not in possession of the father's address in Aberdeen. In the circumstances, I shan't worry any of them for the time being."

"No," said Anthony, "better to wait till something tangible turns up. Then we shall know where we are."

"That's how I feel about it. No need to shout before you're hurt. I propose that we blow along to this house at Puck Willow at once and have a look-see. Do you agree?"

"Entirely, Andrew. And I sincerely hope my fears aren't going to be justified."

They turned past the Mansion House into Walbrook and walked along to Cannon Street station.

"How about getting in?" inquired Anthony.

"I'm going to take a chance," said MacMorran. "I don't anticipate too many difficulties. If it's a Yale I think I've got the 'Open Sesame' for it in my pocket."

The Inspector grinned and added, "Actually, of course, Peter Oliver may have had a sore throat or a bilious attack, taken a day and a half in bed, felt a little better since lunch to-day, come downstairs for an armchair's convalescence by the fire, will hear our knock and conventionally open the front door to admit us to the house of his father, No. 8 Mayblossom Avenue, Puck Willow, Surrey. That's the way it may go."

Anthony shook his head. "Give you 'tens' against that, Andrew. And you can help yourself to a basinful."

"No. I'm not betting," said Andrew MacMorran, "merely filling in the lines of a very possible picture."

3

The stations flashed by, the traffic was light in the early afternoon, and Anthony and MacMorran found themselves alighting on the Puck Willow platform some minutes before they had expected.

The walk to the house in Mayblossom Avenue was soon accomplished. MacMorran opened the gate of No. 8 and used the knocker with the lion's head as Stella had used it before him.

The two men waited in the porch. Anthony shook his head and pointed downwards. MacMorran looked and saw the milk-bottles. Anthony spoke.

"Nobody at home, Andrew. More unused milk. You've saved your money. But it was a pretty picture of yours while it lasted."

Andrew MacMorran nodded and slipped his hand into his overcoat pocket. Anthony saw several keys in the Inspector's palm. The second key did the trick.

"Thought so. Any sign of the little old lady next door?"

"No. She's either passing by or polishing her medals, in all probability."

Anthony dodged into the house behind MacMorran and the latter closed the door gently and quietly. The house was very still. The two men stood on the hall-mat and listened. Anthony pointed to several newspapers and a bill or two that lay on the mat.

"There's nobody in this house," said MacMorran. "Doesn't take me long to sense that."

"Nobody alive," returned Anthony with a shake of the head. "That's a safer proposition, by far."

There were four doors in close proximity to them as they stood there by the front door. And a staircase on the right. All the doors they could see were closed.

Anthony opened the one on the right of the hall as one entered. It was a cloakroom with lavatory, wash-hand basin and mirror. It was empty—in the sense that there was nobody in it.

MacMorran opened the first door on the left, Anthony turned the handle of the second. The first room was a lounge, the second was evidently used as a dining-room and looked out on to the garden. Each was in perfectly normal condition. There was no sign of disturbance or disarrangement in either of them.

Each room looked as it might have been expected to look. On the table of the second room—the dining-room—was a glass of the "pony" description, not clean, and next to it was an ash-tray with the stub of one cigarette in it.

Anthony called to MacMorran to come and look at them. "Well, there's one thing," commented the latter. "There hasn't been anything in the nature of a party to celebrate the absence on holiday of the parent birds. I *have* known some of the more enterprising of the younger generation make a lot of fun and games capital out of occasions like that."

The fourth door which Anthony opened gave access to what modern house-agents' advertisements usually describe as "kitchen and scullery combined". Everything was in order as far as the eye went. There was no litter of any description and the sink was entirely empty of soiled crockery, All doors of cupboard, pantry, etc., were closed and fastened.

Anthony walked over and looked through the window of this apartment to the garden. Like the house, the latter seemed trim and well-kept. There was a large lawn, in excellent condition, and, beyond that, a well-stocked and tastefully laid out rockery. At a quick calculation, Anthony reckoned there were at least a hundred rose-bushes. At the end of the garden was a belt of elm trees and beyond the elms a good-sized field.

Anthony turned and looked inquiringly at MacMorran. "Upstairs," said the latter; "and I'm beginning to think we've spent our time on nothing."

"Wait," replied Anthony, "we haven't finished yet." The two men made their way upstairs. Round the landing were the closed doors of the bedrooms, lavatory and bathroom.

Anthony and MacMorran went to the four bedrooms first, in turn. Starting with the main front bedroom, evidently occupied when they were at home by Mr. and Mrs. Oliver, they then visited the three smaller rooms, occupied respectively and normally, according to Anthony's reckoning, by Peter, his sister and his brother. Let's see what were their names? Margaret and David—that was it.

The four bedrooms at which Anthony and the Inspector looked, seemed, like all the downstairs rooms, entirely in order. No disturbance. Nothing in any way disarranged.

"Wild-goose chase," muttered MacMorran, "mare's nest—and all the other things that you can think of. I was afraid so, when we started. Still, I suppose in the circumstances we had to come."

Anthony opened the door of the bathroom as the Inspector spoke.

He almost recoiled at the dreadful sight which met his eyes.

"Skip it, Andrew," he said quietly, "and come and look in here."

The body of a man in full evening dress lay on the floor of the bathroom.

He lay on his back. His throat had been cut from ear to ear.

"No wonder," said Anthony, "that he couldn't answer the door. Not even, poor devil, for the girl who loved him."

MacMorran took a few short paces into the bathroom. He had been standing behind Anthony. The Inspector looked down at the bath-mat upon which the body was stretched. There was an ugly dark splash on its edge. From the splash to a chair which stood between the bath and the hand-basin was a trail of blood-drops. Anthony counted seven of them, small and separate.

The face of the dead man was ghastly and horrible. From the right side of the neck, from a point just behind the right ear, and running across the throat, almost to the same position under the left ear, was a great clean-edged cut which gaped open—deep, ugly and crimson. The head lolled as a broken doll's might, in a sickeningly awful way towards the left shoulder.

The dead man's face had a greenish pallor, the mouth was the mouth of a mutilated marionette, grim and grotesque, the eyes were wide open and staring and fear, sheer and stark, was reflected in them. A considerable quantity of blood had come from the great wound.

As Anthony took in the full gamut of this horror, an exclamation came from MacMorran. He was pointing down towards the body. Anthony saw what had attracted the Inspector's attention. In the dead man's left hand was an open, white-handled razor of the old-fashioned type.

"Thank Heaven for that," said MacMorran, "that's going to save us an awful lot of trouble."

"You mean?" said Anthony inquiringly.

MacMorran cocked him a searching look. "Suicide. Plain as a pike-staff. The razor's in the dead man's left hand. When I first saw the mess, I had other ideas."

Anthony made no reply. He edged round the side of the body and looked into the bath. It was empty and seemed to be quite dry. He nodded.

"Could be suicide, Andrew. I agree with you." Anthony stood there for a second or so caressing the ridge of his jaw. "Going on what we know, Andrew—reconstruct the affair for me, will you? I'm curious to know just how your mind's working."

MacMorran shot him another critical glance.

"Simple enough. It runs like this, as I see it. Oliver—I've no doubt this is the man we've been told about—left Miss Forrest at Hammersmith station at nine o'clock on Monday evening. He came home here. The folk next door heard him. We know that. The old girl told Miss Forrest they had. He had a bath, shoved on the glad rags to keep another appointment, concerning which the girl Stella Forrest knew nothing, and went out again. Confirmed again by the old girl next door who heard the slamming of the front door. Later on, any time you like in the early hours of the next morning's my guess—he came back, and did himself in. But don't ask me *why* he entered the slaughtering trade—that'll have to come later. Couldn't face something's the probable answer."

Anthony listened carefully to MacMorran's exposition. "Could be," he repeated.

He knelt and examined the soles of the dead man's dress-shoes. MacMorran watched him and shook his head. "Monday was a fine day. And a fine evening, too. No rain. Sunshine for several hours. Nothing like mud anywhere. Besides, as I said, the razor's in his left hand. Good enough." Anthony nodded. "Could be," he said for the third time.

"What's biting you?" said MacMorran suddenly.

Anthony smiled. "Nothing, Andrew. That is to say, nothing in particular. As you say, it looks open and shut. But you can't altogether eliminate Miss Forrest."

"How do you mean?"

"Even if you wanted to," added Anthony.

"How do you mean?" repeated the Inspector.

Anthony shrugged his shoulders. "Miss Forrest says smiling happy Peter Oliver kissed her good-bye at Hammersmith at 9 p.m. Bank Holiday evening. Why then should same smiling happy young gentleman in love with a charming girl, who's returning love for love, decide on such a messy entrance to the Elysian Fields just the matter of a few hours later? I can't link it up yet, Andrew."

"He worked in a bank, didn't he? That's the answer, you'll find. That's where the trouble is, hundred to one on it. Bees and honey. There's a telephone downstairs—I'll use it and get things moving. The sooner the better."

Anthony nodded. "Don't forget one thing, though, Andrew."

MacMorran, who had made the landing, turned back. "What's that?"

"Easter Monday was a Bank holiday." MacMorran stared. "What the hell's that got to do with it?" he muttered as he went downstairs.

4

MacMorran's telephone message brought the men of the "Yard" retinue—complementary and ancillary. The cameramen, the finger-print experts with the insufflator, the pathologist and a couple of uniformed constables.

When they were getting down to it, in their respective functionings, MacMorran telephoned a telegram to Mrs. Oliver, c/o The "Suffolk Hôtel", Bournemouth.

Anthony, who had one or two ideas buzzing in his brain, stayed in the proximity of the bathroom. From one angle, he particularly wished Stella Forrest was there. He wanted another talk with her badly and it was with a generally diminishing interest that he watched the quiet efficiency of the "Yard's" ancillaries.

Dr. Greatorex, the pathologist, addressed him once or twice. On the first occasion he said, "not a pleasant sight, Bathurst." On the second, some minutes later, Greatorex's remark was even more terse. "Jugular," was the word he used.

"Nasty," said Anthony.

"Yes," agreed the pathologist, "spurts a bit, you know." Anthony wandered back to the bedrooms. To the room that he fancied had been occupied by the dead man. He walked to the window and looked out on to the gardens of Mayblossom Avenue. Directly below him, he could see the roof of the Oliver garage. He felt sure, somehow, that his intuition was right and that this room in which he stood had been the dead man's. He came back from the window to the dressing-table. On the table were the remnants of two torn cinema tickets. Anthony nodded to himself when he caught sight of them. For one thing, they tallied with the story which Stella Forrest had told earlier in the day. That she and Peter Oliver had attended a cinema in the Haymarket on Easter Eve.

Anthony fidgeted round for some time and then went back to the bathroom. The camera-men seemed to have finished and had packed up and Greatorex was also tidying up.

"Well, what do you think of it?" inquired Anthony. The pathologist shrugged his shoulders. "Oh, suicide- undoubtedly. The razor was in the left hand and the cut is just what a 'southpaw' would inflict on himself. According to MacMorran, the man was left-handed. There's one thing— he meant doing the job properly, he left nothing to chance. The blade bit deep." Greatorex noticed the expression on Anthony's face. "Why did you ask?" he added. "Anything buzzing under your bonnet?"

"No-o. Nothing that I can actually put a finger on."

Greatorex looked at him again. "What's the trouble, then? No need to look for any, surely?"

Anthony smiled. "Can't get a satisfactory slant on the psychology of it all. That's where I'm 'groping' rather. You know a man must be pretty desperate to slice his throat as this poor fellow seems to have done."

"I quite agree, Bathurst. Every time. But we don't know, do we? Doesn't that partly explain it, at least? How can *we* know what the terror was that he decided to side-step? Good job we can't, if you ask me."

Anthony leant against the bathroom door and lit a cigarette. "Take that as read, Greatorex. No argument with you whatever. Eminently sound—all of it. But come with me mentally and let *me* show *you* something. Listening?"

Greatorex nodded. Anthony began to speak more slowly. "On Good Friday—that's only five days ago, my dear chap, not even a week—this desperate, terror-haunted man takes his girl to Hampton Court. The next day they do a 'flick' at one of the best cinemas. Sunday sees them at Southend and Monday they visit Kew Gardens. Kew Gardens in April, Greatorex. Very lovely, you know. Ever been there?"

Greatorex closed his brief-case and stood up. "What the hell are you trying to say, Bathurst?"

Anthony shrugged his shoulders. "Simply that this man, who's now a corpse, was, but a few days ago, in love with love and life. Doing all the delightfully normal things that a healthy man, with his arms round a pretty girl, wants to do. Are you following me, Greatorex? Friday, Hampton Court, Saturday, the cinema, Sunday, Southend, Monday, Kew Gardens, and Monday night—after kissing his girl good night—off with his own head, and so much for Peter Oliver! Well, Greatorex, does it add up, do you think?"

Greatorex stared at Anthony. He made no answer. "By the way," added the latter, "how long's he been dead? I meant to ask you that before—and forgot."

Greatorex nodded. "Somewhere about the time you said. Round about midnight on Monday wouldn't be far wrong."

Anthony turned away. "Anyhow," he said, "I've told you enough—you see my difficulty.'"

Greatorex avoided the issue. "Yes—the way you've put it, perhaps. But we just don't *know*. We don't know what happened to him *after* he left this girl that you mentioned. *After* he'd kissed her good night. We don't know what he ran up against. Some secret of his past life, possibly. Any one of a hundred possibilities. So to hell with all your psychological mumbo-jumbo. Bathurst, the young fool took his own life." As he spoke, Greatorex held out his hand with a smile. "I must be getting back, Bathurst. And I expect they'll be coming along to remove the body before long. Where's the Chief Inspector—any idea?"

"He went downstairs some little time ago," replied Anthony, "he's 'phoning a telegram to an hôtel in Bournemouth. To some of the family. The mother and sister are staying there. They'll have a pleasant afternoon somewhere about tea-time, poor devils!"

"The father's away too, isn't he? Didn't I hear something about it?"

"Yes. In Scotland somewhere, I believe. That means another sad homecoming. And there's a brother knocking about somewhere as well. On holiday, I mean. I can't tell you where he is for the very good reason that I don't know myself."

Anthony smiled and shook hands with Greatorex. "It almost looks," said the latter, as he turned away to go downstairs, "as though the whole thing might have been specially arranged. All the members of the family scattered as they are. The dead man had things all to himself." Anthony stared after the pathologist's retreating form. Specially arranged! And then the picture of the dead man on the bathroom floor, with the razor in his left hand, came back to him. The same man who had kissed Stella Forrest good night at Hammersmith but a few hours before he slashed his jugular . . . who had been to Kew Gardens with her and seen the joyous earth re-clothing herself with the glory of the blossom and in the amazing Miracle of Spring.

CHAPTER 5

1

Anthony went downstairs and found MacMorran. The latter had evidently just completed his course of telephoning. He seemed hot and bothered.

"Andrew," said Anthony, "Greatorex has just told me that the ambulance men will be along very shortly. That means, I take it, as far as the body's concerned, that you've seen all you want to see?"

"I think so, Mr. Bathurst. All the photographs have been taken, I don't think there's anything more up there that I want to see. For the time being. I can do the rest elsewhere."

"Do you mind, then, if I have another 'dekko'?"

"Eh—what's this? You're very polite all of a sudden. What's the idea?"

Anthony grinned. "Don't be a suspicious old devil. Come with me, will you? I'd like you to be there with me." MacMorran grumbled, but followed Anthony upstairs to the bathroom. Anthony closed the door behind them and the two men stood over the corpse.

"Full evening dress, Andrew. Notice it?"

"Ay! I've already seen it. What about it?"

"Have you been through the pockets?"

"Not yet. No hurry. Do it later. I'm not worried about the case at all. I told you I wasn't."

"Have a look in 'em now, will you? Just to please me."

MacMorran went on one knee beside the body. "Cigarette-case. Silver. Lighter. Wallet. Handful of loose change. Key-ring, five keys on it. White handkerchief. Seems to be the bundle." MacMorran placed the contents on the edge of the bath. "Well, what's next?"

"Door-key on the key-ring, Andrew?"

The Inspector checked on the keys. "Yes. Yale. For the front-door lock. That's the one, without a doubt. All in order."

"H'm. Not what I wanted. What about the wallet? Look through it, will you?"

MacMorran opened the leather wallet and looked through the papers. "Four currency notes. Three for a pound—one ten shillings. Season-ticket. Between Puck Willow and Cannon Street. In the name of Peter W. Oliver. Book of stamps. Three snapshots. Deceased alone and with others. No identity card. Should be here. Prospectus of an hôtel. 'Suffolk Hôtel', Bournemouth. Tariff and regulations. That's where his mother and sister are. Sheet of note-paper. Folded in two. Hallo—what's this? Notes of some kind?"

MacMorran's voice stopped suddenly and Anthony saw that he had unfolded the sheet of paper and was perusing it. Anthony stooped down and looked over the Inspector's shoulder.

"What have you got, Andrew? Anything—really?"

MacMorran passed up the sheet of paper. Anthony read a pencilled scrawl. "If R.G. and D. not too awkward—go ahead immediately after Easter. Must do—80,000 not to be sneezed at. Query—is it too much for me to attempt? Query—disposal of body? Query—murder, query—motive for murder- blackmail or revenge? Query—evidence for suicide? Resolved, to tell her straight what I expect done. After all—you don't keep a dog and bark yourself—if I have an ace of trumps up my sleeve why shouldn't I play it? I *should* be a steam-tug if I didn't."

Anthony passed the paper back. "What do you make of it, Andrew?"

The Inspector shook his head. "Don't know, quite."

"No, you don't, do you? That's how it strikes me. One or two extremely relevant phrases, by the way. No doubt you noticed them."

"Can't see that it makes the slightest difference to the main job if that's what you're getting at. No sense in deliberately shutting one's eyes to plain evidence."

MacMorran replaced the various papers in the wallet. "What I would say," he continued, "is that this fellow was in a 'jam'. That note points to it, to my way of thinking, if we knew enough to interpret it correctly. And the 'jam' suddenly closed in on him as 'jams' have a habit of doing. When he wasn't expecting it, too. Or better still—*before* he expected it. And that closing in took place late on Monday evening. After he'd said good night to his girl. The bloke whose clutches he was in suddenly put him on the spot. Or maybe it was another wench. With the result that Oliver came home knowing that the game was up and butchered himself."

MacMorran buttoned his coat with a gesture that indicated settlement. Anthony, who had been listening attentively to the Inspector, said nothing. MacMorran noticed that his eyes were constantly on the body.

"He didn't run a car, I should say, although there's a garage here." Anthony might have been speaking his thoughts aloud.

"Why not?" cut back MacMorran. "He could have."

"Why—something Stella Forrest told us. Didn't she say they went to Southend on the Easter Sunday by motor-coach?"

MacMorran stared before he nodded. "Yes. You're right. I believe she did say something of that sort."

"Yes. She did." Anthony nodded back. But MacMorran saw again that he was still engrossed with the body. Suddenly, Anthony shot a further question at the Inspector.

"Where was he when he cut his throat, Andrew?"

"How do you mean? In here, of course."

"Yes, I know. But what posture was the man in? Was he standing, looking in the mirror here, sitting on that stool there, sitting on the edge of the bath, or kneeling on the floor?"

MacMorran glanced round the bathroom. "There are three mirrors in here. That long glass on the wall there, and two smaller shaving mirrors. I should say he was standing and looking in the large glass. The one on the wall."

"In that case, then, Andrew, do you think he'd have fallen as we found him—flat on his back and razor in his hand? Wouldn't the grip on the razor relax—the body collapse more and sprawl?"

MacMorran showed signs of being annoyed. "Now look here! Wouldn't all those points that you trot out so nicely have suggested themselves to Greatorex? You're deliberately looking for trouble. Candidly, in reply to your questions, I don't know. And if suicide's good enough for the Crown pathologist, damn it all, it's good enough for me."

"The line of least resistance, Andrew—eh? Well, well, well! And you of all people! We live and learn." Anthony pointed to two parts of a razor-case that lay on the ledge above the lavatory basin. "There's the razor-case from which the razor was taken. But there are at least three safety-razors on the shelf there. Because I've seen them. Also, they all three seem to have been in regular use. Still, there's nothing much in the point, I'll grant you that. We mustn't forget that this is a family bathroom. The cut-throat razor may have belonged to the father years ago. Before the safety type became popular. And, of course, Oliver knew that the house was empty and was likely to remain empty for some time. That's in your favour, too. He could commit suicide in comfort and entirely minus interruption. Yes, the points are piling up for you, Andrew, I can see that."

"Of course they are. Can't understand why you must keep on banging your head against the wall. If there were the slightest—"

Anthony turned suddenly and looked down at the body again. "Have you actually examined the body, Andrew? You—yourself?"

"Only superficially. I left that to Greatorex, really. For once in a way he came along quickly. Right on my heels. Why?"

"There's not so much blood on the collar as I should have expected from a frightful wound like that."

"You can't tell how these jobs go. You never know."

"I say, turn him over, will you, Andrew? I'd just like to have a squint at—"

MacMorran turned the body on to its face. He was startled by Anthony's almost immediate exclamation.

"Andrew, look at the back of that collar! Man, you can't miss it."

MacMorran was slow to comprehend. "Why, what do you mean?"

"Look at it, Andrew! A stiff linen dress-collar, mind you. Not an ordinary soft collar. What does it look like?" MacMorran stood and stared at the back of the dead man's collar.

2

"H'm," he said eventually. "I think I see what you mean. But I don't know that any—"

Anthony cut in summarily. "Half a minute, Andrew. Let's be clear. *What* do I mean?"

"Why you mean that the collar's very much creased and crumpled. But as I was about to say when you interrupted me, I don't know that we need attach *too* much importance to the fact."

"Oh, and why not? I confess that I shall be most interested to hear your reasons."

"Well, the man had been out, hadn't he? Must have been. And we don't know *where* he'd been. But he'd been in somebody's company. When he was there we don't know what may have happened to him."

"On the contrary, Andrew—we know what did happen to him. He got his throat slit. Let's be as accurate as possible."

MacMorran paid but little heed to Anthony's point. He proceeded to amplify his own theory. "For all we know he may have been in a bit of a rough house. From the condition of that collar at the back, it may be that he was run out of somewhere. You know what I mean—by the scruff of his neck."

"Andrew, you're talking sense at last. But it's been a hell of a long time coming. That collar's been badly mauled and it must mean something."

Anthony dropped to the body of Peter Oliver again and turned it over to its original posture. He bent right over and sniffed at the dead man's mouth and lips. "There's no suggestion of alcohol, Andrew. None whatever."

MacMorran thrust his hands into his overcoat pockets. "I could have told you that had you asked me."

"It's not conclusive, I know, but I should have expected a certain amount of alcoholic indulgence coincident with his being thrown out of anywhere on his ear. The two things usually go together. Wouldn't you agree?"

"Maybe. Maybe not. It's not conclusive, as you remarked yourself."

MacMorran jerked his head towards the floor. "Well, are you coming along, or are you going to stop here all day? As far as I'm concerned, the sooner I get away from the contemplation of that 'stiff' on the floor there, the better. The look of him's getting on my stomach. Hark!" MacMorran motioned with his finger. "Unless I'm very much mistaken that's the ambulance rolled up. To take this fellow to the mortuary. Get up from the floor there or they'll shove you on a slab alongside him. And I should hate that."

Anthony stood up and dusted the knees of his trousers. "Thanks for the solicitude, Andrew. Very decent of you. It's nice to know one's appreciated. And you still think that Peter Oliver cut his own throat, eh?"

"I do," returned MacMorran with the utmost composure. He turned to go downstairs again and Anthony followed him. The ambulance was at the door. MacMorran's surmise had been right. He waited at the foot of the staircase for Anthony to continue the point of discussion. But the latter remained silent. MacMorran prodded back. He twitted Anthony with carefully chosen words.

"And you still think that Peter Oliver didn't cut his own throat—eh?"

Anthony shook his head slowly. "I don't know what to think, Andrew. That is to say, with any feeling of absolute certainty. What evidence I've seen so far has been conflicting. But if I were a betting man, my price would be something like 'six to four' on murder."

"And if I were a betting man," responded the Inspector stubbornly, "I'd take you in thousands. But as I'm not—" MacMorran completed the sentence with a shrug of the shoulders and a wave of the hand.

"Even in that contingency," said Anthony, "my price still stands."

The ambulance men went quietly upstairs.

3

When Anthony eventually left MacMorran, later on that evening, the Inspector had promised him all the information which might arise from the photographs or from the work of the finger-print experts as soon as was practically possible.

"You shall have it all, my boy," the Inspector had said, "and in the end, when you've sifted and tooth-combed everything, you'll come to me and say, 'sorry, old chap, I was wrong. That imagination of mine kicked over the traces and led me astray. It was you, Andrew, who was right—Peter Oliver died by his own hand.' "

"That's O.K. by me, Andrew," Anthony had replied; "directly I'm satisfied, you may be sure I shall admit as much to you. All the same, I shall be intensely interested in the fingerprints report. I'm strongly of the opinion that we may get results. And, of course, there are the other domestic considerations."

"Which ones?"

"Mother, sister, father, brother. We don't know if any one of them has anything significant to tell us."

"They can't tell you anything about the actual doings. None of 'em was here.' MacMorran shook his head with emphasis as he replied.

"No, but they can tell us all sorts of things about Peter Oliver himself and his normal household background. Give us an entirely different slant from Miss Forrest's."

"More of the psychology stuff, I suppose?"

"Yes. In a way. Then, in addition to them, there's the bank angle. The manager—or even some of the staff of Delaney's bank—may come across with something. You never know. But at any rate, we shall be able to start filling in the picture a little. Various backgrounds and so on. Extremely valuable."

"If we want it. But take it from me, we shan't, everything'll be straightforward."

MacMorran had extended his hand as he said this and Anthony had taken it. Then Anthony walked back to his flat and to the excellent dinner which the ever-faithful Emily had prepared for him. After dinner he treated himself to a Kümmel and a cigar. His thoughts concentrated on the problem that he had come to call (to himself) "the new Bath Oliver". As he churned and turned the problem in his mind, the time passed almost without his being aware of it. The result was that when he glanced at his wrist-watch and saw that the time was half past ten, he was amazed.

Anthony thereupon decided to throw the problem away for the time being and think about going to bed. He walked to the window and looked out at London by night. It was a favoured habit of his, prior to retiring for the night, and there were few nights when he missed doing it. As he stood there, he heard the sound of quick running footsteps.

Anthony went nearer to the window and looked up the street. Yes . . . he could see the person who was running as she came under the light of a lamp. It was a girl. She ran well—swiftly and easily and gracefully, and with unusually well-controlled feet. Suddenly the noise of the running ceased. Anthony saw that the girl had stopped just outside his own place. There came a ring at the bell and the next thing was that he could hear Emily going downstairs.

CHAPTER 6

1

Emily was soon back. "There's a lady wants to see you, sir. I told her I thought it was much too late. But she—" Emily came to a sudden stop.

"But she what, Emily? Insists that it's terribly urgent?" Emily brightened at the phrase. "Yes, sir. That's just what she did say."

Anthony's grey eyes twinkled. "All right, Emily. You're quite right, of course, with regard to the time, but she may have come some considerable distance and she may be in a jam of some kind so I won't disappoint her by sending her away. Bring her up, there's a good girl."

"Very good, Mr. Bathurst."

Emily turned to descend the staircase again. Anthony kicked a chair into place, put another log on the fire and waited by the door for the returning Emily with convoy. He hadn't long to wait. Emily was accompanied by an attractive, dark-haired girl—about twenty years of age in Anthony's judgment. He was surprised when he saw her—to tell the truth, he had expected his visitor to be Stella Forrest. Emily piloted the girl over the threshold.

"Miss Oliver, Mr. Bathurst," she said in introduction.

"Thank you, Emily. Come in, Miss Oliver, do, and please sit here by the fire. The nights keep chilly and I expect you're cold. Unless your run has warmed you up."

The girl looked a little startled. She was a pretty girl. Dark fluffy hair, dark vivacious eyes and a beautifully creamy-tinted skin.

"My run? How did you—

Anthony smiled. "I both heard you and saw you. When you came along I happened to be standing at the window, you see."

Anthony gestured in the appropriate direction as he took the chair opposite to his visitor. Then he saw that the girl's eyes had recently been ravaged by tears. She looked at him, seemed to draw reassurance and perhaps comfort from what she saw, and started to speak impulsively.

"Please forgive me coming to you as late as this. But I couldn't get Detective-Inspector MacMorran. He's off duty, so I'm told, and I couldn't find his address in the telephone-directory. But I found yours. I'm Margaret Oliver, sister of Peter Oliver—you know all about him, don't you?"

The rising inflexion of the voice, and the note which Anthony detected *in* the voice, gave him a sharp warning. The girl was perilously close to the hysteria border-line.

"Now, Miss Oliver," he said quietly, "take it easy. Don't try to tell me too much at once. Get settled a bit—cool down and take your time, you know what I mean—and then we'll talk things over. Yes? Is that what you'd like to do?"

The girl nodded and the tears came into her eyes—and Anthony thought that she looked prettier than ever.

"You've come up from Bournemouth, of course? This evening. Yes, of course. My very deepest sympathy, Miss Oliver. And your mother? She came with you, I expect? How is she? Putting a brave face on it? I feel terribly sorry for both of you."

Margaret Oliver nodded and gulped down another tremulous sob. "The Police met us at Waterloo, Mr. Bathurst. They were very good and considerate in every way. This Inspector, MacMorran's the name, had made all the arrangements for that to happen. We heard—they told us—how you and he . . . had been to the house . . . our house . . . in the afternoon . . . that's what made me come to you to-night when I couldn't get to this MacMorran man."

Anthony nodded, but he was thinking hard. He decided that he must put a question to the girl.

"I'm just a little puzzled, Miss Oliver . . . wondering, you know . . . but why exactly did you have to see me so urgently to-night? What's the real point at issue? What have you got to tell me that you couldn't have kept until to-morrow?"

He smiled sympathetically as he put the question. Margaret Oliver took a firm grip of herself. Anthony could almost see her doing it.

"I'll tell you, Mr. Bathurst. And I think I'm glad I came to you instead of going to the Inspector. When we first heard this dreadful news . . .

my mother and I at Bournemouth early this evening. We were told that my brother had committed suicide. At least, that was the opinion of the Police. You know that, I take it?"

Anthony would have preferred to evade the question. "Er . . . yes . . . you can assume that to be so. For the time being, that is," he replied.

Margaret Oliver looked at him a trifle critically but went on. She flung a second question at him—which Anthony would have elected to evade even more than its predecessor.

"Please tell me. Is it *your* opinion, Mr. Bathurst, that Peter killed himself? Cut his own throat in our bathroom?"

There was a silence of some seconds' duration. The only sound came from the ticking of the clock on the mantelpiece. Margaret Oliver waited patiently for Anthony's reply to her question. He was gratified that she made no attempt to force a quick answer. At length, after due consideration, Anthony began to speak.

"I am sorry, Miss Oliver, that you have asked me that question. I would much rather that you hadn't. That is to say—to-night. For the simple reason that I do not know how to answer you. For the good reason that I am not sure. Let me say to you this evening—that I have an open mind. Call it fifty-fifty."

Some at least of their grief seemed to be lifted from the dark eyes. "And this Inspector MacMorran, who I understand is in charge of the case, is *he* sure that Peter did this awful thing to himself?"

"I'm afraid that he is, Miss Oliver. When I left him early this evening, I can sincerely say that he was. In the meantime, of course—"

The girl was in like a flash. "Then why aren't *you* sure, if he is? Why is your opinion different from his? There must be reasons."

Anthony shook his head.

"That's not quite fair of you. I didn't say that it was different. I may harbour a doubt or doubts—he does not. Eventually quite soon, possibly—I may find myself in entire agreement with the Inspector."

The girl stuck to him. "Or you may not."

"Or I may not." Anthony spoke gravely.

"Mr. Bathurst," continued Margaret Oliver, "whatever you may say it's clear to me that you do not *yet awhile* see eye to eye with your professional colleague—you must admit that, so I'll vary my question. What is it that makes you think Peter may *not* have killed himself? That is to say, the *reason* of your difference?" Her fingers twisted emotionally as she put the question, and before Anthony could frame a reply, the girl had gone on. "Please answer me, Mr. Bathurst. If only you knew what this means to me, you couldn't hesitate."

Anthony leant forward and looked earnestly at his visitor. "Miss Oliver," he said firmly, "did you come here to ask me that or did you come here to tell me something?"

The girl was startled again. The grip she had recently imposed on herself began to slip. When she replied, the voice had the wild, uncontrolled, frightening ring in it again. "Oh, but you don't understand,' she cried bitterly. "I can't sow seed on stony ground. It will be just a pitiful waste of time."

The unusual, unexpected nature of the girl's reply struck Anthony forcibly. He was impressed. "Tell me more," he countered quietly.

"If you have absolutely made up your mind in any way, I don't wish to worry you. But if your mind is still receptive, and ready to assimilate new facts, I can prove to you that my dear brother has been . . . has been . . ." The last word seemed to stick. But it came at last. Shrill and shattering. "Murdered," cried Margaret Oliver, "murdered by some bloody-minded beast!" And then she began to cry softly and quietly. . . as a child will sometimes when it is distressed beyond measure . . . and as she cried the anodyne of tears came . . . to do its work.

2

Anthony waited patiently while Margaret Oliver cried. He knew that such grief was better out than in. Gradually the tears began to cease until, eventually, the girl looked across at him with something like genuine penitence on her face.

"I'm sorry," she said simply, "please forgive me."

"I understand perfectly," returned Anthony, "please don't worry one little bit."

Margaret gave him a quick nod of thanks. "Well," she said bravely, "can you remember what I said before I behaved like a silly idiot?"

Anthony smiled at her. "Quite a number of things, Miss Oliver. To which do you refer in particular?"

"I said that if your mind weren't absolutely made up I could prove to you that my brother didn't take his own life. Do you remember?"

"Yes. Very well."

"Well—will you let me?"

"It depends, rather, on one or two things. How do you propose to set about the task?"

"You won't *like* what I'm going to ask you to do. I feel certain of that."

"Why not? Why shan't I?"

"Because it's not very nice, you know—comfortable! I want to take you back to the house with me."

She spoke the words doggedly. Anthony was a trifle puzzled. The doggedness had been present in her voice for some little time.

"Do you mean," he said, "that you want me to accompany you back to the house *now*?"

"Yes," she nodded. "That's exactly what I do mean."

Anthony's significant glance went to the clock on the mantelpiece. "I know it's late," said Margaret Oliver, "but this means so much to me. Please come, Mr. Bathurst."

"Won't the house still be there to-morrow morning?"

"I knew you'd say that. Of course it will. But I want to show you something before it's too late."

"Before it's too late? How do you mean?"

"Before it's touched—or altered. That's what I mean." Anthony fell back on reflection. "Where is this something which you want to show me, Miss Oliver?"

"At the house. I said that I—"

"Yes, I know. But where, exactly? In which room?"

Her eyes searched his face. "Why do you ask me that?" she queried.

His eyes twinkled a little. "In order to satisfy myself that it isn't something I've already seen. In that manner, I may avoid the chase of the untamed goose."

Margaret Oliver's reply disposed of his point most effectively. "You *can't* have seen this. Because if you did see it—it wouldn't convey anything to you. It *couldn't*. That's why I want to show it to you. Because I can explain it, and the explanation makes all the difference."

"I see. That certainly strengthens your argument. Tell me, though, which room it's in."

"It's in the bathroom."

The reply made Anthony sit up mentally. He scratched his cheek. "I see. In the bathroom—eh?" There came a few seconds' pause. Then Anthony rose from his armchair. "O.K., Miss Oliver. You win! I'll come back with you as you want me. Collect your things and come round to my garage with me. We'll go by car—and we'll pick up Inspector MacMorran on the way. Although I rather fancy that he'll take much more convincing than I shall. On that account I'll utter a note of warning in advance."

Margaret Oliver stood up and faced him. "Thank you, Mr. Bathurst. Thank you very much. To say that I'm grateful to you is painfully inadequate."

3

Two uniformed constables were outside the Oliver house when the Bathurst party arrived there. After a word or two from MacMorran, one of them accompanied the new arrivals into the house.

"My mother's sleeping with friends," said Margaret Oliver as they entered, "she went straight to them after we'd identified my brother's body. And of course, my father and David won't be back for some hours yet. They *can't* be. As you know, my father's in Scotland and I can't be exactly sure where David is. He happens to be on a walking-tour this Easter week, so you see that we can't tell exactly where he actually is at any given time. But I've done my best and written to where I think he may pick the letter up."

The constable switched on the electric light in the hall. "You stay down here," MacMorran instructed him, "if I should want you for anything I'll let you know."

The man touched his helmet. "Very good, sir."

MacMorran turned to Margaret Oliver. "Now, Miss Oliver," he said grimly, "I'm at your service. Lead on, will you? I understand it's the bathroom you want us to look at."

Anthony gave a quick glance at the girl whose persistence had brought them to where they were. Her face was resolute and determined, with the mouth firm and the lips tightly set.

"Yes, Inspector," she said quietly, "will you come upstairs with me now, please? I'm going to show you something which should prove to you beyond any doubt that my brother has been murdered. It has proved it to me and I pray God that I can, in turn, prove it to you."

"Very good, Miss Oliver. Give us the 'gen'. Then I can be the judge of its real value."

In Anthony's opinion, MacMorran's voice was not too sympathetic. Margaret entered the bathroom in advance of the two men and her finger pressed down the switch of the electric light. Save for the absence of the dead body, the bathroom looked to Anthony just as it had before he had left it. Margaret made her way to the side of the bath.

"Please forgive me," she said, "if for the next few minutes I sound like somebody giving a lecture. I don't intend to do anything like that. But I'm afraid I shan't be able to help it *sounding* something like it. Now will you please look at the narrow end of the bath—the end where you put your feet?"

MacMorran grunted. "Call it the plug-end—that'll suit me."

"Right. That'll suit me, too. Better than anything else, perhaps. Now then again—where exactly is the plug itself at this precise moment?"

MacMorran looked carefully towards the end of the bath before he answered.

"The chain of the plug is twisted round the handle of the right-hand tap—in this case the cold-water tap."

Anthony nodded. "Agreed," he said.

"Right," said Margaret again, "and who would you say twisted the chain of that plug round that cold-water tap?"

MacMorran's reply held no hesitation. "The person who last used the bath. *To bath in*, I mean. When he had finished, he pulled up the 'plug', as we've called it, to let the bath empty of the water and coiled the chain of it round the right-hand tap which happens, in this case, as I said, to be the cold-water tap. That's just a piece of plain-sailing intelligence."

"I'm with you," said Margaret looking more determined than ever, "and now *who* do you say was the person who last used the bath to bath in?"

MacMorran showed signs of surprise at this latest question. "Why, your brother Peter, of course. Before he changed into evening dress—probably, I suggest, to keep an appointment somewhere—don't forget the folk next door heard him go out—he had a bath. Quite a natural thing for a young man to do. After a warmish day in the open air. And there's no doubt about it. Because don't forget that these next-door folk heard the bath-water running down the waste pipe. It all fits to the same pattern, you see."

"You think so, Inspector? Good! Well, then I'll tell *you* something!"

Anthony saw Margaret set her teeth. She pointed dramatically to the two taps at the end of the bath. "You see the set-up here? I want you to look at all of it. There's the end of the chain-plug fastened to the back of the bath. Above that are the two ordinary water-taps. On the left the hot. On the right the cold. Above them, the handle which you move if you want to use the shower. Above the handle, the spray of the shower itself. Have you seen all that I've shown you?"

MacMorran and Anthony both nodded.

"Good. Now this is my point. Perhaps I've been rather a long time coming to it, but I had to explain things carefully. Whenever Peter had a bath, he always finished with a cold shower. Always! It didn't matter what time of the year it was. There was always hot water because there's an electric heater. Please look at the shower handle. It's turned *off*. Now Peter *never* turned it off when he had finished with it, he always left it on. He used to turn off the cold-water *tap*—not the *shower handle*."

Margaret glanced quickly at the faces of the two men she was endeavouring to persuade. Anthony was nodding with what she took to be approval. Encouraged by what she had already seen, she went on more confidently.

"I haven't finished yet. There's something else to my mind even *more* eloquent and more important. Whenever Peter had a bath, and pulled up the plug when he had finished, he *always coiled the chain of the plug round the left-hand tap* the *hot*-water tap! Always, always, always! Why, I could tell invariably, when Peter had bathed here, when I was using the bathroom after him! The evidence was always left behind for me to see. He was the only one in the family who coiled the chain of the plug round the left-hand tap. All the rest of us invariably twist it round the *right-hand tap*. My father, my mother, my brother David and myself. We *all* four of us do it that way. But Peter was left-handed, and I expect that's the reason he always went for the left-hand tap. If you come to work it out for yourself I suppose it's quite the natural thing for a person to do."

She paused and then added, almost vehemently: "Inspector MacMorran, Mr. Bathurst, I'm as certain as I am that night follows day that the person who used this bath on Monday evening *was not my brother Peter*! It was my brother Peter's murderer."

Margaret Oliver's eyes blazed with hate and fury as she made the two statements, and Anthony saw clearly that even MacMorran was impressed by her fervour and intensity.

4

Anthony waited to see what MacMorran would do. And then, for a time, he waited to hear Margaret and the Inspector argue it out together. MacMorran, however, quickly recovered his normal composure.

"Now look here, young lady, you must take it easy—you really must—and not get so excited. I grant you've had a very nasty and extremely sad experience, you have all my sympathy. But now it's my turn to say something. And that's this." MacMorran sat on the edge of the bath. "In a way, young lady, you've been arguing against yourself. I'll tell you why. What you've been at such great pains to prove to me is that your brother was left-handed. Is that so?"

The question came rather too quickly for the girl and she wasn't ready to answer it adequately. "Well, in a way, perhaps—"

MacMorran was relentless. He cut in summarily. "Is that so, or isn't it?"

"All right, yes. Putting it as you have, that answer will do for the time being."

"Very well, then. I've no wish to distress you unduly, Miss Oliver, but when you identified your brother's body, did you actually see the wound in the throat?"

The colour drained from Margaret Oliver's cheeks. "No," she whispered, "not to say that I really looked at it."

"Well, then—now I can tell *you* something. Something that there's no possible argument about. The wound that killed your brother runs from the *right-hand* side of his throat to the left. It is just such a wound as a *left-handed man would make,* using a razor on his own throat."

MacMorran paused for the full import of his remark to sink home. Within a second or so, however, he had followed up. "In addition to all that, Miss Oliver, the razor was in your brother's left hand when Mr. Bathurst and I discovered the body. And I think these facts *more* than counterbalance your testimony with regard to the plug-chain and the bath-taps." He looked across at Anthony. "Don't you, Mr. Bathurst?"

Anthony leant against the towel-rail with his hands in his overcoat pockets. So far he had surrendered the arena to MacMorran and the bereaved lady.

"Well, Andrew," he said, "since you've asked me so directly, I regret to say that my answer's 'no'—and that I must give the credit where it's due—to Miss Oliver. She has convinced me. Let me put it in another way. She has completed what Stella began. Down in the Forrest, let me say flippantly, something stirred. I've always been halfway towards Miss Oliver's position, as you were already aware. This evening she has taken me right over with her. I think Peter Oliver was murdered. But I must admit at the same time—if only in fairness to you, Andrew—there are many things attached to the case which yet awhile I can't even attempt to explain."

There was a silence before Margaret Oliver spoke in a low voice, "thank you, Mr. Bathurst. Now that you have said that, I feel my efforts, and my journey, have not been in vain. Despite what the Inspector has said."

MacMorran was shaking his head cynically. "Well, well, well! Did you ever? Just a colony of left-handed people—all living together. In the country of the awkward, the kack-hander is King. When a vacancy occurs, no right-handed person need apply. The twilight of a great investigator. I give it up." He spread out his hands with a gesture of mock helplessness.

"Just a moment, Andrew—before you cry all is lost. Let me jump in and ask Miss Oliver one or two questions."

MacMorran shrugged his shoulders. "Ask on. I'll listen with an aching heart."

"Your brother Peter, Miss Oliver," said Anthony, "has he always been left-handed?"

Margaret nodded. "Yes. From a little boy. He's always used his left hand in preference to his right. I think I can say in everything. He wrote with his left hand, batted left, bowled left and kicked with his left foot."

"Yes," replied Anthony, "that's just the kind of answer I wanted you to give me. Thank you."

"Why?" demanded the girl.

"I wanted to satisfy myself that this particular physical trait of your brother's was known to a fair number of people. And wasn't merely a family affair. Your answer assures me that it was."

MacMorran seemed to be listening to the new set of exchanges with additional interest.

"Oh, yes, undoubtedly," added Margaret.

Anthony came again. "Now there's one thing about that, Miss Oliver, which I must admit causes me some little surprise. Your brother, I understand, was on the staff of Delaney's bank?"

"That is quite true, Mr. Bathurst. He'd been in their service some years. Peter was attached to the Lombard Street branch. What is it that surprises you?"

"I've always held the idea that banks were distinctly averse from employing left-handed officers."

MacMorran was listening intently now. He knew his Bathurst and he wondered what was coming.

"I wasn't aware of that myself," said Margaret.

"It is so," returned Anthony. "I can assure you of the fact. A cousin of mine was actually refused employment by one of the 'big five' for the reason that he was left-handed. And this after he'd virtually been accepted."

Margaret Oliver shook her head. "Possibly Delaneys are different and don't take that dim view of left-handed people. I've certainly never heard that they raised any difficulty with regard to Peter."

"I see. All right, I'll take your word for it. Now for one or two of the more ordinary type of question. Had your brother any enemies, to your knowledge?"

"None. He was popular everywhere he went." Margaret was emphatic.

"No—er—unhappy love affair? That you know anything about?"

"No. I can truthfully say that. There *was* a girl . . . about a year ago . . . perhaps a little more than that . . . you know what boys are . . . but it seemed to fizzle out. I don't think there was any particular heart-burning on either side. I should say it died a natural death . . . most affairs of that kind do. I fancy that recently there's been a successor—I've an idea my mother knew something of this, you can ask her—but I'm positive that as far as Peter was concerned, there was nothing unhappy about it. Quite the reverse . . . very much so, if you ask me."

"The name Stella Forrest conveys nothing to you?"

"No. But it wouldn't, you see. I had heard no name mentioned at all."

"I see. One more question, Miss Oliver. Had your brother any financial troubles?"

There was perhaps a *soupçon* of hesitation before Margaret Oliver replied.

"No, I don't think so. Not of any great consequence."

Anthony probed. "You aren't perhaps as certain of this as you'd like to be?"

"Yes, I think I am.'

Anthony watched her closely. The Oliver jaws were set. "You'd assert from what you knew of him that he had no financial anxiety of any kind?"

"Nothing to make him take his own life. Nothing of those dimensions."

"That isn't quite what I said, Miss Oliver. Please be frank with me. If we're to help you, you must help us."

Margaret shook her head doggedly. "I understand that. I fully understand that. If I hadn't, I shouldn't have come to you as I have. But I still say 'no' to your question. To the best of my knowledge and belief, Peter had no serious money difficulties. I can't put it more plainly than that, can I?"

Anthony could see that the lady was fully determined to give away nothing and that he would be well advised to drop the line of inquiry for the time being. He turned to the Inspector.

"I don't know whether you desire to question Miss Oliver at all?"

MacMorran rose from his seat on the edge of the bath. "Yes, I do. But I don't want to be too long about it because my bed's waiting for me and its not the only one either. However, I promised I'd come along with you to this house and I did. If I don't feel inclined to change my mind over anything, that's my business. I'm sorry, Miss Oliver, but that's how I feel about everything at the moment."

"I'm sorry too, Inspector. I'd been hoping you'd see my point of view. What are these questions you wish to ask me?"

"One. Perhaps two. Certainly one. Can you tell me of anybody you know within your brother's circle of acquaintance-ship who has the initials RG.

"Yes," said the girl promptly, "my father."

MacMorran stared at her. The immediate answer had surprised him on two counts. He hadn't expected that the answer would come so spontaneously, and he certainly hadn't anticipated the actual form it had taken.

"Your father?" returned the Inspector.

"Yes. His Christian names are Richard Guise—full name Richard Guise Oliver. I'm afraid we're rather unconventional as a family and we habitually refer to him as Richard Guise. He's by way of being proud of the second name, let me tell you. It's a family name. Been in the Oliver family for generations. They're supposed to be descended from the Duc de Guise who was mixed up in that awful St. Bartholomew's Eve business."

"I see. And David is your other brother's name, isn't it?"

"Yes, Inspector. That's right. David Colquhoun. But we call *him* David—only David. He's younger than I am. I came in between him and poor old Peter."

"O.K., Miss Oliver. That'll suit me for to-night. How are you fixed for transport? I take it you're going to where your mother is? Can Mr. Bathurst and I drop you anywhere?"

"Well," Margaret seemed to hesitate again, "I'm staying the night with friends. But . . . er . . . not where Mother is. Could you drop me in Wimblefield? Will you be going back that way? Or will it be taking you off your route?"

"Certainly," replied Anthony, "easiest thing in the world. We shall go through Wimblefield. Tell me where it is exactly you want to go when we're getting near it. Fit? You, Andrew? Good—we'll be getting along at once, then."

The three of them made their way downstairs and out to Anthony's car.

"Your father and brother, I take it, will be coming home to-morrow?" said Anthony as he let in the clutch.

"My father will. But I'm not sure about David. I don't quite know where he is. Actually, he's on a walking tour. But you know that. I told you before."

Anthony nodded as the car turned the corner of Mayblossom Avenue. What the heck was Margaret Oliver so suddenly confused about? A spot of colour burned in each of her cheeks and all her self-confidence seemed to have deserted her suddenly. Anthony wondered if MacMorran had noticed it. As the car gathered pace, the girl relapsed into silence. As they approached Wimblefield High Street, Anthony said, "tell me where I'm to put you down. Don't forget I'm more or less in foreign parts."

Margaret Oliver nodded. She still seemed uneasy and *distraite*.

"You know the railway-station?"

"Very well indeed. So does the Inspector. Don't you, Andrew?"

Margaret wrinkled her brow. "He got very wet there on one occasion," explained Anthony. "Used the most frightful language. Water kept slopping down his neck—I don't think he's ever quite forgotten the experience."

MacMorran grunted non-committally. "I see," said Margaret. "I wondered rather what you meant. Now here's the station—put me down please when you come to the second turning on the left. That will do nicely."

"Not a bit of it, Miss Oliver. I'll take you to the house of your objective. We don't want to spoil the boat for a penn'orth of varnish." Anthony turned the corner. "Which side is it?"

"Left," replied Margaret, biting her lip.

"Tell me when."

"O.K . . . it's not far . . . just a few yards . . . here we are."

Anthony leant over and opened the door for her. "There you are, lady. Service!"

Margaret got out. "Thank you very much for the lift. It's been a godsend. And thank you for everything. Good night, Inspector. Good-night, Mr. Bathurst. And please start looking for the murderer of my brother. Delays are proverbially dangerous."

She fluttered a hand in the direction of the car and turned quickly away towards the house in front of which she had instructed Anthony to draw up. As she did so, Anthony saw a tall, burly-looking figure come out of the gate to meet her. Anthony drove on and turned to the right at the first convenient opportunity.

"So she hasn't even shaken you, Andrew?"

"No. Not even a little bit. I wasn't even impressed by that bath-plug business. If Oliver were upset by something as I maintain he must have been—there's no knowing what he might do in the circumstances. He wouldn't be worrying over plug-chains and water-taps. It's that left-handed cut on the throat I can't get over. Much more eloquent to me than all that girl's argument could ever be."

"There's more than one left-handed man cumbering the earth, Andrew."

"So there may be." MacMorran snapped out the words and then spoke again. "So you've definitely come down on the murder side, eh?"

"Yes, definitely. Not a shadow of a doubt as far as I'm concerned. And I'd like the report of your finger-print men as early as you can let me have it."

"You shall have it. And when you get it, you'll find it'll be another nail in the coffin of your theory."

Anthony grinned at the emphasis in the Inspector's voice.

"O.K. We shall see."

"*And* there's something else," said MacMorran as he looked out of the side window to see where they were, "don't forget what she told us about the initials in that note from Oliver's wallet. So far from representing the name of a villainous and malicious third party, they come back to the domestic picture and undoubtedly refer to the dead man's father and brother. Richard Guise and David. Charity—although we weren't to know—it began at home, Mr. Bathurst."

"Andrew," said Anthony, "you should never flick at the off-ball until you've got fifty on the tins. Believe me, my dear ruffian, it's fatal. And sometimes it's a *hell* of a long walk back to the pavilion."

"I'll risk that in this case," said MacMorran grimly, "and say good night. This is my road."

CHAPTER 7

1

It was past eleven on the following morning when Anthony's telephone began to ring persistently. He reached for it lazily, and heard Andrew MacMorran's voice at the other end. "How now, brown cow?" said Anthony.

"Come up and see me some time," was MacMorran's response.

"Hallo? Is it like that?"

"You heard what I said. And make it snappy. Then you'll be all the more pleased."

"I smell finger-prints," said Anthony.

"Your nose is out of joint."

"That's as may be. But the nostrils are still working. They're still in place. Before many days I hope to fill them with the opening rose."

"Hard or soft? They're both pretty 'niffy' in the raw state."

"No, honestly, Andrew—fingers crossed, how many—how many are there?"

"To the pound, do you mean? No good asking me, I shall have to ring up Billingsgate."

"Come off it. You know what I mean." He heard the Inspector chuckling at the other end.

"Hundreds. The complete box of soldiers! Whorls, loops and spirals. Animal, vegetable *and* mineral. But you can't eat them."

"By Jove, Andrew, as bad as that, eh?"

"No. You've got it all wrong. As *good* as that." Anthony could hear the official chuckle developing at an almost unprecedented rate. "What's more, my lad, they're all the same. The dead man's—as I told you last night. Sorry to disappoint you."

Anthony thought quickly. This didn't add up. "If that's the case, then, Andrew, and bearing in mind your burning passion for truth, why are you so desirous of the immediate parley? As distinctly indicated in our earlier conversation?"

MacMorran coughed. "Well—there is *one* little point I'd like to discuss with you."

Anthony grimaced. He had heard the cough at the other end. He treated himself to a private wink—all on his own. "Oh, I don't know—is it *worth* my coming up to the 'Yard' this morning? If everything's as plain and above-board, as you say, I'm quite prepared to—"

Anthony grinned to himself as he heard the sudden change in MacMorran's voice. There was no mistaking it—he felt certain now that he'd called the old scoundrel's bluff. MacMorran finished what he had to say.

Anthony spoke again. "On the razor you say, Andrew? No? Not? Not *on*? Where, where then, exactly?" Anthony listened to MacMorran's reply. "O.K., Andrew," he said eventually, "seeing as how you've been so matey—I'll be with you in less than half an hour." On the point of hanging up the receiver, an afterthought came to him. He just had time to translate it into words. "Anything yet, Andrew, from any other member of the Oliver family? This morning? In any shape or form?"

"Not unless it's blown your way," responded MacMorran. "Nothing here."

"I see." Anthony hung up thoughtfully.

2

Anthony drove slowly up to Hyde Park Corner.

The traffic was thick and heavy.

He turned into St. James's Park, crossed the park, ran the car quickly up Bridge Street and turned the corner into Scotland Yard. He parked the car in the best possible place and climbed stone stairs (several flights).

When he came to the door of the room that he knew housed MacMorran, he heard a murmur of voices. MacMorran's he was able to detect, but no other seemed familiar.

Anthony thought things over quickly and decided that in the interests of justice the door should be discreetly tapped. The tap elicited no audible response.

Anthony decided to tap a second time. A trifle more loudly, perhaps.

At this second and louder tap, the murmur of voices ceased abruptly and he heard the Inspector's voice inviting him to enter. Anthony shoved his head round the door so that he could take in the scene before he entered.

"Engaged, Andrew? Would you like me to call again?"

"No. Quite all right, Mr. Bathurst. Come in. Nobody could be more welcome, really."

Anthony slipped into the room. "What a greeting," he murmured, "wonders will never cease. Good-morning, Inspector."

A tall powerful-looking man was seated in a chair at the side of MacMorran's desk. MacMorran gestured towards the stranger.

"This is Mr. Oliver. Senior. Mr. Richard Oliver, Mr. Anthony Bathurst."

The tall man rose at once and shook hands with Anthony. "Mr. Richard Guise Oliver—is that it? Sorry to meet you in such sad circumstances, Mr. Oliver. My sincere sympathy. Bad business."

"Very bad business, Mr. Bathurst. And utterly inexplicable to me. My son Peter was as light-hearted a young fellow as you'd meet in a day's march. It beats me absolutely. I travelled last night from Aberdeen. Came straight on here from King's Cross this morning."

Anthony glanced at MacMorran. The Inspector was looking entirely expressionless. He seemed to Anthony to be waiting for something. At the moment, however, his lips were tight and his mouth closed. Oliver went on.

"I'm not used to being in a place like this. Except for one occasion many years ago, my contacts with your people have been non-existent. So you must overlook it if I sort of speak out of my turn—but have you gentlemen considered the possibility of my son having been murdered? You see, I knew him, I brought him up, I lived with him, and you gentlemen didn't." Oliver shook his head as he continued. "Makes a rare lot of difference, that does."

The two men to whom he had spoken looked at him. In silence for some seconds. Oliver had spoken sound sense. Anthony glanced across at MacMorran again. The Inspector knew exactly what the glance meant. He leant forward towards his desk and picked up something. Anthony recognized it at once. It was the razor they had taken from the left hand of the dead Peter Oliver. When he lay on the bathroom floor in the house at Puck Willow. The Inspector showed it to Richard Oliver.

"Ever seen this article before, Mr. Oliver?" Anthony noticed now that the handle was grooved. A fact that had eluded him when he had first seen the razor in the house in Mayblossom Avenue. Richard Oliver took the white- handled razor.

"Well, as it happens, it's not so easy for me to answer that question as you might imagine. But this razor is very much like an old one of my own."

"Why can't you be sure?" inquired the Inspector. Oliver was silent. Anthony saw how worn and worried the man looked. He had been travelling all night of course . . . in addition to the frightful blow which Fate had so unexpectedly dealt him. Oliver was speaking again.

"You see, it's like this, Inspector MacMorran. For some years now, like most people, I've used a 'safety'. But years ago—like most people again—I used a 'cut' . . . er . . . one of the old-fashioned type. And I had one in my possession at that time certainly very much like this one. I'm pretty certain this *is* it! But, as I said, it's years since I either saw it or handled it. That's why I'm not absolutely sure. But actually, though, I think it is the one that belonged to me." He laid it on MacMorran's table again.

"If you're right in that assumption, Mr. Oliver, where would this razor have been last Monday evening?"

The look of worry on Richard Oliver's face grew appreciably. He pursed his lips in apprehension.

"As far as I know, Inspector, in a small cabinet on the wall in the bathroom at home. But as I explained—"

"You mean it's been in that cabinet, as far as you know, ever since you gave up using it?"

"In all probability."

"Why did you *keep* it?"

Oliver shrugged his shoulders. "Why *does* one keep old things? For no reason at all. No more reason than why I didn't do the reverse—get rid of it."

"I see. Well, Mr. Oliver, that's the razor that was found in your son's hand."

"In my son's hand?"

"In your son's *left* hand."

"In my son's left hand." Oliver repeated the words mechanically. The man looked dazed and dizzy. MacMorran interposed again.

"What kind of razor did he use in the ordinary way, Mr. Oliver?"

"Er… Peter… oh—a 'safety'. Always a 'safety'. He had a Gillette. I've never seen him with a razor of that other kind in his hand."

Oliver nodded towards the razor lying in front of the Inspector. Anthony felt that he must intervene if only for a moment.

"Mr. Oliver," he said quietly, "you may rest assured that everything to do with your son's unhappy death will be fully considered and, if need be, investigated. Please don't think that Scotland Yard ever jumps to a conclusion, wantonly, carelessly or light-heartedly. And, of course, there will be ample opportunity at the inquest—"

"Yes. I am fully aware of that, sir. I know my boy'll get justice and fair play. Or rather—his memory. That's why I came straight along here from the train this morning to see you gentlemen."

He reached for his hat and gloves. "I haven't seen my wife yet. And I can't say I'm looking forward to it, either. Peter was *her* boy. The eldest, you know. It usually goes that way. So, if you don't want me any more for the present, I think I'll push off home."

Oliver stood up to his full height. MacMorran nodded and accompanied him towards the door.

"You'll be hearing from us again, Mr. Oliver. And once again—my most sincere condolences."

He patted Oliver's shoulder, shook hands with him and then shut the door. Anthony turned to meet MacMorran as he walked back to his table.

"What was it you wanted to tell *me* about the razor, Andrew? Before Mr. Oliver, senior, turned up."

MacMorran pointed to the chair which Oliver had just vacated. "Sit down," he said, "and take what's coming to you easy and comfortable."

3

"Gertcher," said Anthony, "if you think you sound like Tony Perelli, I can tell you—you don't even look like him." MacMorran grinned. He always enjoyed these verbal passages of arms with Anthony Bathurst.

"Come on, Andrew," continued Anthony, "shed that inferiority complex and spill your bibfull. I'm confident that your patience is nearing exhaustion point."

"Right. I will. I can see you're in the right mood. The properly receptive mood. Sometimes I'm compelled to break through a cr-rust of obstinacy. First of all—finger-prints. There were dozens of 'em, as I told you on the 'phone. On the door-handle—the bathroom door-handle, on the razor, on the towel-rail, on the side of the bath itself, on the ledge over the wash-hand basin, on the razor strop—pretty well everywhere. They were all of them identical. Or in other words, they belonged to the dead man, Peter Oliver. Well, are you down for the count?"

"No. Not yet, Andrew. All the same, I won't deny that I'm far from pleased. It certainly isn't what I wanted to hear. But you haven't finished yet. You carry on."

The Inspector began to speak more slowly. "Unfortunately the other piece of evidence we've picked up is by way of being . . . er . . . contradictory, which fact *may* please you." MacMorran paused.

"Come on, Andrew—don't stall, out with it."

"All in good time. I hate being rushed. I'm just considering the best way to put it. It's to do with this razor here."

"I know it is. You told me that much on the telephone. What is it exactly?"

"Listen and I'll tell you. The razor has been submitted to every known scientific test. And under one process of investigation, a tiny piece—infinitesimal, almost—of yellow fabric has been discovered. In the groove of the handle. Clinging to it. You can see the place if you look. There you are—that's the position."

Anthony nodded. "Has there been any attempt to place, to identify, this piece of yellow fabric, may I ask?" MacMorran was guarded in his reply. "Up to a point— yes."

Anthony began to rub his hands. "Such as the inside of a glove? Yes, Andrew?"

MacMorran was still guarded. "It could be—from the inside of a glove."

"From the inside of, shall we say, a chamois-leather glove? Gents popular wear? All sizes?"

"It could be."

Anthony struck—and struck hard! "Did the expert, who discovered this tiny piece of yellow fabric clinging to the groove of the razor handle, actually nominate a chamois-leather glove as the possible whole, of which the tiny fragment might be the infinitesimal part?"

MacMorran smiled. He knew now that Anthony had him where he wanted him. He surrendered, therefore, as gracefully as possible.

"Amongst other possibilities, yes. A glove such as you describe *was* mentioned."

"You cunning old twister," said Anthony, "making me chase you round the ruddy graveyard like that. You deserve to be kicked to death by wild butterflies."

MacMorran masked his features with innocence. "Not a bit of it," he demurred, "I merely allowed you to follow the point to its logical conclusion. I know how that sort of thing appeals to you."

Anthony fell on silence. After an appreciable wait he said, "well, it suits me, Andrew, that latest piece of information, even though it throws a spanner into some of your works. You must admit that it makes a hell of a difference."

"Of course I must. I do. All the same, though—"

Anthony went on, almost as though he were thinking aloud and hadn't heard the Inspector speaking. "Our murderer wore gloves, Andrew. Which was the very thing I'd suspected. But by the hokey, Andrew, we're up against something. I'll say we are! Bags of craft and unlimited cunning. The left-hand business alone demonstrates that. At long last, I may be confronted with the perfect crime."

"Hold hard a minute," interposed MacMorran, "don't run on quite so fast. You're still *certain*, that young Oliver was murdered?"

"I am, Andrew. Absolutely!"

"Not a shadow of a doubt?"

"Not a sausage, Andrew. As I see it now—it all adds up. As I saw it *before*—as a suicide I mean—in the first chapter—it just didn't. To my eye there was always something wrong. And that's why I kicked."

Anthony paused and then went on again. "Consider the prime factors, Andrew. Stella Forrest herself and what she represents. Margaret's exposition of the bath accessories, and now the more than mere possibility that a gloved hand manipulated that razor lying there—they all *do* add up, and what's more, they cross-cast. Yes, Andrew, I'm satisfied. Aren't you, yourself?"

MacMorran shook his head slowly. "I'm not as convinced as you are. But I'm just inclined, perhaps, to be with you now. And yet to-morrow I might swing the other way again. All the same though, as I was about to say just now, there's a great deal I fail to understand. Because it's not at all clear. A ve-rry great deal."

"You're tellin' me, Andrew. We shall have to return to our beginnings and start on the problem with an absolutely open mind."

MacMorran stood up and began to walk about the room. "If it's murder, the drag-net shouldn't need to be cast very wide to get our man."

Anthony looked up. "Explain, Andrew, please. I don't know that I get that."

"Simple enough, surely? The murderer must be a frequent visitor to the Oliver house—and must be somebody close to the victim. By close I mean really 'intimate'. My dear chap, to get into the bathroom as he did. That sticks out like a poisoned thumb."

"I wonder whether it actually does," countered Anthony quietly.

"Why, what do you mean? How on earth can you—"

"Just a minute, Andrew. Don't you run on too fast. Are we certain that Peter Oliver *was* murdered in that bathroom of his father's house? Let's theorize. Wander, mentally, as a horse grazes. It won't do any harm at this stage of the case. Isn't it possible for him to have been killed elsewhere, and the body brought to the house by car? The murderer may have known that the place was empty. Been informed so by the dead man himself, in all probability."

MacMorran stood and stared as Anthony flung out his theory. "But the razor—what about the razor? How did the murderer get his fingers on that?"

Anthony shook his head. "You hang up on that, too, Andrew. Cast your mind back to Oliver senior. Richard Guise Oliver. Who sat in this 'ere chair less than half an hour ago. What did he have to tell you re your ruddy razor? Was he *sure* it was his? No, sir. Not a hundred per cent. Could he identify it for certain as one of his boyhood collection, all rusty with genuine Victoria era? No, sir, he could not! And don't forget it, Andrew."

MacMorran ceased his pacing and resumed his seat. Anthony's words had gone home.

"Blast you and that tongue of yours," said the Inspector, "sometimes I let you persuade me right against my will."

Anthony came back to seriousness. "Frankly, Andrew, there's only one thing for it. We must do as I said just now. We must start looking at the problem right from the sheer beginning. With completely open minds, Andrew. They're what we simply *must* have. If we don't, we may let an extremely cunning and cold-blooded criminal slip through our fingers. Don't forget what he did."

"Which bit?"

"After he'd polished off his victim."

"What?"

"Had a bath, my dear Andrew. Late at night. In an empty house. Empty that is, bar a stiff. I'm strongly of the opinion that Margaret Oliver's idea is the correct one."

"But why? What made him do that?"

"I should say, Andrew, to rid himself of certain bloodstains and knowing full well that he was perfectly safe from interruption. At the moment that guess is probably as good as any."

"But while he was doing that—where was the body? Don't tell me it was on the bath-mat, by the side of the bath?"

For some seconds, Anthony didn't reply to the Inspector's question. When he did, he spoke quietly.

"I'm not sure *where* the body was, Andrew. When the murderer had his bath. I shall be compelled to give that question a considerable amount of thought."

4

Anthony came away from MacMorran's room at the "Yard", a prey to a conflict of thoughts. He saw very clearly that there was much to be done, before the scent grew cold, if this case were to be brought to a successful conclusion. Peter Oliver's family life, his own personal life, his business life, would all have to be thoroughly looked into, sifted and investigated.

The point that Anthony had made with MacMorran with regard to the actual place where the murder had been committed had been no idle one. For it must be admitted that Anthony at this stage harboured a multitude of doubts. He realized, though, that things on the whole might not be so bad as they appeared. There were so many fields unexplored which might reasonably yield a wealth of data. There was, for instance, the Lombard Street branch of Delaney's bank. And there was Stella Forrest herself. Peter Oliver *might* have given something away to her on a past occasion which the girl might remember . . . something vital which possibly had eluded her but temporarily. There was always a reasonable chance of that happening.

On the other hand, if MacMorran's theory were the right one, that the murderer was somebody very close to the dead man, somebody of intimate relationship who had been admitted to the privacy of the house and the bathroom in all good faith, then the solution of the problem looked like being an extremely tiresome and troublesome affair. For this reason. For this almost invulnerable reason. So Anthony surmised as he drove the car slowly homeward. Almost everybody whom he knew to be familiar with the dead man seemed to have a cast-iron alibi. Take the various members of the Oliver family first of all.

The father, Richard Guise Oliver, had been in Aberdeen. The mother and the sister had been at an hôtel in Bournemouth. The brother, David, was still on a walking-tour somewhere. That is to say, as far as Anthony knew. Stella Forrest herself had said good-night to the dead man at Hammersmith but a few hours before the murder had taken place. Pretty well air-tight, all that lot. This deadlock raised the question in Anthony's mind of Peter Oliver's friends. What friends had he? Again—had he left the house in Mayblossom Avenue on the Bank Holiday evening and returned in the company of another? Or had the murderer come to the house while Peter was there and been admitted by him?

Yet another trenchant query. Why was the murdered man in evening dress? He hadn't been dressed in that manner when he had taken Stella to Kew Gardens earlier in the day. Therefore, he must have changed, as he did, for an appointment elsewhere. Where? That was one vital question, at least, for which the answer must be found if any headway were to be made towards the ultimate solution. Anthony left Hyde Park Corner, wondering what step would be the best for him to take as a starting-point.

There were at least three people who would amply repay him, he considered, for the time spent with them on an interview.

The manager of Delaney's bank would give him a clearer view of Oliver the bank clerk, the woman who occupied the house next door to the Olivers' in Mayblossom Avenue, Puck Willow, might answer one or two extremely relevant questions Anthony desired to put to her, and thirdly there was Stella Forrest, whom he felt he must see again as soon as possible. She was the person who could fill in one background for him, better, in all likelihood, than anybody else. And perhaps—when everything came to be assessed—the most important background of all.

The details of Peter Oliver's private life as it had been lived over the last few months.

CHAPTER 8

1

It was Andrew MacMorran who clinched the issue with a telephone-call almost immediately after lunch. "Glad I don't find you asleep," he opened, "it's what I was afraid of."

"I can feel your relief over the telephone, Andrew. Who woke you up and what's frightening you at the moment?"

"I'm going along to Lombard Street in about half an hour's time. Delaney's bank. Thought you might care to come along with me."

Anthony grinned. "I don't blame you for wanting results, Andrew. That shows you how I feel about it. I'll be seeing you."

"Cannon Street-underground—three o'clock, then. And mind you set the alarm-clock, O.K.?"

"O.K., Andrew." Anthony hung up. "The Inspector's getting busy," he murmured, "who am I to say him nay?"

When they reached Delaney's bank, Andrew Murray received them with his customary urbanity and at once put a message through to his outside office.

"Mr. Fitzgerald," he said, "please understand that I'm engaged and that I'm likely to be engaged for some time now. And on no account am I to be disturbed. And please stand by yourself in case I should need you for anything."

The manager of the bank turned to MacMorran. "Now, gentlemen, please regard me at your service."

"Thank you," said the "Yard" inspector.

"I can guess what you're here about," continued the bank manager.

"I expect you can. It's the death of this young fellow, Peter Oliver, a member of your official staff."

"Very sad, Inspector. Very sad, indeed. Young fellow like that in the prime of life and with his career in front of him. He'd have done well, too. I presume, from the brief report I've seen in my newspaper, that he died by his own hand."

MacMorran gave Anthony a shrewd glance before he ventured his next remark.

"I'm afraid it looks very much like it. Now, that's really what I've come to have a word with you about. We just want to seal the affair up at both ends. No cash trouble here, was there?"

Murray shook his head emphatically. "None whatever, Inspector. You can dismiss the idea entirely, if you ever had it. Oliver had no direct access to any cash at all."

"I see. I can scrub that then, can I? No financial troubles of any kind, eh?"

"No. His duties here didn't touch the handling of cash—he'd done a spot of that sometime back, and I'd shifted him. Last Autumn I fancy it was."

"Oh, why was that? Any—"

The manager interrupted MacMorran's question. "No. No trouble of any kind. My move was in no way a matter of disciplinary action. It was occasioned by normal routine. Staff changes, to be precise. One of my chaps picked up a promotion to another branch and I was compelled, by reason of that, to have a sort of shift round. Quite a common occurrence in a bank of this kind. No, I've no complaints against Oliver of any sort. Excellent youngster in every respect. Actually, his present duties were such as to bring him in contact—"

Murray seemed to pause rather uncertainly. Both MacMorran and Anthony noticed the hesitation.

"As a matter of fact," the manager continued, "I'd made arrangements with Oliver that he should do certain work with me on the Tuesday following the Bank Holiday. That was the reason I noticed his absence from duty more quickly perhaps than I ordinarily might have done. I sent for him, you see, and he wasn't here."

"What was that particular work, may I ask?"

Anthony mentally congratulated MacMorran on the promptitude of his question.

"Oh, merely routine again. I'd been considering for some time now a new form of register for certain securities we hold—foreign securities, they are—and I intended to go through the current book with Oliver on the Tuesday morning following the Bank Holiday and see just what our holdings are. That was all."

"Had you actually informed him of this intention on your part?"

Murray smiled. "Re the new style of register? Oh, no, that's something I've had under my hat for some little time now."

MacMorran shook his head. "No, that isn't quite what I meant. My point was, had you informed Oliver of your intention of going through the present register with him on the Tuesday?"

"Oh, I see what you mean—yes. Well, in a way I had. I had given him instructions on the previous Saturday to report to me first thing on the Tuesday morning following the break and to bring the foreign securities register to my room with him. To that extent, he did know something about it. But no more than that."

MacMorran looked grave. Anthony noticed it and felt sure that he knew why. The Inspector's next question was direct and distinctly to the point. "Nothing wrong, I take it, Mr. Murray, with this register? Did Oliver keep it?"

"Oliver certainly kept it. But there can't be anything wrong with it, in the direction at which you're hinting. That is to say, anything financial. You see, it's merely a register—a book of record. Securities are just 'listed' in it. Just by names and descriptions. I don't see that there can be any—"

MacMorran cut in. "During Oliver's recent absence, did you use this register in the manner that you had previously intended to? In other words, did you do the job on your own?"

"Oh no, Inspector. As Oliver hadn't turned up on the Tuesday morning, I simply pushed the job off until the time when he should return. There was nothing especially urgent about it. My natural impression was, of course, that he'd be away from the bank for a few days at the most. Candidly, I thought he'd probably caught a chill of some sort over the holiday and was having a day or two in bed to get over it. I'd much rather a man on my staff did that than bring the germ into the office and infect half a dozen or so more of the staff. I take a pretty dim view of that sort of thing, because it's happened here more than once. We've had four or five people away at the same time. Damned awkward, I can tell you.

"Quite so, Mr. Murray. I see your point only too well. I suppose you wouldn't mind, just to please me, having a glance at this securities register that you tell me Oliver kept. Sometimes, you know—"

The genial Murray accepted the suggestion without the slightest demur.

"Not a bit, Inspector. Only too pleased to help you in any way. I'm afraid, though, that you'll be wasting your time. I can't see how there can possibly be any jiggery-pokery with the register."

He picked up the receiver of the internal telephone. "Mr. Fitzgerald—bring me in the 'F.S.R.', will you please? Yes . . . please . . . at once. What? In the strong-room? That's all right, that doesn't matter . . . there can't be a lot—and it won't make any difference . . . no . . . that doesn't matter . . . I'm requiring it for a different purpose. Thank you."

Murray hung up, before smiling across at his two visitors. "Shan't keep you waiting more than a couple of minutes, gentlemen."

MacMorran nodded his acknowledgement as the manager placed his finger-tips together. "No, gentlemen," he continued, "I'm afraid the reason for poor Oliver's suicide will be found somewhere in his private life. A love affair, possibly, or perhaps—"

There came a tap on the door. Murray broke off what he had been saying. "Come in," he called.

A tall, dark, oily-haired man entered with a black book in his hand.

"Thank you, Mr. Fitzgerald," said the manager, "on the table here, please, if you don't mind. Thank you very much." Fitzgerald put the book he had been carrying in front of his chief and withdrew.

"Wouldn't think that chap was Irish, would you?" said Murray with a smile and a nod towards the man who had just gone out. "I often tell him he looks much more like a ruddy Spaniard than a Mick."

Anthony smiled back. "The Armada, Mr. Murray, has, I'm afraid, a good deal to answer for."

"The Armada? I don't know that I—" the manager looked at Anthony, evidently for further guidance, but Mr. Bathurst's face was impassive. Murray coughed, therefore, and transferred himself to the main matter in hand.

"Now here we are, gentlemen. This is our foreign securities register. I'll open it for you and show you. It's just what it purports to be. Nothing more—nothing less. In these columns are listed certain securities that have been deposited with us for safety, by various clients of this Lombard Street branch of Delaney's bank. If I tell you it's in the nature of an inventory, perhaps you'll get the idea better and understand its real purport. Do you see, Inspector?"

Murray showed the book, and certain entries in it, to MacMorran. MacMorran nodded.

"I follow. Merely a record, as you say. So that Oliver couldn't have—"

Murray nodded again and began to turn the pages of the register almost idly. He was certainly, as Anthony could see quite well, paying far more attention to the Inspector's words than to any entry in the book at which he was looking.

Suddenly, however, Anthony saw him pause and then bend down towards the register as though he was desirous of scrutinizing an entry therein more closely. MacMorran saw the movement, too. Each of them waited for Andrew Murray to say something.

Murray, however, was silent, but the frown on his face was there for all to see. For the frown held eloquence. The silence was maintained for some seconds. At length, MacMorran judged it opportune to intervene.

"Anything you think you should tell us, Mr. Murray?" It was becoming increasingly clear that something in the book in front of him was occasioning the bank manager a certain degree of embarrassment. Murray was again slow to reply.

"Er . . . yes . . . I'm afraid there is." He caressed his chin. "From one point of view at least. I'm just a trifle puzzled by something I've just seen in here. No doubt there's a perfectly sound explanation, but at the moment I can't quite see it. Examining it as I am, I'm relying entirely on memory—that's the snag."

Murray pored over the register. Then he pushed the book over to the Inspector.

"There's an entry there under date May 11 of last year. On folio 67. See it? The third entry down the page." Murray used the tip of a finger. MacMorran looked at the place indicated. For the moment, Anthony was content to listen.

"Yes," said the Inspector, "I've got the place."

"I shall have to see my chief clerk about it," continued Murray, "but as I remember things, and I've a good memory, Inspector, when it comes to my job here, a gentleman from South America who has extensive holdings in our banks, both in this country and abroad, deposited Bearer bonds to the approximate value of £80,000 with me in May last. That's just on twelve months ago. They had been issued by the Government of San Jonquilo, are secured by the taxes and revenues of that State and bear interest, tax-free, at three per cent."

MacMorran, who had put on his reading-spectacles, nodded. "That's right. I can see the entry all right. £80,000 worth of three per cent Bearer bonds—Government of San Jonquilo, South America. Name of holder, Roderigo Santos Garcia. And on the 17th of March *this* year, according to this register—that's not much more than a month ago—he withdrew from your care half of them. At least, it would appear to me to be so."

"Yes," said the manager slowly, and scratching his chin thoughtfully, "and that's what's giving me occasion to think." MacMorran took off his spectacles and looked up at the man who had addressed him. "You allude, I take it, to the pencilled alteration, the asterisk and the explanatory note— also in pencil—that are all clearly indicated here?"

"I do," returned Murray grimly and with a pale face.

"If I read them aright," went on MacMorran, "I should say what happened was this. Señor Roderigo Garcia intended originally to withdraw £20,000 worth of these bonds from your custody in March last and then changed his mind to double that amount. The original entry of withdrawal was made in the register for £20,000, Garcia seemingly altered his plans while he was here, and the amending entry for some reason or other which I can't yet see was made in pencil and the asterisk note appended at the same time. And it has been allowed to remain in that pencilled state ever since. Am I right in my conjecture?"

Murray looked paler now and much more worried. When he spoke next he spoke with definite emotion. "Inspector MacMorran," he said in an agitated voice. "I'll be perfectly frank with you. I'm extremely perturbed at what we seem to have so surprisingly turned up. I interviewed Señor Garcia myself, as you may imagine would be the case, when he presented himself here on that morning last month and informed me that he desired to take out a portion of the San Jonquilo bonds of his that we had in our keeping. He asked me for a value approximating £20,000. And to the best of my knowledge and belief that was the value he took. It can easily be checked, however, by a reference to the receipt for the bonds which Señor Garcia gave me and which is, of course, in our possession."

Murray's hand went to the internal telephone. "Just a minute, Mr. Murray, before you ring through," said MacMorran. "Was anybody else of your staff concerned in any way with this transaction? In addition to yourself and this man Garcia?"

"Yes," replied Murray, his face drained of all colour, "I'm afraid there was."

"Who was that?"

"Peter Oliver. Peter Oliver was the man who went to our strong-room to obtain the bonds for Garcia and who brought them to me in this room."

2

MacMorran shrugged his shoulders and glanced over towards Anthony. Then he gestured towards the telephone from which the bank manager had temporarily withdrawn his hand.

"Go ahead, Mr. Murray, with what you were about to do. Handle it your own way."

Murray nodded and picked up the receiver. "Mr. Fitzgerald? Come in to me again, will you please?"

Murray replaced the receiver. MacMorran saw that the manager had been badly hit. His confidence had vanished completely. A vein in his temple was earning at least time and a half. The door opened again and the black-haired Fitzgerald made his second appearance that afternoon. Murray motioned nervously to his subordinate.

"Er . . . close the door, Fitzgerald . . . and come in. These gentlemen—you saw them before, I know—are from Scotland Yard. With regard to young Oliver." Murray glanced at the card on his table. "Chief Detective-Inspector MacMorran. Mr. Anthony Bathurst. Mr. Fitzgerald, my next in command. Now take that chair, Fitzgerald, and come and sit here. I want you, primarily, to refresh my memory."

The dark, oily-haired man evinced surprise. "That's not usual, sir."

Murray looked pleased at the tribute. "Thank you. But I'm afraid this isn't a time for compliments. Cast your mind back to last March. The month before this. Can you recall Señor Garcia coming in one morning? He asked to see me specially—one of the cashiers brought him in—and I saw him."

Fitzgerald nodded. "I remember the incident perfectly, Mr. Murray."

"Good. Tell me what happened, will you? That is to say, to the best of your recollection."

"Señor Garcia asked for £20,000 worth of his San Jonquilo bonds. The three per cents. A quarter of his full holding. He'd deposited a large holding with us, when he came over from San Jonquilo. About eighteen months ago I should think. Perhaps a little longer than that. Time marches on."

"Thank you, Fitzgerald. But you're a little out with regard to when Garcia first arrived. Now pop out and bring me Garcia's receipt, will you?"

"Certainly, sir."

Fitzgerald departed. Murray drummed with his finger-tips on his blotting-pad—MacMorran and Anthony waited patiently for the revelations that were to come. Despite the fact that Anthony was feeling much less sure of himself and his theories than had been the case when he entered Delaney's bank. Murray continued his drumming. Anthony's ears began to pick out and recognize a tune. It was the "British Grenadiers". Some minutes passed before the chief clerk returned. When he came back again, he put a slip of paper on the manager's table.

"Receipt for an equivalent of twenty thousand, sir," he announced. "As I said—a quarter of the full holding."

Murray inspected Garcia's receipt and it became obvious to all in the room that his agitation was increasing. He pushed the paper over to MacMorran.

"And as I first indicated," he declared quietly, "you can see that the receipt is for the amount I stated."

MacMorran scrutinized the receipt and passed it over to Anthony. Murray turned to Fitzgerald.

"Now, Mr. Fitzgerald, look at the entry in the F.S. register, will you, please? Look at it carefully and then give me your opinion of it."

Fitzgerald took the register from his chief. He knitted his brows thoughtfully at what he saw before shaking his head in bewilderment.

"I don't understand this at all, sir," he said eventually. Murray waited for the chief clerk to elaborate his statement. Fitzgerald continued. "According to this pencilled amendment and the note below it, Garcia seems to have withdrawn double the amount he's signed for."

"It would appear so, on the face of it. Now tell me this, Mr. Fitzgerald. Those pencilled figures and the words of the note appended—in whose handwriting would you say they were?"

Fitzgerald bent over the entry. "This handwriting is Oliver's, sir."

"Certain of that?"

"Absolutely positive, Mr. Murray."

"I agree with you," returned Murray grimly, "there's no mistaking those Greek 'e's' of his—like an epsilon."

Fitzgerald looked up at his chief, as though something new, in the way of thought, had been born in his brain. "Mr. Murray," he said, "you interviewed Señor Garcia that morning he called here—I only came into it when you informed me of the transaction afterwards."

"That is so. I've explained that already. What's your point?"

"Well, sir. Did you take the bonds from the strong-room yourself?"

"I did not," replied Murray, grim and pale-faced again, "and that's the hell of it. I sent Oliver down to get them. Gave him the key. That is my invariable custom in matters of that nature. I always contact the clerk who happens to be keeping the register. Keeps him in touch. Oliver went down and brought the bonds up here to this room. He gave them to me, and I passed them over to Garcia. Damn it all," he glared, "how the ruddy hell can I run a bank efficiently unless I trust the members of my own staff?"

"I was afraid that's what had happened," nodded the chief clerk, "when I began to piece things together. Well, there's one thing, the matter can easily be settled, sir. We must check up on the value of the bonds still in the strong-room. That'll clinch matters."

"That's the point I was coming to," said Murray, rising from his chair. He went to a drawer for certain keys. "If gentlemen will excuse us for a few minutes," he said.

"O.K.," returned MacMorran, "you'll find us here when you come back."

The two bank officials went out. The Inspector turned to Anthony. "What do you make of it? Also, what did I tell you?" he asked.

"Don't know," replied Anthony, "but the waters seem even deeper than I'd bargained for. What do you think?"

"Oliver committed suicide. My first impression. They're usually the best. It's the old story all over again. When he heard that the old man was going to examine that register as soon as the Easter recess was over and he knew what he'd done, he took fright because it was obvious his little game was up."

Anthony shook his head. "Not so sure, Andrew."

"Why not?"

"The reason's clear, surely? If he knew of this register business with the manager on the Saturday, as we are told he did, why didn't the pangs of conscience smite him then and there? Why should they delay their sinister entry until Monday evening? He was all merry and bright on the Sunday and equally merry and bright until at least nine o'clock on the Monday evening, whereas your way, he most certainly wouldn't have been. No, Andrew, this case isn't solved yet by a long chalk."

Before the Inspector could resume the argument, the door of the manager's room opened again to herald the return of Murray and

Fitzgerald. The face of the former was strained and set. Fitzgerald, biting his lower lip, looked desperately uncomfortable. Anthony waited quietly for the final revelation. Murray sat down heavily on his chair.

"Well, gentlemen, Mr. Fitzgerald and I have checked Señor Garcia's present holding. It seems that something like twenty thousand pounds' worth of San Jonquilo bonds is missing."

The manager bent his head into his hands.

3

MacMorran clinched the issue. "In the circumstances, as you've outlined them, you suspect Oliver?"

Murray, anxious and worried, slowly nodded. In reply, he repeated the phrase that MacMorran had used.

"In the circumstances, Inspector, I'm afraid I have no other course. I need not tell you what a serious matter this is for me personally."

Anthony cut into the conversation for the first time. "Enlighten my financial inexperience, Mr. Murray, please. Are these bonds saleable?"

"Well, it depends rather on what you mean. They *could* be negotiated, of course, on the Exchange, like other stock. And they're bearer bonds, too—we mustn't overlook that. All the same, they're not what I should lay *my* hands on if I started stealing."

He reached forward and picked up the *Financial Times* from a basket-tray on the edge of his table. "Let me see. San Jonquilo Three per cent bearer bonds. They're quoted at 78 this morning."

"That would be a £100 bond, I suppose?" queried MacMorran.

"But would any reputable broker touch them?" asked Anthony. "I should imagine that most brokers would require satisfying in relation to title, would they not? On the other hand a broker who knew you—"

MacMorran interposed. "If you ask me," he ventured, "they'd be disposed of 'under the counter'. Or its equivalent. That is to say through a discreditable agency. At a cut price. They'd sell all right to anybody ready to take the risk. Same as anything else that's 'hot'. You can let me have the series and numbers before we go, can't you? Also Garcia's address."

Murray nodded. "Get them, Fitzgerald, will you?" The black-haired chief clerk responded almost enthusiastically. "I'll see to it now, sir."

But Anthony had more questions. "Mr. Murray," he said, "there's another point, before, perhaps, Mr. Fitzgerald leaves us."

Fitzgerald heard what was said and halted at the door. "It's a small point in a way," went on Anthony, "but I've always been led to believe that most banks looked askance at left-handed people as members of their staffs. In other words, they don't employ left-handed people—the members of a bank staff must use their right hands. Is that true or not?"

Murray shook his head. "*Some* banks may have that rule, Mr. Bathurst, but Delaney's isn't one of them. Or if it is, I've never heard of it. But I'm somewhat puzzled at your question, Mr. Bathurst. Is it . . . er . . . relevant to the case?"

Fitzgerald spoke from the door before Anthony could reply. "Peter Oliver was left-handed, Mr. Murray. I think that's the term of Mr. Bathurst's reference. You, perhaps, weren't aware of it. In the outer office, of course, we *were* aware of it. If only for the way he'd put the pin in, when pinning papers together. Most awkward I can assure you. Productive of . . . er . . . unparliamentary language. I presume that's what this gentleman is referring to?"

"That's quite right, Mr. Fitzgerald," said Anthony. "It was a point I felt I'd like satisfying on."

"O.K., Fitzgerald," said Murray, "get that bond information for me, will you?"

MacMorran came in again. "*I'd* like another word with regard to that, Mr. Murray, if you don't mind. Before we pack up for this afternoon."

"I'm at your service, Inspector. What is it?"

"I'd like you to make full inquiries in addition to those that we shall *officially* make from the 'Yard' with reference to the possible marketing of those missing bonds. See what your own brokers can tell you. You never know. Whispers often float round where you'd least expect them. And if the person who's got those bonds *has* attempted—" MacMorran paused abruptly. "Anyhow, you see what I'm after. Find out, or try to find out, as we shall, if anything's leaked out in the places where such a leakage might be likely."

Murray nodded. "I'll do that for you, Inspector. All the same, it's an extraordinary sort of theft. Candidly, I can't understand it even now. It must have been perpetrated, I'm positive, on the spur of the moment. Can't have been in any way premeditated." Murray stopped, shaking his head doubtfully.

"How do you make that out, Mr. Murray?" inquired Anthony.

Murray looked surprised at Anthony's question. "Well, that must be so, mustn't it? Oliver couldn't have *known* in advance that Garcia would come to the bank last month and ask for those bonds that he withdrew. He wouldn't have been absolutely certain that I should send *him* to the *strong- room*—"

"Wasn't that your customary practice? Unless my memory is at fault didn't you make that assertion—"

"Yes, I did. And it was. But there's always the odd exception, you know. Anyhow—get back to Garcia—Oliver couldn't have *known* that Garcia—"

"Why not? Suppose Garcia had told him previously? Supposing he'd met Garcia somewhere? Socially? At Sandown Park, Twickenham, Stamford Bridge, Madame Tussaud's, St. Paul's Cathedral, Lord's, the Oval, Kew Gardens, the Zoo—"

Murray interrupted. "You're being facetious, surely?"

"Not entirely. Merely attempting to show you what I meant by the possibility of a social encounter between the two men." Murray shook his head. "I see what you mean. But it isn't likely. As I see things."

"You can't rule it out, sir. You can't ignore the possibility by any means. And if you do, I shan't—I assure you. "

As Anthony replied the door opened again and Fitzgerald reappeared. "There are the particulars you wanted, sir. And Señor Garcia's address is below." He handed the manager the paper.

"Thank you, Mr. Fitzgerald. That will do for now, I think. But come in again as soon as I'm free. I'm afraid there are several matters we shall have to attend to at once."

The chief clerk bowed and departed. "Very good, Mr. Murray."

The manager passed the slip to MacMorran. "There you are, Inspector—they're the details you wanted. You'll let me know at once, of course, if you trace anything?"

MacMorran pocketed the slip. "At once, Mr. Murray. And that goes for you, too—if you please."

"Certainly—you may rely on me."

"Extraordinary what comes to the surface when you start digging into things, isn't it?"

Murray nodded sadly. He was a worried, anxious, crestfallen man. "Only too true, Inspector. But even now, I can't see why Oliver had to take either those bonds or his own life. It beats me. San Jonquilo bonds aren't bank-notes, golden sovereigns, or even precious stones."

MacMorran shook hands. "There's always a man's conscience, Mr. Murray. No escaping from it. The still small voice, you know. Got to be reckoned with."

Anthony shook hands also. Outside the bank, he turned to his companion and said: "Andrew, you surpass yourself. That last touch of yours was positively superb."

4

Anthony sat with MacMorran in the latter's room at the "Yard". Anthony took a cigarette and lit up. He offered his case to the Inspector. MacMorran shook his head.

"No, thanks. I'll have a pipe, if you don't mind."

The Inspector began to put the expressed intention into practice. The tobacco burnt well. "At the risk of being monotonous," said MacMorran, tossing away the match-stub, "what about it now? Any alteration of ideas?"

Anthony blew a smoke-ring and watched it ascend. "Some slight alterations, perhaps, Andrew, call them adjustments, in relation to whys and wherefores, but no real deviation from the main line."

"The main line being?"

"That Oliver was murdered. That Oliver did *not* commit suicide. And that's making full allowance," he added mischievously, "for the still small voice that commanded your valedictory eloquence in Lombard Street just now."

MacMorran grunted. He wasn't replying to that—he was painfully aware that the contest would be unequal. "So you're still sticking to that, eh? Going to sink in the last ditch?"

"I am, Andrew. Bar the sink part of it. I don't mind admitting that up to the present I'm completely baffled as regards motive. Although, we do seem now to have stumbled on one most valuable clue."

Mac Morran knew that Anthony's eyes were searching his face. He puffed away at his pipe. "You mean the paper in Oliver's wallet?"

"Naturally, Andrew."

MacMorran began to nod. He nodded several times. "Let's have another 'dekko' at it," he said, as though he were surrendering a position. He took Oliver's paper from his drawer and smoothed it out on his crossed knee. Anthony grinned as he did so.

"Um," said MacMorran after consideration, "in a way it fits, I suppose, and yet it doesn't. It's by way of being damned contradictory."

"How come, Andrew? Instruct the babe, and succour the suckling."

MacMorran screwed his face to one side. "Well, '80,000 isn't to be sneezed at.' So it says here. The figure coincides with the approximate value of Garcia's San Jonquilo bonds that were lodged at Delaney's bank. No doubt you'd noticed that fact?"

"I had, Andrew. Go on, though."

"Well, Oliver didn't get away with the lot, did he? Or anything like it? *And* if you'll bear with me pointing it out—he had the chance of getting away with considerably more than he actually did, according to Messrs. Murray and Fitzgerald. Agreed on that?"

"Agreed, Andrew. They were telling the truth all right. Still—keep going on."

"Well, we then come to the 'query murder—query motive—query suicide' business and to an unnamed 'she' who is to be 'told straight' what she's going to be expected to do. After that Oliver boasts that up his sleeve is the ace of trumps and that he'd be all kinds of a mug if he declined to play it. That, I think, is about the bundle. Or a fair summing up of it."

"Not quite, Andrew, if you'll permit me to make the correction."

"Why, what have I missed?"

"Wasn't there a reference in the note to Easter? The Queen of Seasons Bright? The Day of Splendour? If my memory serve me correctly, Peter Oliver—" Anthony stopped abruptly. "You know, Andrew," he said, "we're taking it for granted that Oliver himself wrote this blessed note which you found in the wallet. It's written more or less in the first person, I know, but that doesn't necessarily—"

MacMorran smiled at Anthony with evident pleasure. "This is where I score." He put the note on his table and called Anthony over. "Remember what the bank-manager said about Oliver's 'e's'? They were Greek, he said. Well, these in this note are made in exactly the same way as those in that bank register were. Do you see them? Look here. I took particular pains to notice. You can take my word for that. The man who wrote this note is the same man who made the pencil scrawl in the bank's register—if handwriting goes for anything. I haven't any doubt about it. And the man who did that bank job was Peter Oliver."

MacMorran sat back looking extremely satisfied with himself.

"It's useful to know that, Andrew, and we'll assume you're right. I'll go on then from where I got to just now. I was about to say, when I digressed, that Oliver in that note you have there makes a reference to Easter. He wrote (according to my memory) that if certain people didn't prove 'too awkward', he'd go ahead '*immediately after Easter*'."

Anthony emphasized the last three words. "Am I right, Andrew?"

"You are. Quite right."

"Well, there you are, you're asking me to accept—if we believe what Murray told us (which we're bound to) as being the reason of Oliver's death, the authentic milk in the genuine coconut—that Oliver, so far from 'going ahead immediately after Easter', started making hay under a shining sun, as far back as the day dedicated to Saint Patrick himself. The seventeenth day of March. Yes, Andrew, I quite agree with you, it's nearly *all* of it contradictory."

Anthony began to pace the room. "Also—there's a lot more I'd like to know, Andrew. Whether, for instance, Oliver had had any previous dealings with Garcia, other than at Delaney's bank."

MacMorran shook his head. "Shouldn't think so. There wouldn't be much affinity between a rich South American, as this Roderigo Garcia appears to be, and a chap who's just an ordinary clerk in Delaney's bank."

MacMorran passed his hand across the note again, to smooth out the creases, and as he did so, his face changed suddenly. "By Jove," he declared, "R.G.! He fits these initials as well as the father—our friend Mr. Garcia, doesn't he? I hadn't spotted that."

"He do and all," returned Anthony, "and supposing he has a wife, who in San Jonquilo was once a gay señorita?"

"Quite likely, I should imagine. With all that dough! What about it?"

"Or even a daughter, Andrew," continued Anthony. "A daughter might do just as well."

"What *are* you getting at?"

"Merely this, Andrew. That the name of either of them, wife or daughter, might conceivably be . . . well . . . Dolores? Then you'd have your R.G. and D., as distinct from the previous suggestion of 'Richard Guise' and 'David'. It's a possibility, I think, distinctly worth our attention. On the other hand, of course, I may be miles off the mark." MacMorran sat and stared at Peter Oliver's note. "Maybe you've got something there," he replied slowly.

CHAPTER 9

1

Anthony stopped the car just beyond Plinner at MacMorran's behest. "Nice place," murmured the Inspector, "very nice place indeed. Not a bit like Wapping Old Stairs. Could do with a basinful of it myself. What do you say?"

"Yes. Quite comfy, Andrew. Better than Tidal Basin or the East India Dock Road."

The house which had excited their comments was detached, its paint was spick and span, its lawns and flower-beds were eloquent of the gardener's skill and everything about it spoke of opulence and the extraordinarily good things of this world. "Wonder where he made his bees—this Señor Garcia," mused MacMorran.

"San Jonquilo," replied Anthony.

"I could guess that myself. I meant in what particular line did he make it."

Anthony shrugged his shoulders. "You can never tell, my dear Andrew—when you're assessing South America. In a manner, possibly, which even you, with your avaricious and predatory nature, would shrink from. To say nothing of your Calvinistic conscience."

"Let me see," went on MacMorran, ignoring the sally, "what's the capital of San Jonquilo? Dashed if I can think of it. Had it on the tip of my tongue just now."

"Santa Guardina," replied Anthony.

"Yes, of course. Santa Guardina. What's its chief business? Is it a port?"

"It is, Andrew. Chiefly noted for coffee, ground-nuts, macaws and brothels. I've been informed through an unimpeachable source that one of the more recent Presidents of this estimable republic made quite a lot of money out of his widespread interests in the last-named activity. And no doubt he had rivals!"

"Really? Still, I'm not surprised. How about it? Seen enough of the externals? Shall we pop along in?"

"I'm fit, Andrew, if you are."

Anthony parked the car and he and MacMorran walked up the beautifully kept gravelled drive that led to the front of the house.

"There's one thing that *has* struck me, Andrew."

"What's that?"

"What's our friend Señor Garcia doing over here? I mean, has he any commercial interests in this country? Business relationships? That's something we could bear to know."

"That bank-manager chap might be in a position to tell us. He should know. At any rate, we can always pick the point up at that end if we think it's necessary. Here we are. I'm ringing the bell."

MacMorran suited the action to the words. To Anthony's surprise an immaculately dressed manservant answered the ringing after an incredibly brief interval. The man was a foreigner—dark hair, flashing black eyes and swarthy skin. MacMorran flicked a card at him and asked a question. About to speak, the swarthy-skinned man paused abruptly.

"Señor Garcia is in—yes. I have no doubt . . . in the circumstances . . . that he will see you. Will you please come this way?"

The man's English was good, although strongly accented. Anthony and MacMorran were shown into a magnificent morning-room which commanded another beautifully trim lawn and delightfully appointed flower-garden. The house seemed to have everything that it takes. The manservant turned to the door.

"You may expect Señor Garcia within a few minutes." He closed the door behind him. Anthony at once beckoned to MacMorran. "Quick, Andrew," he said, "while we're alone. Ten to one this is a photograph of Garcia."

Anthony pointed to a large photograph of a man on the wall of the room. The face was coarse, the lips full and thick, the eyes heavy-lidded. The man of the picture was middle-aged and seemed to be dressed as for a ceremonial occasion. His coat bore decorations. Anthony pointed to them.

"I think I can identify two of those decorations, Andrew. I've met them before. That one at the top is the Grand Order of the Red Star of San Jonquilo and the one immediately below it is the orange and black ribbon of the Republic."

MacMorran was about to reply when Anthony fluttered his fingers at him and spoke from the corner of his mouth. "Somebody coming, Andrew. Hold it. You never know."

They slid away from the photograph noiselessly and were in reasonably appropriate places when the door of the morning-room opened to admit a man very obviously the original of the photograph at which they had just looked. Anthony placed him at somewhere just about the right side of fifty. He was short and fat, his hair and his eyes were black. His skin was dead-white, something like the appearance of a flat fish and his hands were truly remarkable. They were almost exquisitely small—similar to the hands of a child—and they were beautifully cared for.

"Good morning, gentlemen," said the man who had entered, in faultless English. "I am Roderigo Garcia. I understand that you wish to speak to me. I need scarcely tell you that your visit is no surprise to me."

MacMorran was a little taken aback at Garcia's statement. But he quickly remembered that there was such a place as Delaney's bank and Garcia's next words confirmed the remembrance.

"I have heard, of course, from my bankers about my missing bonds and also that you two gentlemen were interested in the affair. So I expected, you see, that you would soon be calling upon me. It is, I take it, that I have the honour and felicity of addressing Chief Detective-Inspector MacMorran and Mr. Anthony Bathurst." Garcia smiled, advanced and shook hands. "And now, gentlemen, please be seated and make yourselves as comfortable as possible."

Anthony and the Inspector took their seats and Garcia himself brought a chair and placed himself between them. "Now, gentlemen, now that you are comfortably seated what is it that I can do for you? Please do not hesitate to ask me anything."

He spread out his hands with a gesture that was eloquent. Anthony and MacMorran had arranged on their journey to Plinner that the latter should take the first stages of the interview with Garcia and Anthony the concluding portion. The Inspector, therefore, went ahead.

"Well, Señor Garcia," he said, "inasmuch as your bank has advised you and you seem well-informed on most of the points, I'll cut the preliminaries. Actually I can save myself a good deal of opening explanation. But I suppose, first of all, there's no doubt that something like sixty thousand pounds' worth of San Jonquilo bonds should be in your safe-deposit at Delaney's bank in Lombard Street, whereas we're told that there's only forty thousand?"

Garcia smiled. "Let me put it my way, Mr. Inspector. Perhaps I am a little more versed in the matters financial than you can ever expect to be. I had eighty thousand pounds' worth of San Jonquilo Three per cents deposited there. For certain private reasons, I withdrew twenty thousand pounds' worth on March 17th last. Now my bankers tell me that another twenty thousand are missing. They *are the facts* as I, Roderigo Garcia, *know them*. I am sorry if I appear meticulous—I do not intend to be."

MacMorran coughed. "Very good, then. That confirms what the bank said and more or less what I said myself. I felt that I ought to check up on the framework of the case, as it were, before I took any drastic steps. Especially bearing in mind the death of this young fellow, Oliver."

MacMorran had come to the point and because of that fact Anthony was closely watching Garcia's face.

"Ah—yes," said the South American, "that was sad— that was very sad. It was, I suppose, suicide? He killed himself, eh?"

"Looks very much like it I'm afraid, Señor Garcia."

"Yes—I, too, was afraid it must be that. I telephoned to the bank manager again—after they informed me about the missing bonds and from what he told me in the conversation that ensued, it seemed to me that in some way which is not at the moment clear, this young man Peter Oliver was unhappily implicated. It is sad for a young fellow to throw his life away like that."

Garcia shook his head sadly. Anthony waited for the sign that he wished to see, but it was not forthcoming. He chose the moment, however, to intervene, because the last thing he had wanted to do when he entered was for himself to drag Oliver into the discussion.

"Had you ever met this young fellow, Oliver, Señor Garcia? Actually come into personal contact with him?"

When he replied, Garcia's manner and demeanour were easy and assured. "Oh, yes. In the bank. Quite an attractive young man I thought, with a distinctly charming personality. I met him on the 17th of March last, the day I took out my San Jonquilo bonds."

"Yes, Señor Garcia," said Anthony, "I was already aware of that. I learned that much from Mr. Murray. Perhaps I should have expressed myself more clearly. I meant—had you ever encountered Peter Oliver socially? Away from the bank?"

This time, perhaps, Garcia was not quite so comfortable. The poise was there, all right, but Anthony felt that it had been deliberately put there.

"Yes, I had even done that." Garcia leant back in his chair and his hand stroked his hair. "I did not think that you meant that sort of meeting. I took it we were discussing him professionally. From the point of view of the bank where he was employed. I had no intention of misleading you."

Anthony deemed a smile diplomatic. "That's all right, Señor Garcia. I quite understand. But the Inspector and I are just trying to fill in Oliver's complete personal background—you get the idea—what he did in his spare time, where he went of an evening, things like that—and it struck me that you might possibly have run across him somewhere. I seem to have struck lucky—you say that you had?"

"Yes," replied the South American, "I *had* met the young fellow away from the precincts of the bank. By a strange series of coincidences, I suppose you would call it. That is the only manner in which one can truthfully describe it. I met him one evening about a fortnight before Easter. In a night-club just off Mayfair."

"Which one?" inquired MacMorran immediately.

" 'The Orange Lizard'," replied Garcia.

MacMorran nodded. "O.K. I know it. Go on, if you please."

Garcia looked a trifle annoyed. "How do you mean—go on? I do not know that I quite . . . understand."

Anthony smiled affably. "You spoke of a strange series of coincidences, Señor Garcia. We shall be interested to hear what they were."

Garcia seemed definitely sulky when he took up the thread of what he had been saying. "It is of little consequence, really. When we first came to this country, my wife and I, we were taken to 'The Orange Lizard' by a young journalist to whom I had been introduced. We are now members of the club with full privileges. This young journalist's name is Bob Dewhurst—he is on the staff of the *Morning Message*. He is engaged to a young lady named Margaret Oliver. Peter Oliver, this young man who has committed suicide in this dreadful fashion, was her brother. Bob

Dewhurst introduced me to him one evening at the 'Lizard' when we were all there. They were the coincidences that I mentioned. Now you know all about it. I hope you are satisfied."

Anthony, by this time, was thinking all sorts of things. He was grateful for MacMorran's next contribution. It seemed to him opportune.

"Now that's most interesting, Señor Garcia. That's just the kind of thing we wanted to know about Oliver. You've been very helpful. You see, we're in a bit of a spot. The police, I mean. What we couldn't understand, in the first instance, was why this young fellow should have taken his life as he did. Well, as you may guess, we made something like the usual routine inquiries, called at his place of business—and as you know, while we were there, we ran into this rather unpleasant complication of your missing San Jonquilo bonds. Which, in turn, led us to you. And, as I said just now, you've assisted us considerably. My grateful thanks."

Anthony wasn't sure whether Garcia looked pleased or otherwise. But he judged the time ripe for a further question. He turned again to the South American.

"Did your acquaintance with young Oliver develop at all, Señor Garcia? Through this young man, Dewhurst?"

"Not at all."

"He never invited you to his house, for instance?"

"In Mayblossom Avenue? No, Mr. Bathurst, nothing of that kind happened."

Garcia bent his head to flick a speck of dust from his trousers. Anthony took advantage of the gesture to give MacMorran a sign that he was content to closure the interview. The Inspector rose.

"Well, many thanks again, Señor Garcia. Hope we haven't taken up too much of your time—and I hope, too, that those bonds of yours will turn up somewhere. For one thing, it would clear the air, and we should all feel better about it."

"Thank you, Inspector MacMorran. I appreciate your sympathy.'

Roderigo Garcia rose and shook hands with the Inspector. Anthony deliberately gravitated towards Garcia's photograph. "If I may say so," he said, "a really excellent likeness of you, sir. Life-like."

Garcia seemed pleased at the tribute. "Thank you, Mr. Bathurst."

"If I mistake not," continued Anthony, closer to the photograph, "the Grand Order of the Red Star of San Jonquilo and the orange and black ribbon of the Republic. Am I right?"

Garcia's face changed—the pleasure was swept suddenly from it. "I must congratulate you," he said. "I had no idea that you were so familiar with our national decorations. Am I to infer from this knowledge that you have lived in—"

Anthony smiled and shook his head. "No, Señor Garcia. I must plead not guilty. The explanation is simple. I once had the pleasure of meeting Sir Beverley Pelham, who was British Minister for some years at Santa Guardina. Did you ever meet him?"

Garcia's face cleared. "Oh, yes. Several times. He was Minister at Santa Guardina during the Presidency of Sebastian Loredana. A charming gentleman, Sir Beverley, with a delightful wife. He and I—and she—got on excellently together. But what is it now?"

Anthony was standing, seemingly, lost in thought. "It's just occurred to me," he declared, "a sort of fugitive recollection—there may be nothing in it, I'm not altogether sure, at times my memory plays tricks with me—but did you marry Señorita Isabella—"

"No," returned Garcia somewhat curtly, "I did not. For once, at least, your memory is, as you say, not so good." He held out his hand. "Good morning, Mr. Bathurst, it has been quite a pleasure to meet you, both you and your colleague. And to have had this conversation. Let me know, please, if the case has any serious developments."

2

"Ha-ha-ha," said MacMorran, as Anthony started the car, "he pushed that last one of yours away beautifully. Didn't half prang it. I'll certainly hand it to him for that."

Anthony grinned. "He's nobody's fool, is he? Our friend Roderigo? What I was after was the Christian name of his missus. And he whanged me over the pavilion for six. He did an' all. Never mind, there are other means of finding out what we want to know. Just a discreet inquiry at the premises of "The Orange Lizard'. I've a hunch and a half that it's going to be Dolores."

MacMorran nodded. "Yes, we can do that. Where are we now do you think, though? Any forrarder?"

"My dear Andrew, there's only one answer to that. The plot's thickening up and the dark waters grow deeper. Oliver, Garcia, Dewhurst, Oliver's sister. Bank. Bonds. Night-club. The links of the chain are beginning to show. *And* twenty thousand pounds' worth of Bonds what should be—ain't! Peter Oliver was murdered all right, don't you worry. There's another thing, too. I wonder whether you noticed it?"

MacMorran laughed. "And don't *you* worry. I spotted it all right."

"Tell me, Andrew. So that we shan't be at cross purposes."

MacMorran laughed again. "I told you not to worry. Why the hell can't you believe me? What I was referring to was Garcia's admission that he was aware of Oliver's address. Previously, when you were scratching at the surface he told you that he'd never visited the Oliver domicile. But he had 'Mayblossom Avenue' on the tip of his tongue all right. Isn't that what you meant?"

"You win, Andrew. What did you think of it, really? Was it significant? Or just one of those straws that float by and don't show you any more about the direction of the wind than you already know. Because he may have picked up the address from the recent newspapers."

MacMorran shook his head. "Can't answer that, yet. Time will tell."

Anthony drove on for some distance in silence. "Do you know, Andrew," he said at length, "that I've never faced a case with a mind so barren of ideas or even theories? As for the question of motive—that ancient bee in my bonnet—I haven't the foggiest idea of anything like one, and that's a solemn fact."

"I'm still thinking in terms of suicide despite all you've said. The bank clerk. Stolen bonds. Night-club habits. Sounds to me like yet another of the oldest stories in the world. Reckless expenditure, diminishing income, debt—and death rather than dishonour. All as per invoice. Good gracious, Mr. Bathurst, the pattern's familiar enough."

This time it was Anthony who shook his head. "No, Andrew. Definitely no. Too many parts of it don't add up. Far too many. Just an occasional one here and there that didn't, wouldn't matter—but in this Oliver business you kick up against them almost everywhere. I shall attack the Stella Forrest link in the chain. There were a couple of kids in love there, and on this occasion in *amore* there may have been *veritas*."

Again MacMorran dissented. "What we have to do is to find out the truth with regard to these missing San Jonquilo three per cents. What has become of them? Whose clutching fingers and itching palm are making contact with them? I *may* get some news today. I've put Chatterton on inquiries of no less than five brokers. The chances are he'll pick up something. If there *is* anything to be picked up. From there, if we're lucky, it may be plain sailing. I'm confident it will be. We shall know why Peter Oliver cut his throat."

"Far be it from me to upset your ruddy optimism, Andrew, but now I'll tell you something. You'll be a week or so yet, before you find Oliver's murderer. And maybe those weeks'll be nearer a month when they're stretched out."

MacMorran laughed. "Well, have it your way. We shall see. But give me ruddy optimism as you call it before puling pessimism—*every time.*"

"Not without due cause or excellent reason, Andrew. Personally I always like to see the old foundation stone. If I can, well and good. If I can't"—Anthony shrugged his shoulders "well, what's the good of ruddy optimism? You can keep it, for my part."

"When I know where those bonds are and who put 'em there," countered MacMorran, "I don't think we shall be long. Here we are, though, at the 'Yard'. Are you coming in?"

"Not now, Andrew. If it's all the same to you. I'll give you a ring either to-morrow or the day after. Cheer-o."

Anthony turned the car, waved to the Inspector and drove off. MacMorran walked slowly up the stone staircase that led to his room.

"Perhaps," so ran his thoughts, "there may be some news in about those San Jonquilo Three per cents. Some of the people have had time to get through to Chatterton. Or he may have had to go after something. Or am I in too much of a hurry?"

He came to the door of his room, little knowing the two stories he was soon to hear concerning the three per cent Bearer bonds, issued by the Republic of San Jonquilo, secured by the revenues of that State and originally purchased by Señor Roderigo Santos Garcia.

3

MacMorran picked up the telephone. "Chatterton back yet?" he inquired curtly. The answer that he received pleased him. "That's good. Excellent! Tell him I'll see him at once. No—never mind what he's doing. Yes, I've only just come back."

MacMorran replaced the receiver with an exclamation of annoyance. Chatterton never allowed grass to grow under his feet and he was in his Chief's room in a matter of seconds. "Sit down, Chatterton. What did you get?" demanded the Inspector.

Chatterton spread out his arms and twisted his face in an attitude of resignation. "Nothing, Chief. Not a bean. Not a sausage, not a funeral note, nor the smell of an oil-rag. Sweet Fanny herself—in person."

MacMorran stared gloomily at his table. "H'm. Not so good. Where did you go?"

"All five of your contacts, Chief. Scrubbed everything else to get round to them at once. Mellon's, Cantrell's, Coster and Waterson's, Delevigne's and finished up in accordance with your instructions at Edgar Durell's. As I said, all blanks, sweet F.A. Everywhere."

"They all told the same story? No deviations?"

Chatterton shook his head. "They all spoke with one accord and with one voice, Chief. Told the same plain unvarnished tale. In fact, they might 'ave rehearsed it together. And the gist of it was this—that no business has been done over San Jonquilo stuff for some considerable time. Certainly not since the date you gave me, March 17th. And, by the way, Chief, Mr. Louis Dickie of Coster and Waterson's asked to be remembered to you very specially. He said I was on no account to forget his message."

MacMorran took a pen and doodled on the edge of his blotting-pad. Chatterton paused momentarily, to continue almost immediately.

"Mr. Dickie said something else, Chief. Said I was to tell you besides the message. Sounded uncommonly like the real McCoy to me."

"What was that, Chatterton?"

"Just this, Chief. That London wasn't the only soapsud down the sink. I was to remind you in case you hadn't thought of it. In other words, traffic in more or less gilt-edged securities, to use Mr. Dickie's words, went on in all the capitals of Europe, to say nothing of certain other financial 'aunts."

MacMorran continued his activities with the men. Chatterton went on airily. "He actually mentioned one of these other 'aunts for your edification, Chief. I suppose he did that because he regarded it as a likely proposition."

"Oh, which place was this, Chatterton?"

"Santa Guardina, Chief," replied Chatterton. "I don't know whether the little old feller knew anything—or whether he was just chancing his arm, as you might say."

Half an hour after Chatterton had returned to his own realms, MacMorran's telephone rang yet again. As he picked up the receiver, the Inspector's temper was not, perhaps, at its best.

4

"Hallo?" he growled . . . yes . . . Chief Detective-Inspector MacMorran speaking. Who is it?"

His face relaxed somewhat as he took in the reply. "Oh, good-afternoon, Mr. Murray. Oh, so-so . . . no, I'm afraid we're not. I agree it's early days yet and there's plenty of time ahead. No, drawn a blank. Yes, a complete blank. So far. What's that? When?"

The Inspector listened interestedly for the reply. "You want *me*—to see *me*—as soon as possible?" MacMorran glanced at the clock. "Well, it's not too convenient but I suppose I can if it comes to that. If it's as important as you say it is. I hope you're not—" He broke off again to listen. "All right, if that's how you feel about it. I'll come along right away. There's one thing, I shan't have to wait very long before I know. What? O.K., then, I'll pack up what I'm on now and come along. Expect me in about half an hour's time."

The Inspector hung up and as he did so his mood of annoyance and fretted temper returned. He frowned almost malevolently at his blotting-pad.

"I wonder what the blazes Murray wants to tell me?" he muttered. "He was mighty mysterious about it. Trust a perishin' bank manager to be scared of his own shadow."

He looked at the clock again. "Before I go, I'll have a word with Hemingway. In case there *should* be any sudden developments."

MacMorran left his room and made his way along the corridor. "Maybe," he thought to himself, "Bathurst is going to be right, after all."

CHAPTER 10

1

MacMorran faced the manager of the Lombard Street branch of Delaney's bank across the latter's table in his private room. To his surprise, rather, Murray looked much more confident and comfortable than he had expected to find him. "Well, Mr. Murray," he said, "here I am, in answer to your summons. Now—what's all the trouble?"

As he put the question, MacMorran formed the opinion that Murray was looking better in every way. Not only less worried than when he and Anthony Bathurst had left him the other afternoon, but almost jaunty and high-spirited. Murray pushed back his chair.

"What time was it when I 'phoned you, Inspector?"

"Just before three o'clock. I happen to know, because I looked at the time. Why?"

"Just a minute and I'll tell you. You say that there's no news which you can rake up with regard to any activity on the stock market concerning the San Jonquilo bonds? You *did* say that, didn't you?"

"That's so, Mr. Murray. Since I saw you last, I've been in touch with several of the leading brokers—who, according to what I've been told, *might* be regarded as likely to have their ears as close to the ground as any. They all report 'nothing doing'. But why do you ask? Don't tell me they've let me down?"

Murray smiled with an air of complete superiority. "You wait. I 'phoned you just before three, you say?"

"That's it. It wanted about a couple of minutes to the hour."

Murray nodded. "Yes, I suppose it would be about that. I returned from lunch about ten minutes past two. I hadn't been back more than five minutes at the outside, when Fitzgerald brought a parcel in to me. There's the brown paper over there it was wrapped in—with the address on it. Have a look at it. You can see what it says."

Murray leant forward and pushed over the wrapping-paper to the Inspector. MacMorran looked at the white panel of label. In printed letters it was addressed to "PERSONAL. THE BANK MANAGER, DELANEY'S BANK, LOMBARD STREET, E.C.3."

"I see what it says all right," said the Inspector, "but what's remarkable about it? Surely you haven't brought me here this afternoon to show me a piece of brown paper?"

Murray laughed. MacMorran had not previously seen him in anything like such good spirits. "You'll be interested in that piece of paper later on. So don't dispose of it too quickly. The proof of the pudding's in the eating and the point of this particular parcel is in the contents. Care to look at them, Inspector? They should interest you more than a little."

Murray pushed four packets of documents over to MacMorran. The latter saw that there was an elastic band round each of them. One glance told him the truth.

"All of them?" he said, "none missing?"

Murray nodded. "All of them. Two hundred in all. Fifty in each bundle. None missing—serial numbers identical and complete. I've had them all checked. Curious business, don't you think?"

MacMorran grunted. "Registered, I can see that. As you say—extremely curious. Don't know what to make of it." Murray spread out his hands. "Why send them back? Why steal them—and then send them back? That's the part that beats me. It's just plumb crazy."

MacMorran picked up the wrapping-paper. "We can trace the Post-Office where it was registered—and the 'somebody' that must have registered it. Maybe a clue in that."

"Very likely, Inspector—but why pinch 'em—and then send 'em back? I want you to explain *that* to me."

"Sorry, I can't do it. They're not the sort of thing that people borrow—say, that's an idea—could they have been borrowed for any purpose? Is such a thing feasible?"

Murray knitted his brows. "You mean to bolster up a shortage and satisfy the auditors somewhere? I hadn't thought of it in that light. You may have got something there. But still, it's pretty far-fetched, isn't it?

These bonds must have been missing from my bank since March 17th. The day Garcia called. That was the one and only opportunity Oliver had to take them. Believe me, he's never had another."

"The serial letters and numbers tally, you say? Yes, that does seem to link it up. You can identify them. There can be no suggestion of substitution?"

"Exactly, Inspector."

"Well, I'm glad they're back, for your sake, and for everybody's sake connected with the bank—must be a relief to you, but it's damned mystifying for all that. I must certainly follow it up."

"Well, there you are, you could have knocked me down with the proverbial feather when I opened that parcel and saw the contents. It was the sort of thing you read about in books. Thought the best thing I could possibly do was to get in touch with you. Which I immediately did."

MacMorran nodded. "You did the right thing, Mr. Murray. I'm glad you did. Whatever it may mean—and I don't know yet what it does mean—the return of the bonds must make a big difference . . . let me have that piece of wrapping paper and I'll wish you good-afternoon."

Murray rose and shook hands. Relief showed in his eyes. "It's a grand thing for me, you know. Because it practically clears the case as far as I'm concerned. I'm sorry about young Oliver, but a man must think of himself and of his position. He wouldn't be human, would he, if he didn't?"

MacMorran nodded. He had no difficulty whatever in seeing the bank manager's point of view.

2

Anthony Bathurst strolled into old man Lambert's restaurant well after "peak-load" time. He was prepared to face with exemplary fortitude the fact that "roast beef" and "roast lamb" would almost certainly be "blue-pencilled" on the menu. For once in a while he would be content to eat of the fragments that remained. For the reason that his meal was not the main object of his presence there.

As he entered the restaurant, he glanced with more than ordinary interest to the cashier's desk. He saw almost the last thing on earth he wanted to see. A greasy-faced-looking brunette, with dark muddy eyes, sat in the seat previously graced by Stella Forrest.

Anthony cursed under his breath, for it was Stella whom he had come to see and this was an undoubted shock for him. He took a seat at a table almost mechanically (for him) and began to work things out. To tell the truth, he had experienced a certain amount of mental misgiving with regard to Stella for some days now, and seeing what he had just seen brought this home to him with redoubled intensity.

Since MacMorran, in accordance with his promise to her, had told Stella of the finding of Peter Oliver's body, there had come no word from her whatever. Stella had just folded up! At first Anthony had accepted this condition in its prime value and interpretation. That Stella was shutting herself up with her grief and mourning her lost love. On that account, he had allowed a reasonable time to elapse before calling at the restaurant to see her, for he knew that he must respect her feelings. Now he had come, Stella was absent.

A waitress came and Anthony gave an order. When the meal was eventually brought to him and Anthony began to eat, he came to the conclusion that the more he saw of things, the less he liked the look of them. There were no two opinions about this. He knew, better than anybody, how Stella's intelligence had translated the truth from Oliver's brief but eloquent absence. He knew how she had felt about the boy—why, then, had she so suddenly disappeared from the arena?

Here was yet another group of figures which in Anthony's opinion refused to add up. From what he had seen of her at that momentous first interview in the room upstairs, Stella Forrest would go through hell and high water to put the noose round the neck of Peter Oliver's murderer. Well then, where was she? Why hadn't she come into the conflict again, either to him or to Andrew MacMorran?

In time the waitress brought Anthony's sweet. As he ate it, Anthony scarcely knew what it was or even what the taste resembled. He shook his head, and his own recent words to MacMorran came back to him. "The dark waters were getting deeper." As he went to the brunette at the cash-desk with his bill, he came to a decision. If it were convenient, he would have a few words with old man Lambert.

An inquiry of a near-by waitress told him what he wanted to know. He found the old man in a room at the back of the restaurant. Anthony produced his card, counter-signed by Sir Austin Kemble, the Commissioner of Police. Old Lambert looked at Anthony critically and then let his eyes drop to the card he held between his fingers. He was in his shirt-sleeves and a dirty brown-coloured cardigan covered his shirt. A grey straggling moustache crawled sullenly across his upper lip and his blue eyes were weak and watery. He was old and fat. When he first saw the card Anthony had handed to him and took in what it conveyed, the expression on his face changed.

"Come in, mister. Come in and make yourself comfortable. What is it you want of me?"

3

Anthony entered the Lambert parlour. "Nothing, Mr. Lambert, that you can't tell me. Without any trouble at all. At least, that's how I hope it will go."

Old Lambert heaved his ungainly bulk into a chair. Anthony judged that the longest things about him were his tooth and his stocking.

"Maybe," returned the old man, "depends what you want. I don't know that, do I? Till I know, I can't say, can I? Reckon that's fair."

Anthony offered him his cigarette-case. "Cigarette, Mr. Lambert?"

Old Lambert took his cigarette and Anthony lit it for him. "Where's Stella Forrest, Mr. Lambert?" inquired Anthony, through the flame of the match.

The old man rolled his cigarette expertly from one side of his mouth to the other. As he performed the exercise, Anthony saw a flickering stab of interest come into his eyes. "Ah," he said, "where's Stella Forrest? Do you know, guv'nor, you've asked me a question I'd very much like the answer to myself. Young Stella was a damn' fine kid. They don't grow 'em like her on every branch. All *I* know is we 'ad a 'phone call, sayin' she wouldn't be comin' 'ere any more."

"When was this?"

Old Lambert pushed aside the grey wisp of hair on his head and scratched his dirty-looking scalp.

"Last Thursday morning. Pretty early it was at that. My missus took the message. I was in Leadenhall market at the time after some poultry."

"Any reason given?"

"Reason?"

"Yes for throwing up her job like that, so suddenly. It wasn't exactly fair to you, was it? It might have placed you in an awkward position."

Lambert shook his head. "Suppose it wasn't, from one way of thinkin', but there you are, I didn't look at it like that. I'll tell you why. There was a special reason behind it. The missus 'eard from one of the other girls that something 'ad 'appened to Stella's 'boy friend'. That's 'ow she put it to me— and I took things for granted, as you might say. I reckoned the kid 'ad taken the knock." Old man Lambert grinned, "when it's Love, mister, you can count me out." He shook his head reminiscently as he added: "I 'ad a soft corner in my heart for young Stella and I can tell you—I'm more than sorry to lose her. Still, girls are like that, the good 'uns never stay with you long. The other sort you can't bloody well get shot of."

Anthony came again. "Did this telephone message that Mrs. Lambert took last Thursday morning come from Miss Forrest herself?"

The old man spat on the carpet and rubbed it in with his foot. The three constituents, after all, were all three his! Anthony, rather fascinated by the exercise, realized this fact and abruptly checked his mental disapproval.

"Now that's funny, mister, but I couldn't for the life of me tell you. I don't think the old girl told me at the time and I'm pretty sure I didn't ask her. 'Ad no reason to—it sounded final to me. The boy friend 'ad 'ad it and Stella wasn't comin' any more—that's all there was to it as far as I was concerned. If you're keen on findin' out where she's gone, you'd better see the Labour people—they'll know if she's in another job. I sent 'er cards along to the kid's address directly I 'eard she'd packed the job up."

Anthony thought things over quickly. "Will you do me a favour, Mr. Lambert? Could I have a word with your missus? About that telephone call? Is she about?"

"Surely," said old Lambert, "where would you expect her to be she's in the kitchen same as every old woman should be by rights. With 'er blasted arms in the sink. I'll fetch 'er along and you can speak to 'er. Park yourself down 'ere for five minutes. I'll be back in a jiffy."

The old man shuffled off. Anthony waited patiently. When the restaurant proprietor returned he was accompanied by a stout old lady whose chief incentive to memory seemed to be a pair of cunning little eyes.

"'Ere you are," said Lambert, " 'ere's the old trouble and strife—now ask 'er what you wanted to. About young Stella's 'phone call."

Anthony got up from the chair in which he had been seated. "Good-afternoon, Mrs. Lambert. I'm so really sorry to trouble you—I know how busy you are at this time of the day—but I believe you took a telephone message last Thursday morning about your cashier, Miss Stella Forrest. Your husband is my informant."

The old woman nodded. "That's right, son. Leastways, I took it—I'm not sure about what day it was. If you say it was Thursday, that's O.K. by me."

Anthony smiled at her encouragingly. "Good. Now tell me, Mrs. Lambert, was it Miss Forrest herself who spoke to you?"

"No, son, that it wasn't. It was a woman's voice. Very different from young Stella's."

"I see. Could you tell me, do you think, Mrs. Lambert, what was actually said? Do you think you could remember?" The little pig-like eyes narrowed. "I can remember all right, don't you worry. What do you think I am? I ain't so old that I didn't go to school. The woman said she was speakin' on be'alf of Stella, that she was throwin' up 'er job, not comin' 'ere any more, and goin' right away. Somethink 'ad 'appened to her young feller. Oh, I know, 'e was dead—that was it. I took the message and passed it on to the Guv'nor." Mrs. Lambert gestured towards her lord and master.

'Sright," he confirmed, "and Stella ain't been 'ere since that day. Never even called for the wages what was due to 'er. Reckon she must 'ave been knocked right over, poor kid." The old man shook his head sadly.

"Where did she live? Hammersmith way, wasn't it?"

"The address was on 'er Insurance cards—I think as 'ow it was in 'Ammersmith somewhere."

Anthony nodded. "I can get it if I want it. Was she friendly with any of your staff here, Mr. Lambert? With anyone in particular? Would any of the other girls be able to—?"

Lambert didn't allow him to finish. "No, she was *not*, mister." There was no mistaking the emphasized certainty of the reply. "Young Stella kept 'erself very much to 'erself—and I didn't blame 'er, I can tell you. She was different from them others. There was a touch o' class about 'er. Cut above the average—there was no mistake about that."

"How long had she been in your employment, Mr. Lambert?"

Lambert worked on his wisp of hair again and scratched his scalp. "Suppose it would be about eighteen months," he answered—"near enough."

"*And the rest,*" retorted his spouse, somewhat contemptuously, "you're a good judge of time, you are, I must say. Wake up your ideas. Good job you never 'ad to do a stretch—you wouldn't 'ave known whether you was comin' or goin'." Lambert turned on her truculently. "Well, 'ow long do you say it is? You're so bloody clever—"

"Use your loaf, you lazy old perisher, then you'd know yourself. And I'll tell you what you can go by. 'Ow long's Uncle Albert been dead?"

"Not long enough," retorted Lambert sullenly, "the old basket."

Mrs. Lambert turned to Anthony. "Take it from me, mister, my old man's a long way out with 'is eighteen months. Stella had been with us 'ere as cashier just on three years. She come to us in the Autumn. It 'ud be three years come next November. 'Im and 'is eighteen months! No idea—and what's more 'e never did 'ave. All 'e ever knows is what *won't* win the three-thirty and 'e can tell you that every day barrin' Sunday."

Mrs. Lambert shook her head in vigorous disparagement of her husband. Anthony could see the old man terminating the interview, if things continued the way they were going. There was an ominous light in the male Lambert's eye. Anthony stepped in, therefore, with another question.

"Where did Miss Forrest come from in the first place, have you any idea? Where her home is, for instance? Or where her people are?"

No answer was forthcoming from either of the Lamberts. The old man, when he had thought it over, eventually offered some sort of reply to the question.

"I don't know where she came from, but Stella was no Londoner. I'd bank on that. No perishin' Bow Bells about her. I wanted a good reliable girl for the cash-desk so I shoved an advert in two or three o' the usual rags. With about forty others Stella answered it. When she came along to me 'ere and asked for the job—I give 'er one look and said, 'when can you start, miss?' She didn't want no lookin' at twice. And I never 'ad no occasion to regret my decision."

"In my opinion," said Mrs. Lambert, in a kind of supplementary contribution, "she come from the country somewhere."

"Why do you say that, Mrs. Lambert?"

"Well, because of 'er ways and 'er manner o' speakin'. Reckon I can usually tell. Country-girls are different to the town sort some'ow. Most of the Cockney stuff these days that get in my way and waste my time are fair bitches, if you know what I mean, mister. Too much blasted education. That's the curse of this country. What's it do for 'em? Makes 'em all too big to do any work. A day's work's three hours—and a day's holiday's 'arf a bloody week! Love on their minds, lipstick on their mouths and next to nothing on their backs. Now, in my young days, when I was a girl, if you as much as—"

"Shut your trap," said old Lambert sharply, "this gentleman ain't 'ere to listen to your bleedin' philosophy, if you think 'e is and if that's all you've got to say, you can get back to the kitchen. Scram!"

Mrs. Lambert flashed a look of supreme indignation at her husband, muttered something like an imprecation under her breath and slunk off. Anthony, feeling somewhat responsible for this rift in the conjugal lute, decided that he needn't encumber the Lambert premises any longer. He proceeded to thank the old man for the service he had rendered him.

"That's all right, sir. Don't you worry about that. I liked young Stella and I 'ope you catch up with 'er. You needn't go through the restaurant again to go out. You can go out the back way. Good 'untin'."

He thrust out a greasy hand. Anthony shook it and turned to leave. His visit to Lambert's restaurant had by no means allayed his anxieties. On the contrary, from whatever angle he looked at the problem, it had intensified them.

4

He walked through the back exit and round again to the front of the restaurant. For one thing he was desperately anxious to avoid anything in the nature of delay or waste of time. As he saw things at this moment, minutes might count in this case.

He entered the restaurant for the second time, passed the sallow-faced brunette at the cash-desk without as much as a glance in her direction and made for one of the waitresses whom he had seen there on the occasion he had first visited the restaurant with MacMorran. The genuinely slack time had already come and the girl in whom Anthony was interested had time on her hands in more ways than one.

"Good-afternoon," said Anthony. "Stella Forrest, the girl who used to be in your cash-desk? Where did she live? Can you tell me?"

"Hemmersmith," replied the waitress, "but I ca'int tell you any mower beyond thet. Ask Thelma, over there—she'll know. They used to trevel together sometaimes."

She indicated with a queenly gesture a waitress near the door.

"I thank you," rejoined Anthony and made off in pursuit of his fresh quarry. Thelma was fat and plump with a fringe of fair hair and humorous eyes. Anthony went up to her.

"Are you by any chance Thelma?" he inquired.

"All day long," said the fat girl, "and resumin' (D.V.) tomorrow. To say nothin' of the rest of the week. What's your individual brand of trouble?"

"Stella Forrest, your cashier. I wanted her address, that was all. I've mislaid it. Hammersmith somewhere. They tell me you might help me."

Thelma regarded him critically. "No funny business, is it? Because I'm not standin' for that. I'm not helpin' anybody t—" Thelma stopped suddenly.

"I can assure you," said Anthony, "that my intentions are absurdly honourable, entirely above-board, thoroughly on the level and wholly and completely friendly."

Thelma nodded. "Skip it. All that and Heaven too? I'll buy it. At the same time, mister, I don't *think* you'll find Stella Forrest at her address in Hammersmith when you get there. I may be wrong, but that's my opinion. Still, no 'arm in tryin'. No. 13 Abraham Lincoln Crescent—not far from the Lyric Theatre. Landlady's name—Gilbert."

"Many thanks. Were you at all friendly with her? Stella— not Mrs. Gilbert?"

"I was *not*. And, what's more important, I shan't be with *you*, if you keep on askin' questions. I'm not the Brains Trust. So, if you should value my friendship, mister—" Thelma moved quickly and lightly towards two customers who had just entered the restaurant and seated themselves at a table.

"If you only knew—I assess it far above rubies," returned Mr. Bathurst to her retreating form, "but I doubt whether you can hear me saying it. Or, if you can, whether you entirely appreciate the assessment. No. 13 Abraham Lincoln Crescent. Name of Gilbert."

CHAPTER 11

1

Anthony lost no time in making for the address of Mrs. Gilbert. He came to Hammersmith and walked quickly in the direction where he knew Abraham Lincoln Crescent must lie. Once near the Lyric Theatre, he quickly located the road he wanted and in addition, by good fortune, he was at the right end of it for No. 13.

The house of his objective looked respectable enough when Anthony knocked on the door, and the thin, pale-faced, tired-looking woman who attended to him was in admirable and appropriate keeping with the house she inhabited.

"Mrs. Gilbert?" queried Anthony, with one of his best quality smiles, and the thin woman nodded in affirmation. "Would you be good enough to spare me a few minutes, Mrs. Gilbert? It's to do with Miss Forrest, the young lady who lodges here."

Anthony thought that a certain amount of anxiety showed on Mrs. Gilbert's face directly he mentioned the name of Forrest.

"Perhaps you'd better come in," she announced lugubriously. It was a grudging kind of announcement and might have been taken to suggest that Anthony had established some sort of advantage by means of a piece of singularly underhanded business.

Anthony said "thank you" and stepped into a passage which took him into a small "best" room of approved respectability. Mrs. Gilbert whisked a chair from a corner of what looked like a small Persian market and, with an aggressive movement of the chin, thrust it at Anthony. Anthony made the necessary physical contact and then saw that Mrs. Gilbert had found another chair for herself. Although she was so spare and thin, she worked with a kind of skimming action and the nonchalance of a class goalkeeper turning a fierce drive over the crossbar for what he hopes will be an innocuous corner.

"Before you tell me anything, Mrs. Gilbert, let me say that my name is Bathurst and that I'm a friend of Miss Forrest's and all that you need let me know is when I can see her."

He used these words deliberately. Mrs. Gilbert bounced up from her chair and realizing that her ace, whenever she played it, could take but one trick, banged it down immediately.

"But the point is, Mr. Batters, the young lady's not here. She's left. She left last Thursday morning. It was a real surprise to me and one of the wrong kind, I can tell you. Miss Forrest was a nice respectable young lady and her cash was always there on the tick. Behaved herself as one of your own might, all the time she was here. I tell you, Mr. Batters, I was real sorry to lose her. I don't mind tellin' you I've shed a tear over it." Mrs. Gilbert began to sniff ominously.

Anthony pulled at his top lip. Things were undeniably getting worse. "I'm sorry to hear that—very sorry. You've no idea where she's gone, Mrs. Gilbert?"

"No more than a fly in the air, Mr. Batters. I hope and trust she's not in any trouble, sir? I should be downright upset to hear that anything like that had 'appened to 'er."

Anthony smiled reassuringly. "Well, that's what I'm trying to find out. And you must help me, Mrs. Gilbert. By helping me you'll be helping Miss Forrest and also helping yourself. Do you see?"

Mrs. Gilbert's thin nostrils quivered but she nodded her understanding.

"Go back to last Thursday morning, will you please? To the time when you say Miss Forrest went away from here. Try to tell me exactly what took place when she left and even before. Tell me everything that you can remember—never mind if it seems to be trivial or of no importance. You never can tell. Sometimes the smallest trifle can mean such a lot. Now please try to tell me, as I said."

Mrs. Gilbert sat bolt upright in what did duty for her chair. It looked to Anthony like something that had fallen off a Burmese pagoda and been brought home between a bunch of bananas and a parrot.

"It was soon after I had finished my breakfast," she opened. "I was just pushin' the egg-shell into the top of the kitchen fire to get shot of it, when there came a tap at the kitchen-door. I wasn't sure who it was so early in the day. Miss Forrest never came down to the kitchen at that time in the morning. She had her bed-sitting-room with me and she used to keep to it. I must say that for 'er. She kept herself *to* herself and knew her place and never so much as took *'alf* a liberty. I've been in the lettin' game too long not to—"

Anthony's insertion was gentle but telling. "And she tapped on the kitchen-door, you say, last Thursday morning?"

"She did that, Mr. Batters. But I didn't know it was her until I called out 'come in' and she came in. Directly I clapped eyes on her, I could see she wasn't herself and was in some sort of trouble. Her eyes were all red and puffy where the poor thing 'ad been cryin' and 'er face was as white as a sheet. She looked so *different*—because most times you saw 'er, Stella Forrest was as pretty as a picture. One out o' the bag, she was, as no doubt you know for yourself, sir. So I says to her, 'Miss Forrest! Whatever is it? Are you ill, my dear, or feeling sick? Can't I get you something?' But she shook 'er head and said, 'no, Mrs. Gilbert, I'm not ill. I've just 'ad bad news that's all— terribly bad news—and I shall 'ave to go away from 'ere. Right away.' "

"I was knocked all of a 'eap, Mr. Batters, to see 'er like that, and to 'ear what she said, but I did manage to blurt out, 'but what about your job at the restaurant, Miss Forrest?' 'That's one o' the things I've come down about,' she says, 'that—and the money I owe you. I'll pay you up to the end of the week, Mrs. Gilbert, because that's only fair to you, and here it is.' She puts the money on the table, Mr. Batters, and then says, 'and would you mind 'phoning Lambert's restaurant for me— there's the number on that little slip of paper—and tell 'em I'm sorry but I've got to leave because I must get away from 'ere at once. Tell 'em,' she says, 'not to bother about any wages due to me, they can keep them to make up for my not giving them the proper notice I should 'ave given.' "

"Well, Mr. Batters, there she was standin' in front of me and I could see that 'er mind was made up and it would be no good of me stickin' my nose into what was 'er business. She shook 'ands, thanked me for all I had done for 'er and that was that. When I went up to 'er room later on in the mornin', she'd packed 'er two suit-cases and gone."

"Clothes, I suppose, in the main? In the suit-cases?"

"Clothes and a trinket-set and a few things like that. And a 'andfull of books. She 'ad nothin' in the way of furniture. It was all mine. I always let 'furnished'. All the drawers of everything are empty—I've looked in all of them, and put clean paper in. I must do, you see. All ready for the next let. Which I'ope won't be long in turnin' up."

Anthony sat in Mrs. Gilbert's front room and thought things over. He was disturbed, worried and anxious. "Tell me, Mrs. Gilbert, did she call a taxi when she went?"

"No, sir, no taxi come here."

"The station isn't very far away, of course, but if she had two suit-cases to carry—"

"She never 'ad no taxi from 'ere, sir. I'm positive of that."

"Do you think she was frightened, Mrs. Gilbert? In mortal terror of anything? From the way she spoke and looked?"

Mrs. Gilbert nodded. "It's funny you should say that, Mr. Batters, but that's just what I *did* think at the time. Miss Forrest seemed all of a dither, as you might say, proper worked up. 'I must get away from 'ere at once,' she said. And it come into my mind at that very moment, as she stood there and spoke as she did, that she was runnin' away from something she was badly scared of. And now you've gone and suggested the very same thing."

"You've no idea, of course, *where* she's gone?" Mrs. Gilbert shook her head. "Not the slightest, Mr. Batters."

"Didn't she ever have any letters come here? From her home? The girl must have had a home somewhere."

"None that I ever saw. But she was an orphan. Her father and mother had both passed over. She told me that much soon after she first come to me. I think she said she'd been brought up by an aunt on her mother's side, but I couldn't be certain as to that."

"How long has she lived with you, Mrs. Gilbert? Some time, I suppose?"

"Three years come next November, Mr. Batters. She come to me when she started at the restaurant. She saw my card in the window one evening when she was lookin' for a room and come and fixed up with me there and then."

This was sound enough, thought Anthony, it tallied and tied up with the information he'd picked up from Mrs. Lambert. He came to a decision.

"Would you mind if I had a glance at Miss Forrest's room, Mrs. Gilbert? Perhaps you'd be good enough to take me up there?"

"I don't mind at all," said the landlady, "if it'll 'elp 'er in any way." She rose and replaced the Pagoda piece in the appropriate department of the bazaar. "Come this way, will you?"

Anthony followed her up a narrow staircase. Mrs. Gilbert walked across the landing and opened a door. "This was Miss Forrest's room, I let it as a 'bed-sit'. Nice and comfortable it is, too, with a southern aspect. If there was any sea in 'Ammersmith you could see it from the front window. Just suitable for a young girl. All the furniture you can see is mine, as I told you. Miss Forrest didn't bring nothink with 'er of that kind. And she's left nothink behind. Look in the drawers. You can see for yourself."

Mrs. Gilbert suited the action to the words. Anthony saw that there was nothing in the chest of drawers, or on the dressing-table. No letters or postcards were tucked away in any corner. Save for a few glass bowls and china pots, the mantelpiece had nothing on it. Anthony, without instituting anything like a close search, nevertheless looked carefully all round the apartment. The one thing which arrested his attention was an old piece of newsprint which he noticed lying near the edge of the frayed carpet close to a leg of the dressing-table. Just two lines of heading. So old that the paper had turned yellow and was curling up. The caption ran, "Gallant Rescuer Walks Away Without Waiting to be Thanked. Holiday Tragedy Miraculously Averted."

Mrs. Gilbert noticed him pick up the fragment and look at it. "That's nothing," she said, "don't waste your time on that. I expect it come out o' one of the drawers when I tidied them. I told you I'd put clean newspaper in all of them. Not before it was wanted, either. Most of the old paper was torn and creased just like that bit is."

Anthony felt that the old girl was probably right. He made another tour of the room and looked inside two cupboards. For all that they contained, they might well have belonged to the ancient and maternal member of the Hubbard family renowned in song and story. Mrs. Gilbert emphasized in words what Anthony was thinking.

"She's left nothin' behind, Mr. Batters. If that's what you're thinkin' and worryin' about. I can swear to that."

"Yes. I can see that, Mrs. Gilbert. I can see that only too well."

He looked at the divan bed in the corner of the room. A thought came to him.

"Did she ever confide in you, Mrs. Gilbert? With regard to anything you must have been a kind of mother to her." Mrs. Gilbert shook her head. "No. Not to say confide. I told you just now, Miss Forrest kept herself to herself."

"Never tell you *anything*? She's lived with you nearly three years, you know. Three years in November. You weren't exactly strangers to each other. Look at the way you must have looked after her! How about her love-affairs, for instance? An attractive girl as she was?"

Another shake of the head from the landlady. "She never discussed them with me, Mr. Batters. I *think* there was a 'boy friend' towards the end of the time, because of the regular way Miss Forrest went out. Just recently, I mean. She did over the Easter holiday that's just gone. Pretty near every day she come to me in the mornin' and said, 'don't expect me in till late, Mrs. Gilbert.' That was the sign, you see, I knew from that that she was goin' out for the day."

Anthony nodded. "What about meals? Did she feed herself?"

"She got 'er own breakfast in this room. 'Er other meals she had out. That's my usual arrangement. I find it suits all parties much the best."

Anthony tried a final shot. "One last question, Mrs. Gilbert. Visitors? Did Miss Forrest have many during the period she was here?"

"Never anybody, Mr. Batters. Not a livin' soul. I can't remember a single occasion when anybody come 'ere to see 'er. No, she lived a very quiet life—she was a real good girl— and I pray to God that no 'arm's come to 'er."

Anthony began to realize that his visit to Abraham Lincoln Crescent had been fruitless. He thanked Mrs. Gilbert for the services she had rendered him.

"Look here," he said in conclusion, "if any communication *should* come along for Miss Forrest, or if anything happens that you feel you'd like to tell me about—there's my address. I've written it down for you on that card which I'll put in an envelope for you. Don't hesitate to telephone, to write, or even to come and see me—whichever appeals to you most at the time." Anthony handed her an envelope. "Good-bye, Mrs. Gilbert, thank you again for your kindness."

2

Anthony walked back to Hammersmith station, jumped into a train and decided that he'd call on MacMorran at the "Yard". If he himself had toiled and caught nothing, that didn't mean that the professional must perforce be in the same boat. MacMorran grinned as Anthony was shown into his room.

"Ah, just the man I wanted. Hawkshaw the detective. Sit down."

"You don't mean to say, Andrew, that you have news for me? Seriously?"

"I've news, all right. I'll say I have. News that'll make you sit up and go pop-eyed. When you hear it I'll guarantee you'll get the biggest surprise of your life."

Anthony smiled back at the Inspector. "O.K., Andrew, I can take it, out with it."

"Just before three o'clock this afternoon I had a 'phone call from the manager of Delaney's bank. He asked me to go over there at once and see him. Urgent *and* important—that was the story. I went over, naturally. What do you think it was he wanted to see me about?"

Anthony smiled again. "Certain missing San Jonquilo Three per cents. In value—approximately £20,000."

"Good man! You've rung the bell in one. The bonds, so Murray informed me when I got there, have been traced." MacMorran attempted to speak with a casual nonchalance. He saw the gleam, though, in Anthony's grey eyes.

"Good man! Returned to you! Where?"

"Have a shot."

"O.K., I will. I'll chance my arm and have a bash at Santa Guardina— capital of the aforementioned State of San Jonquilo. How do I go?"

Anthony saw the smile broaden on MacMorran's face and heard the inception of the inspectorial chuckle. He knew by those two signs that he had blundered.

"I'm wrong, eh? O.K., you tell me."

"I was going to. And this is where you'll sit up and take notice. Substitute for Santa Guardina, Delaney's bank, Lombard Street."

Anthony stared at the Inspector as though his ears had betrayed him. "What? Say that all over again, Andrew." MacMorran repeated his previous statement. Anthony could almost hear the crossing of the "t's".

"Do you mean, Andrew, that they'd never been *stolen*? Never been missing from the Lombard Street branch? Somebody had boobed?"

"No. Not quite that. They were *returned* to the bank by registered post. In a parcel. Brown paper. It was addressed to the manager personally. I've seen all that, so you can take my word for it."

Anthony whistled with astonishment. "Any enclosure— letter or anything?"

"No, nothing. Just the parcel and in the parcel, the bonds—a couple of hundred of them. Four bundles of fifty each. The parcel was registered, I'm told, at one of the offices in the Charing Cross area. I've put a line on it—Chatterton's got it. But I expect you'd already guessed that."

"Well, I know your extraordinary penchant for Chatterton on jobs of that kind. So the missing bonds are back, eh? Well, well, well! Leave them alone and they'll come home, eh? This case has certainly got me guessing." Anthony looked sideways at MacMorran as he spoke. "Still harping on suicide, Andrew? Or have you at last seen the light?"

MacMorran didn't answer. He rubbed the tip of his nose.

Anthony prodded him. "I'm askin' yer," he added facetiously.

Eventually MacMorran came to the boil. "I like the way you put it, I must say, with your 'seen the light'. At the moment, MacMorran coughed into his hand, "I'll admit this. I've more of an open mind than I had in the first place. There are, I'm perfectly willing to concede, certain doubts . . . irregularities . . . if you like that better . . . it's not as plain sailing as I had originally anticipated."

Anthony indulged in inward laughter. "Plain sailing! There's not much that's plain sailing about any of it. Personally, I'm just groping in the dark. Not a glimmer, yet. With the exception of the broad line—murder—not suicide. Something I want to ask you though—been on my mind for a day or so now—what about the inquest? What's the line you're going for?"

MacMorran inspected his finger-tips. "In the circumstances, adjournment. There, now you know. Does it suit you?"

"Well, of course, you're doing the sensible thing. Never mind me. Leave me out of it. *Sine die*?"

"More or less. As I said—*in* the circumstances. Think it's the best line to take."

"The best? It's more than that. It's the only one."

MacMorran nodded and rose from his chair. Anthony waved him back. "Sit down, Andrew, for another few minutes. This 'ere conference ain't over yet. I haven't told you my news. Swop for swop—you told me yours. I haven't been exactly idle, you know, the last forty-eight hours. So sit back comfortably and produce the receptive ear."

"I'm waiting," countered the Inspector. Anthony pushed over his cigarettes. MacMorran took one.

"Stella Forrest has skipped."

MacMorran's match burnt his fingers. He tossed the stub away with an entirely appropriate exclamation. "Skipped?"

"Scrammed!"

"Scrammed?"

"That's what I said, Andrew. In triplicate. Do you like the sound of it?"

"From Lambert's restaurant, do you mean?"

"That—and more. Not only from that estimable eating-house which you introduced me to, but from her 'digs' as well. The last-named were in Hammersmith—but I'm forgetting myself, you have the address."

MacMorran's eyes searched Anthony's face. "You went after her?"

"I did, Andrew."

"What for?"

"I wanted a second impression on several matters. Perhaps even a third. I indicated as much to you a day or two back."

"When did she scram?"

"On the Thursday morning. The day after Oliver's body was found. Got her landlady to 'phone the restaurant for her to tell Lambert she was resigning from her job When did you tell Stella . . . about young Oliver?"

"On the Wednesday evening. Fairly early. Soon after we parted company. I promised I'd let her know, don't you remember?"

Anthony took another cigarette. "She didn't delay, did she? Didn't let the grass come up very much? Why the unseemly haste, Andrew? I don't like it at all, do you?"

MacMorran shook his head.

"I certainly do not. What about the contacts?"

Anthony shook his head. "Nothing doing. Tried to find 'em. Couldn't! They don't seem to exist. No such thing."

"What exactly do you mean?"

Anthony shrugged his shoulders. "Just what I say. There ain't no sich animal."

MacMorran frowned. "Sorry. Don't quite get that."

Anthony repeated the shrug. "According to all my inquiries both of old man Lambert *and* the landlady—Stella came from nowhere and has gone back to exactly the same place."

MacMorran expostulated. "But damn it all, Mr. Bathurst, she *must* have relations somewhere . . . friends . . . it's hardly to be believed that a young girl—"

"You go on thinking so, Andrew. I'm not stopping you. I thought the same as you once upon a time. Now, I know different. The landlady—a highly respectable woman, Andrew —says that Stella arrived one day and asked for a room. Same room advertised by landlady's card in landlady's front room downstairs window. That would be when Stella first signed on with old man Lambert, three years next November, the month of Guido Fawkes, fog, your own namesake Saint and Apostle, and our own Winston Churchill. Stella informed landlady that both her parents were dead."

"Didn't she have any letters?"

Not so that the landlady noticed them."

MacMorran snorted and looked incredulous. "Yes," said Anthony, "I know exactly how you feel and—which is worse for me I can see exactly how you *look*, but everything I tried had both ends sealed up. No parents, no friends, no letters! A girl whose behaviour was absolutely exemplary in every respect."

MacMorran growled. "She sounds to me a ruddy sight too good to be true. I suppose this woman's statements are reliable?"

"I see no reason to doubt them, Andrew. If I'm any judge of persons, she's a really first-class witness. I'll tell you what mainly brought me to that way of thinking. She had the goods with regard to young Peter Oliver and his association with Stella. The stuff was authentic. Let me put it over to you as she handed it to me. These were the words she used. 'I thought there was a boy friend towards the end of the time.' Note that. Then she explained what she meant, why she had made the statement. That she'd noticed certain changes in the girl's personal habits. At Easter, for example, she described how the girl had been 'out' most days and how she had warned the landlady in advance not to expect her home until later. Facts which I knew to be true. No—the landlady, in my opinion, can be absolutely relied on, Andrew. And the one fact that emerges from her is that Stella Forrest, from *our* point of view, is not even a primrose by the river's brim, but just a human *cul-de-sac*. That—and nothing more."

MacMorran fell back on one of his normal exercises. He began to draw grotesque figures on the edge of his blotting-pad. When he eventually looked up, he said, "after all—I don't know that it's of much importance—any of this. Oliver's dead, and his girl decides to fade out. Seems natural to me. When I come to look round it. She's probably taken the knock pretty badly and decided to start afresh somewhere. Quite understandable. Probably her first love-affair—serious—and she's all smashed up. She's one of the highly emotional sort and taken the blow amidships as it were. Some of 'em do. I can recognize the symptoms. Stella Forrest wants to forget."

"That's what you think, eh

"I certainly do. Don't you?"

"No."

"No?"

"No."

"Oh"—MacMorran rolled his pencil back to the pad— "what's your version of the affair, then?"

"I'm not certain. But I definitely differ from you. I think the kid's frightened."

MacMorran came back to incredulity. "Frightened?"

"That's what I said, Andrew."

"What's she frightened of?"

"If I knew that, I should probably know the bundle. Haven't got as far as that yet. Living in hopes."

MacMorran stared at Anthony searchingly. "Any grounds for what you've just said? Real grounds—apart from purely theoretical?"

Anthony considered MacMorran's question before he replied. "Perhaps no *real* grounds. Tangible. But possibly two points of definite support."

"What are they? Let's have 'em."

"The landlady had the same idea as I have. That the girl scrammed because she was afraid of something."

"Based on what?"

"The look on Stella Forrest's face and her general manner on the morning she cleared off from the lodgings in Hammersmith. The landlady naturally took an especially close look at her, because Stella's sudden going was an absolute bolt from the blue."

"Nothing said, though? No hint? No reference?"

"No. Nothing said and nothing hinted at."

"Well, the kid was smashed up as I said. Her world had been knocked all to pieces. Quite suddenly, too. No wonder she looked as you say she did. Surely you can see that?"

Anthony was quiet and impressive in his reply. "There's an enormous difference, my dear Andrew, between looking 'upset', 'smashed up', 'badly hit' or whichever way you want it and looking 'afraid'. Fear! Stark abject Fear! Is there anything *quite like Fear*, Andrew? Any human quality of comparable consistency? If there is, I must confess I don't know it."

"H'm," said MacMorran, "perhaps all the same—you never know," and then the Inspector branched off again. "Two points of support, you said, didn't you? I've heard one. What's the other?"

"You'll grouse at the other one. Grouse like hell. You'll say it's no point at all and that it won't hold water for a second. Probably you'll be right. But it's this. As I see things, for Stella Forrest to be afraid fits the pattern of the crime. As I see it. You've heard me down this particular street before."

The Inspector frowned again. "Fits the pattern? How the heck do you arrive at that?"

"Why, that *she's* afraid, now that *Peter Oliver's* been got rid of. Do you get me?"

MacMorran stared. "What do you mean? That she sees herself in line as the next victim? Is that your idea?"

"That's it, Andrew," said Anthony quietly, "that is my idea."

MacMorran shook his head. "Can't see it myself. On what we know. Candidly, I think you're inclined to look for the sensational."

"What *do* we know, Andrew?" asked Anthony.

MacMorran coughed.

"No, Andrew," continued Anthony, "quite seriously and with no trimmings just exactly what *do* we know? I'd love you to tell me."

Some seconds elapsed before MacMorran replied. "Not a lot, I agree."

"Not a lot? That's how you describe it? If you said 'damn all' you'd be a good deal nearer the mark."

MacMorran shifted uneasily in his chair under the fire of Anthony's criticism. Anthony proceeded to elaborate.

"Let's 're-cap', at this stage of the case—it won't do either of us any harm. Let's 're-cap' and see just what we *do* know. Peter Oliver's found dead after Stella Forrest (entirely on her own) has blown the bugle of alarm. Found by you and me. In other words, you and I were right there when the tapes went up. There's no question, on this occasion, of the scent being cold. *I* think he was murdered, *you* aren't so sure. Naturally—you were born in Aberdeen, I wasn't. What's come along since then? Let's have a look at it. Certain evidence from his sister who comes to us post-haste crying, 'Murder— and let loose the dogs of war.' I *know* then—from her story— that the man *was* murdered. You—still fifty-fifty. Now after that. What? Two things and two things only. One—that certain foreign bonds, with which Oliver was connected professionally, *were missing*—but *aren't so any longer*. Two—that the girl who sounded the

'Tally-ho' for us has seen fit to 'scarper' from the work she performed and from the places which knew her. And *that*, my dear Andrew, is very definitely the bundle."

MacMorran grunted. "Not imposing, I grant you." Anthony came back again. "*Do* we know anything else, Andrew? Have I boobed on anything?"

MacMorran thought it over. "Yes. I think we do. There's Garcia. You didn't mention him."

"No, that's true, I didn't. Do you think we should continue to include him in the clues category? Point is, does he now drop out of the cast? Now that the San Jonquilo bonds have dragged their tails behind them? Does he or does he? Personally, I'm not at all sure about him. What do you think yourself, Andrew?"

"I'm like you. In two minds about him. On the face of it, it looks as though he ought to be scrubbed. All the same, I'm not so sure. Don't forget the Oliver note. The one in the wallet. You haven't mentioned that either yet."

"No, that's one and a half to you, Andrew. I slipped up there when I shouldn't have. You mean, of course, 'Reference R.G. and D.?'"

"That's it. We *must* look further into that. Don't tell me you've discarded your own theories?"

Anthony shook his head and then looked up at the Inspector. "Arising therefrom, it's most certainly indicated, Andrew, that you and I at the earliest possible moment, put in a spot of high living. We'll sample a night-club. In other words, you old scoundrel, we'll make a call at 'The Orange Lizard'."

"Extraordinary," returned MacMorran, "I had it on the tip of my tongue to make a similar suggestion. It *might* pay dividends.'

"That's O.K, then—to-night?"

"To-night? Yes—to-night will suit me very well. We'll take Chatterton with us. We may find him useful."

3

Anthony peered through the windscreen and slowed down the pace of the car. "I thought so. This is Rhapsody Street, Andrew. And there's a little garage, if my memory's to be relied on, at the west end of it, where the terms are very reasonable. If you've no objection, we'll park the bus in there and walk through to Masson Street. If I'm right, it's less than a hundred yards away. O.K.?"

"Suits me," returned MacMorran.

"Right-o, then. That's what we'll do. Come on, Chatterton." The three men alighted at the end of the street and Anthony proceeded to negotiate with the garage proprietor.

"Masson Street, sir? Quite easy. First right and walk through the alley way. Can't miss it. What do you want 'The Lizard'?"

"You're a thought-reader," smiled Anthony, "what's the secret, the trained eye or the discerning mind?"

The man's red face creased and crinkled into good humour. "I get a good many cars come along here all because of the old 'Lizard'. Mustn't grumble. Can't grouse at my bread and butter. Means business for me. The place ain't so hot though. Not so much as you'd expect. Not these days. Slowed up a bit. Like almost everything else. Bit o' most things there, though, so I'm told. Over and under. *If* you should want them. If not —you can always please yourself. O.K., sir—thank you."

The three men came quickly to Masson Street and to the premises of 'The Orange Lizard'.

"As these places go nowadays," said the Inspector as they walked towards the entrance, "I fancy this one's on the mild side. Although you can't always go by reports. It doesn't take long for fresh rackets to spring up and an easy-going comparatively quiet joint can become one of the authentic 'spots'. And it may take some time for the squeak to come through. To begin with, we'll make this a semi-official visit. But no more than that. Are you fit? Square those shoulders of yours, Chatterton. Remember your *esprit de corps.*"

"Yes, Chief," returned Chatterton, "certainly—sorry, Chief." He regarded the pavement, though, with a doubting eye. MacMorran winked at Anthony, took a couple of quick strides and pushed open the door. An attendant barred the way. MacMorran flashed a card at him.

"I'd like a word . . . a friendly word . . . with your Mr. Raymond Hurst . . . your managing director. See to it for me, will you please?"

The attendant swallowed twice, looked at MacMorran, took in all that Anthony had, let his glance linger for one second on a most militant-looking Chatterton and said, "yes, sir. Come this way, sir, will you please?"

4

The attendant preceded Anthony and company along a short corridor, up a staircase with a heavily-piled carpet and then along a second corridor. This second corridor was considerably longer than the first they had travelled.

"Mr. Hurst's office is at the end of this corridor," explained the attendant-guide. He pointed. "Please knock on this door, sir. Then he'll let you know if it's O.K. to go in."

The man turned and vanished. MacMorran walked to a door marked "Private" and knocked. There was no audible answer, but suddenly—and rather to Anthony's surprise—the door opened and a man came out. He held the door open with his hand on the knob. He had raven-black hair, a pale, sallow complexion and dark-brown eyes. He was tall—well over six feet and broad-shouldered. His weight looked to be proportional with his height. He had a deep-rooted, fleshy nose, a small, neatly-trimmed moustache, and full, thick lips. He was in a superbly-tailored evening-dress and his white shirt and collar were equally irreproachable. His white dress-bow would have been difficult to fault if judged by the highest standards possible.

As he stood there with his hand on the door-knob, he smiled at MacMorran—that is to say, his face went through the movements normally associated with the exercise. His teeth, Anthony observed during the smile, were on a par with the rest of him.

"Who are you, may I ask, and what do you want?" he said.

As he spoke, Anthony's left hand bet his right hand an even dollar that Mr. Hurst's birth-certificate would not be obtainable at Somerset House. Evens, queried Anthony? Odds on, he answered himself and both hands agreed.

MacMorran smiled at Hurst's greeting and passed over his credentials. Raymond Hurst's face slipped into second gear.

"Chief Detective-Inspector MacMorran? Indeed! Please come in to my room and tell me why we are so honoured." MacMorran whispered to Chatterton, who remained outside. The Inspector and Anthony followed Raymond Hurst into his room. It was superbly furnished. Anthony saw that Hurst had been an athlete in his time. There were photographs of him in a Rugger fifteen and also in swimming-costume. Hurst waved them to commodious chairs.

"An entirely friendly visit," said MacMorran in explanation as he sank back in the luxurious depths of his chair—"the reputation of 'The Orange Lizard' is still good enough. Regard the call as merely semi-official."

Hurst's white teeth gleamed. "I am delighted to hear you say that. That is indeed excellent news. We always do our very best to—"

"I'm sure you do," returned MacMorran with deliberate intervention "as a matter of fact, Mr. Hurst, I'll be frank with you from the outset. I want you to help me over something. By the way, I'm forgetting myself—this is Mr. Anthony Bathurst." The lips parted and the fangs flickered again—but the dark-brown eyes remained hard, cold and calculating. The thick, rather hoarse voice spoke again.

"I'm delighted to meet Mr. Bathurst, I'm sure." Then Hurst turned away from Anthony to the Inspector again. "I'm just a little surprised though—at what you said just now. You will forgive me. In what way can I be of any assistance to one of the most important officers attached to Scotland Yard?"

MacMorran chuckled and went on to play it off the cuff. Anthony had never seen him quite like this. He positively exuded *bonhomie*.

"Ah, that's it, isn't it, Mr. Hurst? Well, quite a simple business, I'm pleased to say—when we get down to brass tacks. And one that shouldn't give you any trouble at all. It's to do with the . . . er . . . personnel of your club membership."

Raymond Hurst frowned. "Do you mean that one of our members is in any trouble? With your people? If that is so . . . it is most disturbing. . ."

"Come off it," thought Anthony as Hurst so unblushingly dissembled, "or that tongue of yours will bore a hole in your cheek."

"Oh, no," replied MacMorran, "not for a minute. Don't think that. Nothing of the sort. But at the moment there are certain matters . . . of state . . . shall we say . . . rather hush-hush, and on that account I am not in a position to be as frank with you as regards the actual details as I should like to be. Were it in my power to be . . . but there . . . no doubt . . . you're a man of the world, Mr. Hurst . . . you understand."

Hurst nodded with an air of profound sagacity at MacMorran's masterly effort. And then, before he could find words for a reply, the Inspector was in again.

"You keep a register of members, of course, Mr. Hurst?"

"We do, Inspector."

"Oh, good. I felt sure that you would. Now would you be obliging enough to let me have a quick glance at it? Just a few moments—no more—will give me the information that I require. I won't mention names to you this evening . . . no names, no—you know the rest."

MacMorran sat back in his chair with a look on his face of the utmost benevolence. Raymond Hurst, who couldn't keep his eyes off the Inspector's face, seemed to hesitate. He appeared, to Anthony, to be attempting, mentally, to visualize something like the third move ahead. But MacMorran's sudden descent upon him had caught him on one leg . . . and recovery had not yet come to him.

"Oh, yes, Inspector MacMorran," he said (rather too effusively), "certainly . . . by all means. Only too pleased to help." Hurst dropped his hand to one of the lower drawers in the side of his roll-top desk. Anthony heard the noise of the drawer being pulled out. Hurst was bending over the drawer. Suddenly he straightened himself and Anthony saw that he was holding a book in his hand. It was of ledger type but considerably thinner than the normal accountancy ledger and was bound in red. MacMorran smiled graciously as Hurst produced the membership register.

"I won't be inordinately curious," said the Inspector, "or even take any advantage of your courtesy, Mr. Hurst. Because I realize what you're doing for me. Turn to the page where—h'm perhaps that won't do—I was forgetting. Have you the names in there in any sort of order? Or do you just add new members to the list when the occasion demands?"

This time Hurst didn't look so good. There was no fang-flicker or lip-split to add up to anything remotely suggesting a smile.

"Our members' names are kept in alphabetical order— with a separate section for each letter," he answered curtly. "That'll be very convenient for me," contributed MacMorran, "couldn't be better—from my point of view. Now turn to the Gs, will you, Mr. Hurst? G—for Garibaldi. Then you'll be doing very nicely—and I don't mean maybe." Hurst, his eyes full of uncertainty, flicked the pages of 'The Orange Lizard' membership register. MacMorran waited until it was evident that he had found the right page. Hurst, not to be outdone, also waited. MacMorran's smile was more expansive than ever.

"Now, Mr. Hurst, may I just glance at that page? Do you mind? That's all I want. Thank you very much indeed." Hurst turned the register round with just a *soupçon* of ungraciousness and handed it over to the Inspector. MacMorran ran his eyes down the column devoted to the surnames beginning with "G". There were thirty-one of them in all. Without giving Hurst any clue as to which of the names was exciting his interest, MacMorran motioned to Anthony to come alongside him.

Anthony, who had been expecting something of this kind to happen, was quick to respond. He bent over MacMorran's shoulder and read the list of names.

"Anything there interest you?" inquired the Inspector. "Yes . . . I think so," said Anthony, "many happy returns of the day. May your shadow never grow less. Now turn back a couple of pages. I'm interested in another name." MacMorran turned back. "One more," said Anthony, "you can't count."

MacMorran understood the subtlety and obeyed the instruction. Anthony still looked over the Inspector's shoulder. "I thank you," said Anthony suddenly and almost facetiously "I'm satisfied."

MacMorran returned the membership register to Raymond Hurst. "Thank you, Mr. Hurst. Very kind of you. That's about all, thank you. We won't take up any more of your valuable time. Expect you've got plenty on your plate of an evening."

Hurst locked up the red register in its drawer, rose and smiled. "It's a pleasure," he said. Anthony looked and saw the frost in the man's eyes.

"And how," he muttered as a mental rejoinder.

"We'll stay for a drink downstairs," said MacMorran—"may as well have a look round while we're here—the evening's young yet."

"Certainly," returned Hurst. "I was about to invite you. Leave your clothes here and I'll fix you up."

"That's very decent of you." MacMorran turned to Anthony. "I'll tell Chatterton he can scram. This place isn't quite his cup of tea. I don't think I need keep him any longer."

Anthony nodded. "No. That'll be O.K. Good idea."

Hurst took their hats and coats. "You can leave these in my private cabinet. Now come along downstairs with me," he said, "and I'll fix it for you."

Hurst held the door open for them with a gesture of punctilious courtesy. MacMorran went through and spoke to Chatterton. Then the Inspector and Anthony followed Raymond Hurst downstairs. MacMorran's eyelid dropped in Anthony's direction at the first available and safe opportunity. Anthony made appropriate acknowledgement.

As they made their way downstairs, MacMorran was wondering what the size of the strip would be that Hurst would tear off for the singularly obliging attendant who had taken them up to his private room with such despatch and alacrity at their initial entrance. Anthony, on his part, was wondering about a certain two names he had looked for and seen in 'The Orange Lizard' register—'Robert Wykes Dewhurst' and 'Dolores Garcia'. But whereas Anthony had got something, MacMorran hadn't. He was unaware, you see, that the attendant who had been so extraordinarily obliging was also so browned off with his job that he had walked out on it while their interview with Raymond Hurst had actually been taking place.

CHAPTER 12

1

When they came to the foot of the staircase Hurst signalled to one of the waiters. "Find these gentlemen a table on the far side and then report back to me personally."

The waiter seemed to understand immediately. "If you'll excuse me for a time," continued Hurst to MacMorran, "I'll join you again a little later on. I've no doubt you'll be able to amuse yourselves in the meantime."

MacMorran waved to him almost affectionately. "That's all right . . . quite all right, you carry on, old chap. We'll do famously—old campaigners, you know. Don't you bother about us."

The waiter piloted them across the floor-space just as the orchestra struck up for the next dance. Hurst turned on his heel and Anthony saw him go upstairs again. The waiter found the table for them as he had been instructed. Anthony looked at him meaningly.

"Bring us some Scotch," he said.

The waiter nodded and disappeared. MacMorran seemed suddenly overtaken by an attack of uneasiness bordering on anxiety.

"Did I hear you order Scotch? It'll be well over the odds, I expect. Shouldn't we have done better to have—"

"Simmer down, Andrew," said Anthony, "don't yell before the lead's in your tummy—it's on the cards the bottle may come from Father Christmas. You're the white-headed boy here. A blind man could see that. Hurst has taken you to his bosom. Perhaps he's descended from the Royal family of Egypt and has a passion for that sort of thing—who knows? Steady on though, here come the drinks."

The waiter put the glasses on the table with a "split".

"These are with Mr. Hurst's compliments, gentlemen. I was to tell you. When you want me again, just give me the high sign." The man grinned and sidled away.

"Father Christmas it is," said Anthony, "and here's mud in your eye, Andrew."

MacMorran rolled the spirit round his mouth and savoured the fullness thereof. "And not a bad dr-rop of stuff, either. Better than we get at the Police dinner."

Anthony was watching the swaying couples on the floor—according to his reckoning, there were over a hundred and fifty people dancing. The orchestra slid into "When I'm hot, why are you cold, Baby?" and the *tempo* of the place generally was speeded up. MacMorran drank more whisky with the aplomb of the connoisseur. Anthony scanned with interest the faces of the dancers as they swept by the table. The waiters were everywhere, weaving their way to, round, between and from the tables. The whisky began to have its effect on the Inspector. He began to assess finance.

"They take some 'bees' here, in a night," he commented, "you'd never believe it unless you saw it. Why did I ever join the Police? It's a true saying—only 'mugs' work."

Then Anthony said something which surprised him. Anthony had dropped his voice to almost a low whisper.

"Looking for anything, Andrew—or possibly anybody?".

Andrew MacMorran dropped his voice, too, in the reply. "Don't know quite. Are you?"

Anthony maintained the low tone of voice. "Very definitely, Andrew. The murderer of Peter Oliver."

"He's not in this collection." MacMorran's tone was contemptuous.

"Maybe not. Although I wouldn't wager too heavily on that. All the same, the trail that's going to lead up to him may be here. It may even start from here."

MacMorran shook his head and emptied his glass. "Catch that fellow's eye, will you—there's some more where that came from and it might as well be mine as anybody else's."

"I shouldn't be surprised. I'll get him in half a sec. and give him the sign. You spotted those names, of course?"

"In the register? Oh-ay."

"I wasn't so far out, was I?" As Anthony spoke, he arrested the waiter's attention. The man stayed where he was but gave the sign back that he understood.

"The second instalment of firewater from Santa Claus," said Anthony, "is on the way. I managed to convey your desires to good master Cobweb. Or should it be Peaseblossom?"

"Good. Now what was it you were saying about the names? You got what you wanted, didn't you? I gave you the chance."

"I sure did, Andrew. And it also gives *you* what *you* might care to want. You now have your desired trio 'R.G. and D.' As, of course, you've already spotted. Can we add it up to anything?"

MacMorran shook his head. "Doubtful. Very doubtful. No more than an indication at the moment. There's nothing in our pockets yet which you can say definitely adds up. Can't see the skeleton yet—yet alone the flesh to shove on its ruddy bones. No motive. That I can see. Or even remotely think of. Of course, if those bonds hadn't been returned to the bank—" He broke off suddenly. "Don't ask me to think in this atmosphere—with this ruddy band swinging it and Hurst's whisky warmin' the cockles of my heart."

Anthony grinned at the "Yard" Inspector. "Hallo! Here's St. Nicholas again. Bearing down on us in full argosy. With jingle bells and appropriate offering. You'll soon feel better, Andrew. Shift the dirty glasses and make room."

The waiter put more whisky on their table. MacMorran's smile returned. He waited for the attendant to go before he spoke again.

"You heard my remarks about motive," he said quietly, "and you made no reply. Am I to take it that you disagree with me?"

"Not for one fleeting moment, Andrew. That's why I feel we shouldn't keep on barking up the same tree. If, on the other hand, we have a dip in one or two different directions, we might eventually strike something with 'motive' on it in large letters. That's one of the reasons why I suggested it might be profitable for us to come here and play 'Nosy Parker'."

MacMorran prodded him. "There's one thing—you haven't run across the missing Stella Forrest. I don't know whether you expected to."

"Stella Forrest? Not on your life! My dear Andrew, this is one of the last places on God's earth where I should expect to find her. While I've been sitting here, though, I've been thinking about her quite a lot. In fact, I've been beginning to wonder whether we haven't made a howling—"

Anthony stopped abruptly and MacMorran looked over to him in surprise. Anthony was staring towards the entrance with a new light in his eyes. The band had finished a number and most of the couples who had been dancing were making their way back to their respective tables. Anthony spoke to MacMorran in his quietest tones.

"Do you see what I see, Andrew? There—at the entrance? That group of people that's just blown in? Six of 'em all told. Three men and three girls. One girl in pink."

MacMorran looked across to the entrance.

"You and I have already made the acquaintance of two of them," continued Anthony. "Margaret Oliver and Señor Roderigo Garcia. And I fancy, also, without being absolutely sure, that our eyes have rested for a few seconds on a third member of the same party."

MacMorran dissented. "Not mine. Yours may have."

"Yes—yours, Andrew, as well as mine."

MacMorran frowned and looked across at the entrance again. "Not guilty. Bar the two people you mentioned, I don't know any of the others from Adam. You're wrong."

"For a few seconds, Andrew—I repeat the phrase—your eyes have rested on the tallest man in the party. At the same moment that mine did. At least that's my guess, and I'm sticking to it. I judge him to be Robert Wykes Dewhurst, Esquire, journalist, attached to the *Morning Message* and *fiancé* of our little friend, Margaret Oliver."

MacMorran shook his head decisively. "Then you're still boobing I've never met the bloke in my life."

"Gertcher, Andrew—I didn't say as 'ow you'd *met him*. But your eyes have rested on him. That's what I said."

"When was that, may I ask?"

"The night Margaret Oliver took us to her parents' home at Puck Willow—to show us the bathroom."

"What the hell—you're daft, he wasn't there."

"Pipe down and wait for it. Margaret didn't sleep in Mayblossom Avenue—do you remember that—and we took her along to a house in Wimblefield—do you remember *that*?"

"Yes, very well. She said she'd spend the night there. Supposed to be friends. But what's all this to do with—"

Anthony cut in and proceeded imperturbably. "To enter that house, Andrew, Margaret had to knock at the door. We waited in the car while she did. We saw the door opened to her. We—you and I. And the man who opened that door, Andrew, was the merchant whose hand at the present moment is cupping Margaret Oliver's elbow—Mr. Robert Wykes Dewhurst."

"I'd laugh like hell if you were wrong," said MacMorran.

"You're tellin' me," said Mr. Bathurst, "but you won't get the chance."

2

MacMorran drank more whisky. Some minutes elapsed. "What do we do?" inquired MacMorran.

"Do you mean about contact?"

"Yes."

Anthony waited before he replied. "I'm inclined to think that Margaret Oliver will come to us. She hasn't seen us yet. When she does, I rather fancy she'll come and play ball. Garcia may, but in his case I wouldn't rate the chances higher than a bare possibility. If I'm wrong about the lady, and she and Garcia both hang fire, we'll start the ball rolling ourselves. You agree with me that we should?"

"Ever-ry time," replied MacMorran. "As far as I'm concerned, it's too good an opportunity to be missed. There's no knowing what we may learn when some of the tongues loosen up. But I say—where's that waiter feller of ours, why the hell doesn't he do his job properly? Can you see him?"

"You're not lost for it, Andrew, I must say. For sheer unblushing effrontery" Anthony signalled for the third time. "O.K., Andrew. I've located him. The reindeer are on their way again."

"Good. I've always held that there are certain expressions of kindness and good-fellowship which it's a sin not to encourage. Well then—if my friend Hurst—"

The band started a slow fox-trot and Anthony's eyes travelled to the couples who had already taken the floor. As far as he had been able to see from where he was sitting, the Garcia group had already split up and it occurred to Anthony that some, at least, of them were, in all probability, dancing. He hadn't long to wait for the assurance that this idea was correct. For, a few moments after the start of the number which the orchestra was now playing, he saw Margaret Oliver on the dance-floor. She was dancing with the tall man whom Anthony, for the benefit of MacMorran, had labelled Dewhurst. Anthony thereupon prompted the Inspector.

"On the left, Andrew, just passing the curtained alcove—and I think, pretty certain to pass our way within the space of about one minute—do you get it?"

"Miss Oliver—yes, I get it. They'll be in circulation round this quarter before long, as you say. Thank you, sonny. Very nice of you. Put it down there, will you?"

The obliging waiter had brought the third instalment of whisky.

"Yes," said Anthony, "I fancy she'll spot us in about thirty seconds from now. Then see what happens. Watch closely—you never know, it may be informative."

3

Anthony and MacMorran sat back in their chairs and waited for the tide to come in. As Margaret swept by the important table, her eyes took them in and she recognized them at once. Her look however betrayed both surprise and recognition. Anthony smiled back at her and MacMorran, taking his cue from Anthony, did likewise. Anthony watched her closely as the couple swung away. Had she told her partner anything of what she had just seen? Would she tell him or would she hold it and come back later to play it entirely off her own cuff? Anthony thought that he would very much like to know. While Margaret's back was turned for a fleeting second of time, MacMorran spoke from the side of his mouth.

"She recognized us—but that's all. Nothing more. That's as far as we're going to get. For the time being."

"How do you mean?"

"Think she'll come over later and make a fuss of us?"

"I think she'll come over," said Anthony, "somehow! But I'm not quite sure yet which way it'll be. Or even *when* it'll be. Wait till this foxtrot's got cold."

MacMorran grunted. "The first quality needed for a policeman is patience. Likewise the last quality. All day and every day."

"You won't have to wait long, misery—the number's finishing."

Anthony was right. The last bars trailed away. MacMorran drank more whisky. The band stopped and some of them took out handkerchiefs.

"Look," said Anthony, "look what's coming to the patient policeman who was moaning only a few seconds ago. Straight off the top of the Christmas tree. Well, well, well, are Jews and Scotsmen lucky? I'll say they are."

MacMorran looked across the floor. Margaret Oliver had started to come straight across to them.

Under a fusillade of chaff from Anthony, MacMorran prepared himself for the encounter. Margaret came to the table. When she reached it, she stopped. Her face was flushed.

"I suppose," she said almost vindictively, "that I've already been tried, found guilty and sentenced? Yes? For utter heartlessness and the most complete callousness in the history of the world. Well, that's O.K. by me. If I've had it—I've had it. But please remember that sitting at home with a long face and howling my eyes out won't bring my brother back . . . or do the slightest molecule of good whatever. So my *fiancé*, Bob Dewhurst, tells me, and I'm inclined to pay attention to what he says. Well—that's that. And I've got it off my chest. Take it or leave it, as the maggot bites. Now I'll say good-evening. Good-evening, Inspector. Good-evening, Mr. Bathurst."

Anthony pulled a chair for her to sit on. "Good-evening, Miss Oliver. It's charming of you to remember us. Please take this chair. As to what you've just said—for my part—objection sustained."

MacMorran nodded. "What Mr. Bathurst says goes for me as well. Keep a glasshouse myself and I've never been one to throw stones."

"Cheers," said Margaret, "for the relief and for the chair—many thanks."

Anthony glanced at her with keen assessment and some admiration. Her face was harder than it had been on the night she had come to him. The change had taken place in the eyes—they were hard and cold, with a brilliance that was new and unfamiliar. It seemed that a girl had suddenly become a woman and that Margaret Oliver had assumed a mask—for a time at least. She was talking again.

"But what on earth brings you here? The last two people in the whole universe I should have expected to find in here. Why, I should have imagined that 'The Orange Lizard' would have been something like anathema to you. That you wouldn't have touched it with the end of a barge-pole. It only goes to show *you never know*."

"The Inspector's taking over my adult education," smiled Anthony, "he's starting me on a course. It's entitled 'Taking the Lid off'. Tonight's one of the first lessons." Margaret laughed and then looked at him doubtfully. "I suppose it would be wrong of me to ask if—"

"It would," replied MacMorran, "very wrong. So wrong in fact that you really mustn't."

"I see I was afraid that's how it would be. Still, I'm glad I saw you when I was dancing and that I came over and spoke to you. I like to think, when I'm a good girl, that we are friends. It's given me a link with something, that, between you and me, badly needed that link. Will you come and speak to my friends before you go? I'd love you to. And so would they." MacMorran smiled at her. "For all you know, you may be wrong in that last statement of yours. How then?"

Margaret cocked her head at him whimsically. "Must you always look on the worst side? Because you always seem to when we discuss anything. I'll tell you again, and I mean every word of it, that my friends will be delighted to see you. I know they will. Come along over now, please."

"Come on, Andrew," said Anthony, "otherwise you'll cause Miss Oliver to protest too much. And that would embarrass both her and me."

"Thank you, Mr. Bathurst," said Margaret, "for coming over on my side. You put that very nicely. I don't think I could improve on it."

MacMorran grinned. "All right," he said, "the balance of power again. No use fighting against it—waste of time. I give in." He suffered himself to be "convoyed" across the room with Anthony. To the Olivers' table. And to the first of the consummations which Anthony had desired.

4

Margaret led the way and made the necessary introductions. She performed them quickly and unconventionally. "My brother, David, Miss Pamela Hanbury, Mr. Dewhurst, Mr. and Mrs. Garcia—Chief Detective-Inspector MacMorran of Scotland Yard, Mr. Anthony Bathurst. And now let's all sit down."

Anthony noted the English form of address which Margaret used with reference to the Garcias and also the manner in which she had more or less "mixed" the various people. He was curious, too, to take a closer look at David Oliver, the youngest member of the Oliver family.

In the early twenties, he appeared to Anthony to be a younger but larger edition of the dead Peter. The resemblance at close quarters, was striking and bordered on the uncanny and would have been even more pronounced if David had been dark instead of fair.

Pamela Hanbury, the girl evidently with him rather than with the others, was dark, tallish, brown-eyed, slim and vivacious. Probably, Anthony judged, in her late 'teens. Garcia's wife was the most striking member of the party. She was big, blonde, blue-eyed and dominant. In her youth, she must have been an unusually distinguished figure and even now, in middle age, few men would be content on passing her with less than three looks.

Dewhurst was tall and cadaverous. But he had intelligence in his face, he moved quickly and alertly, and Anthony didn't have to be with him for more than a few seconds to realize that his dark, restless eyes missed very little of what was either coming or going.

MacMorran had intervened quickly following upon the terms of Margaret Oliver's introduction.

"As a matter of fact, we have already had the pleasure of meeting Señor Garcia, Miss Oliver. Both Mr. Bathurst and I. I won't claim on that account that we're the oldest of old friends but you'll see that we aren't exactly strangers to each other." He turned and smiled at Margaret. "I think you ought to know that as early in the proceedings as possible."

Now these verbal exchanges were just down the right street for Anthony—they couldn't have been better as far as he was concerned and he watched carefully for the various individual reactions to the Inspector's remark. Garcia himself, he thought, looked more annoyed than anything else. As though he could lay his tongue round MacMorran for not keeping his big mouth shut.

Señora Garcia looked incredulously surprised. As though the veil of revelation had been suddenly torn from something right in front of her and the consequent and entirely unexpected exposure was a shock to her. Margaret Oliver had the appearance of being perplexed and Dewhurst had reacted to MacMorran's remarks in almost the identical manner. The same kind of perplexity was on his features as in the case of Margaret but it soon gave way, Anthony saw, to something else. This something else was much more like studied deliberation.

David Oliver, with his mop of fair hair brushed up from his forehead, looked cynically self-assured. All the confidence of rebellious, iconoclastic youth shone from his features, but his girl friend, Pamela Hanbury, looked as though she was by no means pleased at the turn affairs had taken, although obviously she possessed no real understanding of what it was all about. Anthony thought—you've come here to dance and only to dance—any diversion you'll hate like hell.

Dolores Garcia said to Roderigo, "but you have not told me that you had met this famous detective from Scotland Yard? Why is that? Why have you kept such a thing a secret? Is it that you were ashamed?"

She laughed exuberantly as she put the last question to her husband. Garcia shrugged his shoulders and tried to pass off the incident with a rather malnourished attempt at humour. But Anthony felt almost certain that his initial annoyance had increased. Dewhurst entered the breach. He intended the gesture to smack of gallantry.

"Blame me for this, gentlemen." His voice was charming and unusually well-modulated. "I expect you're thinking it's abnormal for Margaret and . . . er . . . the rest of us . . . to be here . . . in the circumstances. But I suggested she came and when the inevitable argument started, I'm afraid that I threw my weight into it rather violently and turned the scale. So if you're 'thinking things', take it out on me, gentlemen. Revenge yourselves alone on Cassius."

"Don't be absurd, Bob," intercepted Margaret. "To hear you talk, one would think I hadn't a will or a mind of my own or that I was a kid of about five. Don't be so insulting."

Dewhurst shrugged his shoulders and turned away.

"What the hell," contributed David Oliver. "Who cares, anyway?" His voice was thin and precise. To Anthony's ear it had something of a feminine note. David was continuing. "We're here, aren't we? And we're pleased and honoured to be with the bright lights and the sweet music and in the company of Señor Garcia and his wife. I know that *I* am and no doubt the same goes for all of us. What's past is past—the moving finger writes and having writ—well, you know the rest. As I said—what the hell? Dear old Peter would be one of the first to agree with me. And what's more, I don't suppose for one second that either the Inspector or Mr. Bathurst sets himself up as an arbiter of the etiquette of seemly behaviour or becoming conduct. If they do—well, that's just too bad and I hope it keeps fine for them."

Pamela Hanbury giggled several times during David's protracted effort before leaning over to pat him on the arm. "Good for you, David. Quite the little orator—what?"

Anthony was listening intently to everything that was being said. All of it suited his book beautifully. But Andrew MacMorran was in different shape. He was not on duty—he had made that clear to Raymond Hurst at the outset and the whisky—free and flowing—had mellowed him. The conversation, too, to which he was now listening, was an entirely different proposition to him from what it was to Anthony Bathurst. He was still somewhat handicapped, as it were by his dual capacity of Scotland Yard official and ordinary guest but nothing like as much as he would have been ordinarily.

"I still say you're being absurd," said Margaret, "and I'm perfectly certain that neither Inspector MacMorran nor Mr. Bathurst wishes to listen to any more of your excuses. I shall end up by being sorry that I brought them over to talk to you. Anyhow, let's dance! Who's dying to dance with me?"

Before anybody could take up the invitation, Anthony heard the voice of Raymond Hurst, intimate and challenging. And he realized that the one contingency for which he hadn't bargained, when he had walked over to the Oliver table, had taken place. For unless Hurst were considerably dumber than Anthony imagined he was, he would, almost certainly, link up Garcia and Dewhurst with MacMorran's discreetly guarded inquiry concerning 'The Orange Lizard's' register of membership. Anthony wondered if MacMorran's thoughts were running on similar lines.

Hurst said: "I felt I must come and see how you were getting on. I should hate to neglect my duties as your host. I hope they're looking after you—my chaps. You *know* Señor and Señora Garcia? Really, I had no idea! Nice little club we have here, don't you think?"

Garcia answered the inquiry. Although Hurst had not addressed him. "Oh, yes, I have previously met these gentlemen. And if you are in any doubt, Hurst, I can assure you that the meeting was not occasioned by anything to my discredit."

"Of course not, Roderigo," said Dolores Garcia, "there is no need for you to say that. Do not be so silly. Everybody knows it. You are a man of honour—for one thing, you are not in Santa Guardina now. You are in London, the greatest city in the world. In London everybody respects and honours you. The idea! That you should consider it necessary to defend your honour. I am on the verge of being indignant."

David Oliver and Dewhurst laughed. But there was no laughter on the face of Raymond Hurst. Margaret Oliver, though, also began to laugh.

"I'm still waiting for somebody to ask me to dance. I've mentioned the matter before, incidentally! Am I to understand that the age of chivalry is dead—or am I so frightfully unattractive?"

Roderigo Garcia stepped forward. His dark face was flushed as he offered Margaret his arm. "Allow me, Miss Oliver."

"Thank you, Mr. Garcia . . . for steeling yourself to the ordeal."

Garcia and she swung away into the dance. As they swept away, MacMorran looked meaningly at Anthony.

"If it's all the same to you," he said pointedly, "I think we'll be pushing off. I must see the Duchess of Devizes with regard to her emeralds before I go home."

Anthony accepted the hint. "Yes, there's no ducking that, is there? For the moment I'd forgotten all about it." MacMorran turned to Hurst. "Thanks for the co-operation. And the same goes for the hospitality. Very nice of you." "A pleasure, I assure you."

The Inspector looked at the others. "Good-evening, everybody. Mr. Bathurst and I must be going, we've some work to do. I expect you'll be here for some time yet."

Anthony added his own valedictory. David Oliver lit a cigarette and tossed another to Dewhurst. It was not too accurately thrown from the point of view of direction but Dewhurst, diving low to his left, made a brilliant one-handed catch. Anthony smiled his appreciation.

"Say good-evening to Miss Oliver for me, Mr. Dewhurst. Will you, please? When she returns from her dance? Tell her that the Inspector insists on my going back to work. And to Señor Garcia, my salutations."

"Sure," said the young journalist, "only too delighted."

"That goes for me, too," added MacMorran—"please do the honours, will you?"

"I'll be doubly delighted," returned Dewhurst.

As they walked away, MacMorran eyed Anthony doubtfully. "What do you think Dewhurst really meant?"

Anthony grinned. "The same as you think, Andrew. And we're both dead right."

MacMorran frowned and muttered under his breath. "I don't know," said Anthony, with a light laugh, "that I can find it in my heart to blame him. After all, we . . . er . . . weren't exactly his cup of tea . . . "

Then MacMorran began to laugh. "No... I don't suppose we were."

CHAPTER 13

1

Anthony sat with MacMorran again. In the Inspector's private room at the "Yard". "I've a hell of a lot to talk to you about," said MacMorran, "but before I actually start on that, I want you to listen to certain phases of Greatorex's report of his autopsy. I'll read it to you." The Inspector donned his horn-rims and picked up a sheet of paper. "Er . . . ahem . . . er . . . er . . . ahem . . . autopsy on body of Peter Wilton Oliver . . . er . . .urm . . . urm . . . urm . . . blah . . . blah . . . you know all this . . . it's all familiar to you . . . I'll come to the part I want you to hear specially in a moment or so . . . here you are . . . here it is . . . contents of deceased's stomach . . . this is what Greatorex says . . . 'there is evidence that he had partaken of a meal some four or five hours before death . . . fish of some kind was the main constituent . . . the alcoholic content of the stomach was extremely low."

MacMorran leant back in his chair and tossed Greatorex's report back on to his table. "Goes your way, I agree—and not mine. Because it makes it moderately certain that Oliver had little or no food or drink after he had said good-night to Stella Forrest at Hammersmith station. Which means, too, it's a fairly safe bet he didn't go on to 'The Lizard' either then or at some time later."

Anthony nodded. "Yes, I think myself that it almost rules that out. Because it entirely supports Stella Forrest's story—that she and Peter had a meal at a restaurant. And it brings it to this. Whoever came to the house in Mayblossom Avenue, was welcomed and let in by Peter Oliver and finally cut the throat of the man who had admitted him."

"But why?" supplemented MacMorran.

"As you say but *why*? There is one thing, Andrew. You might check. Find out if a telephone call were put through to the Olivers' house in

Puck Willow between, say, nine o'clock on the Bank Holiday evening and midnight. Those two margins should give ample cover. It's just possible, I think, that that's what actually did happen. It was holiday time and many more people would be out of their houses than in. Any person going there for the purpose we're considering would probably not chance his arm. He'd be much more likely to make sure his quarry was at home. Or in other words that his journey was really necessary."

"I've already done it," replied MacMorran, "I saw things as you're seeing them and put a chit through to the P.M.G.'s people. I'm still waiting for their reply."

"Good. It will be interesting to see what turns up."

"I should think we ought to hear by to-morrow morning. In the meantime, there are those other matters I told you I wanted to talk to you about. They're to do with the Oliver family and what we'll call their attachments."

Anthony settled back in his chair. "I'm more than interested, Andrew. I'm all attention."

MacMorran coughed. "Since that visit of ours that evening to 'The Orange Lizard', I've called twice at the Oliver home in Mayblossom Avenue. I've seen the various members of the Oliver family. Don't get me wrong. I've not taken statements from them or anything like that—let us say, just between our two selves, that I've had a conversation with each one of them, individually, and of course entirely without prejudice. I mention that so you can have a clear idea of everything. I don't want you to be in the dark or to misunderstand anything."

Anthony nodded. "I get you, Andrew. Push on."

"I will. Anyhow, you see the position as I've outlined it. All of it voluntary, entirely without prejudice, as I said. The first person I saw at the house was the father, Oliver senior."

"Richard Guise," grinned Anthony.

"That's the idea. Richard Guise. On the day of his son's death he was in Scotland—in Aberdeen, to be exact. He'd been there for some days. On private business. On business to do with the estate of his deceased sister. His story is this. I'd like you to hear it. He didn't stay at an hôtel—he stayed at a private address. With friends of his late sister. When we first communicated with him with regard to the death of his son, we had to ask the Aberdeen Police to take a message to him. According to their version of everything—and we've looked at it quite closely—it was all above-board. As far as I can see on the statements made to us, we can definitely rule him out. Unless, of course, you've spotted something that everybody else has missed and want to argue about it."

Anthony grinned. "No, Andrew, I'm with you. You can eliminate Richard Guise. As far as I'm concerned. I'll toss him to you for the elimination stakes with yelps of delight. Elimination! Blessed word to an investigator. Same stable as Mesopotamia."

"Right. We agree on that, then. Then I had a word with Margaret again and, after her, with the mother, Mrs. Oliver. Let me see—what's her Christian name? I've got it here somewhere." MacMorran referred to a card. "Evelyn. Well, as you know, the evening that Peter Oliver died the two women were at Bournemouth. At the 'Suffolk Hôtel'. Spent Easter there. I contacted them myself at the hôtel by telephone after you and I had done that spot of unpleasant business in Mayblossom Avenue and after I'd 'phoned the telegram. They were certainly at the hôtel on the Monday afternoon and evening. The hôtel people confirm and Mrs. Oliver and her daughter also refer me to Mr. and Mrs. Andrew Murray, the bank manager and his wife, who also spent the Bank Holiday at Bournemouth and whom the two Olivers encountered in the Square at some time during the afternoon. They're not exactly 'Old Chinas', Mrs. Oliver explained to me, but they had met in the past through Peter and they recognized one another."

"Nothing in them meeting in Bournemouth," interrupted Anthony, "there'd be several thousand people in Bournemouth on a fine Bank Holiday. And the Square's the place to run into 'em. You could walk on their heads. Take it from me, I know, I've suffered there. Been pushed off the pavement on innumerable occasions."

"So have I," smiled back MacMorran, "more than once. My old lady's rather partial to Bournemouth. Anyhow, we can eliminate the two Oliver ladies. They're cancelled out. Will you agree on that?"

"Carried nem. con., Andrew. That's three of 'em we've got rid of."

"That's good. We're progressing. Only one member proper of the Oliver family left for inspection. That's David, the younger son. We met him for the first time at 'The Lizard' the other night with his girl friend. You remember him only too well. Well, I had a rather longer conversation with him at the house than with the others. Professionally, he's a teacher in a private school. In Chiswick somewhere. The name of the school is 'Parkin's College'. You know the kind of school it is. What you'd probably call a 'prep.' school. I think he told me they fed Nottborough. Parkin, the old boy who founded the place, is an Old Nottburian, so you can see the idea. Well, David went for a walking-tour over the Easter vacation. On his own. That's his story. The fellow he was going with, according to the original plan, went down with laryngitis a few days before they should have started. This other chap's also at Parkin's. Name of Charles Hassall."

"Where was this walking-tour, Andrew?"

"I've been into all that, and I'm absolutely satisfied. David Oliver went by train from Paddington to Gloucester. He started walking from there."

"What day was that?"

"Hold on, and I'll give you the full details. Then you needn't ask questions. I've been through the whole business with a small tooth-comb. He went to Gloucester on the afternoon of Maundy Thursday almost immediately after his school packed up for the holidays. Spent the night there, slept at a pastry-cook's in the High Street. I had the name and the full address. He was perfectly frank and open about it. Huckle Bros. On the Good Friday he walked to a place called Thornbury. I don't suppose you've ever heard of it. I hadn't."

"You wrong me, Andrew. You wrong me grievously. It's famous for its three Graces."

"How do you mean—Faith, Hope and—"

"No. 'W.G.', 'E.M.' and 'G.F.' The first grew a beard, the second was a Coroner—"

"I get you," growled MacMorran, "skip it! David Oliver slept the Friday night in Thornbury at a commercial hôtel—'Middlewicks' on the Bristol road. On the Saturday, Easter Eve to be precise, our young gent walked from Thornbury to Bristol where he spent the rest of the day."

"He didn't walk far that day," smiled Anthony, "perhaps his feet were sore because he hadn't put enough soap in his socks. But go on. This is all decidedly interesting."

"On the Saturday night, he slept at another baker's shop. At Clifton. Address and name supplied. Messrs. Clarke and Davis. 2A St. Brendans Road. On the Easter Sunday, he walked from Bristol to Bath. Asserts that he went to Evensong in the Abbey and spent the night in Bath. Pub. This time—all the shops shut, probably. 'The Golden Hind' in Hylton-Stewart Circus. That brings us—and him—to the Bank Holiday itself, Easter Monday. Our intrepid walker on that day walked to Salisbury. Spent the night there at a pub called 'The Haunch of Venison', near the market-square. Left Salisbury on the Tuesday morning and plodded his weary way up the Old Sarum road to Nether Wallop. He stayed in this neighbourhood a couple of days—I've got the address. That's where, on the Thursday sometime, the news of his brother's death caught up with him

Anthony was thinking. "Tell me, Andrew. How was that effected? Did you get the details?"

"It was like this. Margaret put me wise to it. David had arranged with her when he set out on this tour that she should write him *Poste Restante*, Nether Wallop. He'd make it his business to pick up the letter or whatever it was—clean shirt and socks, perhaps—at the Nether Wallop G.P.O. sometime after he arrived there. He reckoned, so he says, that it would be somewhere about the Wednesday or Thursday. Actually, he seems to have got there in front of himself. And that's what he says he eventually did—picked it up on the Thursday, I mean."

Anthony was still thinking hard. "You said, Andrew, I think some little time back—that you were perfectly satisfied? Yes?"

"Ye-es. As far as I've gone with it, undoubtedly."

"And how far may that be?"

"Well, I haven't checked the absolute details of the tour with the people at the various places where young Oliver states he stayed. But that's not being neglected. It's going to be done to-morrow. All the same, I'm perfectly satisfied with the boy himself and with the manner in which he told me all the story. Nobody could have been franker. And there's something else I'd say. Nobody could have shown a more genuine desire to co-operate than David Oliver did. I only wish I could say the same of all the people I have to deal with."

"That's the stuff. Pleased to hear you say it, Andrew. Now tell me, who's doing the rest of the check?"

"Chatterton. He's already gone to the West Country as a matter of fact. Left by car this morning. He has all the names and addresses together with the appropriate dates. He can nip from one to the other—the various places I mean. I don't know that I regard it as absolutely necessary, but nevertheless I'm having it done. After all, it's best to leave nothing to chance."

"I think you're being very wise, Andrew. Very wise, indeed. When Chatterton's report comes in, I'd like to have a 'dekko', if you don't mind."

"I'll remember that. No need to remind me."

"O.K., Andrew. Many thanks. Er . . . tell me this. How's Chatterton checking the *identity* as he goes the rounds?"

MacMorran smiled at the question. "Been waiting for that query to come over. And I bet I'll surprise you when you hear the answer. Young Oliver actually lent me a photo of himself as a help. It would be impossible to obtain a more speaking likeness. Chatterton's gone along, armed with it. Shouldn't be much wrong with that, should there?"

"Oliver certainly has been accommodating. Should be plain sailing for Chatterton, as you say. All the same, I'd still like to see his report when it comes through."

"You shall. Well, that's the 'gen' on David Oliver. We can't eliminate him, I'm afraid, as we did the other members of the family, but almost. Just a matter of waiting twenty-four hours for Chatterton to Ŏ.K. him. Well, that's the Oliver family. Oh, something else I'd forgotten. When I was at Mayblossom Avenue I had one more conversation. With Dewhurst. The journalist fellow. He happened to be there with Margaret when I blew along and he got in my way—as you might say." Anthony grinned.

"That's your way of putting it. I've seen similar things happen before. How did it go?"

"Well, as you know, Dewhurst is a journalist. On the staff of the *Morning Message*. He was on duty, he told me, more or less all over the Easter Holiday. Seeing that his girl friend was away at Bournemouth with her mother, I think that's very probably true. In a general sort of way. Ordinarily, with his girl on the spot, I expect he'd have spent some time, at least, round at the Olivers' house in Puck Willow. But with Margaret away at Bournemouth, the attraction wasn't there and he tells me that the Dewhurst nose was on the *Morning Message* grindstone pretty well all the time."

"How was he placed on the actual Bank Holiday?"

"Well," went on MacMorran rather slowly, "that went something like this. Very much a mixed bag. In the morning he says he looked in at the *Message* offices, messed around generally and then had lunch in a pub in Fleet Street. In the afternoon, he went to Craven Cottage and saw the League match between Fulham and Leicester City. After that, he says he went into the West End and did a 'Pub-crawl'. Towards midnight, he popped into 'The Orange Lizard' and joined a party which the Garcias were throwing. According to his story, knowing Margaret Oliver would be away on holiday, they'd invited him to join them."

MacMorran put down certain papers he'd been consulting and pushed back his chair. "There you are. That's the whole bag of tricks. The sum total of those conversational activities I mentioned when you came in."

"Extremely interesting. Thank you, Andrew. For the information and for the confidence. Later on, I must do a spot of sorting-out. Sorry to go off at a tangent for the moment. But I'm intrigued over something. Which, up to the point of going to Press, seems to have eluded me. Peter Oliver was a bank clerk. Richard Guise is a Corporation official. David's a teacher. Do you happen to know which profession or calling the fair Margaret graces?"

MacMorran stared at him in something like wonderment. "I've got it here somewhere. The girl told me in the course of our conversation. But what the hell does it matter? Just at this particular moment?"

Anthony shook his head. MacMorran saw from the expression on his face that he was serious. "I don't know, Andrew—I feel that I'd like to know, that's all. Then I can place all the members of the Oliver family in their proper niches. I like to be able to do that. Authentic background, you know. It usually helps me considerably."

MacMorran clawed at his papers. "You and your niches. Wait half a second and I'll find it for you." He flicked over several sheets of paper.

"Here we are. Margaret Oliver. I'll read you the notes I made after I had my conversation with the lady. The lady who was so sure from the very start that her brother was murdered. Here you are, and there's one for you to work out. Here we are . . . um . . . um, 'employed for the last four years by Messrs. Scarlett, Greene and Rhodes. Literary agents. Address, eleven Henrietta Street, Covent Garden. Typist and confidential secretary to Mr. Lawrence Greene, one of the partners.' Yes, and that reminds me. With regard to that, the girl told me as we went along—you might as well know it as not—that she was 'unusually well-paid for the job and liked both her work and the people she worked for, "very much".' I can tell you a few more facts about them, I looked them up."

Anthony shook his head and smiled again. "No need to tell me any more, Andrew. Thanks all the same. I know them very well, indeed. They're a highly reputable firm of literary agents. Known everywhere for their high standard of professional integrity. They, Bennett, Smythe and Co. and Archibald How, are probably the three best-known literary agents in this part of the world. Even, perhaps, in *any* part of it. Well, well, well—so Lady Margaret's with Scarlett, Greene and Rhodes, is she? Who'd have thought it? I'm glad I know that. May make a difference. And she's Lawrence Greene's confidential secretary? I'll say she likes her job! Very few wouldn't. Unusually charming fellow, Lawrence Greene. Many thanks, Andrew, for the information. You're a veritable human gold-mine."

MacMorran replaced the papers in a file. He eyed Anthony steadily. "Are you on to anything? You sound to me as though you might be."

"Just vaguely perhaps, Andrew. Not an inch more. There *are*, perhaps, one or two little points beginning to look something like the traditional sore thumb. But only 'beginning'. Tell you what I'll do. I'll see you again in a day or so."

"Good. I won't forget Chatterton's report on David Oliver's West-country walking-tour. You shall have that as soon as possible."

Anthony rose. "Very nice of you, Andrew. 'Phone me if anything special turns up."

2

The telephone rang insistently. Anthony leant over from his armchair and picked up the receiver.

"Good-morning, Andrew. Yes . . . I felt pretty confident it was you. I know what the time is. You've always been a consistent worm-catcher. Who? Me? Good lord, I've done a day's work already. O.K., then—I've a receptive ear. Pour the stuff into it."

MacMorran's bantering tone changed. "I've got Chatterton's report on the David Oliver walking-tour in front of me on my table. You asked for the particulars as soon as I had them."

"Ah, Chatterton! That reminds me. Something I've slipped. Before you start it, Andrew, let me apologize and take you back a little way."

"How far?"

"Oh, not so far as all that. Chatterton's previous assignment. Re the surprising and sensational return of the San Jonquilo Bonds. Weren't they registered at a Post-office in the Charing Cross area? Didn't you tell me that? Well, what, if anything, did Chatterton pick up when he ferreted round?"

"Not a lot. I thought I'd told you. That the packet to be registered was handed across the counter by a tall, dark-haired 'foreign-looking' man. According to the girl-clerk—'middle-aged' and 'with something of an accent'."

"No. You didn't tell me. My fault entirely. I forgot to remind you. I'm thinking of that description. Was it Garcia himself, do you think?"

"Garcia's not tall. Rather the reverse, I should say. Wake those ideas of yours up."

Anthony chuckled into the telephone receiver. "Tallness is relative, Andrew. To a girl behind the counter of a Post-office, five feet seven may smack of the family of Anak, especially if her own size is round about five-five. I was going rather on the other points of the description. Dark-haired, foreign-looking and middle-aged. Also—the accent. Still, never mind now—we can come back to it if necessary at some other time. Now get on and tell me about the West-country walk."

"Well, it's quite brief. In a nutshell, Chatterton found it 'okayed' everywhere. He called at the various addresses with which David Oliver had furnished me, and when the different people that Chatterton interviewed saw the photograph he carried with him, they recognized it, according to his report, without the slightest trouble or demur. Actually, Chatterton ran into no stickiness anywhere. Clean sheet at every contact."

Anthony scratched his chin as he pondered these matters. "Where did Chatterton finish up, Andrew?"

"G.P.O. Nether Wallop, my lad. Absolutely the right place. Where Master David picked up the letter from his sister."

"Why didn't David's family use the Radio to find him? Should have been quicker than an ordinary letter."

The Inspector nodded. "I agree. I asked Mrs. Oliver that same question. When I was at the house. It was because David scarcely ever put up at hôtels. That was her explanation. Nearly always at a shop or private house. They argued, that, walking as he was, and staying at places like that, he wouldn't be certain to hear the broadcast news."

"H'm. Something in it, I suppose. Well, what do we do now—eliminate David?"

"We certainly do," responded MacMorran, "in the light of what I've just given you. Nothing else for it. I take it, you don't disagree?"

Anthony scratched his chin again. "No-o. I suppose not. The only thing is, Andrew, the way we're going on, we haven't much left. We're scrubbing all of 'em."

"I couldn't agree more. But one must look facts in the face. To say nothing of the fact that there's the motive question still to be settled. We're just as far off that to-day, as we ever were."

"I'll tell you what you've got to do, Andrew, I keep coming back to it, I know—but you must give it priority, you've got to find Stella Forrest. I've a strong hunch that it would pay fat dividends."

The Inspector shrugged his shoulders.

"Can't see it myself. Dashed if I can. The girl's naturally knocked over and intends to start life afresh somewhere else. But I've told you all that before."

"The difference, my dear Andrew, which you steadfastly refuse to see, lies between being 'naturally knocked over', to use your own words, and scramming for dear and sheer life. Because the latter, in my opinion, is what Stella Forrest has undoubtedly done. Time will prove which of us is right. Anyhow, many thanks for the 'gen' re David Oliver. Bar the question of that telephone-call I spoke to you about, I seem to be up to date on most matters now. By the way, one last question before you ring off—when you went to Mayblossom Avenue for your various interviews, did you happen to have a word with the old lady next door?"

"The old lady next door? I don't know that—why, should I have—"

Anthony interrupted. "Don't you remember? The old girl who passed the time of evening with Stella when she called at the Olivers' house on the Easter Tuesday. Reference bath-water, morning papers and milk-bottles."

"I did not. I didn't see that it was indicated. I still don't see. Why? What's your point?"

"Nothing specific that I could lay a tongue round. Just generalities. You never know, you know, with the really genuine 'old girl' type. Amazing what they pick up in the course of the day's nose. For all we know, this one that prattled to Stella in the porches may well be the eyes and ears of Puck Willow. Think, my dear Andrew, what a Golconda she might turn out to be from our point of view—properly handled."

"You're a ruddy optimist, no more and no less, if you think you'll be able to—excuse me for a moment, there's an interruption."

Anthony waited. He could hear MacMorran talking to a third party at the other end of the line. The interruption lasted for some little time. Eventually the Inspector's voice came through to him again.

"Sorry to keep you waiting. However, I'm clear now. And you didn't wait for nothing. The interruption was highly opportune. It was the reply to that query about that possible telephone-call. To Peter Oliver on the Bank Holiday evening. Or rather *to the house* where he was. Well, the answer's the one you want. Right down your street. There *was* a call. The P.M.G.'s crowd have traced it. Got to congratulate you again, I suppose."

Anthony's lip curled in a grimace. "Skip it, Andrew. Cut the cackle. There's a murderer running loose somewhere while we're nattering and Stella Forrest hasn't been found. What time was the call? Did you get that?"

"You bet I did. Twenty-three minutes past ten."

"From a call-box, of course?"

"How right you are."

"Near at hand. That's my guess—no, not a guess, much more than that, a three-starred nap."

"I said how right you were. To be exact, the call-box is about one hundred and fifty yards from the Oliver house in Mayblossom Avenue. And that's straight from the pillar-box's mouth."

"I thought so. Sorry, Andrew, but I must say it. That was to confirm that Peter was in, and also, by inquiry, if he were alone. All the same, Andrew, why use the old man's 'those were the days' razor? Don't get that, do you? Still, Andrew, once again, many thanks for the 'gen'—I'll be seeing you." Anthony hung up. There was perhaps the vital ray of light just beginning to filter through.

CHAPTER 14

1

The time had most certainly come, Anthony thought, as he sat in his chair following on MacMorran's telephone conversation, for him "to take stock". He always liked to do this with a problem when it was proving unduly difficult and obstinate. Which was very definitely the case with this "Oliver Bath" murder. Unhappily for Anthony's peace of mind, Stella Forrest had disappeared. According to MacMorran there was no news of her from any source. And he hadn't the slightest notion of how to find her, bearing in mind the awkward condition that MacMorran of all people regarded the girl's defection as relatively unimportant.

The exercise of "taking stock", however, merely served to bring home to Anthony only too clearly the fact that, as an investigator, his cupboard with regard to the present problem was distinctly on the bare side. In addition, he had certain doubts which refused to be dissipated.

Should he make one more contact before he sat down for his customary essay into the territory of elimination (not necessarily of the MacMorran type) or should he burn his boats and get to work with fountain-pen and paper at once? Anthony mentally debated the question from all angles. If only he had been enabled to have had that second interview with Stella Forrest. After the discovery of Peter Oliver's body. Wherever his thoughts travelled to, they invariably and inevitably came back to that point. And he was forced to admit it to himself—there was still the second impasse. Motive! The detective's eternal headache. The age-old question. Where was there any semblance of motive in the problem under review? Had the murder been fortuitous? Born of sudden and venomous passion? Or had the murderer on the other hand made the telephone-call, spoken to his intended victim, and gone to the house with deliberate murder in his heart? If so, how could the choice of the weapon be accounted for? An old razor belonging to Oliver senior. *Unless the murderer had known it was there.* Yes, there was something there perhaps. Something, too, which narrowed down the field from which the murderer could come. How many people in the cast *would have known* of the existence of that ancient razor?

There would be Richard Oliver, David, Margaret, Evelyn the mother—and just possibly Margaret's *fiancé*, Dewhurst. No doubt upon occasions, such as Christmas perhaps or Summer week-ends, Dewhurst might well have stayed with his *fiancée's* family and used the Mayblossom Avenue bathroom.

Five of them! And every man Jack and woman Jill in these five had a perfect alibi. Stay, though—that statement wasn't inexorably true. Much of Dewhurst's alibi for the Easter Monday was unverified and unsupported. Anthony ran over it in his mind. Hung about in the morning. Football match in the afternoon. After that, a round of pubs in the West End. Towards midnight (Anthony remembered the words) had joined a Garcia party at "The Orange Lizard". Good lord, not much real alibi in any of that. Surely MacMorran could see that? Just a minute, though! Wasn't there something he was forgetting? Margaret's original statements with regard to the bath?

Anthony marshalled his thoughts.

There was something of the highest importance here—he felt positive of it—if he could only grasp it before it eluded him. He must make no mistake.

The murderer had deliberately staged the crime so that it indubitably cried "suicide". Razor in dead man's hand—left-handed gash in the throat. Murderer must have known, therefore, that the dead man was left-handed. Right! That, then, was established.

But and the vital point was contained here somewhere— the murderer had a bath after the crime was committed. Or before? *Each* was possible— but the former the more likely. Still, that for the time being wasn't of paramount importance. And, when it came ultimately to be investigated, the bath which the murderer had, would, like the murderer's act, surely be laid at the victim's door. "Peter Oliver," everybody will say, who comes to investigate the affair, "bathed himself at sometime during the evening."

But, according to Margaret Oliver's statement, the murderer either *forgot* or *didn't know* Peter Oliver's invariable habit concerning the disposal of the plug-chain when he had finished his bathing. So that directly she saw the conditions of the used bath she *knew* for a *certainty* that the man who had last been in it *had not been her dead brother.*

"Now where have I got to?" thought Anthony. "What people in the cast are there who knew *(a)* of the existence of Richard Oliver's old razor, *(b)* that Peter Oliver was left-handed but who *didn't* know *(c)* of Peter's post-bath habit with the plug- chain?"

Anthony worked out the answer and then when he arrived at it, began to shake his head. It seemed to him that all the people who were aware of clauses *(a)* and *(b)* knew, too, of clause *(c)* and—which was altogether worse and more discouraging from Anthony's own point of view—all the people who qualified for *(a)* and *(b)* were also the *only* people who could *not* do similarly for clause *(c)* as he had constructed it. In other words, all he had tried to effect had led to complete stultification and cancellation.

Anthony tried again. Clause *(a)* was particular—and the people who qualified for it must be limited as regards number. Clause *(b)* was general. Doubtless included many. Clause *(c)*, however, was as particular as clause *(a)*, and by reason of its *negative* nature came to this state of cancellation. Anthony mused over his problem.

To arrive at the identity of Peter Oliver's murderer he wanted a man (or woman) who knew of the father's razor, who was familiar with Peter's left-handed propensities, but who was ignorant of his personal post-bathing habits. It seemed to him, as he thought it over, that Dewhurst was the one and only possibility. Unless—Anthony rose from his chair and began to pace the room.

Supposing the murderer was a cunning scoundrel who budgeted for the possibility of the suicide bluff being called? What then? He might have. It was well on the cards. The wisest murderer is he who covers as many of his tracks as possible. Yes, it was a likely contingency all right. The killer in this murder wasn't deficient in intelligence by any means. The brains were there. Consider the cool business of the bath itself.

Anthony could see that this new idea which he had conjured up held a vista of several intriguing possibilities.

Take the murderer's possible reasoning, to begin with. If the police did reject the suicide theory and came down on the side of murder—despite all the subtle precautions that had been taken and cleverness used—the man who *then* knew all the answers might well have a large label marked "Guilty" pinned securely to his coat. There'd be a healthy focus of spotlight on him for a certainty. It might well be a good thing *not* to know all the answers.

Anthony sat down again in his chair wondering whether he'd really got somewhere at last.

There was one thing at least which loomed large in front of him— something that he *must* do.

He must reconnoitre the ground in the vicinity of the Oliver house at Puck Willow. He had not been there since he, MacMorran and Margaret Oliver had come away from Mayblossom Avenue on the Wednesday of Easter Week.

The evening—Anthony's thoughts began to wander again— when Richard Oliver had been in Aberdeen, when Margaret and Evelyn had been in Bournemouth and had received the message emanating from MacMorran that Peter was dead and the evening when David had been in the neighbourhood of Nether Wallop in the county of Hants. Waiting for a letter from his sister.

2

Anthony walked from Puck Willow station in the early hours of the evening. Much in the same way as Stella Forrest had walked when her heart and intelligence had told her so persistently that all was not well with her lover, Peter Oliver.

He had two main objects in view. One—to look over the lie of the land generally, which he knew he should have done before, and two—to visit the old lady who, as he had indicated to MacMorran, might prove to be, under judicious handling, the eyes and ears of Puck Willow.

The first thing that Anthony desired to find and to look at was the telephone-kiosk from which, on the night of the murder, the call had been made to the Oliver residence. Now that he knew for certain about this call, Anthony had definite ideas with regard to this telephone-box and wanted to put them to the test.

Actually he came to the turning named Mayblossom Avenue before he was able to find the telephone-kiosk for which he was looking. Which fact, to his pleasure, tallied with his memory. For the reason that he had not noticed any telephone-box when he had come to Puck Willow previously. He recalled the terms of MacMorran's statement. "About one hundred and fifty yards away from the house." In that case, he argued to himself, the box must be in the opposite direction to that in which I've been travelling. Anthony therefore walked down Mayblossom Avenue past the Oliver house. He came to the end of the avenue. There was no kiosk in it anywhere. Which way should he turn now?

Anthony looked to the right and to the left. There seemed to be more houses to the left than to the right so Anthony chose the former direction. It turned out that he had taken the turning he needed.

The telephone-box was on a corner, about sixty yards distant.

Anthony came to it. What he saw pleased him. It fitted the theory he was beginning to nourish.

The red, glass-panelled box stood on the corner of what was really no more than a lane. A few paces away from the box was a clearing—a patch of waste ground, covered with grass and small, partly cut-down trees.

Once upon a time, Anthony guessed, it had been fairly thickly wooded and reasonably like a small plantation. Anthony walked towards it, that he might see the place better and in greater detail.

When he came alongside it, his pleasure increased at what he saw. He was considering this piece of ground now from the point of a man in a car.

In a car at night. Anthony endeavoured to reconstruct certain incidents as it occurred to him that they might well have happened. The car could be halted on the corner where the telephone-box stood for the driver to alight, slip into the box and use the telephone. There would be no necessity to conceal the car from the public until it was established for certain that *(a)* Peter Oliver was at home and that *(b)* he was *alone in the house.* Which questions would arise from the telephone-call and be answered either one way or the other.

Then, as a natural sequel, would come the question of concealing the car. It would be a sound proposition, from all points of view, if the car remained well in the background of events. The fewer the number of people who saw it, the fewer would remember it, and the fewer that remembered it, the better.

Well as Anthony looked at the place in front of him—what could be more convenient for the activities he had just depicted to himself? This was a most isolated spot and the car could be easily run on to the grass behind the telephone-kiosk, the lights switched off, and who would be the wiser? This effected, the murderer of Peter Oliver would be in a position to complete the journey to Mayblossom Avenue on foot. And nobody would be in a position to cry either "wolf" or "car" when the time came for the crying. If ever indeed the time *did* come.

3

Anthony walked slowly back to Mayblossom Avenue. He felt positive now, from what he had just seen, that the murderer had come by car on that Easter Monday evening. The man who had cut Peter Oliver's throat knew where the razor was, the old razor that hadn't been in service for years, knew that his victim was left-handed, may or may not have known the essentials of the plug-chain in the bath, and in addition, drove a car.

David didn't drive a car, in the ordinary course of things. He had spent the Easter break on a walking-tour. Keen motorists aren't, as a rule, too fond of Shanks's pony. Even if it were possible to prove that a man might—Anthony shook his head impatiently at himself. The usual irritating things were crowding upon each other, a step forward and then, almost on its heels, a step back again. To the tantalizing territory of status quo.

And then, as he walked towards the houses again, yet another thought popped up in Anthony's brain. Supposing there had been *two* men concerned with the murder? Supposing, that is, the murderer had been accompanied? In the car. Which might have belonged to the other man. This other man might have driven the car.

And, going on from there, this other man might, conceivably, have remained in the car after the telephoning while the murderer made his way to the house in Mayblossom Avenue and did the job. He might even have cruised round *in* the car while the job was being done. Round and round the houses. Not stayed put anywhere.

Just a minute, Anthony was thinking again. The car might even have been a "taxi". Hired. An ordinary taxi-cab plying for hire. "Put me down by the telephone-kiosk at the corner of Thingumajig Road—that will do me very nicely—I'll show you where I mean, driver, when I come to it." That would be a good deal sounder than definitely booking the taxi to Mayblossom Avenue. Far less risky, in case questions were asked afterwards. "Here we are, thank you, driver, this will suit me nicely, what's the damage? Three half-crowns, sir, and—thank you, sir. Lovely day it's been, hasn't it? Marvellous. Thank you very much, sir, and all the very best. Good-night to you, sir." A taxi. From town? Or merely from Wimblefield?

Again Anthony fell to wonderment.

Either contingency would have met the purpose. But it would mean two lines of inquiry. He must see MacMorran about both of them directly he got back.

In the meantime he'd do the sensible thing and kill the second Puck Willow bird with the one stone. He'd see the old lady who was the neighbour of the Olivers. What was the name now? Ah, yes—Edwards. He was almost on the house now. He must be. Anthony checked his position. Ah, yes, he thought, he couldn't be far away. Three doors off.

A few more strides and Anthony had walked up the path, made the porchway and knocked on the front door. When it slowly opened, Anthony saw the old lady herself. Her old-fashioned spectacles had slipped almost to the tip of her nose and her hair was grey and wispy. But the eyes which the spectacles covered were bright, beady and inquisitive and the glance which shot from the venerable face betokened, at least, no small measure of native shrewdness and feminine curiosity. Anthony raised his hat gallantly. "Good-evening, Mrs. Edwards. My name is Bathurst, and here's my card. Can you read it in this half-light or shall I—"

Interruption came with immediate annoyance. In the shape of a reedy voice from somewhere in the recesses of the house.

"What is it, Alice—tell them we've got plenty or that we don't want any—and come in."

The sound of the man's voice was quickly followed by the sight of the owner of the voice. A thin, scraggy, nervous-looking man appeared in the depths of the hall—all nose, dental china and Adam's apple.

"What is it?" he cried again querulously—"and who are you—we don't all want to be murdered in our beds. One's enough to be going on with."

Alice, his wife, passed Anthony's card on to him. He found glasses and peered at it, while Anthony waited, as though it were some strange new kind of Life which was confronting him in the reality of which, despite the evidence of his senses, he could scarcely believe. Alice, the old lady, said something to him in a low voice.

"All right," he said in a mumbling kind of reply, "all right. Have it your own way. *Personally*, I'd much rather keep myself out of this kind of thing. It usually leads to any amount of bother to say nothing of actual trouble—which at our age we can very well do without."

Alice spoke again. "I know," he replied peevishly—"I know all about that. I *know* we're supposed to help the Police—I don't want you to tell me. But we needn't go out of our way to—"

The old girl cut into his verbal complainings without further ado. "Will you please come in, Mr. Bathurst? I can see where you're from and it hasn't taken me long to guess what you've come about. I may be old, but I'm not daft—yet. One's enough in a house."

Her eyes were greedy with interest and avid with curiosity. Anthony felt, as he entered the house, that as far as "type" was concerned, she was, for him, a Heaven-sent blessing and a golden opportunity even though the husband attached might be just about as useful as a sick headache.

Anthony found himself in the best room—in Alice Edwards's lounge. Mr. Edwards had gone ahead and switched on the light. The room was cold but Anthony realized as he sat down that he would be forced to put up with that discomfort. Edwards had switched on the light—that was quite enough expenditure for one evening—he certainly wasn't switching on the electric fire.

"We've been wondering, Mrs. Edwards," Anthony opened, "if you'd be kind enough to let me have a little further information with regard to the evening when that unhappy affair next door took place. That is to say, the evening of Easter Monday—the Bank Holiday. Chief Detective-Inspector MacMorran, of Scotland Yard, has suggested that I come to see you. He is inclined to think that my information from you will be of the highest possible value."

Edwards looked across the room at Anthony. The look was heavy-laden with apprehension. "What is it, sir—murder? Because if that's the case, it only comes back to what I said to the wife in the first place—"

Anthony smiled and shook his head. "No. We mustn't jump to conclusions. The Police have still an open mind, Mr. Edwards. At the moment we're sifting everything. Every tiny piece of evidence which comes our way."

"Ah," said Edwards eloquently, "I understand." He shook his head profoundly, crossed his legs and clasped his knee between his hands.

Anthony thought, "wrong again, old chap" and as the thought registered, in came Mrs. Edwards.

"What was it you came to ask us about to-night, sir?" And then her voice changed—her eyes shone with the glint of sheer naked inquisitiveness. "Do the Olivers know you're in here with us? Or is it a secret operation?"

"No-o, Mrs. Edwards," replied Anthony sizing up the true merit of the situation, "the Inspector insisted that I should see you and you only.

Not the people next door. He was strong on the point. He made no bones about it—'Mr. and Mrs. Edwards—they're the people,' he said. 'And in their own house'."

The old lady's face was wreathed in pleasure and satisfaction at the Bathurst tribute. She edged nearer to him on her chair. "Please go on, sir. What was it you wanted specially to know?"

"Well, this is the question. Did you hear a car that night? Call next door? At *any* time during the evening?"

"No. Did we, Ernest?"

"No," replied the man of the house.

"I take it," continued Anthony, "that in the normal course of events comparatively few cars would come down this avenue? It leads nowhere much, does it?"

"I agree," said Edwards, "nearly all the cars that do come down here do so to bring folk to the various houses—either people living in the avenue or people visiting friends here. I reckon that's how you figured it out, didn't you?"

"I did, Mr. Edwards

"Well, you're quite right."

"Good," smiled Anthony—"now then and going on from there you heard the front door of your neighbours slam fairly late during the evening. You originally thought—and very naturally, too—that it was Peter Oliver going out. Now, of course, in the light of what has transpired, that's by no means so certain. It may *not* have been Peter Oliver. And it's to do with that incident which I've just mentioned that I want to ask you another question. You've stated that you heard the front door slam at about half past eleven. That is so, isn't it?"

Mrs. Edwards nodded eagerly. "That's quite right. I'll stick to that. As near to half past eleven as could be."

Anthony leant forward. "Well, then, try to take your minds back to that moment. Did you happen to hear a car anywhere in the avenue fairly soon after you heard the front door slam?" The old lady looked across at her husband directly Anthony put the question. Edwards returned the compliment and gazed at her. Each slowly shook a head. Edwards began to reply in his thin, querulous voice.

"I wouldn't say anything like 'soon after' because candidly I can't remember. I always think it's difficult to look back on a *period* of time and say afterwards how long it actually was. Very difficult indeed."

Edwards shook his head again as though disclaiming his own doubt. But he brightened up and continued almost immediately. "As a matter of fact, though, now that you've mentioned it, there *is* something that I *do* happen to remember. It's suddenly come back to me. No doubt your question prompted it. And it's this. Not so very long after the wife and I heard the front door shut next door—she went up to bed and I started to bolt up for the night. My usual job of work—the very last thing I do. Well, when I went to our front door to draw the bolts, I looked through the glass panel of the door and I noticed that the front gate wasn't shut. One of the tradesmen that called here during the day had probably not taken the trouble to close it properly and it had swung open. Well—it may be a whim or a kink of mine—I don't like my front gate open. In fact, I dislike it very much. The blessed dogs are such a nuisance. Leave their cards everywhere. Ought to be a tax on the whole dam' lot of 'em. So on the spur of the moment I went out and closed the gate. And as I did so, a car went by. Now I *did* happen to notice that, because in my opinion, for what it's worth, it was travelling extremely fast. Much faster than average. Now your question of a moment ago brought all that back to me."

Mrs. Edwards looked at her husband approvingly. She was delighted with this latest effort of his. He was proving worthy of her. In the meantime, Anthony had listened with keen interest.

"You've no idea, I suppose, what kind of car it was? Colour, size, make—anything of those natures?"

Edwards laughed a throaty laugh. His Adam's apple worked well under pressure.

"Too dark. It was getting on for mid-night. Far too dark for me to see anything like that."

"I was afraid you'd say that. But you'll be able to answer my next question. In which direction was it travelling?"

"Up the road. That is to say—going towards Puck Willow village and of course the railway-station."

"Coming from—'no man's land'?"

"If you like to call it that—*or possibly* from one of the houses lower down the avenue."

"But the avenue is quite short and you said the car was travelling extremely fast. Doesn't that seem to indicate it had come from somewhere farther away?"

Edwards nodded. "I get your point. Yes, you're quite right. It must have come, I should say, from somewhere farther away than any of the houses down the avenue. But is it important? Personally, I can't understand why—"

"That remains to be seen, Mr. Edwards. The Police hold certain theories and while they hold them, each one has to be tested."

"Of course, of course," said the old lady—"how many times have I told you that, Ernest, when we've been arguing? Why, I can remember, in the case of the Bognor murder—when the poor girl was found buried on the beach—there was no end to the trouble the Police took. My sister knew the railway-guard who was on the train—"

Anthony nodded. "You've an amazingly fine memory, Mrs. Edwards. Remarkable indeed for your age. I don't know that I've ever met its equal." He rose. "I won't take up any more of your valuable time," he said engagingly—"please accept my best thanks for the information."

He shook hands with the old lady and her husband. Edwards accompanied him to the front door. "If it *should* come to a murder-trial—could you scrounge a couple of tickets for me and the old lady? I've always wanted to hear the words of the death sentence and see the black cap go on."

"I assure you, Mr. Edwards," said Anthony. "I'll do my best for you."

4

Anthony walked to the top of Mayblossom Avenue, hesitated on the corner for a matter of seconds and then turned back again. After all, he argued to himself, there's no point ever in neglecting an opportunity whether it be an open goal or a ball hit in the air. The Gods that be have a disagreeable habit of not forgiving people who squander opportunities such as these.

So Anthony retraced his steps and knocked on the door of Number 8 Mayblossom Avenue—the house of the Oliver family. To his pleasure and satisfaction, it was Margaret who opened the door to him. Her face flashed into warm welcome. Unless she were an exceptionally gifted actress, she was equally pleased to see him.

"Mr. Bathurst! Oh—but please come in. Am I pleased to see you? Why didn't you 'phone us and say you were coming?"

Anthony smiled at her warmth. "It's not too late, then, for me to come in and have a talk?"

"Late? At this time of the evening? I should say not. We're not early birds in the Oliver family, I'm afraid."

Margaret closed the door and shepherded Anthony into the hall. "We're all at home with the exception of David. It's just gloom in this house these days. Mummie and Daddy are knocked right out by our trouble. I suppose it's only what one can expect. I'm afraid they'll never really recover. They're too old for one thing—and of course, for another, Peter was the son and heir. But the house is a Morgue."

"I understand," said Anthony.

"Bob's with them," added Margaret—"that does take it off a bit. I'll take you in. We're all in the dining-room. Come along." Anthony went in on Margaret's announcement and she made the necessary introduction.

Mrs. Oliver was the one occupant of the room whom he had not met before. It was easy to see that in her youth she must have been extremely attractive for she was a good-looking woman even now in her middle age. She was tall and graceful, with full blue eyes and a well-shaped nose. Her glittering white hair showed signs of meticulously careful dressing and contrasted elegantly with the black dress she was wearing.

Dewhurst rose abruptly as Anthony entered the room. If Margaret were pleased at Anthony's arrival and showed it, Dewhurst certainly wasn't and didn't. But he camouflaged his real feelings with an overplayed smile as the two men shook hands. Anthony explained and confessed that the reason behind his call was not entirely social.

"Actually," he concluded, "I wanted to meet you, Mrs. Oliver, because I'm wondering whether you'd help me by discussing one or two matters with me. I should have come to see you before this but I had no wish to seem precipitate. Your daughter has doubtless told you about our first meeting—hers and mine I mean, of course."

"Yes, Mr. Bathurst, Margaret has told me all about it. I must thank you. How she came to your flat on that dreadful Wednesday evening." Evelyn Oliver spoke simply and well. "But I'm sorely afraid," she went on, "that I can't tell you very much."

Richard Oliver moved rather uneasily in his chair and looked anxious at the turn the conversation had taken. He glanced at his wife with evident concern.

"My wife isn't too well, Mr. Bathurst as you may well guess after all this business. I hope you won't tax her too much or worry her unduly."

Dewhurst added his semi-protest. "Mr. Oliver's quite right, you know, Bathurst" he said rather effusively. "I hope that we *can* rely—"

Anthony cut in. "Please don't worry," he smiled. "Actually I feel you're being just a trifle uncomplimentary to me. I shall have to appoint Miss Oliver as my advertising agent if you're going to look on me as a human scourge. Get her to prepare the way for me."

Margaret showed appropriate indignation. "Please, Mr. Bathurst," she said almost heatedly, "don't take any notice of them. You ought to know better, Bob. Fancy imagining such a thing. And please remember what Mr. Bathurst has already done for me. Just to help me. He need not have done. Had he pleased himself in the matter, he needn't have raised a finger, he could have ignored me and my requests—altogether."

Bob Dewhurst grinned. "Seem to have put my foot into it, don't I? Not the first time, though—or the last, I expect. All right then, forget what I said."

Mrs. Oliver herself closured the argument. "Please don't fuss. What was it, Mr. Bathurst, that you wanted to ask me? Then all my champions who have so suddenly sprung up will be able to see for themselves that you're not ill-treating me. There's one thing, though, I must say it's shown Bob in a new light. I've never known him to be so solicitous on my account."

Dewhurst heard the crack and shrugged his shoulders rather ostentatiously. Anthony came back to the position that had been his some little time previously.

"What I'd like to discuss with you, Mrs. Oliver, is quite simple and straightforward. And there is nothing secret about it either. It doesn't matter, for instance, if everybody in the room with us now hears the discussion."

Evelyn Oliver nodded. But she looked prim and her lips were set. "Is it about my son, Peter?"

"Yes."

"Very well, Mr. Bathurst, ask me then—and if I can I'll answer you."

"You can answer this all right. I feel pretty certain. Had your son spoken to you recently with regard to any sentimental attachment that he had formed? In other words, Mrs. Oliver, was there a lady in the case?"

Evelyn's face cleared suddenly. "Yes, I can answer that. And the answer is 'yes' again."

"How long ago did this happen, Mrs. Oliver?"

Evelyn considered the question. "I can tell you the exact day. It was on Shrove Tuesday. I made an extra supply of pancakes for Peter's dinner that evening when he came in from the bank. That's how I can remember it."

"That's excellent. Did he tell you the lady's name?"

"Yes. Stella something. I'm sorry I can't recall the surname, but I *think* it began with an 'F'. Was it Fulton? Or something like Fulton? That seems to be the name in my mind."

Anthony shook his head. "Not—not Fulton, Mrs. Oliver, but I know what you mean and I think I get the association. It was 'Forrest', wasn't it?"

Mrs. Oliver nodded. "Yes, that's it. 'Forrest'."

"Good. Now did your son tell you something about the young lady?"

Evelyn wrinkled her brow. "General things, do you mean, or particular?"

"Well—particular, chiefly. That was the idea in my mind when I asked the question. Did he give you any details about her?"

"Yes. There was one thing he told me—that the girl worked as a cashier in a restaurant fairly near Delaney's bank—I mean fairly near to Lombard Street. I think he said that was where he had first met her."

"Good again. Anything more than that?"

"That she was young—I forget the age that Peter said—and, of course, amazingly lovely—they always *were* that. Either 'perfectly marvellous' blondes or 'absolutely smashing' brunettes."

Anthony wasn't sure if the tone of her voice held bitterness or merely ironic humour. "Nothing about the young lady's family?""

"Nothing."

"Or where she came from?"

"Not a word, Mr. Bathurst. Nothing whatever with regard to her antecedents or family or anything like that."

"Well, that's explicit enough, Mrs. Oliver, to suit anybody." Anthony knew that everybody in the room had been listening intently to the exchanges of the conversation and none more keenly than Robert Dewhurst. He very carefully worded, therefore, his next question.

"Was this information that your son passed on to you, Mrs. Oliver, with regard to this love-affair of his, to be regarded as confidential? Was that *his* intention?"

Mrs. Oliver hesitated before she answered. Anthony cut in again before she could find words.

"Let me help you, Mrs. Oliver. What I meant was this. Did you son say when he confided in you, 'now—this is between you and me, Mother—please don't tell anybody else'?"

"No. He certainly did *not* say that." Mrs. Oliver gave the answer and paused. "At the same time—I'd like to make myself clear I regarded it—what he had told me, I mean—*in the nature of* a confidence. Actually, I *kept* it to myself. Er . . . more or less."

Anthony was in like a flash. "Not entirely?"

Again, Mrs. Oliver was slow to reply. "Well . . . I want to be truthful. *Absolutely* truthful. And careful what I say. Because I've got sufficient common-sense to know that if I'm *not* absolutely truthful in the answers I give you I shan't be helping you. I *did* tell one or two people . . . just in a general sort of way. No more than that. I couldn't be really specific and tell anybody any details because I didn't know the girl's full name . . . to be absolutely sure of it. I'd forgotten it. And if you're talking romance to people and don't know the young lady's name—well, Mr. Bathurst, I ask you!"

Anthony nodded. "I can take it then, that you gave *nobody* the full name of Stella Forrest in connexion with any love-affair of your son Peter?"

"You can, Mr. Bathurst, very definitely. I can assure you the fact. As I said just now, until you mentioned the name a few moments ago, it had eluded me most successfully. I doubt whether it would ever have come to me again."

"Thank you, Mrs. Oliver. You've been of tremendous assistance to me. In a way I'm sorry you've answered as you have, because your replies don't exactly suit one or two little theories I'd formed, but there you are—I must put up with that. I can't always have things go my way and the absolute truth's the best for everybody in the long run."

"No more questions?" smiled Mrs. Oliver.

Anthony shook his head. "No. No more questions."

"I'm pleased to hear that," contributed Richard Oliver. "I was beginning to get a bit worried as you kept on. I don't want the wife's strength overtaxed."

Anthony turned to Margaret. "It's your show now, Miss Oliver. But it will be very brief and distinctly to the point."

Dewhurst was still looking as pleased as a dog with no tail. Margaret's smile in Anthony's direction failed to improve matters—at any rate not so much that you'd notice it.

"What do you want to ask me?" opened Margaret.

"Just this. When exactly did you write your first letter announcing your brother Peter's death?"

"That's easy to answer. My first letter—early on the Wednesday evening. At Bournemouth. Not very long after we'd had the telegram and those dreadful Police messages had come through to me on the telephone. There were a few minutes to spare before Mummie and I caught our train from Bournemouth Central. The time would be about half past seven. If anything, a little later."

"Where did you actually write the letter, Miss Oliver?"

"In the Beaumont Lounge of the 'Suffolk Hôtel'. If that's conveying anything to you."

"Oh, yes. I know it well. Too well, perhaps. The last round of drinks that I had there cost me just on thirty bob. Four of us there were—not fourteen."

"That's the place," affirmed Margaret with a nod of the head. "I can recognize that you know it."

"You wrote, I suppose, because it wasn't convenient for you to telephone? I mean to the intended recipient?"

Margaret seemed a trifle mystified by the question but suddenly her face cleared. "Oh, I see what you mean," she replied after a slight pause—"yes, I wrote to David. My young brother. I couldn't get him on the 'phone as you know. Because I didn't know exactly where he was. He was away on that walking-tour."

Anthony nodded. "Yes, I guessed as much, Miss Oliver. That it was your brother to whom you sent that letter. What did you do to make sure he'd get it—address it to a Post-office somewhere—*Poste restante*?"

"That's exactly what I did do. You see, David had previously told me to write to Nether Wallop, if I had anything to tell him of any special importance while he was away, and he'd arrange to pick up the communication there somewhere about the Thursday of Easter week. As it was, it was just as well he had made the arrangement. I was able to get in touch with him."

"As you say, Miss Oliver. Now for the crucial question—to whom else did you write? Besides your brother?"

"On that Wednesday evening, do you mean?"

"Yes."

"Oh, no one. No one at all. You see, there wasn't time, Mr. Bathurst. Even if I'd wanted to. Before the train left, I mean. There wasn't a hope of writing to anybody else."

"I see. Well, thank you, Miss Oliver—I haven't any more questions with which to worry you."

"I'm glad," returned Margaret with a simple candour, "some of them frighten me."

"You're no more glad than I am," interposed Dewhurst sharply, "because I can't see the slightest point in any of the questions. All the same, none of 'em frighten me. Of course that may be because I'm not—Bathurst." He broke off and shrugged his shoulders as he turned away.

Anthony smiled at the young journalist. "No—as you say, you're not Bathurst. But 'were you Bathurst and Bathurst Dewhurst there would be a Bathurst'—well, what a difference just three little letters *can* make, to be sure." Dewhurst smiled. Margaret frowned. And this time it was Anthony who turned away and shrugged his shoulders.

CHAPTER 15

1

It was precisely at this somewhat embarrassing moment that Richard Oliver came back into the conversation. The look on his face and the tone of his voice when he spoke were equally grave.

"I think, Margaret, that you should inform Mr. Bathurst, seeing that he's on the subject, how you contacted me in Aberdeen. From Bournemouth. If it doesn't affect anything else, it will at least assist him to clear the slate. I take it that's what he's trying to do."

"I didn't contact you, Daddy. It was Mummie. Don't you remember?"

Mrs. Oliver made the next contribution. "Yes. Margaret is quite right. I telephoned to my husband, Mr. Bathurst. From the hôtel. I telephoned to him—it took me some little time to get through—and Margaret wrote a quick short note to David, as she has already explained."

"I guessed that's how it would be," returned Anthony, "please don't worry any more about it. There is just one question, though, that I'd like to ask Mr. Oliver. I don't consider that there's anything particularly private about it so there's nothing to stop my asking him now. And I don't think, either, that he'll mind my asking it. I take it that all of us here in this room at the moment believe that Peter was murdered and did not on any account commit suicide?"

There were murmurs of assent from the others though Anthony couldn't be certain as to whether Dewhurst was a proclaimed party to the agreement. Anthony went on.

"Well . . . then . . . in that case . . . seeing that there's such a measure of general agreement and seeing, too, that you all knew Peter and that I didn't . . . can anyone of you suggest anything like a motive for the murder? I'll ask Mr. Oliver himself first."

There were headshakings round the room from everybody but the person named. Anthony waited for Oliver. He had noticed that Oliver hadn't shaken his head yet. Oliver leant forward from his armchair and knocked out the dottle of his pipe into an ashtray on a table at his side.

"Well, it's rather strange that you should ask me that. Because during the last day or two, I've been asking myself pretty much the same question."

Oliver paused. The murmurs of assent became buzzes of incredulity. Anthony congratulated himself mentally on his adroitness in framing the question. Was he going to dig up something at long last? Oliver turned to him.

"Do you remember that morning I saw you and Inspector MacMorran in his room at the 'Yard'? The morning I came back from Scotland?"

"Yes, Mr. Oliver, I remember it."

"Do you remember something I said? I can't recall the exact words I used, but I said something like this. That I'd had no previous dealings with the Police except for an occasion that went back to the year dot? Remember?"

"Yes . . . I . . . er . . . noted your remark."

Anthony took a glance round the room as he replied. Mrs. Oliver was gazing at her husband with a look of startled fear of revelation to come. Margaret had a look on her face of mock indignation and Dewhurst looked merely and ordinarily surprised. Oliver himself wasn't oblivious of the various personal reactions.

"Don't worry," he said drily, "I can't produce any skeleton from the Richard Oliver cupboard to amuse you or shock you as the case may be. It's nothing of that kind. Sorry if I've disappointed anybody. No, it's just a little matter of an ancient crime in which I was called upon by Fate to participate. My . . . er . . . participation, however, took place on the side of Justice." Richard Oliver turned to Anthony again. "Do you remember, Mr. Bathurst, the case which the more sensational Press featured as 'The Man with the Patched Elbow'? Thirty years ago—quite."

Anthony nodded. "I remember the affair, Mr. Oliver—by reading about it. I was comparatively young when it happened. A young girl was killed in the East End of London and her body found in an alleyway. Where was it, now?"

Oliver was on the point of supplying the information when Anthony checked him. "Don't tell me, Mr. Oliver. Let me see if I can recall some of the circumstances."

He paused and then began to speak again more slowly. "The girl was killed in a cul-de-sac at Leybridge. Her name was Florence Dennison. Of course, you were the passenger in the tram from Leybridge to North Ham—you gave information to the Police concerning the murderer. He travelled with you on the evening of the murder and you subsequently identified him. His name was Canham. Joseph Canham. Am I right?"

"You are," said Oliver quietly, "and I must congratulate you on a remarkable effort of memory seeing that it was I who brought the matter up. I was a junior clerk in those days, working for the North Ham Council. I used to attend Accountancy classes at the Leybridge Technical Institute. That's how I happened to be travelling in the same tram as Canham. And it was my evidence, I suppose, that really brought him to the gallows. But can you remember anything else with regard to that case, Mr. Bathurst?"

Anthony considered the question for some seconds. "No. I don't think so. Do you mean in any particular direction?"

"Compare the affair with our trouble, Mr. Bathurst."

Anthony nodded. "Yes," he replied quietly, "I've caught up. Florence Dennison's throat was cut. Canham was a mad killer, no doubt, but in those days the psychologists weren't so active as they are now, and he took the nine o'clock walk. Today he'd be sent to Broadmoor and be politely referred to as a 'patient'." He changed his tone. "What's your real point, Mr. Oliver? I'm certain you're going to produce something."

"Merely this. While Canham's trial was on I had a threatening letter . . . that if he were sentenced to death, the same fate would be mine, even if the method were different. After the trial, and of course the verdict, I had another letter similar in tone—my days were numbered, etc., etc."

"What did you do with them?"

"Passed them over to the Police, of course. I was in close touch with them as you may guess and it was the natural thing for me to do. They didn't worry me particularly—the letters. I was a philosophical sort of bloke in those days, and nothing more ever transpired from them. Until this affair of my son. Which, I'll be perfectly candid, has made me think twice during the past few days. Maybe my idea's all boloney."

Anthony's brow was furrowed. "Why exactly, Mr. Oliver, have you begun to think in this way?"

"I've had two reasons, Mr. Bathurst. Neither of them may appear to you as particularly potent. Firstly, that I can't see the *vestige* of any other motive for anybody to kill poor old Peter, and secondly, the similarity in the way the two victims died. That has made me wonder whether that Canham chicken had come home to roost.

Anthony thought hard. "These letters that threatened you, Mr. Oliver how were they signed?"

"There was no name in the ordinary way. As a signature. The writer put at the bottom of the script the rather theatrical phrase, 'Blood is thicker than water.' Just that—no more."

"Which would seem, assuming that there *was* something behind them, and that they were authentic, to indicate that the writer was a relation of Joseph Canham's. Do you agree?"

"Oh, yes. That's how it struck me at the time. I don't know what ideas the Police had, if any. They just collared the letters and stuck to them."

"H'm," commented Anthony, "you've certainly given me a new line of country with this idea. But how do you explain the terrific interval? It's a rusted revenge, if ever there were such a thing. To stay your hand for something like a matter of thirty years. To me, it's almost incredible."

"There *might* be a reason for the delay," contributed Richard Oliver quietly. "I've thought of one or two, actually. Just possible reasons. I wouldn't claim them to be any more than that. Would you care to hear them?"

"I would, by all means."

"Well, the man concerned *might* have been in prison and therefore been rendered incapable of carrying out his threats."

Anthony shook his head decisively. "No. I refuse to accept that one. Sorry. The 'stretch' is too long. Far too long! The man would have been released long before thirty years had passed. Any more?"

"Yes," replied Oliver imperturbably, "this one is a trifle more on the fantastic side, perhaps, but it's one which *has* occurred to me. That the killer deliberately waited until Peter was the same age as Joseph Canham was when he was executed."

Anthony frowned. "Before we discuss it, is that actually something like the fact?"

"To the best of my memory Canham was about twenty-five or twenty-six. Roughly the same age as Peter. At any rate there wouldn't be a lot in it."

Anthony was silent for a time. So were Margaret, her mother and Robert Dewhurst. Richard Oliver sat quietly in his chair and watched Anthony's face intently.

"No soap?" he queried at length.

Anthony began to shake his head.

"How did the murderer gain admittance or entry to the house, Mr. Oliver? It's heavy odds that Peter himself admitted him. This Canham projection, from your past, must have been in a practical issue, a stranger presenting himself at the door. Under what pretext could he prevail on Peter to let him in?"

Oliver filled his pipe slowly, pressing the tobacco down with his thumb with meticulous care and precision.

"I admit all that, Mr. Bathurst, and it's all eminently sound, no doubt. I've thought of it just as you have. But—and no disrespect meant to you—how do we know, any one of us, who this Canham association *is*, and therefore what he or she looks like? As I see things, this Canham avenger—let me call him that to distinguish him properly—may be somebody whom Peter knew as somebody else. Somebody entirely different. Surely the attack when it came would be treacherous and . . . er . . . insidious?"

Anthony made no reply. Oliver followed up quickly. "It occurs to me that he might have been well known to Peter socially. That he might have met him somewhere—somewhere quite respectable so that there was no hint of suspicion attached to him, and Peter therefore accepted him in perfectly good faith for what he pretended to be."

It was at this juncture that Dewhurst broke in. "Well, if your conjecture's got anything in it, Dad, the field must be well narrowed down. On the score of age, alone. Joseph Canham, the executed murderer you've been talking about, would have been, had he lived, according to the data you've supplied, somewhere in the 'sixties. And it's reasonable to assume that this 'Blood is Thicker than Water' bloke would be more or less contemporary with him. Well, how many people did Peter know well, who were anything like *that* age? That's the question that requires answering."

Anthony had listened to Dewhurst with more than ordinary interest. "I take your point, Mr. Dewhurst," he said, "and it's a good one but it's not altogether a certainty. I'll tell you why. Revenge is sometimes a legacy for a succeeding generation. Handed down as a family feud. I've known it work that way. Canham *might* have left a son, either legitimate or otherwise, to whom the fire of the feud had been passed on by a brooding and purposeful mother."

Anthony turned to Richard Oliver. "Was there a Mrs. Canham in the case, can you remember?"

Oliver shook his head. "I'm not sure. It's so long ago now. Actually, if I had to answer I don't fancy there was. But still, don't rely on me for the information. I may be quite wrong. As I said, it's too long ago for me to have retained any necessarily accurate impression. Well, now we've had all that chin-wag about it, what do you really think of my idea? Anything in it?"

Anthony smiled. "To be perfectly frank, I'm not attracted by it. But of course it holds a possibility. And when I've looked at it more carefully, there's the chance that it may grow in attraction. Beyond that, I can't say. Prefer to reserve judgement. But I'll tell you what I *will* do. When I get back, I'll have the files of the Canham case turned up and I'll examine them. There may be something there which'll stick its neck out. If there is I'll pounce. We'll see."

"Good," returned Richard Oliver, "that's an idea." He rose from his chair. "Well? Far-fetched? Fantastic? Perhaps it is. *Probably* it is. For myself, I don't know." He paused and shrugged his shoulders. Then he said, "But it's the only motive that *I* can think of for anybody to have murdered my son. To have come into this house and cut my boy's throat." A catch came into his voice.

"Don't, Richard, please," implored Mrs. Oliver, "for my sake."

2

Anthony 'phoned MacMorran immediately upon his return. "Listen, Andrew," he said, "I may have got something. What? No, no plumes for my bonnet. I'm out of it this time. It emanates from Oliver senior. Yes . . . that's right. Richard Guise of the ilk. I'm not strongly attracted by it, but as he's put it up to me we mustn't entirely neglect it. Do you remember the Leybridge murderer—name of Joseph Canham? The man with the patched elbow? A few years, I should say, before the '14-'18 war. Cut a girl's throat and left the body in a cul-de- sac? Have I rung the bell yet?"

"Ancient memories, aren't they? I'll say! I think I do just remember it—I was a constable at the time. But what about Canham? Are you going to tell me he was left-handed?"

Anthony could hear the Inspector's chuckle. "No, I'm not," he replied, "the point that I am going to tell you concerns the aforementioned Richard Guise. How? I'll tell you how. Look up the files of the Canham case and you'll find that it was his evidence of identification which told strongly in sending Joe Canham to the execution shed. What? Of course I know. You wait for it . . . don't be so impatient. Oliver, at the time of the Canham trial, had threatening letters sent him . . . which quite sensibly he turned over to the Police. They were signed with the phrase, 'Blood is Thicker than Water'. This affair of his son has revived the whole business in his mind. So much so that he's inclined to put two and two together and make it twenty-two."

"Good God," came MacMorran, "do you mean he scents revenge? After all this time? Why, man, it's donkey's year-rs ago." The accent of Aberdeen peeped through.

"That's how it is, Andrew. That's how Oliver is beginning to look at it. Anyhow, to satisfy him, and me as well, have the dossier turned up for me, will you? See if there were any likely cadets of the clan Canham who *might* have survived the menace of the years and been tempted to have a bash. It'll be as well to seal it off. Seeing the way Richard Guise feels about it."

"All right. I'll look into it for you. I'll let you know what I find."

"Thank you, Andrew, I knew you would. By the way—any glimmer anywhere of Stella Forrest? From any quarter?"

"Not a shred, not a whisper. Sorry, but there it is."

"I'd like to be sure that girl was still alive," replied Anthony, "that shows you how I feel about things."

3

MacMorran rang off and Anthony replaced the receiver. He was extremely thoughtful. The extraordinary nature of this Oliver problem was the *number* of incidents to do with it which were so entirely abnormal. Anthony began to make a list of them. He listed them in what he regarded as the order of their respective importances.

(1) The return of the bonds which had been missing from the bank.
(2) The sudden and immediate disappearance of Stella Forrest.
(3) The complete lack of information as to Stella's antecedents and the strange suggestion of monasticism with regard to the life she had led at Mrs. Gilbert's house in Hammersmith.
(4) The Garcia link-up with Dewhurst and the Olivers by means of 'The Orange Lizard' *plus* his association with Peter Oliver professionally.

(5) Garcia's reticence with his wife concerning the call on him at his private house by MacMorran and Anthony, and
(6) The cryptic reference in the note found by MacMorran in Peter Oliver's wallet to "R.G. and D." which fitted the two Garcias, man and wife, absolutely, in addition to Oliver senior and his son.

There were certain other abnormalities in addition to these which Anthony had already listed—he knew that very well, but for the time being he decided to concentrate on those which he assessed as "principal". He took them one by one—in the same order as he had listed them.

The return of the San Jonquilo bonds, by registered parcel.

By a man who, according to description, might have been Roderigo Garcia—the lawful owner of them. Anthony shook his head—here was something he was unable to understand. Unless Peter had been made to steal them in the first place, under threat? Then, when he was dead, and removed from the picture—Anthony broke off again. Where the hell was the sense in it?

And then, the complete effacement of Stella Forrest. Within but a few hours of her hearing of the death of Peter Oliver. Why?

Fear was the dominating impulse, undoubtedly. The landlady with whom the girl had lived for just on three years had no hesitation in subscribing to this same theory. But fear of what? Fear of whom? Was Peter Oliver's murderer known to her? If so, what were the conditions attached to him that made her so afraid of him? Why didn't she come out in the open and denounce him? Seeing the measure of her affection for her murdered lover?

Did the whole business go back in some strange manner to Stella's past life? Anthony shook his head again, but travelled smoothly from the mental point he had reached to the third item on his list.

According to the statements of Mrs. Gilbert, the Hammersmith landlady, Stella had possessed but the flimsiest of those contacts with the ordinary social world which in the normal way would be exercised by a young girl of Stella's age and attractiveness. No friends, no visitors, no letters, no relations, no acquaintances, no home! Over a period of nearly three years.

With the exception, of course, of the very recent love-affair with Peter Oliver. Again—why? What could be the reason? Why in the name of goodness should Stella Forrest be a human cul-de-sac? Anthony could produce nothing intelligent enough to satisfy his own powers of reasoning. If Stella had something to hide, he was forced to confess to himself that he hadn't the slightest idea of what it was or even what it might be.

He moved on to a further consideration of the Garcias—Roderigo and Dolores. He was determined to collect every detail and every item of which he knew, that concerned this husband and wife from Santa Guardina. Both the Garcias knew Robert Dewhurst. According to the story given him, the original meeting between them had taken place at 'The Orange Lizard'. Well, that was all right, nothing suspicious or sinister about that. Through Dewhurst, the Garcias came to know, naturally, Margaret Oliver.

Then, adding more links to the chain, through Margaret, her brothers Peter and David. One of whom, the elder—and the man who had been murdered—was employed professionally at the particular branch of Delaney's bank which Garcia used and where he not only kept his current account but had also placed in his safe deposit San Jonquilo bonds to the value of approximately £80,000.

More than that, when Garcia had called at his bank for the purpose of reducing his bond holding, the very man who had handled the bonds en route to the manager had been this same murdered Peter Oliver.

Anthony took out his handkerchief and wiped his brow. Because it was being brought home to him very forcibly—that he was getting just nowhere! Travelling round in futile circles like the playful puppy chasing his own tail!

Never mind though, he'd finish the job properly now he'd started it. What else was there in connexion with these Garcias? There was the note MacMorran had taken from the dead man's wallet which might or might not refer to them and there was that significant omission on the part of Señor Roderigo Garcia to inform his wife that he had been called upon by an Inspector of Scotland Yard in relation to the supposed theft of his San Jonquilo bonds.

Anthony had labelled this omission as "significant". Now that he came to think it over in cold blood, he wondered whether his choice of adjective was either happy or intelligent. He knew only too well that many men never trouble their respective wives with any matter to do with business. There was often soundness and sense behind this practice. Anthony also knew that, only too well. Was Roderigo Garcia a man of this type and habit?

Anthony came to the conclusion that he might well be—which in that case meant that nothing of much importance should be ascribed to the reticence he had displayed in the matter which Anthony had been considering. All the same, Anthony thought, it might be as well to keep it in mind, in the event of anything happening in the future to disturb this conclusion, which would then invest the incident with a new importance. Anthony's mind then moved to the minor abnormalities . . . there were several of them. One which interested him rather more than the others arose from the arrangements made concerning David Oliver's Easter walking-tour. Anthony found himself seriously contemplating the case of the teacher, Charles Hassall . . . employed on the staff at Parkin's College, Chiswick . . . who had suddenly gone down with an attack of tonsilitis. No, not tonsilitis—laryngitis.

4

Anthony travelled to Chiswick in the morning and when the sun was shining, and on the strength of one discreet and well-placed inquiry was able to locate Parkin's College without undue difficulty. It stood on the corner of a road leading down to the river and, as Anthony had expected, had once been a well-built and spacious private residence. The premises extended for some considerable distance down the side road and Anthony saw with some interest that the enterprising Parkin (or possibly his predecessor) had had the garden asphalted to serve for a reasonable attempt at games and also as a drill-yard.

As Anthony looked at it, however, over the wall of the side-turning, and for the first time, the garden-space was empty, so he concluded that other educational matters were for the moment occupying the curriculum. Before he had started out that morning he had also put through a judiciously worded inquiry to a well-informed quarter in the district as to the personnel of the staff of Parkin's College and he had been informed that in addition to Frank Crabtree Parkin, B.A. (Aberystwith), the proprietor of the establishment, the staff numbered but three. Namely, David Colquhoun Oliver, Charles Edward Hassall and a lady—a Miss Antonia Purnell. Parkin himself lived on the premises— the other members of his staff returned to their respective homes each afternoon when their educational labours were finished.

When Anthony was informed of these details, they afforded him a strong measure of satisfaction. If he took a 'dekko' at the school and found a young teacher who obviously wasn't David Oliver—there would be no sorting out process for him to do—because by mere elimination, the young man must be Hassall —the very chap with whom Anthony was desirous of having a few words.

Anthony looked at his wrist-watch. It was a quarter to twelve. According to his calculations, based very largely on what he knew, the pupils and staff of Parkin's College would "break" at noon. If he had any luck, he might be able to contact Hassall soon after that. In all probability, he thought, the man would leave the College to have lunch somewhere. At any rate, there would be a reasonable chance of this happening. As he had walked to the College earlier that morning, Anthony had seen at least three café-restaurants which looked likely providers of a lunch for even an impecunious teacher. Anthony walked a few yards down the side-turning and then retraced his steps to the main road. But all the time he kept his eye on the principal entrance to the establishment. Minutes passed with Anthony killing time with various walking exercises and then, suddenly, the vernal morning air was sharply sundered with a volley of noise. From the gate of the seminary there poured a stream of boys. Boys of all ages, shapes and sizes. The one thing and the one thing only which they appeared to possess in common was an entire absence of good manners. They poured into the roadway and then began to vanish in a variety of direction.

When the road and its vicinity began to clear of this human cascade, Anthony took up a more strategical position from which he could control his vision of the main College gate. He reckoned that if Hassall *were* leaving the premises for lunch, a snack or even the walk of abstinence, he would be soon appearing in sight.

Within five minutes Mr. Bathurst's powers of deduction were rewarded. A tall, thin, bare-headed young man with a long slender nose, his hands thrust deeply into a shabby-looking "mac", came out of the College building, walked up the path and passed out of the main gate.

"If this isn't my man," said Anthony to himself, "it will be just too bad. For both of us."

He swung into the tall man's tracks, at a respectful distance, and followed him into the main road. As Anthony had previously guessed, the pursuit didn't turn out to be of long duration. For the bare-headed figure in the old mackintosh turned into a small shop of the restaurant type but a short distance down the main road.

Anthony looked at the name over the doorway, "The Windmill Café", as he himself exercised imitative action. The man he had followed was just sitting down. The table he had chosen was entirely vacant. Anthony saw that it was unique in this respect and dropped into a chair opposite his quarry.

An elderly waitress with bags under her eyes and tiers under her chin was quickly alongside waving a soiled-looking card. Anthony's companion chose corned beef and salad. Anthony ordered a steak pudding and deliberately opened a newspaper. He must be careful not to rush things—"give him time, give him time," he muttered to himself.

The waitress brought the plates and Anthony was quick to notice the comparatively generous helpings. The popularity of "The Windmill Café" had been speedily made manifest. He put his newspaper on one side and looked approvingly at the plate in front of him. As he started to eat he made his eye catch the eye of his *vis-à-vis*. "They do you well here, I'll say that for them." Anthony had opened the exchanges.

His companion nodded. His face had become both friendly and agreeable. Anthony knew now that all was going to be plain sailing for him—money for chocolate!

"Ra-ther," came the reply in a curiously refined voice, "that's why I'm sitting here. I've a flair for good grub. I like my nose-bag as well as the next man."

"Same here," said Anthony, now well in, "different from some places I've been in recently. Could I tell a tale!"

"Oh, where was that? In London, do you mean?"

Anthony fixed his eyes firmly on the other fellow's face. "I say," he said, with almost a hint of apology, "aren't you Mr. Hassall from the College round the corner? Or am I—"

"Guilty, my lord," said Hassall genially, "but I didn't know that I was so—"

Anthony came in again. "My nephew's pointed you out to me once or twice, that's how I know."

"Oh, does he attend our mausoleum? What's the little beggar's name?"

"Smith," replied Anthony promptly.

"Good lord, we've a positive gaggle of Smiths. What's his—"

Anthony took his courage in both hands. "He's the little chap with the dirty face and untidy hair. Generally looks as though he'd been pulled through a hedge backwards. But I was talking about grub and the wretched stuff they serve in some places. It has to be seen to be believed. And it isn't always London where the worst crimes are committed."

"So I'm told," commented Hassall, "what an absolute godsend this food shortage must have been to thousands! All the mean, stingy, parsimonious rats have had the time of their lives. Cut things down—pared here, scraped there, shoved their tongues in their cheeks, talked about patriotism and the urgent need for saving, and then proceeded to indulge themselves in a perfect orgy of meanness and ha'penny-saving. Makes me sick."

Anthony guided him gently back to the main avenue—the avenue where he wanted him. "I think you're right," he said, "I agree with you all along the line. And when people tell you, as they often do, that things are quite different in the country and that it's a land flowing with milk and honey, you tell 'em from me to take a run. Why, a friend of mine recently had a walking-tour in the West Country. About a fortnight before Easter. He started from Melksham in Wiltshire and finished at Painswick in Gloucestershire—you ought to hear him moan! Told me the other evening that in ten days' walking he reckons he had no more than a couple of decent meals." Anthony pushed away his empty plate.

"Go on," said Hassall, "is that a fact? Depends, of course, the kind of show you stay at. I'll tell you what makes me say that. Actually, bearing in mind what you've just said, it's rather interesting. By something of a coincidence a colleague of mine has just come back from that same spot of country that you've mentioned. Well, roughly the same. He was down there for Easter. He started from Gloucester and worked up past Salisbury Plain somewhere. He reports more favourably than your chap. As I say, it just depends on the show where you elect to hang your hat up. Sometimes you strike lucky, at other times you're in the dirt. What have they got for sweets to-day any idea?"

"I don't happen to have the menu but I fancy I spotted some hefty wedges of Boiled jam roll in convoy a few moments ago."

Anthony was thinking quickly, but there was no need. Hassall opened the door for him almost effortlessly. Hassall grinned, "as a matter of fact," he continued, "I nearly went to the West Country with the chap I just mentioned. He asked me to accompany him originally and I accepted the invitation—but in the end I cried off." Hassall continued to grin.

"Oh," returned Anthony quietly, "how was that? Not too fit or something?"

The thin face opposite to him was still wreathed in humour. "That was my alibi. I cried off on the score of laryngitis. But it was 'phony'. There was nothing wrong with the old throat at all."

Anthony pretended that he was somewhat bewildered. "Why? I don't quite get that. What was the idea?"

Hassall's face became serious. He was about to reply when the list of sweets was presented to him. "You're right," he said to Anthony, "the old Boiled jam's still functioning. It's not bad, either! Fills up the crannies. Shall I order a couple?"

"Please. Many thanks."

"Good. Two Boiled jams."

The waitress left the table. "Why did I stall the walking-tour?" said Hassall. "Well, that's not too easy for me to answer. I think I jibbed it. You see, it comes down to this. You've got to be great pals with a bloke for the two of you to spend a whole week together. I wasn't sure whether we'd fit in . . . just before the time we should have started off. . . say three or four days before . . . my bloke developed a hell of a temper . . . groused and moaned at every little thing . . . and fairly put me off. He showed me a side of his character I'd never seen before . . . and candidly, I began to think twice about things. Do you know it seemed to me somehow as though the bloke didn't really *want* me with him . . . that he'd repented of the invitation he'd extended to me . . . and was doing his level best to choke me off. Maybe I was quite wrong, but that was the way I felt."

Hassall's seriousness departed from his face. The Jam rolls came and his grin returned with them.

"So I invoked the aid of an imaginary attack on the jolly old larynx. If I hadn't, I might have been able to give you my opinion of West Country grub. As it is, I just can't. Too bad, isn't it?"

Anthony smiled at him. "Ah, well, that won't matter. It'll be all the same in a thousand years."

Hassall nodded. "Too true—we shall be dead a hell of a long time. Not bad these, are they? Something to get your teeth into."

"Quite good. I shall certainly come here again. The place shines like a good deed in a naughty world. I may even bequeath the knowledge of it as a rich legacy unto my heirs."

"In case you don't know," intervened Hassall, his face creased in smiles, "it's called 'The Windmill'. I thought perhaps you mightn't have noticed the name."

"The Windmill', eh? Well, my dear Hassall, it's one at which I shall never tilt."

"Good for you," grinned the young schoolmaster.

CHAPTER 16

1

Anthony travelled back from Chiswick, a prey to conflicting thoughts. Was *anything* ever going to emerge clearly from the eddies of this fantastic problem? He had never yet investigated a case where confusion became so repeatedly, and so regularly, worse-confounded.

The luck he had turned up with Hassall, to begin with, had soon run against him. And in such an aggravating and annoying manner. He had set out with the intention of satisfying himself whether the throat attack had been genuine, only to discover that it had been *Hassall* who had declined the walking-tour at the eleventh hour. That it had been Hassall himself and not David Oliver who had applied the quietus.

And what had he discovered? That Hassall *had* made the break, that the illness *had* been faked, and that, in a way, David Oliver had deliberately for some days worked up "an atmosphere" and skilfully brought it to something like boiling-point at the psychological moment.

Anthony saw himself in the precarious position of being between two stools. How much of David's tantrums was real, and how much belonged to Charles Hassall's imagination? Margaret had written to David to the Post-office at Nether Wallop in Hampshire early on the Wednesday evening. When Peter had been dead for two days.

In the afternoon of the Easter Monday when Peter was in Kew Gardens with his Stella, Margaret and her mother had met in the Square at Bournemouth, Mr. and Mrs. Andrew Murray. Anthony began to wonder whether either Margaret or Evelyn Oliver, her mother, had made any mention of David in the conversation with the Murrays which subsequently must have taken place. He *might* have been mentioned, thought Anthony. It was just on the cards. Peter certainly would have been . . . as Peter was the one link between the families . . . and from Peter, it was quite reasonable to suppose that the conversation would travel to David.

If so—David's holiday would almost certainly be discussed—it was a hundred to one on that Mrs. Oliver would say "Oh, David's on a walking-tour, somewhere down in Gloucestershire," and she might have mentioned the actual town where David was supposed to be, by walking schedule, on the Easter Monday.

Anthony was more than ordinarily interested both in that town and in that daily itinerary of David Oliver. A man can do so much when he is all alone . . . and a long distance away from relatives, friends, and even acquaintances.

2

Directly Anthony got home, he 'phoned Andrew Murray, the bank manager at the Lombard Street branch of Delaney's bank. Murray soon came on. Anthony recognized his genial tones.

"Mr. Bathurst . . . oh . . . good afternoon! What can I do for you?"

Anthony laughed. "Good afternoon, Mr. Murray. A rather unexpected request, I'm afraid. Take your mind back to Easter Monday, will you?"

"That's easy. Mrs. Murray and I were at Bournemouth. For one thing the wife hadn't been too well since Christmas and for another it's our normal haunt for Easter—over the weekend that is. What about it?"

"You met Mrs. and Miss Oliver in the Square at Bournemouth on the Bank Holiday afternoon. That O.K.? Miss Oliver's my informant."

"Yes. Quite O.K. I can confirm that. Although I wasn't actually present at the encounter, personally. It was like this. I'd popped into a tobacconist's for some cigarettes . . . they were pretty tight down there over the Easter . . . and I'd told my missus to walk on and I'd catch her up . . . when I came out of the shop and walked along to find her . . . I found her talking to the two Oliver ladies. They'd run into her about a hundred yards up the road. I just passed the time of day with them and we broke up. They were going along to Boscombe—and we weren't."

"Your conversation with them was strictly limited, then?"

"I'll say it was. Just the ordinary commonplaces. How are you—fancy meeting you—it's a small world, isn't it—and cheer-o, hope you have a good time. That, I should say, just about sums it up."

"I see. That's rather disappointing. I'd hoped for something better."

"I'm sorry to hear that—but we aren't much more than acquaintances, you know. Peter Oliver was here . . . as you know . . . only too well . . . and we live at Horton Hatch which isn't a great way from Puck Willow where the Olivers live. We've met on the train several times and in that way the ladies have got to know each other. But this sounds all very mysterious—what are you really after?"

"I'm trying to find out—strictly between our two selves—where exactly a certain member of the Oliver family was on that Easter Monday. And I'd considered the possibility that Mrs. Oliver, in the course of a perfectly innocent conversation, might have given it away."

"I see. No—sorry—can't help you there. Just airy nothings and conventional chatter—nothing more than that."

"Ah, well, Mr. Murray, if you can't help me, you can't, and that's all there is to it. Many thanks for putting up with me for so long."

Anthony hung up. What he had already said to Murray was true. He *was* disappointed that he hadn't been able to collect more.

He went to his armchair and thought things over. Then an idea struck him. And the more he thought it over, the more attractive it became. It was only an ordinary idea—nothing brilliant about it and it followed very naturally and logically upon his previous idea.

If Andrew Murray's conversation with the two Olivers at Bournemouth on Easter Monday had been entirely empty and conventional *Mrs.* Andrew Murray's might not have been! She had "got in" on the conversation several minutes, possibly, before her husband had arrived. While he'd been chasing cigarettes. Anthony nodded to himself. He would go and have a pleasant little chat with Mrs. Andrew Murray.

3

Anthony came to the rather dainty little suburb of Horton Hatch in a somewhat subdued state of mind. Reference to the telephone directory had provided him with the address that he required. Mrs. Andrew Murray resided at "Fontenoy", Chandos Avenue.

Anthony came to the house by car because he realized from the start that the interview might require careful handling and that the personal side of it might prove an important factor in the way it eventually turned out. Anthony drove up to the house quietly and rang the bell. It was well built and charmingly situated.

"Not much change," said Anthony to himself as he waited at the door, "out of five thousand quid." It was evidently Mrs. Murray herself who answered the door. She was dark, with a high white forehead, and of medium height. In age, judged merely by appearances, she might have been anything between thirty-five and fifty. Her lips were a trifle sullen . . . petulant, but her voice was cool, low-pitched and unusually pleasing. She looked inquiringly at Anthony. He smiled and explained himself. For a little while, Mrs. Murray frowned. Anthony continued to smile. Gradually the frown disappeared and Jean Murray looked at Anthony and smiled too.

"Come in," she said simply, "and let me see if *I* can help you."

Anthony was conducted into the lounge—roomy and tastefully furnished. Anthony chose a chair. Jean Murray sat near to him.

"Now amplify," she said, "what you said to me before, Mr. Bathurst. Andrew has told me, of course, that you were interested in the mystery of young Oliver's death, but I never thought that I could possibly help.

She smoothed her skirt over her knees. Anthony amplified as she had requested him to. Jean Murray listened attentively before nodding her agreement.

"It's perfectly true, as my husband has told you. I ran into the Olivers, Mrs. Oliver and her daughter, while Andrew was in a shop. Tobacco, or something in that line—I really forget, but it's usually that, or cigarettes. It was in the Square at Bournemouth on the Bank Holiday afternoon. The Olivers and we are only acquaintances—no more than that. But you know what it is when you're away on holiday and you run into a familiar face. Gets you all nostalgic, I suppose, and you stop and speak. Whereas if the same thing happened at home you'd just nod and pass on. Well, that's what happened in this instance. I was with them some minutes I should think—quite. Andrew was some time putting in an appearance. There was plenty of excuse for him, though. The place was absolutely crowded with people—even walking wasn't an easy matter."

Anthony nodded, "Yes, that's just how I've pictured it. Now tell me, Mr. Murray—this is the point I've really come about—did either Mrs. Oliver or Miss Oliver mention the other son? David? In the course of the conversation?"

Mrs. Murray's lips parted in what was very nearly a mocking smile. "Mrs. Oliver mentioned the whole Oliver family, Mr. Bathurst. I had to listen to a rare rigmarole—in which I really wasn't very interested. I suppose she told me all the details to explain why she and Margaret were at Bournemouth on their own.

"That's the idea, Mrs. Murray—that's just what I wanted to hear. Now can you all me,more or less, just what the lady said?"

Mrs. Murray examined her fingertips critically. "I think I can. She told me that her husband was away in Scotland somewhere through a death in the family, that Peter was spending Easter with a young lady to whom he had just be come engaged—she couldn't tell me the girl's name, she said, she hadn't actually seen her yet—and that David, the younger boy, had gone on a walking tour somewhere in England with a colleague of his. Isn't he a teacher in a school somewhere? I've got that idea in my head, but maybe I'm all wrong about it. That's the gist of the lady's conversation, Mr. Bathurst. You should thank your lucky stars you've come to somebody with a good memory." Mrs. Murray smiled. "Will you have a cup of tea with me? Have you got time?"

Anthony thanked his hostess and accepted the invitation. Mrs. Murray made tea and brought it to him.

"No sugar, please," said Anthony.

"Heavens, what a god-send you are," said Jean Murray. Anthony thought hard as commonplaces of conversation were tossed to and fro. Suddenly he cut in.

"Going back, Mrs. Murray, just for a second. To David Oliver's walking-tour. Can you remember if Mrs. Oliver mentioned an actual place where he was, would be or might have been?"

Anthony smiled at her. "Yes," said Jean Murray, "I think I can. Now you've revived it in my mind. I fancy she told me she'd had a picture post-card from him from Salisbury."

"Salisbury, eh? I see. Now let me make a careful note of that."

"Why? Is it important?"

"It might be. I can't tell yet."

"More tea, Mr. Bathurst?'

"Thank you." Anthony surrendered his cup. The conventionalities of conversation took the stage again. Anthony didn't mind now. He had the ancient name of Sarum in his note-book.

"I little thought," prattled Jean Murray as she poured out tea, "that when I asked Andrew to take me away for a few days at Easter it would mean that I should be called upon to help the Police in a mysterious affair like this death of young Oliver has turned out to be."

"You never know, Mrs. Murray," contributed Anthony.

"How true that is, Mr. Bathurst. Of course we're fond of Bournemouth, my husband and I. We often spend a few days there. But not in the summer, for a long stay. Just at odd times. We like it better that way—when there aren't *quite* so many people."

Anthony drank tea. "When you met the Oliver ladies on the Bank Holiday afternoon, that, of course, was your first encounter with them?"

"Oh, yes. Of course! We had only two days there. Well, two and a bit. We went down by car on the Saturday afternoon. I'd been sleeping terribly badly for some time. So I had prevailed on Andrew to take me as soon as he was clear of the bank. My doctor had recommended it strongly—said the sea air would do me a world of good. I was lucky. We had two really lovely days. On the Sunday and Monday the weather was superb. Sun nearly all the time and hardly a cloud in the sky. *Couldn't* have been better for the time of the year. We left just after dinner on the Monday evening, had a lovely run up and were home here before ten, listened to the radio till about half past ten perhaps and then went to bed. By the way, that reminds me of something."

Jean Murray stopped her chattering and Anthony could see from the expression on her face that she had thought of something which she at least regarded as important. Anthony felt that it would be discreet on his part to intervene with a question. There was undoubtedly something on Jean Murray's mind.

"And what has your return journey from Bournemouth reminded you of, Mrs. Murray? Anything important from my particular point of view?"

Jean Murray moved the spoon in her tea-cup almost absent-mindedly. She began to speak. She had been silent for some little time and now she spoke at a slower rate than she had used at any previous time during the interview.

"It's funny," she said, "seeing the line your questions have taken. But I've just remembered something. Goodness knows whether it's important or not. My talking about our journey home brought it back to me. On the way home we passed the Central railway-station. Mrs. Oliver and Margaret were going in as our car flashed by. I saw them both—distinctly. It's all vivid in my mind—the picture of them going in, I mean. They didn't see us, but I saw them. Andrew didn't see them either, he was driving—all eyes on the road."

Anthony began to think again. "And what time was that, Mrs. Murray? As nearly as you can remember it?"

Jean Murray considered. "About twenty minutes to eight. *Is* it of any consequence?"

Anthony shrugged his shoulders. "All the facts help, Mrs. Murray. Whereas ignorance of them may seriously hinder. We'll leave it at that for the moment. But at any rate you'll be able to see from what I've said that you've assisted me considerably. My very best thanks."

Jean Murray flushed with pleasure. "Another cup of tea, Mr. Bathurst? There's plenty in the pot—and it's not *too* awful."

Anthony surrendered his cup for the second time.

4

He hadn't been at home for much more than half an hour when MacMorran rang him.

"Hallo Andrew? What is it this time?"

"Something you asked me to look into. Transport to Puck Willow on Easter Monday evening. Remember?"

"O.K., Andrew—I get you. Picked up anything?"

"No, nothing. Chatterton's been nosing round on it for some days. According to his own story he's interviewed every driver of every motor vehicle that runs on wheels. No luck at all. He can't trace any hired car or taxi-cab that was commissioned for the job. Either from town or from Wimblefield itself. So there you are, pick the bones out of that! We don't move much, do we?"

"Oh, I don't know, Andrew. I'm feeling just a wee bit more confident these last twenty-four hours. One or two ideas are beginning to take shape. Nothing definite yet, but tending that way. Anyhow, many thanks for the information. I'll be seeing you."

Anthony hung up. Then he returned to his armchair. A hazy idea had taken possession of his brain. Was it too entirely fantastic—or was it? He suddenly felt excited and knew instinctively that his pulse had quickened. There wasn't the slightest doubt that Mrs. Murray had told him the truth—he was certain of that. Well, then, if that were so, it *could* have been possible for the murder to have been committed in the manner he had begun to visualize.

Anthony rose and paced the room. He paced the room for some minutes, his brain busy with a hundred details. Then he seated himself again and his fingers went to his waistcoat pocket and to the frayed piece of newsprint he had picked up on the floor of Stella Forrest's bed-sitting-room in Abraham Lincoln Crescent, Hammersmith. From the paper that had been used to line one of the drawers, so said Mrs. Gilbert, the landlady. Anthony wondered. He looked at it again and examined it carefully.

Suddenly he seemed to make up his mind. He rose quickly and walked to his writing-table, where he snatched a sheet of note-paper and an envelope. Anthony wrote quickly, before putting the letter into an envelope together with the frayed fragment of newspaper. He sealed down the envelope, wrote "Personal" across the flap and addressed it "Laurence Greene Esq. Messrs. Scarlett, Greene and Rhodes, Henrietta St. London W.C.2."

"This," he said aloud, "is going to catch the next post, from the nearest Post-office. I'll run along with it myself."

CHAPTER 17

1

Anthony was aware, of course, that Margaret Oliver was Laurence Greene's confidential secretary. She had told MacMorran so herself, and the Inspector had passed on the information to Anthony. When Laurence Greene opened Anthony's letter he had seen the special marking on the back of the envelope—he looked across the table at his secretary and blinked at her through his big horn-rims.

"Bathurst," he said, "Anthony L. Bathurst—didn't you tell me the other day, Miss Oliver, that he was interested in your brother's affair?"

"Yes, Mr. Greene. And you told me you knew him— fairly well, I gathered."

"H'm. Quite so. He's written me here asking me to do something for him. Something rather up my alley. Here you are—here's his letter—you can read it for yourself. Don't suppose for a moment it's anything to do with the death of your brother. Go on, read it for yourself."

Margaret Oliver took Anthony's letter and read it.

My dear Laurence,

If you're frightfully busy—please forgive my bothering you. But there's something I'd very much like you to do for me. I enclose a fragment of newsprint heading which may or may not be of vital importance to me. You told me once—and this letter is clear evidence that I believed you—that you could recognize or ascertain the name of any newspaper of which you were shown even a small fragment— provided that it was of bona fide publication. Will you kindly oblige in respect of the present enclosure? If so, my dear Laurence, I shall then sign myself,

Yours, eternally gratefully,

Anthony L. Bathurst.

P.S. When you reply, please regard the details of the matter as entirely confidential.

Margaret looked up from the letter at her chief. "There's no enclosure here," she said.

Laurence Greene shook his head. "No, Miss Oliver. I have it here. I removed it—for safety. There's so little of it."

"I see. Can you," she went on, "do what . . . er . . . Mr. Bathurst says you can?"

Laurence Green smiled. "Oh, yes. I can recognize newsprint all right. It's been a hobby of mine for years. Bathurst himself can do the same with regard to the big stuff—but he can't do what I can do when it comes to local newspapers. You know the *Hogsnorton Herald* or the *Chipping Sodbury Chronicle*. Publications of that variety. That's where I come in. I'll tell you what you can do for me, Miss Oliver. It will save my writing to acknowledge. When you've a minute, get on the 'phone to him—the number's on the letter there—and tell him O.K. and I'll let him have what he wants within a couple of days. Thanks. And now for some real work. Got your book? Good. Letter to Charles Wogan, Esq.

"My dear Charles,

Many thanks for yours of the 19th inst. I've good news for you. Our Paris office have had an offer for your Reluctant Lady *from Jean de Marsac. He offers £500 on publication . . ."*

Margaret's fingers worked fast but her thoughts ran even faster.

2

Anthony looked at the clock on his mantelpiece. He was in two minds as to the better course for him to pursue. Should he see MacMorran and persuade him to move quickly or should he bide his time and endeavour to make certainty doubly certain? If his fingers had now firmly grasped the true threads of the case and he felt almost absurdly confident that they had—it was going to turn out to be the most amazing problem that had ever come his way for solution.

Which course should he take? MacMorran had all the resources of Scotland Yard behind him—if he *could* persuade the Inspector to follow his advice—Anthony shook his head. He knew, beyond any doubt, that if he went to MacMorran with the story of the Oliver Bath crime as he now saw it, MacMorran would be profoundly sceptical and in all probability refuse to believe him. Anthony knew that this left him with but one course. It was essential that he must find—

At that precise second of his thinking, his telephone rang, almost at his elbow. There was a peremptory note about the ring which caused Anthony to grimace at the offending instrument. He turned and lifted the receiver.

"This is Kensington 55855 . . . Bathurst speaking."

The sound of a woman's voice came through to him. "Is that you, Mr. Bathurst? Oh, good. I was afraid you'd be out and I shouldn't be able to get you. It's Margaret Oliver speaking."

"Oh, good-morning, Miss Oliver. I'm honoured."

"I'm glad you think so—myriads wouldn't. But listen, please. I'm speaking from 'Red, Green and Dusty'."

"And who on earth—"

"I'm sorry I forgot you didn't know. That's what we're always called in the inner circles of the world literary and I'm so used to saying it on the 'phone. Er—'Scarlett, Greene and Rhodes', I mean. Now do you get me? I'm speaking on behalf of Mr. Laurence Greene. You knew I was his secretary, didn't you? He asked me to give you a tinkle. You wrote to him yesterday—he's just got your letter."

Anthony grimaced for the second time that morning before he replied to her.

"Oh yes, Miss Oliver. That's all right. You mean, I take it, that he's given you a message for me? Is that the idea?"

"Yes. That's it, Mr. Bathurst. He wants me to tell you that he'll be pleased to do what you've asked him and that he'll send you the information you require in the course of the next two days. That will suit you, I suppose, Mr. Bathurst?"

"Many thanks, Miss Oliver. Please convey my compliments and thanks to Mr. Laurence Green and tell him how much I appreciate his kindness."

Margaret Oliver's voice changed. "Tell me, please," she said, "are you any nearer the truth . . . about poor Peter?"

Anthony replied gravely. "Very much nearer, Miss Oliver. Within a week, I am confident that Inspector MacMorran will have made the arrest. What do you say to that?"

He heard her gasp at the other end. Then her voice came through again. "Are you really serious . . . when you say that?"

"I was never more serious in my life, Miss Oliver." Anthony waited for her reply. But none came—there was silence. Margaret had hung up.

3

Laurence Greene's reply came through in even less time than he had promised. For by the evening post of the day following Margaret's telephone conversation, Anthony received the letter for which he had been waiting.

Anthony opened the envelope quickly and read the contents.

My dear A.L.B.

Didn't expect this so quickly, did you? Just shows you, doesn't it? Class will tell! Herewith the slip you forwarded, returned. I'm afraid it's almost on its last legs, so if it's any value to you, treat it tenderly. Which brings me to the point. It's a portion of a local weekly paper published in Bristol, circulating Bristol, Gloucester and their vicinities under the title of the Western Clarion. *Of that you may be certain. We Greenes never let a man down. How do I know, say you? That you sent me a portion of the W.C. (dear me that sounds shocking)? Well, it's through my own special knowledge added to that of somebody else with whom I've conferred on the matter. If you write to the Editor, Western Clarion, 9a Voyce St., Bristol, and tell him what you desire to know, you should get from him all the details required. Is thy servant worthy of great reward? Even so and so be it!*

Yours always,

Laurence E. G. Greene.

(The man who lives up to his reputation.)

P.S. This is all between you and me in accordance with your expressed wish.

Anthony sat back in his chair and thought things over. Bristol! Gloucestershire generally! The *Western Clarion*! His letter to Greene had turned up trumps after all. Was it possible—even now—that his latest theory of the crime was going to prove the correct one?

One thing annoyed him—he wasn't able to *act* yet. He was still delayed. He couldn't go haring off to Bristol on a purely chance shot such as this was. He must wait for the "all-clear", and to obtain that meant that he must write yet another letter. The Editor of the *Western Clarion* at Bristol must supply him with the full paragraph of which he possessed but the headlines.

Anthony felt for his fountain-pen. The letter must be written—it was imperative—so the sooner he got down to the job the better. How should he word it? It required care, skill, discretion and discrimination. So that the editor should be aware of its urgency and yet not overwhelmed by it.

Anthony wrote steadily for a few moments, before stopping to read carefully what he had written. What he read evidently pleased him. He signed the letter, with a certain amount of flourish. At last the sands of the killer's hour-glass were fast running down!

4

Once again, Anthony sat with MacMorran in the latter's room at Scotland Yard.

"I asked you to come along," said the Inspector, "with a definite purpose. But before I tell you what it is, you tell me something." MacMorran grinned. "How's tricks? Are you moving at all?"

He stared at Anthony with speculative eyes. Anthony lit a cigarette and chucked the case over to MacMorran. Through smoke he spoke.

"Yes. Definitely. Moved several paces forward since we last met. Waiting for the last link in the chain."

MacMorran looked at him with eyebrows cocked in inquiry. He whistled. "As close as that?"

"Think so. But I can't possibly put it in front of you *until* I'm satisfied with regard to that last link I spoke about."

MacMorran rubbed his jaw reflectively. "H'm. I see. Well, you've never let me down yet, so I'll continue to put up with you. Now, you listen to me. I asked you to come along this morning to meet Murray, the bank manager. He'll be here at eleven o'clock. When I arrived this morning, there was a message on my table asking me to 'phone him directly I came in. I did. He told me he wanted to see me about something in which he thinks I may be interested. Actually he'll be here within a few minutes now. I asked you to come along."

"Many thanks, Andrew. What's it about—any idea?"

"All I know is it's to do with Garcia. That's all he'd tell me on the 'phone. Can't blame him. Bank managers are like doctors and priests. The private room, the surgery and the confessional. All hush-hush and bated breath. The result was that I didn't—"

A tap on the door interrupted him. "I expect this is Murray. Come in."

Andrew Murray was at the door with a constable. MacMorran welcomed him. "Come in, Mr. Murray. Take that chair, will you?"

"Good morning, Inspector. Good morning, Bathurst. I can't stay long, we're very busy at Lombard Street, and I'm not sure now whether I'm doing the right thing in coming here. After all, I'm a bank manager, and a client's a client. But I had this letter this morning. That's all. A client's a client, as I said, but murder's murder all the world over. And Oliver was a young fellow on my staff. We both worked for Delaney's. That means something, you know. Anyhow, read the letter, Inspector, and then give it back to me."

Murray tossed a letter on to MacMorran's table. "There may be nothing in it," he added, "but it occurred to me that there'd be no harm in your knowing."

MacMorran opened the letter and read it. When he'd finished he put it in Anthony's hand. Anthony saw that the address was Plinner.

Dear Mr. Murray,

I shall be calling upon you at half past two on Tuesday next to close my current account and to withdraw my holdings and deposits. I regret to inform you that certain business complications in San Jonquilo which have suddenly come into being make it imperative that I return to that country almost immediately. Actually, my wife and I have booked air passages and we leave on Friday of next week. With thanks for the many assistances which you have rendered me.

I remain,

Yours sincerely,

Roderigo S. Garcia.

Murray came in again. "Have I acted rightly in coming to you, or not? As I said just now, I'm hanged if I know. I've no *business* to have told you, but there you are, Garcia's going to skip, and the knowledge of it worried me rather, so I 'phoned you, Inspector. Is it fishy—or is it?"

MacMorran saw that the bank manager was genuinely perturbed. He looked in Anthony's direction but the latter's face was expressionless.

"Well," said the Inspector, caressing his chin, "it's difficult to say at the moment. It *may* be all serene—on the other hand, it may not. But I agree with you that it looks a bit on the suspicious side, and by and large, I think you did the right thing in letting me know."

Murray's face cleared a little. He used a handkerchief to wipe his forehead. "Good. You don't know what a relief to me that is. It's not all honey, the responsibility of a bank manager. It was the suddenness of this Garcia business that made me blink."

MacMorran nodded. "Yes. It *is* the suddenness, as you say. All the same, I don't see what I can do about it."

"Wise words," murmured Anthony.

"I know," said Murray, "nobody better. That's the awkwardness of it all."

"At the same time," went on MacMorran, "we're forewarned. Thanks to you, we know Garcia's intentions. We can take steps to deal with him should we regard such a procedure as desirable. And we've got something like ten days in which to do it. In other words, we're no worse off, and it may turn out that we're very much *better*. We must wait and see."

Anthony then came in with a surprising question. At least it surprised MacMorran and it may have had a similar effect on Murray.

"Mr. Murray," he inquired, "does anybody else at your bank know anything about this? That is to say, as far as you know?"

Murray thought over the question. "As far as I know, one person only. That's my chief clerk, Mr. Fitzgerald. You've met him."

"I see. Did you tell him?"

"Oh, no. But it's his duty to open the inward post. So that everything's ready for me when I arrive in the morning. He would open all letters with the exception of those addressed to me personally and marked 'Personal' or 'Private', or, perhaps, 'Confidential'. All that's my own arrangement. And Garcia's letter had none of those marks."

Anthony nodded and repeated his previous remark. "I see. Only Fitzgerald. Thank you, Mr. Murray."

Murray looked at MacMorran. "You can go, Mr. Murray. I won't detain you any longer. Very many thanks for what you've done. Great help."

Murray's face flushed with satisfaction and pleasure. He waved and slid out. MacMorran turned to Anthony. "Garcia, eh? Scramming out of it. I agree with the bank manager. Fishy! Decidedly fishy!"

"Going back to Santa Guardina, Andrew. Where the lights are bright and the señoritas even more attractive than those provided by Raymond Hurst of 'The Orange Lizard'. By the way, did you notice the likeness between Hurst and the businesslike Fitzgerald?"

MacMorran, stung by the remark, stared at him in wonderment. "What the hell are you talking about?" he said curtly. Anthony grinned. "Fitzgerald," he replied, "of Delaney's bank, Lombard Street, and . . . er . . . Hurst . . . presiding genius of 'The Orange Lizard'. Extraordinarily alike, to my eye."

CHAPTER 18

1

The editor of the weekly newspaper entitled the *Western Clarion* came up to scratch handsomely. Not only did he thank Anthony in his letter of reply for the interest exhibited in his newspaper, but he avowed that to serve Anthony in the degree of supplying information was to him an occupation of sheer and supreme delight. To that end it was his pleasure to enclose the full paragraph from the *Western Clarion*, of which Anthony had furnished the headlines.

Mr. Bathurst would see, so wrote the industrious editor, that the actual edition of the paper which originally contained the paragraph of Mr. Bathurst's interest had been published just on four years ago. But after all, he continued, what was a matter of four years? Just a flash—nothing more—in the pattern and design of Eternity!

He concluded his most interesting letter by declaring that if there were any other service he could perform on Anthony's behalf, the latter must not wait a second before demanding it of him.

Anthony smiled as he read this epistolary effusion, and it says much for his patience that he read it before he turned to the paragraph which the editor of the *Western Clarion* had forwarded.

Because, if Anthony's theories were sound, there was the chance that this paragraph *might* contain the clue for which his fingers had been groping for so long a time.

Anthony noted the exact date of the paper's publication and read the paragraph.

It ran as follows:

Visitors to, and local inhabitants of, Weston-super-Mare, had a thrill if they were near the beach yesterday morning which many of them, we do not doubt, would very well have done without.

A young girl swimmer who was some considerable distance from the shore was suddenly observed to be in serious difficulties, but happily her cries for help did not fall on deaf ears. A young man, in bathing costume, who was standing on the beach, immediately swam to her assistance and most gallantly brought the young lady to shore apparently none the worse for her frightening experience.

It was generally agreed amongst the large number of people who witnessed the rescue, that, rarely, if ever, has more courage been displayed than that shown by yesterday's hero.

Unhappily from the point of view of those desirous of seeing a fitting conclusion to the rescue, the gallant rescuer, after assuring himself that his protégée was safe and sound, walked away from the scene in a cloud of complete anonymity.

It has been rumoured since that he was a foreigner unable to speak English but we are not aware whether there is any truth in this idea.

The young lady who underwent this terrible ordeal and who was most upset because she was unable to express her gratitude to the man who had saved her, is, we understand, a Miss Stella Forrest of 19 Pimpernel Cottages, Worle.

"At last," said Anthony to himself as he reached over to his book-case for the copy of the ABC that he knew was there.

2

Anthony frowned at what he saw. The ABC railway-guide referred him to "Paxton and Worle". After turning up the joint reference, Anthony's frown developed considerably and he decided that his best proposition was train to Weston-super-Mare and thence by bus to Worle. Paxton could go hang and take care of itself. The Crystal Palace likewise. Anthony's mind was like that—a creature of sudden twists and turns.

He packed a suit-case with commendable celerity, had dinner on the train and stayed the night in a reasonably comfortable hôtel in Weston-super-Mare. He would deal with the Worle matter in the morning.

When morning came it was fair and sunny and Anthony set off soon after breakfast in high spirits. The omens were generally good.

Since he had made up his mind to come to Somersetshire, everything had gone propitiously for him. Would his luck hold when he came to the village of Worle? Well, he would soon know whether his journey had been fruitless.

Anthony alighted from the 'bus which had brought him into Worle and set out at once to look for the Post-office. The task was not an arduous one. It seemed to Anthony as he looked round that the population would be somewhere round the two-thousand mark.

A thin man stood behind the Post-office counter. Anthony went in, smiled cordially and wished him "good-morning" The thin man mumbled something in reply. Anthony wasted no time. He made straight to his point. The thin man listened. When Anthony finished, he nodded.

"Ay, mister," he said, "you haven't done so badly coomin' 'ere. I can direct you all right—as far as the address is concerned. I mind the lass well. One o' the prettiest that ever this little old village turned out. But—and I just hate to disappoint you, mister—I haven't clapped eyes on her for years now—not since she went 'oop to Lunnon."

Anthony's heart sank at the words. He was hearing what he had been afraid he might hear. He knew, too, that if his own idea were the right one and Stella *had* fled back to her own village because of the fear that haunted her, this man in the Post-office would know. There would be no concealing the fact in a country village such as this was. All the same, he would inquire at the house—something *might* emerge from the conversation.

"Tell me, please," he said to the thin man behind the counter, "how do I find my way to Pimpernel Cottages?" To his further dismay the thin man shook his head.

"T'ain't no manner o' use you be goin' there, mister. The Forrests be all gone from there. Let me tell you now! Young Stella and 'er sister Winnie lived there with their widowed stepmother. When Stella went 'oop to Lunnon, Winnie started courtin'. When Stella was 'ere chaps wouldn't look at 'er sister, they was all for Stella—but when she took 'erself off, that was all changed. Well, Winnie got along with the chaps and eventually married a young feller from Bristol, I think it was, and went there to live. When she went, 'er mother went with 'er. And that was the last us in Worle see o' the Forrests."

Anthony's discomfiture was now almost complete. He felt that he would do no good by remaining in the Post-office and subjecting the thin man to a barrage of questions. It was as clear as day that Stella was *not* in her native village—that she had *not* come back to it.

Anthony thanked the thin man for the information he had given him and made his way out of the Post-office. Outside in the street, he stood on the pavement for a little time wondering. It appeared to him now that his best course, almost his only course, was to get back to MacMorran without delay. To stay where he was seemed an absolutely profitless project. Stella Forrest had not returned to her native heath—nostalgia had not had its way.

Anthony began to walk away from the Post-office. He tried to reason out his new problem. If Stella hadn't come back to the village of her youth—*as he had felt certain she would have—* where had she gone? That was the essential point. But to search elsewhere for her, minus a clue of any kind, would be akin to looking for the needle in the hay-stack. He had neither the time nor the inclination to indulge in that procedure. His old fear came back to him. Had the murderer caught up with her . . . and removed her as he had removed Peter Oliver?

Anthony still continued to walk on, until he realized that he was leaving the village behind. He must retrace his steps, there was no point whatever in his wasting time.

He turned, therefore, determined to make his way back to the bus terminus. Suddenly, as he walked and wrestled with his problem, he looked up and saw on the side of a wall in front of him the name in black on a white ground. "Pimpernel Cottages." There were two rows of cottages, about a dozen on each side. Anthony looked at the humble dwellings which Stella Forrest had known in her youth. It was a far cry from here to Hammersmith.

He pictured her living here, running along the road, playing on the grass, full of the rich red wine of youth. And then leaving the tranquillity of Somerset fields, "so full of sap and sunny", for London and its bright lights. For Lambert's restaurant and Mrs. Gilbert's bed-sitting-room.

Where had she run to, or where had she been when the killer had stolen up behind her? Anthony sorrowed for Stella Forrest. There was the village of her youth almost in front of him and a cottage which now knew her not.

And then, as he sorrowed, an idea came to him. Now that he had come so far in search of her, he would not leave Worle without making inquiry for her at her cottage of the Pimpernel. There was always the hundredth chance!

3

Anthony walked up to the tenth cottage on the right-hand side. A long, winding path led to a small front door. Wallflowers were in sweet-smelling profusion in the front garden. There was neither knocker nor bell on the door. Anthony rapped with his bare knuckles. A middle-aged, florid-faced woman came at the summons. Anthony smiled and doffed his hat.

"Be it the insurance?" inquired the woman, "because if it be, we doant want any"

Anthony explained that she was heading in the wrong direction. He gently and courteously diverted her. The florid-faced woman listened. Eventually the frown which had come to her face disappeared and her features cleared generally. At last she nodded, and Anthony thanked whatever gods there be, for their august and majestic reception of the hundredth chance. The woman of Number 19 Pimpernel Cottages began to speak.

"As it happens you've done the right thing, mestur. Doant 'e mind what you 'eard at Post-office. Although, o' course, you can't rightly blame 'im up theer for what he told yer. 'E didn't know no better! But that yoong leddy you speak of *did* coom 'ere. Late one night it was. A week or two back, not more. She coom inquirin' for 'er flesh and blood—joost as you said she might ha' done. My 'oosband see her at door 'ere—'e coom out into kitchen afterwards and told me."

Anthony listened, probed and quested for details. But he met with scant success. The florid-faced woman was unable to add anything of value to the story as she had first told it. The little house where Stella had lived as a little girl and Stella herself had passed like ships in the night.

Anthony thanked the woman for her assistance and went back to the main road and his own depressing thoughts. The tempo of the case persisted—invariably every condition of acceleration was inevitably attended by the reverse exercise of "slowing up".

Anthony looked back on the innumerable occasions when his spirits had risen on a wave of confidence only to be almost immediately dragged back to despondency. His visit to the West Country had been cast in similar mould. There was nothing for it but to return to Weston-super-Mare and then, after that, to London and Andrew MacMorran.

Anthony walked back to the bus terminus and climbed on to the bus which was waiting there. He would lunch at his hôtel and catch a train back to Paddington in the early afternoon. After that? Anthony shrugged his mental shoulders. *Without* Stella Forrest's confirmation of his theory, he would be forced to move warily and to take a chance. *With* her corroboration, he would have moved—and moved quickly, struck—and struck hard.

The bus brought him to his destination. Anthony alighted. The hôtel at which he was staying was about a quarter of a mile's distance. The walk took him through the town. Anthony strolled along comfortably, he had ample time. Suddenly, like the blue-hurled bolt, Anthony stopped with a gasp of amazement. At the cash-desk of a baker's shop, which advertised "morning-coffee, lunches and teas", sat Stella Forrest!

4

Anthony stood and watched her and spoke to himself. "So I was right after all. Home is the hunted, home from the hill." He scribbled quickly on a visiting-card and entered the shop. Walking quietly to the cash-desk, behind a stout woman of many baskets, he put the card on the desk-ledge. Stella's eyes were downcast as he did so. The card bore the words—*when and where can I see you so that we can talk?*

Stella looked up from the card incredulously. Her eyes met Anthony's. There was recognition in them and anxiety—and also, perhaps, relief. Anthony was by no means sure with regard to this last-mentioned condition. He waited in patience for Stella's reply. Either spoken or written. He saw her fingers reach for a pencil lying close by. Stella began to write on the card. Below the message he had written to her. When she had finished, she pushed the card back to him.

"Thank you," said Anthony. He walked out of the baker's shop into the street. At a few yards' distance Anthony read what Stella Forrest had written. *3 p.m. on the corner where the hoarding is.*

Anthony looked for the indication and saw at once where she meant. He would have lunch at his hôtel and meet Stella at the time she had named. The break for which he had waited had come at last.

CHAPTER 19

1

When he met her he said simply, "where can we go? I want to talk to you." Stella nodded. "Yes, Mr. Bathurst, I know. Come with me. There's a little tea-shop where we can have tea at half past three. It's not very far from here."

Anthony made no demur. He was assessing her—her looks, her demeanour, her general attitude. She was very lovely, but something had gone from her eyes since his last meeting with her. The girl had become a woman and the way had been hard. The grey lass sorrow had held her hand and guided her to the escarpment of maturity.

Neither of them spoke again until they reached the rendezvous which Stella had nominated. The little shop was empty—it was comparatively early and the afternoon-tea rush had scarcely started. Stella went to a side-table and Anthony sat with her. He saw that she knew the woman who came to attend to them.

"Order what you like," he said to Stella, "and make it for two."

Stella nodded and Anthony waited. After she had poured out the tea, she looked at him. "How did you find me? Even now, I can't really believe it's happened."

Anthony told her of the cutting from the *Western Clarion* and how he had found the fragment in her room at Mrs. Gilbert's.

"That was wonderful of you."

Anthony said, "Perhaps. But today was sheer luck. No bouquets, please. Why did you run away? You were afraid, weren't you?"

Stella nodded. "Yes. Terribly. I knew that if I told everything, I should be in great danger."

Anthony said again, "Let me tell you a story, Miss Forrest. The story of everything as I see it. If I go wrong anywhere, please interrupt me and put me right. Is that agreed?"

Stella drank her tea, put down her cup and nodded. "Yes, I'll do that, but I don't understand how you can possibly—"

But Anthony had started before she could complete what she had been about to say.

"The real starting-point shall be the day when you were swimming in the sea out there"—Anthony gestured in the appropriate direction—"and found yourself in difficulties." Anthony dropped his voice a little as he went on. "The local Press, when it reported the incident of your rescue, hinted that the man who had acted so fearlessly *might* have been a foreigner. You didn't know . . . for some time. . . you didn't know . . . who he was . . . until he came back to you and disclosed his identity. Am I right, Miss Forrest?"

Stella nodded again. "Yes . . . you are perfectly right."

"I was afraid I must be," Anthony went on. For what seemed to Stella, listening eagerly, an interminable time. Every now and then he stopped suddenly and questioned her, so that his recital was punctuated by a series of nods or denials (mainly the former), from Stella. Anthony gradually brought the story up to date. He began to speak more slowly. "Now, of course, I'm not quite so certain as to what happened. After you met Peter Oliver and you fell in love with each other. I may be inaccurate with regard to a number of the details. But I presume that you and Peter Oliver went one night to 'The Orange Lizard' and Garcia was there—am I right?"

"Yes . . . we had been introduced to 'The Orange Lizard' some little time before . . . you guessed that, I suppose? And who took us there?"

This time it was Anthony's turn to nod. "Yes, and you were invited to the house at Plinner—am I right?"

"Yes. Peter was working late at the bank and he picked me up outside to take me to the Garcias' house."

"And that was the night which brought matters to a head?"

"Yes, I'm positive it must have been. Because we had been so careful before that happened. Peter should never have risked it."

Anthony was silent. When he spoke again, he said, "he signed his own death-warrant, poor chap. The seed of suspicion, then merely sown, germinated over the Easter week-end into the flower of certainty and the whole diabolical and treacherous plot began to take shape."

Anthony paused again. Stella began to cry, softly and very quietly. He ignored the tears . . . deliberately. "Tell me," he said, "have you been actually threatened... since?"

"No."

"Nobody knows where you are? You're certain of that?"

"Only you."

"I wouldn't be too sure of that," countered Anthony grimly; "all the same, I don't suppose you'll be—" He broke off.

"What are you going to do?" said Stella, dry-eyed now.

"Put a match to the fire. Something may happen. Rats abominate a house on fire as much as they dislike a sinking ship. Tell me again, Miss Forrest. This baker's where you have managed to get a job—they sell biscuits, I suppose?"

Stella said simply, "The man it belongs to sells everything in his different shops. From bread to borax and from borax to boot-polish. Surely you've seen his name on the carts? Grocers, bakers, butchers, chandlers—he's got shops all over the town. *And* in Bath—*and* in Bristol."

"All the better for my purpose," said Anthony, hard-mouthed and grim-lipped. "Get me a biscuit if you can, known as a 'Bath Oliver'. There should be some about down in this part of the country. Bring it to me here at this time to-morrow afternoon. I'll tell you what it's like . . . it's a kind of . . . "

2

On the following afternoon, Anthony waited in the same tea-shop for Stella Forrest. She was a few minutes late in coming but she came all right and put a small bag in front of him on the tea-table.

"Your biscuits," she said, "they're real Bath Olivers. You said bring you one, but I've brought you three."

"All the better," replied Anthony grimly, "we'll administer three shocks in succession instead of the one that I had in mind. That ought to shake a certain person's complacency, and it might even do better than that—it might yield very tangible results."

"How do you mean?" asked Stella.

Anthony ordered tea before he answered her. Then he turned to her and said, "my snag's going to be *proving* the case. British Juries require more than brilliant essays in deduction, Stella. It's going to be darned difficult, my child, believe me. Give me one of the biscuits."

Stella obeyed. Anthony continued, "I've provided myself with an envelope of strong Manilla paper and of just the right shape. See how nicely it fits?"

Anthony took out his fountain-pen and addressed the envelope. Stella watched him with a look of fascination on her face. The waitress brought the tea just as Anthony had finished addressing the envelope. Suddenly, Stella leant forward and grasped him by the arm.

"What's the trouble, Stella?"

"Why," she said, "I've just thought of something. Something important. You mustn't post that *here*!"

The grey eyes mocked her. "Why not? Afraid it'll break in the post?"

"Of course not. Don't be so absurd. Think!"

Anthony thought. "Yes," he said slowly, with the slowness of considered agreement, "yes, Stella. Good for you! You're right. It will be put down as coming from *you*, because of the postmark. The postmark will awake memories."

"Of course," she whispered.

"Yes, and in that case it wouldn't accomplish what I'm hoping—" Anthony paused. "I'll take it back with me and post it in town. Better still, I'll—" Again he paused. When he went on again, he said, "even though there may be a suspicion that this first one emanates from you, I'll take good care that no such doubts are entertained with regard to number two and number three. When they're removed from their respective envelopes, I assure you it won't be in accompanying thought-terms of Stella Forrest."

Stella nodded her acquiescence and understanding. "How long will the interval be," she asked, "between them?"

"What do you think yourself?"

"I should make it short. You know, follow up quickly. I think it would be better that way."

Anthony grinned as he lifted his cup of tea. "Right hook to the jaw, eh—and then the left to the solar plexus? Not bad. Not at all bad! Lady, I'll take your advice. That's how it shall go."

"What will happen?" asked Stella simply. Anthony shrugged his shoulders. "Difficult to say. But I'm hoping for a 'scram'. Or panic—translated in some way that MacMorran and I can pick up."

Stella shook her head. "I don't think that will happen. When I look back on things, and think, I don't think it'll go like that."

"Why not? This is something quite new, don't forget. No contingency of this sort has ever had to be faced before. I don't see how you can tell what the reaction will be when a person is faced with a set of circumstances that are entirely unfamiliar."

Stella still shook her head. "I know. But all the same I think time will prove me right."

This time it was Anthony who shook his head. "You allowed yourself to be dominated by a stronger will than your own. Look at that semi-monasticism which was imposed on you when you lived at Hammersmith with Mrs. Gilbert. No friends, no parties, no letters from anybody. All dictated by fierce jealousy and an almost insensate possessiveness.

Stella nodded. She clasped her hands on her lap. The tears were in her eyes again. "Yes. It was wrong of me. Worse than just wrong. Wicked, in the first place. But you don't always realize that you're doing wrong until it's too late, and then you can't draw back. I've paid, though, for my sins. Dearly. I couldn't have paid more dearly. I shall never forgive myself. If it hadn't been for me, Peter would never have been murdered as he was."

"Don't reproach yourself too much, my child. We all make mistakes and you aren't to blame anything like as much as you think you are." Anthony moved his cup and saucer so that he might lean his arm on the table. "When I think how nearly I was to missing the vital point, I begin to shudder. If it hadn't been for that left-handed business, I might still have been in the dark. Eat that other pastry. Looks something like cream on it. And I'll take care of this pile of ammunition.' "

Anthony took the envelope and bag which contained the biscuits. Stella Forrest began to pack the used tea-things on to the tray. "When are you leaving?" she asked.

"Almost at once. I've settled with the hôtel people. When I say good-bye to you, my next move will be in the direction of the railway-station. There's a train just before five o'clock."

"Shall I . . . shall I . . . have to appear as a witness if you . . . make the arrest?"

"That's looking too far ahead. Don't worry about that until later on. Let's see how things pan out first."

"I should hate it," said Stella, "having to give evidence . . . like that."

"Don't think about it. Staying on down here? In the shop?" Stella smiled at him bravely. "I think so. For a little while. I must. I've my living to get."

Anthony smiled and held out his hand. "Good for you! Well, *au 'voir* . . . good-bye for the present. I'm bound to see you again sometime." Stella took the extended hand.

"Thank you, Stella," said Anthony, "for all the help you've given me."

"It is I," replied Stella, "who should say that to you."

3

Anthony returned to Paddington and straightway consigned his special envelope to the care of the Postal authorities. No sooner was he back at his flat than he telephoned to the "Yard" and asked for Andrew MacMorran. The Inspector was on duty and answered the call.

"I'm back," said Anthony, "strange though it may seem. During our unhappy separation I have passed through many trials and much tribulation. But I am still ready for more. To that end I shall be in your office at nine forty-five tomorrow. Ack emma, as ever was. So remember to be early for once in your chequered career."

MacMorran spoke at considerable length. Anthony heard him out. "You, Andrew," he said at length, "are merely the 'grim wolf with privy paw' which 'daily devours apace and nothing said'. You could have saved all your breath and then employed it to a better purpose such as tankard-emptying. I tell you here and now that the Oliver bath problem is solved! I know 'why' and I also know 'who'. Now shout for joy, you old reprobate."

Anthony could hear MacMorran's heavy breathing at the other end of the line. He went on talking. " 'Sfact, Andrew! Commencing at nine forty-five tomorrow—ack emma as aforesaid—the tale, like a draught of spicy nut-brown ale, shall be poured into you."

MacMorran cut in again. "Where the hell have you been?"

"Zummerzet, Andrew. The luscious fields thereof. Junket and cider brew."

"Can we move at once? I mean—arrest?"

"That's the snag, I'm afraid. That's what we shall have to talk about to-morrow, Andrew. It ain't goin' to be all straight and above-board. That's the worst of it. But it's a beautiful case, Andrew! I wouldn't have missed it for all the tea in China. A wonderful murder! By an amazing criminal. I quite expect serious difficulty in convincing you. You'll be pinching yourself to assure yourself that you're wide awake. Still, I'll live on in hopes."

MacMorran began again. The dissertation developed rapidly. Anthony listened for a time, sleepily. "Oh, blast you, Andrew," he said at length, "I'm tired. I've had a hell of a long day. I'm going to Uncle Ned. Possess your Aberdeen soul in patience until morning gilds the sky. It can wait, believe me."

Anthony hung up without further ado. MacMorran sat in his chair and glared at the telephone. Without looking up he said bitterly, "and you!"

A second later, however, a comfortable smile broke over his face.

4

Anthony knocked on the door of MacMorran's room at a quarter to ten on the following morning. The Inspector grinned at him as he entered. "Hope you had a good night's rest."

"You bet I did, Andrew. Take a better man than you to upset that. And I reckon I wasn't the only one."

Anthony crooked his foot round the leg of a chair and pulled it towards him. MacMorran frowned.

"How do you mean—you weren't the only one?"

"Well, what about yourself? Didn't the news I gave you last night make you sleep better? I'll say it did. No tossing and turning for you last night. The official boat safe home in port again, rent cordage, shattered deck—but nevertheless in port? Good lord, Andrew, don't sit there looking all Ridley and Latimer."

MacMorran coughed. "Your news was good, certainly. But I'd like to hear the details before I put down the red carpet."

"Andrew, you shall. That's what I'm here for. Now, listen—and I'm afraid you'll be listening for some little time!" Anthony tossed a cigarette to the Inspector, crossed his legs and began his story. "The yarn starts in the West Country, and may almost be said to finish there. No, that wouldn't be altogether true, the finish isn't in sight—*yet.*"

MacMorran put his arms on his table and leant on them. Anthony was by now well in his stride. Every now and then MacMorran uttered an exclamation of incredulity. Suddenly he came in with an interruption.

"Are you sure of this? It's not that imagination of yours a bit over-heated? You know—you're asking me to—"

Anthony treated the diffidence with but—scant ceremony. "Gertcher, Andrew. Can't you see how all the bits and pieces fall into their proper sockets? It's a beautiful case—didn't I tell you so on the 'phone last night? It all *fits*.

"Can't you see that, Andrew? Right from Stella Forrest in her bathing-costume to Stella Forrest in the cash-desk at old man Lambert's restaurant and finally to her engagement to Peter Oliver—her going to 'The Orange Lizard' and then finally to her meeting Peter after he had been working late at the bank and going with him to Garcia's house at Plinner. And—which is more than *anything*, Andrew—*my* solution is the *only possible one*! That's the chief reason why it pleases me so. Oh, yes, it's a beautiful case all right, Andrew. You and I aren't likely to meet another down the same alley."

MacMorran "doodled" on his blotting-pad. "What do we do? Since you're so hundred per cent certain?"

"Oh, I forgot to tell you. What I did last night, first thing this morning and what I shall do early this afternoon." Anthony produced his third Bath Oliver letter, and gave MacMorran the details. The Inspector furrowed his forehead.

"When was the first received? When should it have been?"

"This morning's post. It will disturb the killer's complacency. The second will mean distinct agitation. The third, I hope, *may* be translated into something like panic. We shall have to wait and see."

"And that's the third that you have there?"

"Correct, Andrew. This is B.O. Number Three."

"You intend to post it this afternoon, you say?"

"That *was* the idea."

"It'll be received, then, to-morrow morning?"

"First delivery, Andrew. Unless there's a technical 'itch."

MacMorran shook his head. "I don't think we can take any risks. Dare not! You never know how the cat may jump. We should have full cover right from the start. I must see Chatterton."

"Suits me if that's how you feel about it."

MacMorran was emphatic. "I most certainly do."

Anthony began to speak more slowly. "Since you have used the word 'risks', I've been thinking, Andrew." He pulled a sheet of note-paper towards him and started to scribble on it. MacMorran sat and watched him without speaking. After a few seconds Anthony pushed the paper back to the Inspector. "Look here, Andrew, that's where the vulnerability is—do you agree?"

MacMorran read what Anthony had written. "Yes, I agree."

"Well, then, our best plan is to attack on those lines. Although I admit it's not going to be easy. But Stella's the ace, whichever way you look at it. All the way through. We could create the impression that Stella had partly opened her mouth and talked . . . just a little . . . to the Police, I mean . . . and that pressure was being put on her to talk still more . . . with her mouth open wider . . . do you get the idea, Andrew?"

MacMorran scratched his cheek. "How could we best do that, do you think?"

"You could do it, Andrew. You could do it yourself."

"You mean—the personal call?"

"Of course. What could be better? You could handle it better than anybody. You could take with you a nice big packet of 'suspicion' seed and sow it so deftly and so judiciously, that even when you smiled, the air would be full of black caps and condemned cells. And then leave Chatterton to do the rest."

MacMorran changed from scratching his cheek to rubbing the side of his nose. "Ay," he said cautiously, "it's not such a bad idea. I could handle it all right . . . the way you say. I could put the fear-r of Almighty God into Lucifer himself . . . if the circumstances were right for me. This one'll be child's play. When do you think—the sooner the better?"

"Every time. Why not this evening? Shall we say—between the biscuits? Certainly before Friday. To-day's Wednesday."

"Why before Friday. What's the urgency about Friday?"

There was a twinkle in Anthony s grey eyes as he replied. "Wasn't it a certain gentleman's intention to leave by air for San Jonquilo on Friday next? I seem to remember something of the kind."

MacMorran nodded. "I get the point. You *would* think of that, wouldn't you?"

CHAPTER 20

1

Anthony returned to his flat and waited impatiently for the sound of the horn. The horn which in all probability would be a telephone. But horn or telephone—either would do. For the message which Anthony awaited in either case would be the same—"that the hunt was up".

The first note was sounded late on the Wednesday evening when a 'phone-call came through from MacMorran. Anthony couldn't help feeling a little anxious as he answered it.

"Bathurst speaking . . . O.K., Andrew."

"Guessed you'd be sitting by the telephone."

"Not quite that, but near enough. Well, tell me the worst. Did you cast the line?"

"Yes. I took your advice. Popped along early this evening. As a matter of fact I've only just got back to civilization."

"How did it go? Any pleasing signs?"

"Well, I had to clear the stage a bit—as you may guess—before I could really get down to anything. But I'm distinctly hopeful. You were quite right, of course—the lady was the master-card. Gave much food for thought, I can tell you."

"Good. Any doubts still lingering in the old brain-box, Andrew or have they folded their tents?"

"No. No doubts now. The guilt showed plain enough. You're on the target all right. Trust you!"

"That's very nice of you, Andrew. Any biscuit-crumbs observable?"

Anthony could hear MacMorran laughing. "Not so's you'd notice."

"But you said you were distinctly hopeful, Andrew. I noted the words particularly. How come?"

"Well, I'm never the ruddy optimist that you are, but I *think* that the next step *may* be the old 'run-out powder'."

Anthony was sharply inquiring. "Why, Andrew? You must have spotted something to say that."

"Never satisfied, are you? Must know everything? Well, well, well! All right, I'll come clean. There was a current copy of the *ABC* almost centre stage. May be nothing in it of course, but the sight of that gave me hopes. There you are—now I've told you."

"Open? The *ABC*, I mean?"

"No. Shut. You want it *all* your own way."

Anthony ignored the thrust. As far as he was concerned this was no time for flippancy. "Where's Chatterton?" he asked.

"Just where you're thinking he is. Plus Evershed. Plus Davidson. Three of 'em on it. Don't worry about that. All the holes are being watched."

Some seconds elapsed before Anthony replied. "Something in my bones tells me you've pulled it off, Andrew. That it's going the way we want it to. Almost in the bag! Don't know why, exactly—but I've suddenly come over tremendously confident. I don't think we shall have to wait very long, either."

"Depends what you mean by very long. I know what I think myself."

"What's that?"

"*Somewhere round the week-end.* And early rather than late at that. And you'll find I shan't be very far out."

"Maybe. Maybe not. We shall see. One word before I hang up. We're up against a cunning criminal who won't be taken without a struggle. Tell the Chatterton squad to be on the look-out for a fast one. A real 'quickie'—one out of the bag."

MacMorran laughed confidently. "Don't you worry about Chatterton. He's got eyes in his—excuse me, my internal 'phone's going."

2

At ten o'clock on the following Saturday morning a man descended the steps of an important London sub-way. Primarily, to ninety-nine observers out of every hundred, he looked an ordinary man. There was nothing extraordinary about his height. There was nothing particularly noticeable with regard to any quality of physique. His clothing was indeterminate. His walk and his carriage generally were entirely inconspicuous.

But the two "Yard" men, who had been more than ordinarily interested in his movements for some days now, "tailed" him inexorably as he made his way along the sub-way.

Chatterton, for he was one of the two, had noticed that the quarry, on this latest public appearance, was carrying a large suit-case. A suit-case which had not been carried previously by him on that same Saturday morning. He was wearing—and the recording of these details is important—a brown hat (dark), brown tweed overcoat, brown lounge suit and a pair of extremely well-polished dark brown shoes. Their toe-caps positively scintillated in the morning sun, with that attractive combination of shade—red and brown—known to the boot-polish trade as "ox-blood".

He walked some distance up the sub-way and then turned a corner marked "Men's Conveniences". Chatterton and Evershed, his assistant, ranged themselves strategically.

The man in front of them walked sharply, but without the slightest suggestion of undue haste or hurry. As he turned into the space where the lavatories were, he looked to the passers-by just as he intended to look—an ordinary, commonplace man going about his everyday business.

Meanwhile, Chatterton and Evershed waited patiently for his reappearance. After a time, Chatterton glanced somewhat anxiously at his watch. Ten minutes had passed. And the quarry hadn't shown up.

Chatterton looked across to where he knew Evershed was standing. The latter, almost imperceptibly, shook his head. Chatterton frowned, although he didn't know that he was frowning. He was absolutely positive that the man whom he had been trailing had not come out from the place into which he had recently passed, ergo, he must still be in there.

And just at the precise second that Chatterton's brain registered that thought, a man came from the Public Lavatories and passed him. He was not so tall as the man who had gone in. Or was he? He was not so stout. Perhaps. His shoulders were different—one sagged a little as he walked. Besides, his clothes were altogether different. The hat was grey, the light overcoat was grey, the trousers looked to be of grey flannel and the man's shoes—Chatterton's eyes happened to notice the shoes, the shoes of this second man. They were the same kind of shoes that the quarry had worn!

Chatterton's brain was stung into understanding. They were the *same shoes*! There could be no mistaking them. The shade of colour, the terrific shine—the tiny, slightly discoloured mark on the left foot—Chatterton was after this second man like a hound after a fox.

Evershed also saw, understood, and took up the running. Chatterton could see the man's face now—and all his doubts and misgivings came back to him. The face was different! No doubt about that. There was a small moustache, there was a pair of broad black-stemmed horn-rim spectacles, the eyes were more protuberant, the cheeks were more fleshy, the mouth was altered—it had a kind of quirk now, the ears were more red, the nose was wider and broader, the transformation was amazing—the transformation was complete! But the shoes . . . and the suit-case . . . they were the same! Chatterton's pulses began to work overtime.

Evershed caught up. Chatterton threw words at him over his shoulder. Evershed understood.

The man in front hurried to a bus-stop and swung on to a west-bound vehicle.

Chatterton boarded the bus on his heels. The quarry went nimbly to the top deck. Chatterton parked himself inside—in one of the seats commanding the conductor's platform and the staircase.

Chatterton knew he was safe enough there and he thought he knew, too, what the first destination would be. This bus spelled "Paddington" to Chatterton if anything ever did. The grey-hatted man didn't disappoint him. He moved down the platform to the booking-office with the stride of an athlete.

Chatterton on his heels turned his back as his quarry bent to the booking-clerk's pigeon-hole. But he heard the pregnant words "Stratford-on-Avon".

Chatterton retreated a few yards, bought a ticket for himself and picked his man up again making for the appropriate platform. The quarry passed the barrier. "How long before she goes?" asked Chatterton.

"Two minutes," replied the official at the gate. "Hell," said Chatterton, "I'm taking no chances. It's that or bust."

3

Evershed reported back to the "Yard". He stood in front of Chief Detective-Inspector Andrew MacMorran and the grey- eyed man whom he knew as Mr. Bathurst.

"What the hell do you mean?" demanded MacMorran. "What you say doesn't make sense to me."

"Well, sir," said Evershed defending his position, "what I'm afraid of is that Chatterton's made a boob. I can't understand it—straight I can't. This bloke he's gone after—well, he's nothin' like the feller we were tailin'. Can't make out myself why Chatterton fell for it like he did. There we were, waitin' as I explained to you, and I'll take my livin' oath our man hadn't shown up again, when Chatterton suddenly moved off like a crowd of perishin' women after nylons and gave me the tip what I was to do. I scarpered back here—they were the orders."

MacMorran scowled. "I suppose Chatterton knows what he's doing."

Evershed shrugged his shoulders. "Well, sir, he should, but you never know with a perishin' superior officer—as often as not they make a perishin' pills of—"

The rage in MacMorran's eye warned Evershed just in time. The latter coughed behind his hand. "Er . . . sorry, sir . . . my mistake."

MacMorran looked towards Anthony. "Means we must wait for Chatterton. He'll get something through to us, you can bet. First chance that comes his way."

"Looks like it. Well, I'm not disappointed. That's one thing about it. The rat has run."

"Yes. And in a clever way, too. Up to ten o'clock this morning according to Evershed—no departure from the normal." The Inspector looked at the clock on the mantelpiece. "I said it would be the week-end, didn't I? Wasn't far out."

Evershed coughed again. This time to call attention to himself. MacMorran took the hint. "All right, Evershed. You can scram. Stand by till you hear from me again."

"Very good, sir." Evershed vanished with remarkable celerity. When the door closed behind him Anthony said, "what about me? What do you want me to do? Stay on the boil?"

MacMorran, who had lit his pipe, spoke through a haze of tobacco-smoke. "Suppose you'd better." He drew a deep breath and sat back in his chair. Anthony saw that his nerves were on edge.

"I agree with you, Andrew. With regard to what you're thinking. I'm thinking the same myself."

MacMorran growled. "What do you mean?"

"You know what I mean. You're thinking 'what the hell is Chatterton doing?' Don't trouble to deny it. I'm thinking much the same—"

MacMorran glared at him and swallowed hard but said nothing.

"All we can do," went on Anthony cheerfully, "is to wait. For Chatterton. And it's no good chewing the cud over it. That won't get us anywhere."

"Which," remarked MacMorran with mordant sarcasm, "is a hell of a lot of satisfaction."

Anthony rose and strolled over to the window. He stood there for some few minutes looking out. His hands were thrust deep into his trousers pockets. Anthony jingled coins.

"And for the love of Mike," snorted MacMorran from the depths of his chair, "don't DO THAT!"

Anthony grinned. "Sorry, Andrew. I deserve your censure." He wandered back to his chair. MacMorran's eyes went to the clock again. Anthony made an interpretation. "Getting near lunch-time, Andrew. What do we do?"

"Don't worry. You won't starve! We'll have it sent in. No difficulty about that. I'll see to it now."

MacMorran picked up the telephone. He gave an order which sounded all right to Anthony. MacMorran replaced the receiver. "It's astonishing to me," he said acidly, "how some people are able to eat food no matter what the circumstances. No finer feelings, I suppose—that's the most likely explanation."

Anthony made no reply to the crack. He was trying to put himself in Chatterton's place. When the two lunches arrived, he hadn't got very far. By the time they'd been disposed of, he was still in much the same condition.

MacMorran looked at his plate and said, "do you know, I could scarcely tell what I was eating all the time I was eating it. That shows you."

Anthony said, "neither could I. But the reason was different. And it didn't show me anything."

MacMorran rang for the two trays to be removed. Anthony put his feet up and smoked cigarettes. At 1.33 the 'phone rang. MacMorran grabbed at it with both hands. He listened and looked across at Anthony. His face had changed completely.

"It's Chatterton," he said, his hand covering the mouthpiece, "he's speaking from Leamington station. I told you there was nothing crawling on Chatterton. He's got eyes in his—O.K., Chatterton, I'm listening."

4

Anthony also listened—somewhat anxiously—but his listening was confined to what MacMorran was saying. After a comparatively short conversation, the Inspector replaced the receiver in its cradle and looked across at Anthony.

"He wants us to follow up. We can be at Leamington by four o'clock. He'll 'phone us there as soon after four as he can make it. We must get cracking. I'll give you the details in the train. Fit?"

"Right now," replied Anthony.

"I'll see about the car, then. I'll 'phone down at once."

"Right-o, Andrew. I'll meet you in the front in five minutes. As far as I can remember, there's a train from Paddington round about two o'clock. Gives us bags of time."

"O.K. I'd rather have it that way. I hate having to rush things. Getting too long in the tooth. The bags are all ready, nothing to worry about there."

Anthony dashed out for a word with Evershed to whom he listened very carefully, but despite this interruption, was ready and waiting in the front for both the Inspector and the car. They caught the train with ample time to spare as Anthony had predicted and eventually, at an appropriate moment, he prodded the Inspector.

"Now, Andrew, let's have it up to the fall of the last wicket. Right from the time that Chatterton sent Evershed back to report."

MacMorran growled. "Some hopes! Now you know how long Chatterton was on, and you heard what I said to him." Anthony grinned. "I want to know what *he* said to *you*. In other words, Andrew, what's cooking?"

MacMorran proceeded to fill and light his pipe. Very deliberately, and with an infinite taking of pains. "It's like this," he said slowly. "Chatterton's got a headache. Says he feels certain he's after our man, but he can't quite make out why he looks so different."

"I don't get that, Andrew. Chatterton must know why—"

"It's no good chewing the rag over it, because I don't know enough. No details. Chatterton didn't have time to tell me. But he did say this. The destination for the moment is Stratford-on-Avon. You have to change at Leamington. Where he 'phoned from and where he'll 'phone us at four o'clock."

Anthony blew a smoke-ring across the compartment. "Don't know that I like the look of things, Andrew. Now you've told me what Chatterton said on the 'phone. As I hinted, I was afraid of a real 'quick one'—still, no point in meeting trouble halfway. What I would like to know is what made Chatterton string along as he has. He must have had an extraordinarily good reason. From what you say he seems to be both certain—and uncertain! That's what I don't get." Anthony shook his head pessimistically.

"I told you," said Andrew, "it's no good having a 'p.m.' on it. Much better wait till we get to Leamington. But I'll tell you what I do wonder about. Why Stratford?"

"Intelligent selection, Andrew. During the Shakespearian season which started about a fortnight ago, place full up! With all sorts and conditions. American plus! Bald, bearded—and an incalculable number of rather appalling, long-haired, horticultural specimens. You should see them gather in strength for the 'elevenses'. The cafés crawl with 'em. No, Andrew, our man knows what he's doing all right. At the same time—had I been asked—I should have doubted his chances of getting accommodation at short notice."

MacMorran looked at his watch. "Half past three. In about half an hour's time we ought to hear more. "

Anthony nodded. "And let's hope it's good when we do hear it, Andrew. For—if you ask me—this is a lousy way to spend Saturday afternoon."

"It might be worse," commented MacMorran, "all I've spent so far will go on my expenses sheet."

Anthony made his way into the corridor. He stood there for some time. Suddenly, he leant down to MacMorran and pointed away to the left. "There you are, Andrew," he said, "Leamington! Prepare for the worst."

CHAPTER 21

1

The time was a quarter past four before Chatterton telephoned to Leamington station. In the meantime, MacMorran and Anthony had occupied the station-master's office patiently and expectantly. MacMorran took the call when it came and again Anthony listened with some degree of anxiety. But on this occasion MacMorran's replies were short and sharp.

"What name did you say? Shipston-on-Stour? The White Bear'? What's that? Car from Stratford? O.K., Chatterton. What's that? You do and you don't? Well, we must put it to the test, that's all. Can't tell till we've had a go, can we? O.K.!"

MacMorran turned to Anthony. "Did you hear that? We've to make for a place called Shipston-on-Stour. 'The White Bear'. Ever heard of it?"

"Yes, Andrew. It's a place of two counties. Used to be in Warwickshire, now it's in Worcestershire. Or the other way round. I can never remember which is which. How does Chatterton seem now? Still in two and a half minds?"

MacMorran shrugged his shoulders. "Can't make him out. It's not like Chatterton. Something extraordinary must have happened. He'll tell us more, though, when we get there. I'll tell you what we'll do. We'll go by car straight from here. Better than hanging about for a train. I'll see the station-master again—get him to recommend us a garage. Come on. No point in wasting time."

Anthony rubbed his chin. "Just a moment. Where do we meet Chatterton? Did he arrange anything specific? Or do we just blow along and hope for the best?"

"In the bar of 'The White Bear'."

"H'm. Walking straight in, eh? Rather like taking a risk, isn't it? If our friend the killer gets an eyeful—"

MacMorran cut in. "Well, for some reason which I can't quite make out, Chatterton didn't seem to think it would matter."

"Curiouser and curiouser," murmured Anthony.

2

Anthony and MacMorran came to Shipston-on-Stour in the cool of an April evening. Anthony looked out of the car window.

"Stop here, Andrew," he said, "by the church. And ask the way to our rendezvous."

The Inspector rapped on the glass. The car came to a halt. Anthony got out and waited for MacMorran. "Round to the market-square," said the latter after he had dealt with the driver, "only a few minutes' walk."

As they turned into the square, Anthony felt a touch on his arm. It was Chatterton. The latter saluted MacMorran, from force of habit in all probability, and said to the Inspector, "walk the other way, sir, for a few minutes. Our man's in the bar at the present moment and I'd like to put you gentlemen wise to one or two matters before you take a 'dekko' at him."

"That's the best news I've heard this evening, Chatterton," said Anthony, "apart from any opinions Inspector MacMorran may have."

Chatterton grinned, but Anthony saw that it was not his customary grin—there was something lacking. Chatterton addressed himself to the Inspector.

"You see, sir, it was like this. From the moment we picked him up this morning everything went Sir Garnet until 'is 'Ighness dived down a subway and made for a 'Gents'. I was on his tail and Evershed was O.K. too, all alongside." Chatterton proceeded with his story, giving a generous supply of detail. Anthony listened with meticulous attention. Until Chatterton came to his conclusion.

"Well, there you are, sir, now you know the whole story. But it's a marvellous disguise if it *is* our man. If it's not, and I've made a colossal boob—well, sir, I shall 'ave 'ad it!"

Anthony was thinking hard. "He hasn't spotted you, I suppose, Chatterton? Doesn't realize that you've tailed him all the way? No chance of that?"

Chatterton shook his head. "I never gave him an earthly, Mr. Bathurst. The only time he saw my old clock was when I swung on the bus that took us to Paddington."

MacMorran nodded. "Good. Well, as I see things, Mr. Bathurst and I must get to close quarters with him. All the same—I'm puzzled. Don't mind admitting it. I never ran across an amateur disguise yet that would have foxed me."

Chatterton shrugged his shoulders awkwardly. "I can take it, sir," he said gruffly.

"Is he staying at 'The White Bear'? Are you sure of that?"

"Not absolutely sure, sir. But I think you can take it so. I can tell you this. He came into the bar just now from somewhere upstairs and he's havin' dinner very shortly."

MacMorran stopped walking. The others halted with him. "Well, shall we turn round and go back? Now that you've given us the time of day?"

"I wonder," remarked Anthony, "if it would be possible for you and me, Andrew, to have dinner with him? Whether it could be arranged with the landlord of 'The White Bear'? If we could arrange it that way it ought to tell us a hell of a lot. We should certainly know 'yes' or 'no' by the time the meal was over. How does the idea strike you, Andrew? Chatterton could sink some wallop in the bar and be ready for action in case he should be needed."

"Sounds very nice, Mr. Bathurst," contributed Chatterton cheerfully, "don't think you could have a better suggestion."

"I'll manage it," said MacMorran grimly; "when I tell mine host who I am, he'll find us some grub all right."

"Excellent, Andrew. In that case, then, we'll slide gracefully into action."

The three men turned and Chatterton took them to "The White Bear." "Wait here a jiffy, sir," he said. He indicated a courtyard entrance and promptly disappeared. He was back almost immediately and whispered to MacMorran. " 'Is Grace 'as finished lookin' on the wine when it's red and is now knockin' back a goodly portion of roast beef and two veg. You come in now, sir, and do your stuff."

3

Twenty minutes after MacMorran had put his card and his request to the landlord, he and Anthony entered the dining- room. The landlord ushered them in.

"Company for you, Mr. Hopkins," he announced jovially to the one occupant of the room, before turning to the new guests with the heartening declaration, "your meat pie'll be along in a couple of minutes, gentlemen."

Hopkins, seated at the end of a long table, looked up at the two newcomers. Anthony felt that he looked upon a complete stranger. He wondered how MacMorran was thinking.

"Good evening, gentlemen," said Hopkins. Anthony's ears strained for the accent and the cadences of the voice. Were they familiar—or were they?

He and MacMorran returned the salutation. Anthony took careful stock of this man, Hopkins. He looked the typical American, both in manner and general sartorial effect. Anthony as he gazed upon him had no difficulty in sharing the misgiving which had so disturbed Chatterton. The man's manner was perfect. He drank his coffee and pushed away the cup and saucer gently but firmly. Anthony's observation was directly on the man's fingers. He thought that they trembled, just a trifle. Hopkins spoke, rather hesitatingly.

"You gentlemen here on the same errand as myself? I guess you are. The Shakespeare Festival? But you haven't travelled the thousands of miles I have. Not on your life! All the way from Wisconsin. Well, I guess Shakespeare was well worth the journey. He was a darned smart guy and he sure said a number of exceedingly wise things."

Anthony murmured conventional phrases.

"Years back in Madison," went on Hopkins . . . "that's my home town— we put on a show of *All's Well That Ends Well* but I guess the darned play didn't live up to its title. Maybe we'd a done better with *Hamlet, The Prince of Denmark.* If only for the generous amount of killin' there is in it . . . or even with Macbeth and them witches."

MacMorran was attacking his portion of meat pie, so once again Anthony entered the conversational breach. If this man were not what he was pretending to be, it was a consummate piece of acting. Superb indeed, because it was so splendidly sustained. Hopkins rose from his chair.

"I won't bore you any longer, gentlemen, no doubt you want to get on with your meal, and you're tired after your journey. You'll find me in the smoking-room."

Hopkins went slowly to the door and went out. They heard his steps descending the staircase. Anthony waited for MacMorran to speak. He had a shrewd idea that the Inspector might rise to supreme heights. As it was, MacMorran almost choked. "What the merry hell Chatterton thinks he's playing at, I for one—"

Anthony interrupted his flow of language. "I don't know, Andrew," he said quietly, "I just *don't know*. Once or twice when he was speaking just now, I felt he was too true to be good, if you know what I mean. Of course, it's a wizard performance, I grant you—he knows full well that the real secret of playing *any* part successfully is to convince yourself that you *are* that part. That is, of course, if he *is* phoney." Anthony paused, and then went on again. "I shall find out before bedtime, Andrew," he concluded very quietly.

MacMorran answered impatiently. "How the blazes shall *I* know? When *you* know? That's the part that's giving me a headache. The fellow may be armed, we can't dither."

"Get Chatterton to watch all the exits. Tell him at once. And then we'll join our friend for a smoke as he suggested. If I hand my cigarette-case to Hopkins, you do the necessary."

MacMorran was plainly nervous. "Yes, that's all very well. I can't afford to make a mistake, though." His forehead showed drops of sweat.

Anthony replied quietly. "I won't ask you to move, Andrew, unless I'm absolutely certain that Hopkins is our man. If I harbour the slightest doubt, I promise you, I'll hold my hand. But remember this. The height's about right and also the colour of the eyes."

"Oh—and what colour's that?"

Anthony nodded. "I know what you mean. It's hard to describe. Sort of nondescript. No particular shade predominant. But as I remember things, it's not too bad."

"Seems to me," growled MacMorran, "that you're deliberately looking for justification. Doesn't make me any more confident."

The landlord brought them coffee. "We'll drink this, Andrew, and then, after you've seen Chatterton, we'll find our Stratford pilgrim who thinks Bill Shakespeare was a wise guy. Do you agree? Dar'st thou, my good Andrew, now leap in with me into this angry flood and swim to yonder point?"

"O.K.," replied the Inspector. The reply must be regarded on all counts

4

Hopkins was less talkative when Anthony and MacMorran rejoined him. The three of them had the room to themselves, a condition which afforded MacMorran no small measure of satisfaction. Anthony threw out several carefully selected lines of conversation but Hopkins, in a big-armed chair by the fireplace, remained reticent and entirely at his ease. MacMorran fidgeted to nuisance standard. Suddenly Anthony switched the talk back to Shakespeare. Hopkins again flew the flag of enthusiasm. Eulogy followed panegyric. "I remember in Madison one fall, our local club put on *As You Like It*. We turned people away in hundreds. Yes, sir. Night after night! Hundreds turned away."

"Did you take part in the show yourself?" questioned Anthony.

"Yes, sir! The name of Cyrus P. Hopkins was in the *dramatis personae*."

"What did you play?"

"I clowned as Touchstone. Donned the motley! And I hit the high spots. Yes, sir!"

Anthony nodded agreement. "It's a good box-office play, *As You Like It*. I always think it's helped largely by the forest scenes." The penultimate word bore just a touch of emphasis.

Hopkins coughed and his words jerked out, "maybe you've got something there."

His fingers drummed nervously on one of the arms of his chair. Anthony noticed the movement and found himself listening to it with a kind of curious fascination. His hand went slowly to his pocket to feel for his cigarette-case. He took the case out. It was MacMorran's turn to watch now. Anthony held the case to the man in the armchair.

"Cigarette, Mr. Hopkins?"

"I thank you, sir." Hopkins extended his hand. MacMorran rose, hesitated for a split second, and then grasped the nettle!

"Andrew Murray," he said, "I arrest you for the wilful murder of Peter Wilton Oliver . . ." the rest of the charge followed but Anthony scarcely heard it. His eyes were fixed intently on the man whom MacMorran was holding.

"Don't be a damned fool . . . " the words came from the lips of the man who had called himself Hopkins . . . but suddenly the falsity of the environment seemed to begin to leave him . . . gradually . . . like a cloak slipping slowly from his shoulders . . . and the reality of Murray began to come back and oust the character that had been so skilfully assumed. He stopped speaking and slumped back in his chair. Then he shrugged his shoulders with an air of resignation. "All right, Inspector," he said slowly and wearily, "I give in . . . I've had enough . . . *more* than enough. Cowards die many times before their deaths . . . I'm tired of all of it . . . I'll come with you quietly."

He rose unsteadily from the chair. MacMorran spoke to Anthony. "Get Chatterton in, will you? We must see about transport."

5

Two evenings later, Anthony talked. In the lounge of his own flat—to Andrew MacMorran.

"Full confession—eh, Andrew? Well, that's satisfactory from our point of view. In a way, I think I expected it. The man's had enough, as he told us when he stopped being Hopkins." Anthony rubbed his hands. "All the same, Andrew, one of the most interesting of all our cases."

MacMorran nodded and then drank beer. "I shall be pleased to take part in the usual post-mortem. What put you on to him personally? I never got as far as that."

"Well it started, I suppose, from Margaret Oliver and the left-handed business concerning the bath. The murderer had known of Peter Oliver's left-handedness. The throat wound proved that conclusively. But he *hadn't known* of Peter's habit with the chain of the bath-plug. I always bore those two points well in mind. They seemed to me of vital importance. Margaret also said that Peter's use of his left hand was generally well known. And yet, . . . take your mind back, Andrew . . . Murray, Peter's own chief . . . at his *daily place of business, mind you* . . . told us that he was unaware of the habit. He lied, Andrew. I didn't know it was a lie, then, but I tucked away carefully for future reference."

MacMorran drank more beer. "A good point. I'll hand it to you. In the confession he says—"

Anthony cut in. "Don't tell me the details, Andrew. Let me see if I can fill in the picture myself. If I go off the rails anywhere, put me right."

MacMorran nodded, and lifted the tankard again.

"I'll go on," said Anthony, "in this way. When I began to look for motive, I simply could *not* get away from the disappearance, almost immediately after Peter Oliver's death, of Stella Forrest. I felt pretty certain that the '*fons et origo*' of the crime lay, in some obscure way, close to *her*. Her landlady had no doubt whatever that Stella had panicked badly and had run because she was terribly afraid. So there I was, you see, beginning to tinker with one or two interesting ideas and possibilities with regard to Stella Forrest and our friend at Delaney's bank.

"But against all that, of course, were the San Jonquilo bonds. Which belonged to Señor Roderigo Garcia from Santa Guardina. First they were stolen . . . with the finger of suspicion pointing strongly (according to Murray) to Peter Oliver . . . then they're most surprisingly returned in a registered package . . . addressed to Murray. This fact proved conclusively that if Oliver had stolen them, he certainly hadn't returned them. . . dead men aren't particularly partial to actions of this kind. We are also informed (again by Murray) that on the Saturday preceding the murder, he had instructed Peter Oliver to produce to him on the following Tuesday a certain book, which Oliver kept, as part of his duties with the bank, to do with foreign securities . . . and that if Oliver had been guilty of a theft which was now certain to be discovered . . . here was ample motive for the thief to commit suicide. Lot of Murray about the house, wasn't there, Andrew?"

Anthony paused.

When he continued he said, "I then began to concentrate on the Stella/Murray angle. Dare I consider the idea that she had been his mistress *before* she became engaged to Peter Oliver? To me, at that stage, it seemed eminently worth while considering. I began to gnaw hard at that particular bone, Andrew, and gradually the pattern of the crime began to appear more clearly. I remembered something that seemed to me most eloquent. I'll mention it to you later. Remind me if I should forget.

"Let us suppose—and a good deal of this is truth and *not* mere supposition—that an unusually attractive young girl falls violently in love with a well-preserved middle-aged man who rescues her one lovely summer morning from the ghastly death of drowning. There you have the genesis of the Andrew Murray/Stella Forrest affair. A fragment of newspaper that I was fortunate enough to pick up in Stella's room put me on the bottom rung of the ladder for that, but I deserve some marks, Andrew, for following up something which *might* have seemed of but trivial importance."

The Inspector nodded again. "The Weston-super-Mare incident is mentioned in the confession. But go on."

"When the affair began, each was desperately in love with the other. The man wasn't unhappy at home—superficially he was quite ordinarily happy but his passion for Stella was on another plane entirely. He placed her in a job in London, near his own, and saw that she found decent and adequate accommodation. His possessiveness was colossal and the entire affair from beginning to end was conducted with the utmost secrecy. When they met, it was invariably miles away from any of their respective daily and regular haunts. He ran no risk ever of being seen with this girl into whose life he had swum so powerfully.

"For a time, blind with gratitude and passion, Stella willingly and gratefully accepted these conditions which he imposed. Accepted them, I should say, with as much delight as anything else. No man should ever mean anything to her . . . but Andrew Murray!

"But youth calls to youth, Andrew, and bright eyes to bright eyes, and Peter Oliver, lunching at Lambert's restaurant one day, looked at Stella and Stella looked at him, and Dan Cupid did his stuff and Andrew Murray, the middle-aged—had had it!"

"I get it," said MacMorran with a look of profound wisdom.

"Good for you, Andrew. Well, there we are. At the point where Stella went wrong. She told *neither* man the circumstances of the other. The consequences, however, were, in the march of Time, inevitable. Although Oliver had no suspicions whatever concerning Murray, the middle-aged lover was nobody's fool, and it didn't take him too long to discover the change that had taken place in his lady-love.

"But Stella gave nothing away. All his efforts to discover 'if she had a lover' were of no avail. She was careful that all her meetings with Peter took place well away from the bank premises except perhaps on one special occasion when he was working late and when the murderer *may* have had the first shadowy notion as to the existence and identity of his young rival. Until the afternoon of Easter Monday when Mrs. Oliver in the Square at Bournemouth gives enough away to Mrs. Murray of her son Peter's love-life as to make Murray reasonably certain of the identity of the man who has supplanted him in Stella's affections, when his wife relays the gossip to him.

"From the details passed on to him, he became relatively sure where previously he may have entertained but strong suspicion. Stella herself has helped me to dot the i's and cross the t's with regard to what I've already given you, Andrew, but from now on I must draw largely on my own imagination. The terms of the confession, though, may enable you to check me."

"I can do that all right," affirmed the Inspector.

"Well," continued Anthony, "there we are with the Murrays in the Square at Bournemouth. The Olivers have proceeded on their way to Boscombe. Murray himself knows the worst—the *facts* of what he has been fearing and dreading for weeks, and all his passion and consuming jealousy for Stella rise in his heart and engulf him. He cannot live without the sweet companionship of this girl who has come to mean everything to him!

"And gradually, the monstrosity, the sheer enormity of the triangle comes home to him with bitter, mordant, soul-searing intensity. To think that he should be robbed of his *own lovely darling by one of his own junior clerks*! God, he said to himself, I don't stand for that, and the seed of murder which was already in his heart, as just a possibility, germinated and came to life as a strong and powerful plant."

Anthony paused again. "He begins to think things over—the details of what Mrs. Oliver has told his wife. Only Peter at home, all the others away. Peter has spent the holiday 'with his girl friend', and the murderer, lusting for his young rival's blood, whispers to himself, 'now might I do it pat'. He and his wife return from Bournemouth that evening and reach their house.

"How can he effectively counter the presence of his wife? His mind, I suggest, toys with this problem all the way up from Bournemouth, and he reaches a cunning solution. His wife has recently suffered from insomnia. The doctor to whom she had gone for advice, had prescribed sleeping tablets. When she took these, they induced some hours of heavy sleep. If, when they reached their house he could manage to—"

MacMorran interposed. "You're quite right. He asked for coffee soon after they arrived at Horton Hatch and he knew where his wife kept the tablets. When he left the house in the car for the Olivers' she was already in a deep sleep. When he returned round about midnight, she was still asleep. Actually he says that he woke her. When that happened, she had no knowledge whatever that he had ever been absent from the room."

"I thought that was probably the answer. Now I'll tell you how he went to work with regard to Peter Oliver. He telephoned first from a call-box to make sure that the young man was at home. Then, I suggest, he flung out a rather attractive invitation of some kind. Something of this nature. 'I say, Oliver, old chap, it's Murray this end—hope I'm not taking you too much by surprise, but I'm at a loose end. Got a couple of tickets for a late dinner and cabaret show at the— fill in here what you choose, Andrew—but my missus is off-colour. Can't possibly make it, old chap. I suddenly thought of you, knew you were on your lonesome, ran into your people at Bournemouth. What do you say? How about coming along with me? You'd have time to slip into the glad rags, wouldn't you?" "

MacMorran smiled. "You're almost exactly right. He asked him to the 'Trocadero'. Oliver was rather flattered—invitation from 'the old man', etc., etc., something most unusual. He fell for it. Subsequently—"

"Hold it, Andrew. Let me have another go. Don't deprive me of my petty triumphs. Or should it be scanty? He left the car somewhere near the call-box and walked up to the house. Right?"

"Right."

"He was dressed ordinarily, but in the car had been his suit-case from Bournemouth—evening dress in it. He took it along with him. When Peter opened the door to him and he took his time, of course, before he actually showed up—Peter was all ready for the festive occasion. The murderer, however, wasn't! How about this, then, for the ensuing conversation? 'There's just one thing, Oliver, old chap. Didn't bother to dress at home. Came straight round to you. Can I use your bathroom, and could you possibly lend me a razor? Shan't be much more than a quarter of an hour. Oh, I forgot to mention it, I always use a cut-throat. One of the old-fashioned type, you know.' Am I right, Andrew?"

"Can't say. He hasn't gone into details like that. But you catch me bending a bit there. How could he have been certain that there would be a razor of that type in the house? And if there *hadn't* been, which was more than likely, how could he have committed the murder? What other weapon had he?"

Anthony grinned. "With his own razor of the same sort, of course, which was ready in case. But the domestic razor, if he could possibly get hold of one, found in the dead man's left hand, would make it almost a cinch for suicide. In fact, I'm aware of one distinguished member of the 'Yard' who was absolutely convinced—"

"That's O.K.," said MacMorran, "we know! Going back, though, if *Murray's* razor had been found in the dead man's hand if the other one hadn't been forthcoming—it might have proved awkward for the killer."

"Not very, Andrew. Do you think it would be a simple matter to identify a razor purchased in all probability many years ago?"

MacMorran shrugged his shoulders. "I'll proceed," said Anthony. "Well, the rest was easy. He started getting ready in the bathroom, began to shave with his own razor, inveigled Oliver in on some pretence—quite a simple thing to do—got behind him, and farewell Peter Oliver! Then came the various steps—the donning of the gloves, the Oliver senior's razor placed in the Oliver junior's left hand, his own hot bath and general clean-up of self and razor, clothes put back into suit-case, etc., etc., knowing all the time that he was almost safe from any interruption. Certainly safe enough to take the chance. And then the car home to Horton Hatch and his sleeping wife."

MacMorran nodded again. "You're near right enough. It tallies pretty well with the man's own version. One point, though you said 'hot bath'. Are you certain of that? The house had been practically empty—unoccupied—for some days, there had been no fire, I should say—"

"Immersion heater in the bathroom cupboard, Andrew. Didn't you notice it?"

"You're right. I did."

"There isn't a great deal more," said Anthony, "except perhaps two points. Firstly, the note we discovered in the dead man's wallet. It gave us both, if you remember, 'to furiously think'. Actually it had nothing whatever to do with the crime. Margaret Oliver, as you know, is employed at a literary agency, the well-known firm of Scarlett, Greene and Rhodes, and Peter had ideas of writing a mystery story and using her influence to push it. To the cognoscenti her people are always referred to as 'Red, Green and Dusty'. The allusions are obvious. Hence the initials we ran our heads against. The other point is this. When we arrived at Delaney's bank, the red herrings of 'suicide' were carefully and deftly laid on the plate for our consumption. The inquiry into the Securities register, the missing bonds—there was the motive all dressed up like a dog's dinner for us to swallow. But, of course, all emanating from the one guilty source. When I tested one or two other lines of attack, none of them pleased me to the extent that the Murray one did. And then I thought of something else, Andrew. The point I told you to remind me about some few minutes ago. When Stella was worried to hell about Peter Oliver, before she tossed the trouble into *our* lap, did you notice that there was one particular—and natural—action which she did *not* take? Which nine people out of ten, placed as she was, would have taken? She did *not* ring up Delaney's bank! If there *were* any water in my theory, Andrew, her reluctance to communicate with the bank was right down my alley. So I felt more confident about matters than ever."

"Yes. I *had* spotted that bank business with Stella. I think I mentioned it to you in the early stages. She was keeping away from the boss."

"She was that, Andrew! And when she scrammed, she was afraid that her association with him might come to light and that he would be prepared to go to any lengths, to keep her mouth shut. You see, in some instinctive way, she felt within her that she knew the truth of the murder."

"Yes. She had the 'gen'. Nobody else was in that position. One more point, though, before I make tracks. When we were waiting in that room at Shipston-on-Stour, when neither of us was certain whether Hopkins was genuine or not, what made you certain he was our man? The decision seemed to come to you suddenly."

Anthony smiled at MacMorran's question. "I'll tell you, Andrew. I've been waiting for you to ask me. The disguise was marvellous. I've never seen a better. I don't think I ever shall. He'd seen to almost everything. Wig, his eyes had been treated to make them bulge, his cheeks filled with 'plumpers', small moustache, glasses, and a completely different style of dress from his normal in almost every respect. And, *plus* all those sartorial externals, he'd accomplished what everybody must do, if they hope to succeed in carrying off a successful deception. He'd fitted himself *into the skin of Hopkins*, so that all the time he was persuading himself that he actually *was* an American from Madison, Wisconsin, who had travelled thousands of miles in the cause of Shakespeare. If he could persuade and convince *himself*, how much easier to inflict the identity on us? That was why he kept so cool when we walked in on him."

MacMorran interrupted. "But even now I don't see how you—"

"How I saw through him?" Anthony chuckled. "Well, I shook him just a trifle when I slung the word 'forest' at him rather unexpectedly. The shock threw him back on one of his own personal mannerisms—a real Murray one, nothing to do with Hopkins. He drummed on the table with his fingertips. *He had done this in his room at the bank when we first interviewed him!* On that first occasion I had been interested to hear him tap out the opening bars of 'The British Grenadiers'. It's a tune that's comparatively easy to recognize. In that room at Shipston-on-Stour *Hopkins also regaled us with the same tune!* I could scarcely believe my ears, the coincidence was too utterly miraculous to get by. Overjoyed, I offered him my cigarette-case. You know the rest."

There was admiration in MacMorran's eyes. "One out of the bag," he declared, "absolutely!" He eyed his empty tankard with disfavour. "And certainly a case which calls for some little celebration. It would be a thousand pities not to . . ."

Anthony found another bottle. "I should hate to disagree with you, Andrew," he replied. He opened the bottle and extended his hand. "That tankard of yours, Andrew. It's a pleasant sound . . . the pouring out of beer . . ." MacMorran took the tankard from him, almost reverently, and drank. "Good show," he said, "jolly good show!"

THE END